Praise for bestselling author Debra Webb

"Debra Webb is endowed with an incredible
imagination and an impressive ability to create
multi-dimensional, realistic characters."
—*The Romance Reader.com*

"Webb doesn't let her readers down."
—*RT Book Reviews* on *First Night*

"A chilling tale that will keep readers turning pages
long into the night, *Dying To Play*
is a definite keeper."
—*Romance Reviews Today*

"Hot sex, an evil villain and a courageous hero
make this a thrilling *Situation: Out of Control*."
—*RT Book Reviews*

"A mismatched couple's frantic race
to stop a demonic killer makes Debra Webb's
Full Exposure a chilling page-turner."
—*RT Book Reviews*

DEBRA WEBB wrote her first story at age nine and her first romance at thirteen. It wasn't until she spent three years working for the military behind the Iron Curtain and within the confining political walls of Berlin, Germany, that she realized her true calling. A five-year stint with NASA on the Space Shuttle Program reinforced her love of the endless possibilities within her grasp as a storyteller. A collision course between suspense and romance was set. Debra has been writing romantic suspense and action-packed romantic thrillers ever since. Visit her at www.DebraWebb.com or write to her at P.O. Box 4889, Huntsville, AL 35815.

DEBRA WEBB

Situation: Out of Control

Full Exposure

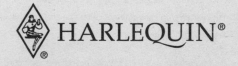

HARLEQUIN®

TORONTO • NEW YORK • LONDON
AMSTERDAM • PARIS • SYDNEY • HAMBURG
STOCKHOLM • ATHENS • TOKYO • MILAN • MADRID
PRAGUE • WARSAW • BUDAPEST • AUCKLAND

Recycling programs
for this product may
not exist in your area.

ISBN-13: 978-0-373-68817-3

SITUATION: OUT OF CONTROL & FULL EXPOSURE

Copyright © 2011 by Harlequin Books S.A.

The publisher acknowledges the copyright holder of the individual works as follows:

SITUATION: OUT OF CONTROL
Copyright © 2004 by Debra Webb

FULL EXPOSURE
Copyright © 2004 by Debra Webb

This edition published by arrangement with Harlequin Books S.A.

For questions and comments about the quality of this book please contact us at Customer_eCare@Harlequin.ca.

® and TM are trademarks of the publisher. Trademarks indicated with ® are registered in the United States Patent and Trademark Office, the Canadian Trade Marks Office and in other countries.

www.eHarlequin.com

Printed in U.S.A.

CONTENTS

First I'd like to take this opportunity to say a special thanks to all the wonderful folks at eHarlequin.com. You provide authors and readers alike with a home away from home, a wonderful place to chat and meet new friends. And to read great stories! Thanks for all you do!

This book is dedicated to a handsome young man I'm certain has a bright future ahead of him. He's not only good-looking, but intelligent and loyal—the best traits a man can possess. This one is for you, Chad, a terrific nephew! Love, Aunt Deb.

SITUATION: OUT OF CONTROL

CHAPTER ONE

Victoria Colby-Camp stared out the window of her new home, watching the scene that would have once torn at her heart with an unbearable ruthlessness. Children, backpacks swinging, rushed to climb into minivans and SUVs. Harried mothers slid behind steering wheels all the while calling off the usual morning checklist. "Buckle up!" "Do you have your lunch?" "Where's your coat?"

Victoria had missed out on most of those tender years with her son. She'd scarcely gotten him through first grade before evil had descended upon her family.

She drew in a deep breath and pushed away the pain that lingered still. It was over now. Her son was home and safe from the bastard who had tortured him. Jim Colby was healed, for the most part. However, there were changes not so easily overcome. The brainwashing techniques that had been used on her son had lingering effects. But he was strong. Just like his father had been. He would continue to improve, continue to regain the life that had been stolen from him. And, most important, he had a woman who loved him close at his side.

Victoria smiled. Another woman besides his mother. Tasha North had proven a vital element in his recovery. Victoria thanked God for her each and every day. Jim and Tasha were currently spending a much-needed getaway in the Caribbean. The doctors had agreed to a two-week hiatus from treatment after three long months of intensive therapy. Though Victoria missed him immensely, she knew that her son was in capable hands with Tasha.

The smile faded from Victoria's lips. Despite the joy of having her son back and knowing that Leberman was rotting in hell, there were still questions related to his legacy of terror. Questions that had to be answered, though she was loath to admit as much.

Lucas was right. They had to discover how Leberman had gotten his information and they had to find the man who had helped him kidnap Jim all those years ago. He would have answers they desperately needed.

Victoria would never believe that a member of her own staff had knowingly betrayed her. Never. Nothing anyone could say would convince her. However, she did recognize that there were ways of getting information without a person's knowledge. Even her seemingly invincible Colby agents were human. That, in her opinion, was the only way the information Leberman used could have come from her agency.

With that solemn realization, she had reluctantly agreed to Lucas's plan. An internal affairs investigation would launch today. She swallowed, a knot of emotion making the task near impossible. No matter how much sense this step made, no matter how good the man in charge of the investigation, Victoria couldn't help feeling guilty.

She felt like a Judas.

Everyone at the agency insisted that they understood and welcomed the scrutiny. And yet, it felt utterly wrong. But it was the only way. She could not accept the risk that the second man involved with Leberman's long-ago plot to destroy the Colbys might learn of some future tactic that involved Jim. The doctors had repeatedly acknowledged that some parts of Jim's memory could not be unlocked.

As a longtime secret agent for the United States government, Lucas knew far too much about mind control techniques to assume that the inaccessible parts of Jim's memory were harmless. It would be just like Leberman to have built in an encore—a backup plan in case his machinations failed. All it would take was the right word or set of circumstances and a deeply embedded neuro command might just overtake Jim's ability to think for himself. Might force him to do the unthinkable.

That possibility represented a risk Victoria would not take.

She had to trust Lucas as well as the man he'd chosen to oversee this investigation. Someone outside the Colby Agency. Someone who would be completely objective.

Cole Danes.

Victoria had only met him once, but she had immediately sensed a coldness about him. He appeared distant and untouchable, unfeeling actually. His reputation marked him as relentless, savagely so.

But Lucas trusted him.

She had to remind herself of that all-important fact.

She glanced at the clock on the mantel—8:00 a.m. The meeting would start now...and she couldn't be there. Lucas had given her orders to stay clear of the investigation. Any interference on her part would be detrimental and only prolong the discomfort.

This had to be done.

She understood that.

But she didn't have to like it.

"I've prepared your favorite breakfast," Lucas said as he came up behind her.

She hadn't heard him come into the room. How long had he been watching? Unguarded, her every thought had certainly etched the echoing emotion on her face. He would have easily read each one. He knew her so very well.

Her husband slid his strong arms around her waist and pulled her against his reassuringly strong body. She felt the steady beat of his heart, experienced an instant sense of relief. "You have my word," he whispered softly against the shell of her ear, "that all will be well."

Tears brimmed before she could suppress another abrupt surge of emotion. How she prayed he was right. She gave herself a mental shake. How could she doubt Lucas? He had never failed her. She leaned her head against his shoulder. "I know."

"This will be over very soon."

She nodded. Cole Danes had assured her that he would waste no time. He knew what to do and he would do it without hesitation or question. He was the best. His reputation unparalleled in the arena of internal affairs.

Still, the worry gnawing at her would not be allayed. Victoria placed her hand over Lucas's and said out loud the words that filled her heart with tormenting dread. "But nothing will ever be the same."

Lucas didn't have to say anything. He knew, just as she did, that this step would forever change the dynamics of the Colby Agency. There was no way to pretend away the inevitable.

Nothing would ever be the same.

CHAPTER TWO

Inside the Colby Agency

Heath Murphy surveyed the conference room as the remainder of his colleagues at the Colby Agency made their way to fill the vacant seats around the long mahogany table. He nodded a greeting to Ric Martinez, the guy who'd taken Heath under his wing the past couple of months to show him the ropes. Ric and his lovely wife, Piper, had acquainted him with Chicago's nightlife and cultural offerings, as well, since Heath was new to the city in addition to being new at the agency.

More greetings were exchanged and coffee cups filled before the room settled, leaving the quiet crammed with simmering anticipation. Heath recognized all the faces, had been befriended by most. There were a couple folks from research who kept to themselves, offering only a cursory acknowledgement of other humans when absolutely necessary. Heath imagined that those guys spent so much time in cyberspace that they'd forgotten how to be truly social with like life forms.

Maxwell Pierce, Ethan Delaney, Nicole Reed-Michaels and Mildred Parker, just to name a few others, were the ones who went above and beyond the call to make the new feel welcome on a daily basis. Heath gave one person in particular an extra wide smile. Mildred, the secretary/personal assistant to the head of the agency.

She kept everyone straight. Knew the Colby Agency
inside out. He doubted there was a person here who
could do without Mildred's special brand of guidance
from time to time, especially a newbie like him.

The door closed and Heath glanced in that direction.
Simon Ruhl and Ian Michaels, both second in command
only to Victoria Colby-Camp herself, moved to the front
of the room. Neither man looked particularly happy this
Monday morning. Heath couldn't actually blame them.
Like everyone else at the agency he'd been briefed on
what was about to take place. And, like the rest, he
felt somewhat less than comfortable with the situation
though he didn't have a real problem with the process.

As a former police officer he was aware of what
an internal affairs investigation involved. Depending
on the investigator in charge it could get pretty ugly.
But then, this wasn't an official police proceeding, this
was a civilian firm. He doubted the inquiry would be
anything like the real thing. He surveyed the polished,
professional group seated around the table. He couldn't
see these people tolerating the kind of crap cops had no
choice but to endure. Heath clenched his jaw hard and
forced the bitter memories away. He'd been cleared,
eventually. No point going back down that road again.
He wasn't a cop anymore. He was a private investigator.
At one of the most prestigious firms in the country.

He didn't have to rehash the past.

He would not.

This was his home now.

Forcing himself to relax once more, he tuned out
the past and focused on the pep talk Simon Ruhl had
launched.

"We've all been briefed on the necessity of this investigation," Simon said. "I've been assured that it will

be accomplished in as efficient and nondisruptive a manner as possible. However—" his gaze moved from face to face before he continued "—Ian and I will be available for anyone who wishes to talk or who has a problem with any part of the proceedings." He looked from one attentive listener to the next. "Do not hesitate to come forward at any time."

Acknowledging nods jogged through the group. Simon's words had the intended effect. Heath could feel the change in the atmosphere of the room already. Tension relented and anticipation receded to a degree. There was no reason to be concerned, that was the message Simon wanted to impress. No one present really believed that a traitor existed among their ranks.

Heath was too new to speculate but his gut feeling was that the internal affairs investigation would be an exercise in futility, not to mention a monumental waste of time. These were the good guys. He'd worked with enough bad guys to know the difference.

"From this moment forward and until this investigation is completed," Ian Michaels said, taking the floor, "you will take your instructions from Mr. Danes."

A new kind of hush fell over the room. Heath frowned. The apprehension ratcheted back up a few notches. Maybe the staff wasn't as prepared as he'd presumed. A ping of dread made his own instincts flinch, but he quickly dismissed the uneasiness. Semantics, method of delivery, those were the reasons for the sudden reversal in the climate of the room. From his observations Heath had noted one distinct difference between Simon Ruhl and Ian Michaels. Simon went the extra distance to smooth ruffled feathers, to inject calm. In vivid contrast, Ian's demeanor was distant, quietly intimidating. The man did not mince words. Yet he was well liked. Two very different men, both very good at their work. Like everyone else employed by this agency. Heath couldn't help feeling a little rush of pride at having been brought on board. This was his new home. He liked it and intended to make a fresh start here.

No looking back.

"And just when are we going to meet this Mr. Danes?" Mildred piped up with her usual blunt flair. Heath smiled. She was a definite original. One of a kind.

"Now is as good a time as any."

Every head in the room turned to stare in the direction of the unfamiliar voice. A stranger leaned casually against the wall next to the door. Heath felt certain he wasn't the only one who had not heard the newest arrival enter the conference room. As the man pushed off the wall and strolled leisurely to the front of the room, a different level of uneasiness nudged at Heath. Just who the hell was this guy? Anyone who could catch a room full of highly trained agents off guard was good.

Damn good.

Heath's gaze settled on the man in question as he assumed the position of authority as smoothly as drawing a breath. Simon and Ian stepped aside, giving him the floor without further ado. Ian settled into a chair next to his wife, Nicole, and Simon took the last remaining seat on the opposite end of the table. The whole transition of power took a single second with no pomp and circumstance.

The man at the front of the room braced his hands behind his back, assuming a typical military stance of attention. But there was nothing typical about his expression. He surveyed those seated around the table with a kind of primal intensity that spoke of extreme confidence and uncanny perception. This man would not only be very good at his work, he would also enjoy every moment of the effort as well.

Heath would bet almost anything that Mr. Cole Danes was not only ex-military, but ex-CIA, too. Or perhaps some group more subversive. Heath had met his kind before. Nothing would get in the way of the job. Ruthless was the word that came to mind.

Cole Danes trusted no one. Heath sensed with wrenching certainty that ice likely filled his veins. The man epitomized the phrase "commanding presence." Tall; broad-shouldered; deep, authoritative voice. Total control. He would accept nothing less. His tailored suit, while elegant, suggested careful attention to detail. All business. But his overlong hair gave him the untrustworthy look of a shady character from the wrong side of the tracks and the silver hoop that winked from one ear only strengthened that perception. A dichotomy.

"My name is Cole Danes."

Heath's attention shifted forward once more. Now the games would begin.

"As Simon told you, I will conduct this investigation as quickly and with as little disruption to the status quo as possible. Each of you will be subjected to close scrutiny that will involve extensive background investigation and repeated interviews."

A tiny smile tugged at one corner of Heath's mouth. He didn't see the big deal in that. Hell, he'd been through that already just to be considered as a Colby Agency investigator.

"You may believe that you've been exposed to this very sort of investigation before." Danes's gaze settled on Heath as if he'd spoken his thoughts aloud. "Perhaps when you were hired."

Heath felt the hairs on the back of his neck stand on end. What was this guy? Psychic?

"Let me warn you now," Danes went on, his penetrating attention, thankfully, advancing to someone else, "this will be a new experience. That I can assure you. When I'm finished—" that relentless gaze moved from face to face while the room held its collective breath "—I will know more about you than you know about yourself."

"That sounds strangely like a threat, Mr. Danes," Ian Michaels suggested in that quietly intimidating tone that marked him as a man who refused to be disconcerted by mere talk.

Danes relaxed his stance ever so slightly. His mouth quirked into a casual smile but there was no sign of amusement in his expression. "No, Mr. Michaels, that was not a threat at all." The smile vanished, ferocity lit in his eyes. "It was a promise." He turned back to the room at large. "Any questions?"

HEATH DIDN'T HANG around in the conference room when the briefing was over. He went to his office and closed the door, as did most everyone else. No one wanted to linger and risk being the first to be sacrificed on the Cole Danes altar of supremacy. Though Heath had only been at the agency a couple of months, he felt certain that no one had ever seen Ian Michaels and Simon Ruhl as furious as they were by Danes's cocky answer to Ian's question. Danes clearly didn't give a damn. He had his job to do and wasn't about to play nice.

Heath pushed aside the whole subject and directed his attention to reading reports. Simon had suggested that he read the past year's case reports in order to get a better handle on how the Colby Agency conducted business and the level of insight expected from him. He'd already worked on a couple of cases with other investigators. Soon he would get his first assignment. He wanted to be prepared. The internal affairs investigation notwithstanding, he really liked it here. He wanted to fit in and do a good job. It had been a while since he'd felt right with his life, professionally or personally.

Despite this morning's overbearing announcement by Danes, Heath wasn't worried. Cole Danes was looking for someone who'd fed information to Victoria's longtime enemy over a period of years. The guy, Leberman, had been eliminated before Heath received news he'd been hired. He had nothing to worry about in this investigation. Still, Danes made him uncomfortable.

Someone very much like Cole Danes had ended Heath's career as a cop. Well, that wasn't exactly true. Heath had been the one to resign on his own. But it was the kind of cold intimidation tactics he saw in Danes that had made him walk away. The distrust and suspicion heaped upon him had been a rude awakening for a guy who'd put in eight good years. Had never once gotten out of line or failed to do his duty.

In the end that hadn't counted for squat. He'd been looked upon as just as guilty as his partner until Heath had been cleared. What happened to innocent until proven guilty? Apparently during an internal affairs investigation there were no innocents. That was the part that bothered Heath the most. He'd trusted his partner and look where that had gotten him. Maybe Cole Danes wasn't so far off the mark. When things got down to the nitty-gritty a guy could only trust himself.

A cold hard fist of memory hit him square in the gut.

And then there were those times when he couldn't even trust himself.

A quick rap on his door jerked Heath from the troubling thoughts just as it opened.

"I need a few moments of your time, Mr. Murphy."

Cole Danes entered Heath's office and sat down before he could assimilate an appropriate response. Damn. Maybe this guy could read minds and wanted to make sure Heath didn't feel left out.

Heath set aside the report he'd been reading. Might as well get this over with. "What can I do for you, Mr. Danes?"

Piercing blue eyes studied him for what felt like a mini-eternity before an answer was forthcoming. "I'm aware that you've gone through an investigation of this nature before during your days on the police force in Gatlinburg, Tennessee."

Tension tightened in Heath's gut. "That's right."

"Although you were cleared of any guilt you walked away from a promising career."

"I did." He scarcely kept the rest of what he wanted to say in check. What the hell did his past matter? What did it have to do with here and now?

"Then you're aware a certain level of intimidation is necessary to accomplish the mission."

The impulse to grind his teeth was irresistible. Oh yeah, this guy read minds all right. He'd known exactly what Heath had been thinking this morning. "I'm aware that people in your position appear to think so."

Danes's mouth quirked with a less than polite smile. "Touché, Mr. Murphy."

Heath considered briefly whether he should relax or get worried. He decided on the former. Cole Danes was only doing what he did best, unsettling his target's piece of mind.

"I understand you've worked a couple of cases with other investigators here at the agency."

Heath nodded. "That's right."

"Good. I spoke with Victoria this morning and she agrees with my decision on the matter at hand."

That announcement surprised Heath. He hadn't figured Danes for the sort who would take advice from anyone, much less seek it out.

Danes pinned him with that laserlike gaze, demanding full attention. "Since this I.A. investigation doesn't actually pertain to you, I intend to put you to work for me."

"Come again?" Heath must have misunderstood. He was brand new here, hadn't worked a single case on his own. Not to mention that Danes clearly saw the I.A. investigation in his past as a black mark whether he said as much or not.

Danes explained, "The only lead I have at the moment regarding Leberman's connection to the Colby Agency is a man named Howard Stephens. Lucas Camp believes Stephens worked closely with Leberman. I need to find this man."

"Okay," Heath said slowly, drawing out the syllables. "What do you know about him?"

"Not very much. He's former military, a black operations unit within the realm of Special Forces. Twenty years ago his family believed he left the military to join the CIA. According to the intelligence Lucas has collected, Stephens's wife died five years ago and he has made the rare appearance to see his only child, a daughter, since. She's the sole link we have to the man."

Heath considered the information for a moment. "Is he still CIA?"

"He never was CIA. According to military records, Howard Stephens died eighteen years ago. We believe that's when he started working for Leberman, but we have no conclusive evidence."

"So the only hope you have for discovering Stephens's whereabouts is through his daughter?" Heath didn't like where this was headed.

"Therein lies the trouble," Danes went on. "She *is* our only link to him—however, I doubt she knows where he is any more than we do. From what I've gathered, he simply shows up from time to time. She never knows when." Another of those utterly fake smiles twisted Danes's lips. "Kind of like a kid waiting on Santa Claus. Sad, wouldn't you say?"

A sickening sort of dread pooled in Heath's gut. He could feel the worst coming. "You're going to use her to find her own father."

"Actually—" Danes leaned forward a bit "—*you* are."

The impact of those three words slammed into Heath. Every instinct shot to a higher state of alert. "Why me?" He had the least experience of anyone on staff. He understood that he was the only employee exempt where the I.A. investigation was concerned, but surely that alone was not qualification enough for such an important mission. Bottom line: he didn't like this. He had a bad, bad feeling about it. Heath didn't like using people period. Not like this certainly.

Danes shrugged nonchalantly but his expression was anything but casual. "You're the only investigator clear of my suspicion at the moment. You know that."

Heath also knew that there was much more to this

decision. A man like Cole Danes would never pin something so important on so little.

"I also know that I'm the least qualified." Heath stated the obvious that Danes appeared to overlook or to skirt. "Being a small-town cop doesn't prepare you for investigations involving guys like Leberman and Stephens. Even homicide detectives don't get the James Bond super-spy course. You want to share the real reason you picked me for this assignment?"

Another of those disingenuous smiles. "Jayne Stephens works as a tour guide and volunteers on a mountain rescue team in Aspen, Colorado. Your mountain-climbing skills are essential."

Ice spread through Heath's chest, freezing everything in its path in a single heartbeat. "If you know as much about me as you think you do," he said tautly, "then you know I don't do that anymore." A dozen painful memories flashed through Heath's mind before he could stop the soul-shattering process. He clenched his jaw and squashed the images. He would not go there.

"That's right." Danes looked thoughtful for a moment. "Your girlfriend fell to her death. It was an unfortunate accident, of course. Those things happen," he offered glibly, "even to the best."

And Heath had been the best. That's what made the whole situation so unbearable. Heath never met a rock face he couldn't scale. He'd stayed in shape more for that hobby than he had for his job as a robbery/homicide detective. It wasn't like there was a lot of crime in his town, but living in a tourist hot spot like Gatlinburg had ensured that he'd met all kinds. A couple of skiers from Utah had changed his life. They'd invited him rock climbing in what they called the real world. Not the kind of uphill hiking he'd done his entire life in the

Blue Ridge Mountains of Tennessee, but the vertical treks up the Rockies of the West. The true danger zone. The kind of challenges an adrenaline junkie couldn't resist.

He'd loved it, had lived for the thrill. And then he'd made his one mistake. He'd wanted to share his passion for climbing with the woman he loved. Had told himself he could teach her all she needed to know...could keep her safe.

"You picked the wrong man for the job," he told Danes, his voice strangely emotionless as he dragged himself from the place that still gave him nightmares in the dead of night.

Danes shook his head. "I'm never wrong, Murphy. Trust me on that." He tossed a file onto Heath's desk. "Study it. You leave tomorrow."

Heath's gaze riveted to the manila folder as if it contained a contagious, deadly virus. He hadn't skied or climbed in three years. Had sworn he would never...

"Let me know if you have any questions."

Heath's attention jerked upward. "Wait."

Danes hesitated at the door, an unmistakable impatience in his posture.

"I'm not sure you understood me," Heath said flatly. "I can't do this." Uncertainty quaked through him, leaving a too-familiar tremor of weakness. It was out of the question. Impossible.

"Fear can be a good thing," Danes told him, "if you use it to feed your determination."

Anger pushed Heath to his feet and he held up both hands, stop-sign fashion. "Just a damned minute." The fury rushed through him, burning away the chill of remembered pain...the regret and fear that ate at him still. Who the hell did this guy think he was? He was playing

God here. Messing around with things that were better left alone. "Even if I did agree to do this, which I won't, how the hell do you expect me to get the information from this woman? Howard Stephens is her father. She isn't going to roll over on him without some big-time motivation."

Silence hung in the air for a pulse-pounding second that felt like ten with Danes's relentless glare boring straight through Heath.

"Any way you have to," Danes told him. "Coerce her, seduce her—whatever it takes. Just get the information."

Heath shook his head. "You said her father just pops into her life," he argued. "You said yourself she likely has no idea where he is."

"Correct," Danes allowed. "I'm certain she doesn't know his location any more than we do."

Heath scrubbed at his forehead and the tension nagging there, hating the fact that his hand trembled with the effort. "Then what the hell is the point?"

"I've put the word out that we intend to get to Stephens through his daughter," Danes said bluntly. "I'm certain that will get our target's attention. We shouldn't have to wait long."

A new blast of outrage obliterated all other emotion. "Doesn't that put her directly in the line of fire?" Heath demanded. Who knew what a guy like Stephens would do to protect himself? Surely Victoria Colby-Camp hadn't sanctioned this kind of maneuver.

"Right again, Murphy. She's the only connection we have. The only bait." Danes opened the door but hesitated once more before exiting, that Arctic gaze pressed in on Heath with renewed ferocity. "I would suggest that you get on the case before he has time to react to the news. Blood isn't always thicker than water."

Danes walked out, closing the door behind him with a succinct thud of finality.

Heath could only stand there, trying to get his fury back under control. What kind of man was this bastard? Obviously the kind willing to risk an innocent life to accomplish his mission.

"Dammit." Heath dropped back into his chair and stared at the folder on his desk. He closed his eyes and forced away the memories that tried once more to resurface. How the hell could he do this? He'd come to Chicago to put the past behind him. He never wanted to think about the mountains again. Never again wanted to see the way his family and friends back home looked at him. It was his fault she was dead. He knew it. They knew it. He hadn't been the same after that. If he had, he'd have picked up on his partner's dirty game before it was too late. But he'd failed there, too.

He'd let the woman he loved down and he'd let the Gatlinburg police department down, as well.

All he wanted now was to start over.

He could talk to Ian or Simon. Maybe get one of them to call Victoria and get something done about this.

Heath braced his forehead in his hands, kneaded the tension throbbing there. Then they would all know the truth about him.

He was a damned coward.

Afraid of a couple of ghosts from his past.

Scared to death he'd make the wrong decisions all over again if presented with a similar scenario.

How the hell was he supposed to do his job when he couldn't get past the fear?

Reluctantly, his fingers trembling in spite of his every

effort, he opened the folder. Big green eyes stared back at him. Long brown hair and a smile that, despite being captured in a mere photograph, took his breath away. Jayne Stephens, 24, soon to be 25, he noted. Her birthday was only a few days away. She looked young and innocent, but there was something else in those eyes that Heath hadn't seen in his own for a very long time. Happiness. This young woman had the world by the tail and her whole life ahead of her. She was in love with life. He could see it in her smile…in those incredible eyes. But that wouldn't last long.

She had no idea that her own past was about to come crashing into her present. Could she possibly know who and what her father was? Though Heath didn't get around much to seeing his own parents anymore, they did talk on the phone fairly often. But that was his fault. He'd made the choice not to go back. Yet, no matter how he felt about his past mistakes, he would still do anything to protect his folks.

This woman would be no different.

Heath read her file from cover to cover. Absorbed the details and facts that made Jayne Stephens who she was. Her life was quiet, organized and predictable. She had nothing to hide. Avoided the limelight and always gave credit to her team members rather than herself after a rescue.

Then he did the only thing his conscience would allow, he called the airline and booked himself on tomorrow's earliest flight to Aspen.

He refused to consider what the weather would be like there right now with February making up for January's lack of potency. Lots of snow. Lots of tourists. Valentine's Day weekend was coming up. Couples just wanting to enjoy a weekend getaway while hard-core skiers and climbers piled into the town like an overdue avalanche.

When he reached the page that outlined his cover profile a laugh choked from his throat. An investigative journalist? Oh yeah, that was perfect. He'd been cleared by the owner of a local guide service, Jayne's boss in fact, to do a piece on the mountain rescue team. He'd have to give Danes one thing, he'd tied up every detail in a neat little bow. The way had been paved with gold bricks for Heath's entrance. All Heath had to do was show up…and pretend that the past didn't matter. That the snow and the mountains hadn't cost him far too much already. He swallowed back the emotion that scaled into his throat.

He needed the Colby Agency. He couldn't fail, couldn't walk away from his first assignment. Even the shrinks would say that it was past time he'd come to terms with the ghosts that still haunted him.

But that didn't make it any easier.

He flipped back to the photograph of Jayne Stephens. He'd much rather stay here and be stuck right in the middle of the maelstrom this I.A. investigation would surely generate than to set foot on a snow-covered mountain.

Heath closed the file and stood. Well, considering that Danes had already put out the word that Jayne Stephens was a target of this investigation, Heath had little choice but to do what had to be done.

Every instinct he possessed warned him that her father would want to make sure she kept quiet about him.

There was no way to gauge what Howard Stephens

might be capable of or willing to do to assure his own safety.

Jayne Stephens's quiet, organized life was about to spin out of control.

CHAPTER THREE

Move it or die.

Jayne Stephens plunged forward, climbing at a relentless pace over and through the snow, her snowshoes sinking into fresh powder and dragging at her determined efforts. White was all around her, interrupted only by the occasional fir tree. She focused on the goal: the avalanche beacon that would ultimately save the lives of three trapped climbers.

As team leader, Jayne kept moving, not slowing even as her forty-pound rescue pack dragged at her weary shoulders and the lung-searing cold puffed in and out of her mouth like blasts of frozen fog. The four-man "hasty" team she led would reach the victims first, do what they could and prep for the arrival of the "support" team. The support team, weighted down with a full rescue load, couldn't move as quickly and efficiently through the morning's fresh snowfall. A full twenty-four inches had fallen in the wee hours before dawn, the snow-packed ice beneath making for perfect avalanche conditions. The absolute crappiest conditions for a rescue.

Jayne glanced at the oddly dark sky. More snow would fall. Soon. If they couldn't get those climbers out this morning, they might not make it out at all. The coming storm would force both teams back.

It was the first rule of rescue: Create no new victims.

But Jayne had no intentions of failing those hikers or her team. They would all make it out.

A new rush of adrenaline urged her onward, pushing her body past the point of exhaustion…past the dark timber of subalpine fir. Just a little farther now. Move faster. Push harder. Don't think, just move it.

Despite the fierce cold a line of sweat slid down her neck. All she had to do was make that ridge and rappel over the side to reach the trapped climbers. Assessing health condition and treating anything life threatening was the most pressing order. Then fuel for the body, solid and liquid, both of which she carried in her pack. By the time the support group arrived she and her team would have the victims ready for transport.

Then all they had to do was make it back down to Express Creek trailhead so the helicopter could lift the victims out of here. The rescue teams would walk out if possible. If not—if the brewing storm had blown in— they'd hunker down in a snow cave until the helicopter came back for them after the weather settled. Every member of the team was prepared for waiting out the worst. Clad in Gore-Tex, polypropylene and Nomex protective wear, maintaining body heat wasn't an immediate issue. Still, with the recent heavy snowfall, they were all walking avalanche triggers. The utmost care had to be taken while maintaining an emergency pace.

Jayne leaned into the thirty-mile-per-hour wind and forced another step and then another until she reached the peak at the south end of Richmond Ridge. She stared back at the members of her team. Little dots floated across her line of vision like defects in her corneas. She squeezed her eyes shut for a few seconds to clear them away. Better. The snow would do that…play games with your vision. With the mind, too, if one wasn't careful.

A quick glance over the ridge and relief rushed through her. An upside-down flag, the universal distress signal, showed her exactly where the climbers had dug in. Thankfully the group had possessed the foresight to wear avalanche beacons and to dig in, making a snow cave for protection from the weather, once they'd realized they were beyond climbing out of their predicament. The latter had likely kept them alive through the bitterly harsh night.

"I'm going over," Jayne told Chad, the first member of her team to reach her position.

"Gotcha."

Chad Wade would serve as the "edge man," ensuring the safety rope stayed in place. The safety rope was swiftly rigged along the ground beside the edge of the cliff, then tied to two solid anchors, one being Chad. After anchoring her rappelling rope, Jayne clipped her harness to the safety rope and stepped over the edge into thin air.

She controlled her descent, stopping long enough to prop her feet against the cliff face, then leaned out, almost horizontal, and began the rigorous journey down to the jutting edge where the climbers had taken refuge after one member of their group had fallen. Adrenaline pumping through her veins, Jayne's mind automatically went through the steps she would need to perform once she reached that precarious ledge.

She'd done this dozens of times. No need to be apprehensive. But somehow today felt different. She couldn't shake the uneasiness that increased with every foot she moved downward. She had no way to contact the trapped climbers other than to call out to them when she'd moved a little closer. A call from a cell phone had alerted the sheriff's office that they were in distress and the avalanche beacon had led the rescue team to their position but attempts at further contact via the cell phone had failed. Either the battery had died or…they had.

She wouldn't accept that. She gritted her teeth and pushed the worst-case scenario aside.

The radio strapped to her chest squawked. "You all right down there, Little Boss?"

Jayne couldn't help a smile. She was the only woman on the team. After the men had finally gotten used to having a female among them they'd eventually taken notice of her skill. Now she was second in command, the little boss. It only took one glimpse of her standing alongside the boss, the rescue team's leader, Walt Messina, for anyone to get the joke.

"No problems," she assured her watchful edge man. The other two members of her hasty team would be preparing for the arrival of the support personnel. Litters would need to be lowered if, as she suspected, the victims were unable to be hauled up with a mere harness.

"Mountain rescue!" she shouted downward. "Can anyone hear me?"

When her voice had stopped echoing, silence hung heavily in the frigid air.

Not good.

Almost there.

She readied herself for stepping onto the ledge. It wasn't more than seven or eight feet wide. Nothing but a jutting boulder from the rock face.

Reaching out for footing, Jayne stretched her right leg toward the ledge at the same time she reared her arm back to dig into the wall with a rock pick.

A jerky tug on the line made her freeze. She glanced upward a split second before the abrupt drop. Her heart rocketed into her throat, accompanied by the whiz of nylon and steel as she struggled to slow her fall.

Shouts and curses blasted from overhead.

Jayne grappled with her rope, trying to catch herself. The line rushed through her gloved fists like water pouring through a sieve. She swung her body like a pendulum, aiming for the rock face. Anything to slow her momentum.

She butted the mountain, then dropped another fifteen feet. The line jerked hard and she flopped against the rock face again. She groaned.

Three or four seconds passed before the realization penetrated that she'd stopped plummeting downward. Her heart sank back into her chest and started beating once more.

"Jayne, you okay?" Carl Brownfield's frantic voice rattled over the radio.

"Yeah, yeah." She sucked in a shuddering breath. Damn, that was too close. "I'm good. What the hell you guys doing up there?"

"The brake failed."

No kidding. Another deep, bolstering breath and she was ready to start the ascent required to regain the ground she'd lost.

"We're gonna haul you up, Little Boss." Chad's reassuring voice vibrated across the airwaves. "Just keep your balance. We've gotcha."

"Make sure you don't turn loose," Jayne offered with as chipper a tone as she could muster. Her edge man's strained chuckle told her she wasn't the only one nervous here, but she was the one suspended a few thousand feet above the ground. She stole a glance downward and shivered. Long ways down.

As she moved upward her attention returned to the

trapped climbers. No response yet. There was always the possibility that they couldn't hear her through the thick, insulating cave of snow.

"Mountain rescue! Can anyone hear me?" she called as she grabbed onto the ledge.

"Paul is on his way down," echoed from the radio.

Jayne glanced upward long enough to acknowledge that EMT Paul Rice was rappelling down to join her. She hoped like hell his services would be needed…she wanted this to be a live-victim rescue not a body recovery.

Jayne dug into the fresh snow that covered the small cave opening. "Mountain rescue," she repeated, her voice strained with equal measures exhaustion and determination. "Can anyone hear me?"

The sound was very nearly inaudible. A moan or sigh. But it was all she needed to resurrect hope. A gloved hand reached out to her and she smiled through the tears blurring her vision.

Thank God.

THE RETRIEVAL TOOK nearly two hours and the new storm had blown in before they were finished hauling the injured climbers from the ledge. Two of the men suffered from mild hypothermia, but the third man, the one who had initially fallen, was far worse. The various scrapes and bruises were nothing. The real problem was a flail chest—possible broken ribs with fluid buildup. This man would die if he didn't receive medical attention in a hurry.

Jayne and Paul, with the help of two from the support team, rushed the injured man to the waiting helicopter as quickly as possible with the wind and snow blinding their every step. With the victim's condition deteriorating rapidly the helicopter had no choice but to go without the other two. The rescue team would carry the remaining victims out on litters. It wouldn't be easy nor would it be the first or the last time that kind of rescue would be necessary.

The best they could hope for was that everyone would survive.

Jayne pushed harder, sending up a silent prayer as her body strained to obey her commands. *Please God, no new victims.*

NIGHT HAD SETTLED over Aspen like a velvet, snow-capped blanket by the time the day's adventure was truly behind Jayne and the other members of mountain rescue. Coming down was like surfacing from a deep-sea scuba diving journey, the sense of returning to a different world. Home...but not quite. It would be hours, maybe days before the sensation passed.

With the battle between man and nature and the race against time behind her, real life slowly came back into perspective. Her job as a backcountry trail guide, from which she would now be on hiatus until the elevated avalanche advisory had been lifted. Her tiny apartment above the Altitude Bar and Grill in the middle of downtown.

Here she was just another face in the crowd of locals who made a living off the thousands of tourists who flocked to the little resort town during the skiing season.

Statements had been given to the reporters who always showed up to cover rescues. The adrenaline was fading and bone-melting exhaustion had set in.

And still the victory party roared on. Rafe Gonzales, the owner of the Altitude Bar and Grill, provided steak, the trimmings and beer for all involved in the treacherous rescue. The camaraderie was nice, but about the only thing Jayne really wanted to do was slip into a steaming hot tub and then sleep like the dead. Rafe was having none of that. And he was right, she supposed. She did need to eat. Fuel her body to have the strength to make it through a bath before collapsing in bed.

"I thought you were a goner there when that brake failed," Chad said to her as he leaned close and offered his beer mug for a toast.

She managed a faint laugh. "Me, too."

"I should have kept a better check on the equipment." His face had turned far too solemn. He clearly blamed himself for the incident. Like man, things created by man failed from time to time. No one was perfect.

"It happens, Chad." She clinked her mug to his. "Equipment fails. Some things just can't be foreseen. Don't beat yourself up."

Paul Rice dropped into a vacant chair at their table. "He's gonna make it," he announced before taking a long draw from his beer.

"Good." Jayne knew he meant the climber with the flail chest. "He was damn lucky."

"Damn lucky," Chad echoed.

They were all damn lucky.

Jayne finally allowed herself to relax as she watched her teammates do the same. The day had been hell, the weather seriously evil. But they had rescued the victims and hadn't created any new ones. In the end, that was all that mattered.

She ate, drank a couple more beers and then said her good-nights. She was dead on her feet. Had to call it a night or go to sleep right there on the table in spite of the music and the crowd of revelers. The guys gave her the usual ribbing, calling her a sissy but tonight she didn't care—didn't even bother retaliating. She'd get them for it later. Mountain rescue teams underwent periodic training, intensive training. Whenever Walt couldn't be there, she was in charge. They would pay. A smile slid across her lips. Oh, how they would pay.

Jayne trudged through the storeroom and up the backstairs to the second floor. The upstairs portion of the building had been renovated years ago into two apartments. A large one that took up most of the floor space for the owner and his wife who had passed away a couple of years ago. And the second into a mother-in-law suite. But the mother-in-law was long gone, too. Rafe was all alone now. He and his wife had never had children so the extra room was rented out. Jayne had moved in three years ago and had never left.

The place provided all that she needed. She opened the door and went inside, not bothering to lock it. She didn't have to worry about security. Rafe had a state-of-the-art system on the first floor for after hours. During opening hours the kitchen and bar staff made sure no unauthorized persons entered their territory.

Jayne liked it here. She'd spent most of her time until age twenty-one either in chilly Chicago or sunny California and, in her opinion, Colorado was the perfect balance. Nice summers with amazing winters. The white-capped mountains were awesome all year round. She adored the feel of small-town living in Aspen, though when the tourists and seasonal dwellers arrived the population more than quadrupled.

After her mother's death she'd stayed in California a while but eventually she'd needed a change and this had been it. Becoming a member of mountain rescue had given her the physical and mental challenge she had longed for but hadn't been able to find. Apparently she was an adrenaline junkie just like her father. Living on the edge, surviving danger appeared to be the only obsession that satisfied her lust. Too bad she couldn't share that with anyone. Most of the time it didn't bother her, but once in a while when the guys would start talking about their families, she felt a little left out. She always got over it. That was a lesson she'd learned long ago.

Don't dwell on things you can't change.

When the tub brimmed with steaming water she peeled off the layers of Nomex and Gore-Tex and long underwear. The soothing water welcomed her like a lover. In fact she couldn't imagine any man giving her the satisfaction that the hot, enveloping embrace a long, hot soak offered. But then, she was a little cynical when it came to men. Not men in general, just lovers and husbands.

She'd watched her mother waste away, in love with a man who was more apparition than husband. Jayne's first love affair had ended badly in college, mainly because she had managed to maintain a higher grade point average and get through her classes faster, ultimately leaving him behind. Men didn't like to be outdone it seemed. Maybe that's what had gone wrong the last time, as well. The man she'd thought was special apparently hadn't been able to deal with her rescue work. So, like her old college beau, he'd dropped out of her life without so much as a goodbye. Poof…he was gone.

Still, there were men in her life. Her father, though she saw him only rarely. She'd long ago forgiven him for basically deserting her and her mother. He had done and still did what he had to do. Her teammates. She cared deeply for each one, respected them all as equals. But even among those fine men she saw the primal beasts that roared beneath their civilized exteriors. They loved the adrenaline rush of a rescue, would risk life and limb regardless of wives and children at home. They would take days on end off work to go on a rescue, ensuring a constant state of financial chaos.

But how could she hold against her teammates the very defect she recognized in herself? She couldn't. Though to her credit, she didn't have a spouse or children. Probably never would. Jayne frowned. How did one trust anyone that much? Love was one thing, because she certainly loved her father, cared deeply for her teammates, Walt and Rafe. She smiled at the thought of her landlord who was more family than friend. The crusty old man was like an uncle to her. Her only family actually since she so seldom saw her father. Loving a man wasn't the real problem, it was the "in" love thing, she supposed.

Trust was an altogether different animal. She trusted the team and her close friends here. She just wasn't sure she could trust anyone with her whole heart and her body. Sex was nice, but falling "in" love…hmm… she'd have to think about that sometime when she wasn't totally exhausted.

Or never.

She didn't need a husband to be complete.

Jayne Stephens was happy.

She drew in a deep, contented breath and sank deeper into the water. Her life was as close to perfect as one could get. She lived in the perfect town, had great friends who didn't get into her business. What else could she ask for?

Pushing away the hint of doubt that lingered, she washed her hair and soaked a while longer before reluctantly dragging her wholly relaxed body from the cooling water. She wrapped her dripping hair in a towel then pulled on her ancient terry cloth robe without bothering to dry off. She'd draped the robe over the radiator to warm it while she soaked. The heat wrapped around her now, making her moan appreciatively.

Hot cocoa. That would be the ultimate ending to the evening. Then she planned to sleep for at least twelve hours. It would be days before the avalanche advisory would be lifted and that gave her a nice break from work. Maybe she'd even get to spend her birthday doing something totally frivolous like shopping.

Twenty-five. She shuddered. Somehow that sounded *so* old. Pushing the thought away, she reminded herself that she was still twenty-four…at least for a couple more days.

She filled the kettle with water and lit the stove eye. A hefty mug, a couple of marshmallows and one-fourth cup of milk added in for richness and she'd be in business. The cocoa might be instant but she'd learned how to doctor it up making it taste almost as good as the pricey concoction they offered at the coffee shop across the street.

A soft rap on her front door drew her there. The kitchen and living room were one fairly spacious room. A tiny hall opposite the front door led to her bedroom and bathroom, which were admittedly cramped. Despite the lack of actual square footage, the soaring, beamed ceilings of the ancient architecture and the massive front window overlooking snow-laden sidewalks and twinkling storefronts made the place at once cozy and chic.

Jayne pulled the door open without identifying the

visitor. This was a close community, everyone knew everyone else.

Walt Messina, the rescue team's commander-in-chief—so to speak—and her boss at Happy Trails, towered in her doorway.

"I heard about the brake failure," he growled. Walt was like a big old bear. But, to those who knew him well, he was all bark and no bite. Another man she felt intensely fond of.

She nodded. "Gave me a bit of a scare but Chad took control of the situation." She opened the door wider and stepped back for her boss to come inside.

He shook his head. "I don't want to intrude." He noted her robe. "Just needed to ask a favor of you."

Jayne's senses went on alert. Walt didn't ask for favors, he gave orders, generally without justifying them first. For the second time today a sense of things not being right nudged her.

"What's up?" She propped against the door, her weary legs reminding her she'd been through a lot today.

Walt stared at the floor a moment. "Well, I've got an old friend at the *Denver Post* who needs something from me."

Jayne raised her eyebrows in question. She hadn't a clue what this could have to do with her but obviously her boss did. "You're originally from Denver, right?" she asked for lack of anything else to say.

He bobbed his head up and down. "He wants a real-life piece on the life of a trail guide and a mountain rescue member. Says it's real important to his publisher."

Jayne shrugged. "You don't want to give him the interview?" Sounded like an easy fix to her. A frown inched its way across her brow at his hesitation to answer her question. Judging by Walt's expression there wasn't anything easy about it.

After several moments of deliberation, he confessed, "He doesn't want it from me. He wants a woman's perspective."

It took a few moments for the words to infiltrate the nice little buzz the beer she'd had for dinner and the relaxing bath had cloaked around her brain. "A woman?" she parroted. He couldn't mean…

"I need you to do this for me, Jayne. I owe this guy."

Her head was moving from side to side of its own volition before the words were fully out of her boss's mouth. "I don't need some reporter dragging around in the snow with me, Walt. You have to know what an added risk that would be. You know the rule *don't create any new victims*. You're the one who came up with that slogan."

He hung his head. "I know. But I'm desperate here. This is important. Can you help me out?"

She crossed her arms over her chest and rolled her eyes. "For how long?" She had to be out of her mind to agree to this. If she didn't love her big old cuddly boss so much she'd tell him to forget it. But clearly this was a big deal to him. He either owed this guy big-time as he said or he wanted to impress him by showing off a member of his team. A *female* member, which was admittedly a rarity.

"Three days tops," he said quickly. "As soon as the avalanche advisory passes you can take him on a private tour of whatever peak you prefer."

She lifted one eyebrow skeptically. "Can this guy even ski? I'm not risking my life so some lowlander can scramble up a mountain. He'd better be a skilled climber or he can forget hiking up any peak that would interest me."

Walt blushed to the roots of his gray hair. What was up with that?

"He…ah…he's a skilled climber," her boss assured her. "Has a lot of experience. He won't be a liability."

Jayne still wasn't convinced. "I'll be the judge of that," she countered, annoyed. "He'll have to pass a competency test before he goes anywhere with me." There. That should scare off the cocky reporter. She felt certain once her boss explained to the guy just exactly what a competency test involved he'd be ready to hightail it back to Denver.

Walt suddenly stepped to one side and another man came into view. Jayne's heart skidded to a near stop. Tall was the first detail her mind wrapped around. Dark hair and eyes…the darkest brown eyes she'd ever seen. And those dark orbs were glittering with amusement at her at that very moment.

"When would you like to start?" he asked.

The deep, husky sound of his voice shivered over her skin like a gust of summit wind…only it warmed her on the inside while it raised goose bumps on her flesh.

"Er…Jayne, this is Heath Murphy. He's the investigative journalist my friend at the *Post* sent to capture this story." Her boss gestured to the man at his side. "Mr. Murphy, this is Jayne Stephens, the best trail guide and rescuer on my team."

Heath Murphy thrust out his hand. "It's a pleasure, Ms. Stephens."

Her eyes still glued to the mesmerizing ones analyzing her so thoroughly, Jayne placed her palm against the one offered. Something electrical sizzled up her arm setting off alarms in her head. Startled, she jerked back her hand. Her bewilderment instantly morphed into renewed irritation. What the hell was wrong with her? The beer maybe? The weakness left behind after a wild adrenaline rush...whatever the problem she had no intention of acting like a starstruck adolescent.

"I wish I could say the same, Mr. Murphy," she said bluntly. "But you see, in my line of work, the unknown can get you killed."

A smile stretched across that handsome face and her knees almost buckled at the sensual intensity of it. "Don't worry, Ms. Stephens, I can assure you I know how to handle myself in any situation."

Oddly, that was the part that scared her the most.

CHAPTER FOUR

A sultry mix of rhythm and blues whined from the speakers tucked neatly into the Altitude Bar and Grill's classic decor. The jukebox filled with classics was set on continual play—the spirits flowed like a river. The place was crowded with impatient skiers infuriated by the avalanche advisory that had kept them off the slopes that day. Threats of skiing tomorrow, whatever the conditions, were tossed about like speculations on the rise or decline of the stock market, with every bit as much vehemence.

Heath shook his head. Stupid tourists. Whether they were skilled skiers or not, getting out in this kind of weather was suicide. Two more feet of snow had been dumped on the area just yesterday, making conditions ripe for trouble. Those who'd doled out the cash for one-week stays in one of the country's premiere ski resorts had a single goal in mind—getting their money's worth. They'd come here for the snow, what was the big deal?

Not smart.

Jayne Stephens had done a stellar job ignoring Heath for most of the day. He'd watched her leave her apartment practically before daylight to go for a five-mile run. He had to admit he hadn't gone five miles in a while. Over the past couple of years he'd gotten kind of lazy, putting in no more than the perfunctory two or three miles per day that being a cop required. Just enough to keep in decent shape.

The cold combined with the altitude hadn't made this morning's extra effort any easier. Once he'd nearly been certain she'd noted his presence, but then she'd gone on as if she'd seen nothing at all.

Still, he had a feeling she'd known he was there.

After a shower and change of clothes she'd moved on to errands and shopping. She'd dropped by the post office, cruised a couple of women's boutiques, then popped in the supermarket. She'd parked her decade-old SUV behind the bar and trudged up the back stairs, both arms loaded with bags of groceries.

She hadn't come out of her room again until 5:00 p.m. when she'd joined Rafe in the bar to work. That move had surprised Heath. He hadn't read anything in her file about her working at the bar and grill from time to time, but according to Rafe she helped him out fairly often. Good help was hard to find, he insisted. His best waitresses were always leaving town with some rich tourist.

Considering every waitress Heath had seen thus far was not only young but attractive, he could see that happening. He wondered what kept Jayne Stephens hanging around. He sipped his beer and watched her now. Her thick brown hair was pulled back into a braid that hung to her waist. Those green eyes were attentive and the smile...well, the smile was pretty damned gorgeous. Every male in the room noticed, even those accompanied by a wife or girlfriend.

The only person who didn't seem to take note of the attention was Jayne herself. She stayed busy, never slowing or taking extra time to chat. He wondered at that. A young, attractive woman like her should have a steady social calendar, but from what he'd learned so far she scarcely dated and hadn't had a single long-term romantic interest since her arrival in Aspen three years ago.

She took her work seriously, too seriously maybe. Appeared to have no interest in pursuing anything beyond the degree in geology she'd already achieved.

Content.

A frown tugged at Heath's brow. That was the word. Jayne Stephens seemed content with her life just as it was. Definitely unusual this day and time. Satisfaction was a difficult state to reach and maintain. Even he couldn't call himself content. There were holes in his life, past and present. A kind of emptiness haunted him that never really went away.

Heath took a sip from his beer and pushed the thought away. The past was gone…dead. No point rehashing any of it.

Work was what he did now. The occasional date accompanied by sex and then nothing. Eventually he'd stopped bothering, focusing solely on getting a new career off the ground. He had reason to cut himself some slack. He wondered what was her issue. She had to have one. People didn't turn off certain needs without a reason.

"Okay."

The subject of his reverie dropping into the chair across the table from him jerked Heath from his unsettling musings. His gaze clashed with hers before he could completely disguise his surprise at her sudden move.

"Why are you watching me, Mr. Murphy?" She placed her tray on the table and propped her elbow next to it to rest her chin in her hand. Those clear green eyes studied him with a curiosity that was at once disconcerting and appealing.

He gave himself a mental shake. "Heath. Call me Heath."

She leaned back in her chair and studied him a bit longer before continuing. "All right. Heath. Why are you watching me like this? I thought you were here to cover mountain rescue or hiking in the backcountry. What does my waiting tables have to do with either of those things?"

"I'm interested in all aspects of your life. This—" he gestured to the room at large "—is part of what makes you who you are."

She cocked her head and eyed him skeptically, apparently searching for the ulterior motive. "Really?"

Cute, he decided, even annoyed as she was. "Absolutely."

Jayne pushed to her feet and picked up her tray. When she would have walked past him to attend to her customers she leaned down and whispered in his ear, "Just one pointer—you're going to have to run a hell of a lot faster if you plan to keep up with me."

A self-deprecating grin slid over Heath's lips. Oh yeah. She'd noticed him this morning. He watched her move back to the bar to place an order but this time his attention wasn't drawn to her long hair…those swaying hips snagged his complete interest. He wasn't supposed to focus on those kinds of details, but she had a great body. Running wasn't all she did to keep in shape, he'd wager. A little body pump, maybe yoga for flexibility. A person, man or woman, had to have tremendous upper-body strength to be a climber, especially one trained to rescue the injured.

Her legs were long, well muscled but still womanly.

Very nice curves—dangerous curves—completed her stature. This morning's running attire had included frame-forming material from the waist down. Great legs, great ass. Both of which he could objectively appreciate as a man, he told himself. The assessment was a fact, nothing more.

She turned just then and objectivity went out the window. His heart rate surged as if he'd just scaled to some unseen peak. What was it about her innocent beauty that disturbed him so? She could very well be hiding information about her father. She could know exactly where he was, who he was, everything.

But the sharpest instincts Heath possessed refuted that conclusion. She didn't know what her father did… had no idea who he was. Her life was far too serene to be hiding a secret that unsettling. If this mission played out the way Danes wanted it to she would soon learn both things about her father. Maybe that was the part that got to Heath. Her life of simple contentment was about to end and his participation represented the catalyst.

As a police detective he had used people, generally dirtbags, to glean the information he needed. He'd hurt people, even killed once. All in the line of duty.

But never, not once in his life had he damaged the innocent. And this time there was no way around it. He clenched his jaw and stared hard at his glass of beer. If he could find anything on her, some wrong thing she'd done, some knowledge of wrongdoing she possessed, his conscience might just let him slide on this one, but his gut told him that wasn't going to happen.

She was clean.

Innocent.

He closed his eyes and exhaled.

Whatever it takes.

Cole Danes expected him to use her no matter the circumstances or the fallout.

Heath opened his eyes and asked himself the question he should have asked before he surrendered to this assignment.

Would Victoria Colby-Camp have allowed this underhanded strategy? Would she have directed him to use this young woman in whatever way necessary? Heath didn't know Victoria very well but he understood one thing with complete certainty: Victoria was a woman of principle. One who would never compromise those principles. So, the real question was, just who was Heath actually working for? The Colby Agency or Cole Danes?

He had his orders.

She, his gaze followed Jayne as she weaved her way through the congested tables, was his assignment. Whatever it took to reel in her father. No questions, no hesitation. Her emotional well-being would be part of the collateral damage, but Heath would do everything within his power to see that she didn't lose anything else. Keeping her safe, maintaining control over her physical well-being, was paramount.

As she headed back to the bar with an empty tray a rowdy patron snagged her by the arm. Heath went on instant alert, sat up a little straighter. He'd noticed this guy flirting with her all evening. The jerk stood, taking the tray from her and setting it aside as a new, achingly slow R & B melody floated through the air.

Smiling politely, Jayne attempted to beg off the unwanted advances, but her pursuer didn't let go. Heath pushed to his feet as the jerk tugged her to the dance floor. It was clear that she had grudgingly relented to the dance to prevent a scene.

Before he realized he'd even moved, Heath was at the guy's back, fury pounding in his skull. He tapped him on the shoulder.

"Get lost," the guy tossed over that same shoulder.

In one fluid motion Heath gripped the man's arm and turned him around. Before the jerk could spit out whatever he'd intended to say, Heath warned, "This is my dance, pal."

The lethal intensity of the words sent the guy staggering back a step. "Whatever," he muttered. He released his hold on Jayne and shuffled back to his table and friends.

She looked as annoyed at Heath as she was at the other guy. "It wasn't a big deal," she protested. "Rafe would have stepped in if he'd thought I needed help."

One glance at the bar told Heath she was right. Rafe was watching, his gaze narrowed suspiciously even now.

Heath shrugged. "Looked like a big deal to me."

When she would have walked away Heath stopped her with a hand on her arm careful to keep his touch gentle. "You mean after all that I don't get the dance." He couldn't say what possessed him to make such a move. Maybe Danes's words about seduction echoing in his brain, or maybe just plain old lust. Whatever the case, he wanted this dance…wanted to hold her like that.

She surveyed her tables and tossed a look at her boss before meeting Heath's gaze. "Sure." She halfheartedly hung her arms around his neck and gave him a look that said she had better things to do. "I wouldn't want you to miss out on anything that makes me tick."

Oh, the lady had an attitude problem. He smiled, slid his arms around her waist and scooted her real close.

She gasped, startled by the bold move. Heath's smile widened to a grin. "Thanks. That'll make my job a lot easier."

The dance floor was crowded, which ensured that they stayed close. The music drowned out all else. After about thirty seconds Heath gave up on pretending the dance was about the case. Instead, he lost himself to the sweet smell of her. Lilac. Not perfume. Bath oil maybe. Or shampoo. Soft and subtle. Sweet and enticing. He inhaled deeply, allowing her scent to permeate his senses.

The heat…the response she generated in his body surprised him, caught him completely off guard. The man-woman thing, physical attraction. That's all it was. Basic chemistry. But the conclusion didn't ebb the tension tightening inside him. If anything, the mental denial only pushed him closer to some crazy edge on a physical level.

Another couple bumped into them and Jayne's arms tightened around him. His own reacted in kind. Protective instinct, he told himself. But when his jaw brushed her soft temple he knew his speculations were way off course. Want seared through him, burning down too many defenses for comfort.

It was crazy but he couldn't stop it. She felt good in his arms and somehow he needed that. Like going shopping without having eaten for days and buying everything in the supermarket. He felt starved for just this kind of touch…her touch. No strings, no emotional luggage. Just the simple pull of attraction. He hadn't realized how badly he'd wanted to feel that again.

Impossible, the voice of reason insisted…but every sway of her body, every touch of her against him shook him up inside…made him want her more. Incredible…

but true. His hands slid down her back, pulled her closer still. He felt the little hitch in her breathing…felt her tremble. And then he stopped, unable to do anything but look at her and wonder at how a total stranger could make him react so irrationally.

The music faded away and she stepped back, her eyes round with surprise or something on that order.

"I have to get back to work."

She left him standing there…watching her walk away.

Heath shook off the haze of lust and made his way back to his table. What the hell had just happened?

He looked at his empty beer mug and decided another was in order but damned if he'd risk having her get close enough for him to order one.

He pushed a path through the thickening crowd, slid onto the one empty bar stool and waited for Rafe to notice his presence. The bar was a sharp contrast to the tables behind him. Most of the folks seated on the stools spoke quietly to each other or basically peered silently into their drinks. The rabble-rousers and dancers were all taking up space around the numerous tables.

He gave himself a mental kick for going stupid on that damned dance floor. Maybe he'd just gotten caught up in the moment. Everyone else was partying the night away.

Yeah, right. And maybe he'd lost his mind. That was the more likely scenario. Lust. He'd neglected his social life far too long.

Jayne rushed up to the bar a few feet away and belted out an order. Thankfully four or five occupied seats separated her from Heath. He refused to look her way but, as bad luck would have it, their gazes collided in the mirror behind the bar. She looked away first.

Damn.

Twenty-four hours and he'd already lost control of the game. Not a good sign for his future career. He had a feeling Cole Danes was not the sort of man who readily accepted failure.

Rafe placed an icy mug of brew on the counter in front of Heath. "You look a mite unsettled, Mr. Murphy. Is everything all right?"

So they were back to Mr. Murphy. This morning the old guy had been pleased to be on a first-name basis.

"Everything's great," Heath allowed, pinning a smile into place.

Rafe propped on the counter and leaned slightly toward him. His words were spoken just loud enough for Heath's ears only. "Look, young fella, I don't know what your game is, but I don't like what I just saw. I thought you came here for a story. I don't like people taking advantage of my hospitality."

"I'm here for the story, nothing more and I would never take advantage of your hospitality."

Whether Rafe saw the sincerity in Heath's eyes or simply decided to leave it at that, he added, "We all have stories, Murphy, but this little gal's like a daughter to me. Don't *write* anything to hurt her."

Heath shook his head adamantly and shimmied his answer somewhere between the God's truth and a flat-out lie. "That's not my intent here."

The older man's analyzing gaze turned hard. "And when you go, don't take anything you didn't bring with you. Got it?"

"Got it."

"She was hurt by a stranger like you a couple years ago, I don't want her to go through that kind of grief again." With that said, Rafe went back to tending bar and Heath drifted back into self-disgust.

Twenty-four hours and he'd lost his perspective.

How the hell had it happened so fast?

JAYNE LOCKED HER apartment door for the first time in a very long time. She sagged against the door and questioned her motives.

It was him. He made her feel insecure…uncertain.

She didn't like that. Didn't appreciate some stranger coming into her life and making her feel…afraid.

Peeling off her T-shirt, she hesitated. Was that all she'd really felt when he'd held her in his arms? She tossed the garment aside. No, that wasn't all she'd felt by any means. Attraction, she'd felt attraction for a man she didn't even know. She pushed off her jeans and shoes. Okay, so it wasn't the first time she'd had the hots for the new guy in town. But that had only happened once and he had, apparently, realized she wasn't the girl for him since he'd left without even saying goodbye.

Would she be smarter this time? Avoiding Heath Murphy would be the smartest thing to do. But that wasn't possible. Her boss wanted her to spend time with Heath Murphy…to give him the story he wanted. She dragged her fingers through her hair, releasing the braid, and allowing the long tresses to fall around her shoulders.

Jayne looked at herself in the mirror and wondered why of all the women in the bar tonight he'd stayed so focused on her. It wasn't like waiting tables would be a pivotal part of his story. Even she knew better than that.

She hadn't been the most beautiful girl there tonight.

There had been plenty of uninhibited young ladies who could have shown him a good time for the night. Something resembling jealousy trickled through her.

Jayne laughed at herself. She was taking all this far too seriously. Mr. Heath Murphy would blow out of town just as quickly as he'd breezed in. All she had to do was give him the story he wanted and then he'd vanish. The last thing she needed to do was let him take a chunk of her heart when he left.

With a sigh, she stripped off her bra and pulled on a nightshirt. Trust was something she gave only to her rescue team members. She couldn't trust this guy. No matter how innocuous his reasons for wanting to hang around her. There was always a chance…

The telephone rang, derailing the one subject she'd put off dealing with. She preferred to stay away from that place. It hurt too much to even consider the possibility.

"Hello."

The silence on the other end of the line sent her heart into a faster rhythm.

"Jayne."

A rush of affection soared through her, overshadowing the doubt and uncertainty.

"Dad!" She sank onto the side of her bed and leaned against the mound of pillows. "It's so good to hear from you." A part of her would never understand why he couldn't manage to visit more often, or at least call on a regular basis, but when he finally did call or visit it made the whole wait worth it.

"How's my girl?"

She suppressed a sigh. He had no way of knowing just how close *blue* came to describing her mood tonight. "Fine. And how are you?"

The pause before his answer made her frown. "I'm good, honey. As always."

This time she was the one who paused to analyze his tone, the words he used. Not nearly as jolly as usual. Definitely not his customary choice of verbal play.

"I missed you at Christmas," she admitted, feeling as petulant as a five-year-old. This was the first time for as long as she could remember that he'd missed calling on a holiday.

"Sorry about that. I was out of the country. Couldn't be helped."

Work. Her father's work kept him from sharing his actual job description with her. But she'd read between the lines and seen enough movies to put two and two together. He was undoubtedly a spy of some sort. Probably for the CIA since he spent so much time out of the country. Her mother had concluded as much, but neither of them had ever really known. He neither confirmed nor denied their conjecture.

"But I promise I'll make it up to you. Soon."

Her fallen expression lifted. Making up usually involved a visit. She hadn't seen him in…more than a year. A visit would be terrific.

"When?" He had to hear the anticipation in her voice. She was such a child whenever he called. It was like twenty years ago all over again. His every call, every visit was like Christmas any time of the year. Even when he'd stopped coming at all for months on end, sometimes years, she still anticipated his arrival like most children did Santa Claus or the Tooth Fairy.

But it hadn't been the same for her mother. She'd heard her mother talking with friends. Had heard her use the word desertion in connection with her father. Had watched her mother steadily grieve herself into an early grave. Yet, Jayne couldn't stop loving her father, not even for his past sins. She had no one else. No siblings, no cousins she knew of. No one. He was all she had left in the world. And she had every intention of hanging on until the end.

Besides, her father was fifty-five. Retirement had to be right around the corner. He'd promised to retire here. In Aspen where they could spend his twilight years together. She pictured the strong man her father was and somehow twilight just didn't fit.

"I need a favor of you, Jayne."

The subtle change in the nuances of his tone set her on edge. Something was wrong. She hadn't heard him sound like this in years…not since he disappeared that one time. And back then she hadn't heard from him for a whole year after that tense conversation. She'd only been six at the time but she remembered it vividly. She remembered the tears as well. Not hers. Her mother's. Night after night for months she'd heard her mother crying through the thin walls of their home. And then there had been the hasty move to California, as if staying one more day in Chicago would have been too risky.

"Sure, Dad, anything."

"I want you to be very careful. Especially now. Remember I've always told you that I have enemies." She nodded but, of course, he didn't see her, but he knew she understood. "I've always been able to keep you separate from that unpleasant business but I'm not sure I've managed this time. *This time is different.*"

Jayne sat up, her pulse skittering as much from his tone as from his words. "What do you mean?"

"There are people who want to hurt me and they will do anything to get to me." A heavy breath hissed across the line. "Including using you, I fear."

"They know about me?" Fear trickled through her veins. She moistened her lips and bit it back. She would not be afraid. Her father had taught her to be stronger than that. He'd kept her a secret and she'd done the same. It was the safest way.

"I have reason to believe that they do." Another unsettling pause. "I hate to have to do this to you, honey, but I would feel a lot better if you got out of there. I'd like to stash you away some place safe for a while."

The grown-up Jayne warred with the obedient daughter who still lived for these rare and precious moments. "But, Dad, I can't do that. I—I have commitments."

"I know you do, that's what makes the request so difficult, but it would mean a great deal to me if you could indulge me this once."

This once.

Hard as she tried Jayne couldn't help resenting that statement. She and her mother had indulged him for a lifetime. How could he use her emotions against her? She loved him, desperately, but this wasn't right. To ask her to do this—to possibly give up everything—it just wasn't fair. These phone calls, rare visits were all he'd ever given her and she clung to them. But this was too much. Even she, despite the child deep inside her who would do most anything for his approval, recognized the injustice of this request.

"Dad, you know I love you and I'd love to help. Really I would, but I can't do this. You're asking too much. As soon as the avalanche advisory is lifted I'll be in the backcountry twenty-four/seven."

Her soul ached, cried out for her to take back the words, but she held her tongue, stayed strong. She couldn't do this, not even for her father.

He chuckled softly. "I thought you might say that. So, I'll ask you to at least do one thing for your old man."

Relief gushed through her with such force that it momentarily stole her voice. She simply couldn't bear being on the outs with him. No matter how little impact he'd had on her everyday life, their connection was a powerful one.

"What would that be?" she ventured, her voice warbling, giving away the emotion she so wanted to shield from him.

"Take extra care in all that you do. Beware of any strangers who come into your life."

She smiled through the tears crested on her lashes. "You know I always do that, Dad, but I promise to be extra careful."

"Good. Just one last thing—"

"You mean there's more?" She swiped at her eyes, her heart aching to beg him for the whole truth. Something was very, very wrong. She was an adult now, why couldn't he tell her the truth?

"No matter what anyone tells you, Jayne, always, always remember that I love you."

And then, with a simple click, he was gone.

Jayne stared at the receiver for a long while after that. He'd called to warn her. He was in trouble. It didn't take someone in the secret agent business to figure that one out. He was in deep trouble and he feared for her life.

Beware of any strangers who come into your life.

At the moment there was only one stranger in her life....

CHAPTER FIVE

"He made contact."

"I know."

Heath had thought he was prepared for this exchange but he'd been wrong.

"You know?" How could Cole Danes know before Heath reported in?

"The place is wired, Murphy. Do you think I'd leave anything to chance? That's not my style."

He should have anticipated that, Heath thought scathingly. He should have and he hadn't.

A man like Danes covered all bases up front. "In that case, is there some point to my being here?" Heath returned, irritated that he hadn't been told about this in the mission briefing—if one could call the demand that he take this assignment a briefing.

"Your job, as you well know, Murphy, is to keep our bait viable until we have what we need."

Rage burned its way through Heath's gut. "Not to worry, Danes," he shot back, allowing his irritation to show, "that's my primary mission. I won't be letting anything happen to our *asset*."

"I'm sure you won't. He'll be close now. He knows you're in place. She may be suspicious of you for that reason."

Heath resisted the impulse to suggest that Danes had likely given Stephens his name and description just to be sure the man recognized the enemy in a timely enough manner. But he kept his mouth shut. He had a job to do. He couldn't let his distrust of Danes interfere with that job.

"You know what I need," Danes reminded before ending the call.

"Yeah, I know," Heath muttered to himself as he closed the phone and tossed it onto the bedside table. He liked this guy less and less. Cold and relentless is what he was, that much was crystal clear. Uncaring about who he hurt to accomplish his mission. Heath hadn't signed on to work with men like Cole Danes.

But the internal affairs investigation would be over soon. If Danes got what he needed from Stephens then perhaps the Colby Agency could return to normal. Again he couldn't help wondering how Victoria felt about all this. If Heath was unhappy with the situation he could only imagine how the woman who'd turned the Colby Agency into the thriving, well-regarded firm it was today felt.

Heath studied the image on his laptop. Jayne worked hard and slept the same way. She hadn't moved a muscle since she'd climbed into bed two hours ago. He'd situated the monitors in her apartment to cover all doors and windows, had installed a listening device on her landline as well as her cell phone. His monitoring of her activities would be strictly on the up and up, allowing her the privacy she deserved when she undressed or bathed. To take advantage of a situation like this would be reprehensible. His observations were for her safety, not for his carnal pleasure. Admittedly, the desire to study her every move for more than simply business had flared more than once, but he'd squashed it without hesitation. He wasn't that kind of man. She needed his protection, not his lust.

He closed his eyes and thought of the sweet expression on her face when she'd spoken to her father. That call had thrilled her. She loved the man. Missed him. Didn't suspect for a moment that he was a bad guy. Her eyes had shone brightly with emotion. After she'd hung up the phone, she sat for a while, hugging her arms around her knees, looking as vulnerable as the little girl Stephens had literally abandoned nearly two decades ago.

She'd needed a father then, needed him even now. Heath slowly moved his head from side to side. No wonder she looked at the owner of the bar and grill like an uncle, and the guys on her rescue team like family. She needed that male influence in her life to make up for the past…for the one man she'd longed for all these years. Heath now knew with certainty that her father was the reason she'd avoided long-term romantic commitment. Trusting her male friends was one thing, but she wasn't about to give another man her heart; the single most important male figure in her life had already broken it.

What a waste.

Those feelings of protection had welled inside a hundredfold as Heath watched her sleep. But there was no way to make his part in this right. Howard Stephens was guilty of the unthinkable, the worst of which included helping to steal Victoria Colby-Camp's son and torturing him for nearly twenty years. The bastard was evil incarnate in Heath's opinion with only that one black mark against him. But there was more. He and Leberman had killed Victoria's first husband, James Colby. The small group of mercenaries that had once operated within Leberman's dominion had to be stopped once and for all. That couldn't happen without cutting off the head of that poisonous viper, Stephens.

Jayne would be devastated when she learned who and what her father was. If Heath had possessed any doubt about her innocence in this, it was undeniable at this point. He would be the deliverer of that horrible truth. She would hate him for it. Her life would never be the same.

Fury swept through Heath all over again at the thought of the call from Danes. That her every move and word was funneled into Heath's laptop hadn't bothered him because he performed his job with the utmost respect. Would not take advantage of the opportunity. But the idea that Danes might be watching as well as listening... that bugged the hell out of Heath. Danes had apparently set up the monitoring system's software to live feed both Heath's receiver and one back at the agency. That move was, as he'd so eloquently put it, a part of his "not taking any chances."

Heath blew out a disgusted breath and dropped his feet to the cold floor. No way in hell could he sleep. Somehow he had to put a stop to this obsessing about Danes's character. Heath had a job to do just as Danes had been hired to accomplish a certain mission. He, from all accounts, was very good at doing his particular work. Who was Heath to say if what he did was right or wrong? He didn't have all the facts, Heath told himself as he blew out another heavy breath. The only thing he could do was carry out his mission, which was to protect the asset while luring in the target.

He'd spent too much time already analyzing Cole Danes. Heath had his assignment. He had to remember that things were never completely black and white.

Hadn't he learned that lesson the hard way in his last career?

Pushing up from the bed he decided a perimeter check and a snack were in order. No point lying here watching Jayne sleep via the monitor while the likelihood of his sleeping grew more remote.

That was just another thing he had to get back under control.

He had to stop thinking about her as a woman. She was an asset. One who needed his protection. He couldn't stay sharp if he let this case get personal. Maybe he wasn't as ready for his first assignment as he'd thought. He'd spent eight years in law enforcement working cases and doing a hell of a good job keeping objective—what was the problem now? It was this place, he knew. It reminded him too much of the past he wanted to forget…perhaps the setting was throwing him off, making him feel unsure of himself and allowing doubt to take root.

But he was here. End of subject.

Heath slipped from the small room and moved quietly down the short corridor, which led directly into the kitchen of the Altitude Bar and Grill. Rafe had told him to make himself at home in the kitchen when he'd offered the only vacant room within the city limits.

Every hotel, motel and resort cabin in the Aspen area had been booked even before Heath arrived. Ski season was at its peak, not to mention some sort of junior Olympics event was in town. Walt Messina, Jayne's boss and the owner of Happy Trails guide service, had hit up his buddy Rafe for the proverbial "back room." Walt knew Rafe had remodeled the bar's back room into a one-room efficiency when he first took over the establishment. Originally the room had served as a bunk for

Rafe's first bartender whenever the snow got too heavy for him to make it up to his cabin or for whenever Rafe was on the outs with his wife of half a lifetime. Nowadays it served mostly as a place for visiting friends to crash when they'd indulged in a little too much of the bar's offerings.

Heath felt confident that Rafe's decision to let him use the room had more to do with his desire to keep an eye on Heath than out of hospitality. The old man was very protective of Jayne. Walt Messina had no reason to suspect Heath since his friend at the *Post* had vouched for him. Of course Heath had never met the gentleman at the *Denver Post* but Cole Danes had. The guy owed him a favor.

Heath scratched his chest as he maneuvered his way through the dark kitchen. He wouldn't want to owe Cole Danes any favors. Heath immediately chastised himself for going back down that road. He had to give Danes a chance, let him do his thing. Trust, or at least patience, was his new watchword. Heath's trust had taken a beating from his former homicide partner, but he couldn't let that disappointment keep him down.

Harsh light blared from the refrigerator when he pulled the door open. Heath blinked against the brightness. He'd been so absorbed in keeping an eye on Jayne tonight he'd failed to eat. But that wasn't unusual. As a police detective he'd always gotten caught up in his cases to the point of letting everything else go.

As he perused the ready-sliced meats and cheeses, he couldn't help wondering what made this time different. Yes, he was fully focused on his asset, but the whole Cole Danes issue kept butting into his perspective. He had to forget that guy and put the I.A. investigation out of his mind. Whatever lurked in the Colby Agency's past had nothing to do with him. This case would be best served if he remembered that fact.

Deli-sliced ham and provolone cheese made his gut rumble. He grabbed the selections as well as the mayo and eased the fridge door closed with one hip. He blinked a couple of times to adjust to the darkness again and set the items on the nearest counter. The overhead light switch was all the way on the other side of the room next to the door leading into the bar. He'd definitely need some light to locate the bread.

The creak of a floorboard alerted him a split second before his gaze zeroed in on movement in the dark near the storeroom door.

He had company.

Heath froze. Let his senses do the work. The intruder moved slowly into the room. There were a couple of exterior windows but tonight's cloud cover ensured virtually no light whatsoever from the moon. A few more steps and his company would be at the end of the long stainless steel island that separated them.

An almost inaudible but sharp intake of breath warned him that his presence had abruptly been noted.

He had to move.

Heath was over the island and on top of the intruder before he could take another step.

The soft scent of lilacs and silky feel of feminine skin exploded in Heath's senses as he pinned the intruder to the cold, steel surface of the counter.

He grabbed something long and solid right before it collided with his head.

Wood.

Baseball bat.

"The police will be here any minute!"

Jayne.

Heath hadn't really needed the threat to recognize her. He'd known who she was the moment he touched her, smelled her. That her lithe body was trapped beneath his against the unyielding steel penetrated his awareness next. As strong as she looked she felt incredibly soft beneath him. Those well-defined and toned muscles were still undeniably feminine, warm and desirable to his touch.

"You'd better let me go you son of a—"

"It's me," he said, cutting her off and jerking himself from the momentary trance he'd drifted into. He pulled the bat from her hand and stepped back. "Heath Murphy."

She whirled away from him and stamped toward the door and the light switch there, the hard slap of her bare feet on the wood floor declaring her fury loud and clear. Oh hell, someone should have told her he was staying here. Obviously it should have been him. He'd assumed Rafe would fill her in.

"What the hell are you doing here?" she demanded as she flipped the switch, flooding the room with fluorescent light. The long bulbs blinked erratically then hummed into full bloom.

Heath looked at the baseball bat he'd wrestled from her then back at the woman. "Do you always wander around in the middle of the night with a deadly weapon?" he teased, hoping to defuse her anger. He laid the bat on the counter, not wanting to look intimidating or threatening in any way.

"Answer the question, dammit." She crossed her arms over her chest and stalked back in his direction.

He wished she had taken the time to don a robe so he wouldn't be distracted by her shapely legs. The night-shirt hit mid-thigh, leaving plenty to derail his concentration. He gave himself a mental shake. It wasn't like he hadn't seen her in that getup already. Somehow the real thing was vastly more appealing than the image on his monitor or maybe he just felt free to appreciate the view when she was aware he was looking.

"I'm staying in the back room." He hitched his thumb in that direction. "The hotels were all booked up. Rafe kindly offered me a place to bunk."

If he'd hoped that assurance would calm her outrage, he'd been wrong. She looked even more furious now.

"Are you telling me," she countered hotly, "that Rafe okayed your staying here and didn't say anything about it to me?"

"Obviously." Heath cleared his throat and gestured vaguely. "I'm sure it was just an oversight. It was a last-minute decision this afternoon and with the busy night in the bar he probably forgot."

"This was Walt's idea, wasn't it?" she accused, those green eyes glowing with ire.

Damn, he could just imagine if all that fury were to morph into another kind of passion…

"Er…yes," he confessed. "Walt suggested it."

Jayne shook her head, none too happy to have her suspicions confirmed, then that sizzling gaze whipped back to his. "You could have mentioned it."

He shrugged, then wrapped his own arms around his chest. He'd never been shy about his body, especially with a woman, but he suddenly felt utterly naked in front of her. He hadn't bothered to drag on a shirt, hadn't expected to encounter anyone.

"I should have, yes." He lifted one shoulder in another apologetic shrug. "I guess I didn't think about it." He let his gaze settle fully onto hers. "I was a little distracted."

He didn't have to spell it out…she knew he meant the dance. Recognition flared in her eyes.

Dammit. The impact of his dark eyes was very nearly more than Jayne could bear. She had told herself that he couldn't affect her that way, but she was wrong. He made her shiver in spite of her fury and that only made her angrier.

A new suspicion broadsided her. Her gaze narrowed. "Are you trying to seduce me, Mr. Murphy?" Didn't guys like him always think they could have it all? Just because she was the subject of his story didn't mean she was easy, dammit!

The look of surprise that skittered across that too-handsome face gave her the answer even before he spoke. "No! I…" He looked around as if searching for some better explanation. He pointed to the food he'd dumped on the counter. "I just came in here for a sand wich. I assumed everyone else was asleep."

He was telling the truth. Jayne reasoned that it was her father's call that had unsettled her so, had made her more distrusting than usual. She outright refused to consider that maybe she was simply attracted to the guy and that his overpowering sensuality wasn't really his fault. He was just too damned good-looking. And that hair. Thick and tousled as it was. She wanted to run her fingers through it.

She squeezed her fingers into fists of determination and resisted the impulse to tap her foot. What the hell was wrong with her? He might not want to seduce her, but this guy was still a stranger. She had to remember her father's warning. She had no way of knowing who really sent this man. Walt had never even met him before. His name might not even be Heath Murphy. He could be some sort of spy. A killer maybe.

Yet, her hungry gaze roamed his big, masculine body once more—he looked utterly adorable right now. A killer wouldn't look like this…would he?

"Maybe you'd like to join me?" He gestured to the ham and cheese. "I'd love the company."

It was 2:00 a.m. He had to be out of his mind. Or maybe she was because she very much wanted to join him. A pang of hunger sliced through her, but she wasn't sure ham and cheese would do the trick.

She swallowed back the want that rose in her throat and tried to relax. "Sure. A sandwich would be nice." She told herself that the best way to figure out if this guy was lying to her was to spend more time with him— question him. See if she could catch him in a lie or trip him up somehow. But she had an awful feeling that she was fooling herself.

Walt wouldn't have any friends involved in the spy or murder business. She joined Heath on the refrigerator side of the island as he found the bread and started sandwich preparations. She was being ridiculous. He was just a reporter. A friend of a friend of Walt's. She trusted Walt. Trusted Rafe. If they liked this guy—trusted this guy—who was she to argue?

Jayne pushed away her father's nagging warning and decided to do this her own way. If Heath Murphy was here to get at her father or to harm her there was only one way to find out.

When Heath's masterpiece sandwiches were ready for debut and Jayne had filled two glasses with milk, she pulled up an old wooden stool on the opposite side of the counter from him. She wanted to watch his facial expressions as they talked. At least that's what she told herself. It wasn't a hardship, but it was necessary, wasn't it?

She had to know if this guy was for real.

"I've never cared for Denver," she told him bluntly. "Have you always lived there?"

He washed down a mouthful of sandwich with a big swig of milk. "Actually I live in Chicago. I'm a freelance writer so I do articles for a number of publications around the country."

Uneasiness slid through her. "So you don't actually work for Walt's friend?"

He shook his head. "I do but I don't." A slow, easy smile widened that full mouth. "Does that make sense?"

Wow. She blinked, averted her gaze from that megawatt smile. "Yeah, sure." She took a bite of her sandwich to buy some time for contemplating her next question.

"Aspen has always been home to you?" he asked before she could decide on her next move.

"I lived in Chicago until I was six." She supposed that gave them something in common, in a roundabout way. She resisted the urge to roll her eyes. Why in the world would she care if they had anything in common? He was just a minor nuisance in her life that would be gone before she could decide if he was friend or foe.

"Really? Where? Maybe I live in that same neighborhood." He flashed that smile again.

"Oak Park." She remembered the little house they'd owned there. She'd hated the basement. Wouldn't even go down there with her mother. But the neighborhood had been nice enough the best she remembered.

"Do you miss it?" he asked. "Chicago, I mean."

"No." Jayne's appetite vanished. Somehow the subject of Chicago always had that effect on her. Maybe it was because that's where everything had changed. She, her mother and father had lived what felt like the perfect life then. At least, to the extent she could remember. He had come home more often, even stayed for weeks at a time. Her mother had kept the house filled with scents of cookies baking and pot roasts simmering. She'd had lots of friends at school and in the neighborhood.

Then suddenly it all ended. Her father disappeared and she and her mother moved away.

"Earth to Jayne."

She blinked. "What?" She hadn't realized he'd said anything. Nor did she like the way he was looking at her now. Analyzing her. Trying to read between the lines of her answers, as well as her distraction. She was the one who needed to be analyzing. Instead she'd gotten bogged down with the past. She hated when that happened.

"I was asking where you ended up after Chicago."

"Sacramento, California." That her tone still sounded distracted flustered her. Her father's call had her off balance, that's all. She refused to consider that it might be this damnable attraction to the man facing her at the moment. They'd only just met.

She wished now that she hadn't been awakened by his late-night plundering. Somehow her gaze shifted downward from his face, to rest on his bare chest. For a desk jockey he kept in great shape. Those broad shoulders were sculpted much like a climber's. She already knew how strong he was by the way he'd pinned her to this countertop and taken the bat away. She shivered and focused on the barely touched sandwich on her plate.

"I'll bet it took some time to adjust to that kind of change."

Again Jayne found herself scrambling to catch up with the conversation. He'd said more, but the words hadn't penetrated the haze of lust she'd slipped into.

"It wasn't that bad," she lied. She'd hated California. No one had liked her. The school had been so different from the one she'd attended in Chicago that she'd been utterly miserable. That's when she'd started her climbing hobby.

Memory after memory of her climbing high in the trees in her backyard flashed one after the other through her mind. She'd started out being satisfied with reaching the lower limbs, but then the need to go higher and higher had become an obsession. It had been the perfect escape. High above the rest of the world. Looking down on all those who treated her as an outsider.

She'd been in love with climbing ever since.

"I learned a lot about myself there," she said out loud, more to herself than to the man staring expectantly at her. She settled her gaze on his. "I learned I could be anything I wanted to, all I had to do was work at it."

And she had. She'd gotten through school, had herself a degree in geology but never once had she felt inclined to teach or do research. She'd rather just revel in the natural beauty and wonders that God had created. That need for adventure had brought her here. Just for the winter she'd told herself. After college she'd wanted, needed, a break before making a decision on what to do with the rest of her life. Her mother was gone. There was nothing holding her anywhere.

She'd come here that winter for the season and she'd never left. Her hard work and perseverance had paid off. She explored nature's beauty for a living and helped show others what the world at twelve thousand feet above sea level had to offer. It was amazing.

She didn't drive a fancy SUV, just an old clunker she'd picked up from a local. She didn't own her own home. But none of that mattered. All that mattered was that she was content. No ties, no commitments to anyone but herself. Well, other than the mountain rescue team and the occasional lost climber.

She didn't need anything else. She'd learned from the best—never look back. Not once had her father ever attempted to explain his sudden disappearance or his long absences. He simply showed up and pretended that all was as it should be.

"What about your folks?"

Heath's question snapped her back to attention. She had to stop zoning out like that.

"My..." She started to tell him that her mother was dead and that her father visited occasionally but she caught herself in time. She blinked, taken aback that she would stumble so badly with this man. Bolstering her defenses, she dished out the standard story, "There's no one but me." She produced the requisite sad smile. "Well, no one besides Rafe and my friends here."

He spotted the lie as soon as it was out of her mouth. She didn't miss the detection in his eyes before he disguised his surprise at her response. That unsettled her just a little. What did her family, or lack thereof, have to do with anything? Why would it matter if she chose not to talk about her family?

Beware of any strangers who come into your life.

Maybe she should heed her father's warning. Heath Murphy was the only stranger who had come into her life, other than tourists, in a very long time. His sudden appearance just prior to her father's warning might not be coincidence.

"I'm sorry to hear that," Heath said with a kind of sincerity that couldn't be faked, giving her something to puzzle over. "It's tough losing the people you care about."

He spoke from personal experience; she heard an old, lingering hurt in his words. But even bad guys had loved ones. However sincere he appeared, that didn't mean she could trust him. No one knew that better than her.

"Well, you know—" she pushed to her feet "—that's life." She picked up her plate and glass. "Good night, Mr. Murphy."

Rafe didn't like anyone dirtying up his sink once the kitchen was clean. Jayne quickly dumped the remains of her sandwich into the trash and deposited her dinnerware into the empty dishwasher. If Mr. Murphy was smart he'd do the same. Or maybe he wouldn't and Rafe would kick him out.

She could hope. Turning from the sink she came face-to-face with the man who had an uncanny ability to completely disorient her. At first she'd thought he'd decided to follow her example and clean up after himself, but instead he set his dishes on the counter next to her. Her gaze followed the movement, slid up those powerful arms and rested on that awesome chest. She hated herself for the weakness but she was only human.

"Look, I apologize if I brought up a tender subject when I asked about your family," he offered quietly. "I've got a few of my own. I can assure you I didn't intend to make you uncomfortable."

Jayne took a deep breath and gave her head a little shake. "Look, Murphy, why don't I just tell you the truth, okay?" Her heart started to pound when her brain caught up with her mouth. She'd always preferred honesty. Never had learned to hold her tongue the way she should. But this startled even her. "I don't know you," she stated bluntly, knowing full well it was too late to turn back now. "I don't trust you. And I have no intention of sleeping with you."

The last statement sent heat flooding to her cheeks and utter humiliation racing through the rest of her body. She could have left out that part. Dammit.

Instead of saying anything he took his time loading his dishes into the dishwasher, still blocking her escape with his body and giving her more than adequate time to grow utterly flustered. Cutting him some slack, she had just said a mouthful. Maybe he needed a moment to come up with a rebuttal.

Finally, after what felt like forever with him bending and reaching and making her feel more restless by the moment, he straightened and looked directly at her. She swallowed tightly and suddenly wished she had left the room at good-night.

"I'm sorry my presence disturbs you." His voice was soft, his expression concerned. "I'll try not to overstep my bounds again."

"I would appreciate that," she admitted, relieved to have the tension broken.

He shrugged, the movement drawing her attention like a fly to honey. "As for the sleeping together thing, I can't say I hadn't thought about that myself." He paused just long enough for the words to send a bolt of heat scorching through her. "But I would never compromise my principles. Good night, Ms. Stephens."

He walked out.

Her mouth dropped open in disbelief.

She was supposed to be the one to walk out. To have had the last word, the final warning.

Instead, he'd left her there feeling like a total idiot.

Not to mention she'd same as confessed that she'd thought about sleeping with him.

Uncertainty trembled through her. But she didn't want to sleep with him. Clearly he didn't want to sleep with her. What the hell had she been thinking admitting that to him? Temporary insanity! She'd lost it. Well, he'd certainly put her in her place.

A new blast of fury set off a minefield of outrage. Oh, he would regret that arrogant rebuke. Whether he'd intended to insult her or not, she would make him earn every word of this story the hard way. If he wanted to know what it was like to be a member of the mountain rescue team, she'd show him up close and personal.

Heath Murphy would rue the day he showed up in her town.

CHAPTER SIX

Heath poured himself a second cup of Rafe's famous wake-the-dead coffee and resumed his position at a table a few feet away from Jayne and the mountain rescue team members gathered for a weekly breakfast meeting.

She hadn't spoken to him this morning. Rafe had banged on his door at 5:00 a.m. and passed along the info about the meeting. Jayne had either forgotten or chosen not to tell him since this was a regularly scheduled event. Considering her father's warning, he was prepared to work harder at earning her trust. Her oversight hadn't slowed down his reaction since he'd been awake already. The motion detectors already installed in her room warned him whenever she moved through any interior doors as well as the one exterior door that led into the upstairs corridor.

The meeting had started at six o'clock sharp. In the past hour they'd covered upcoming training sessions as well as traded humorous tourist stories. It had been the same in Heath's hometown. The locals couldn't help getting a laugh now and then at some of the overenthusiastic tourists who showed up determined to portray themselves as professional skiers, snowboarders, hikers or climbers. Only when they broke a leg or got lost in the wilderness did they admit to their true amateur status.

Aspen was considerably larger and more popular

than where Heath had grown up. Tucked away in the picturesque Roaring Fork Valley at the base of a towering mountain, Aspen had it all from what he'd seen so far: an abundance of shops ranging from gourmet restaurants to bars and pubs, from discount five-and-dimes loaded with tourist memorabilia to ritzy art galleries visited by the rich and famous—most within easy walking distance to the best hotels and resorts. The nightlife ranged from glitzy and glamorous to raw and untamed.

In his opinion Aspen was where the beautiful people came to ski and be seen in an extreme wilderness setting that, despite the haute couture, had managed to maintain its natural raw edges. But none of that meant anything to Heath. In fact, he used every ounce of determination he possessed to block out the insignificant details of the scene around him and to focus only on his mission. He didn't want to *experience* this environment.

He had to be here but he didn't have to soak it up.

So far, with the avalanche advisories still in place, he'd been able to avoid entirely *outdoor recreation*.

"So, we'll meet at the cabin at six tonight to do a gear check."

Heads around the table nodded.

Heath was surprised by that. Tomorrow was Jayne's birthday. He'd expected some sort of party or get-together in her honor. Maybe that was the purpose of tonight's meeting. If so, no one had let him in on the secret.

The mountain rescue cabin was located on the west end of Aspen's Main Street. The team's extra gear, topographic maps, communications system and most anything else they needed to perform rescues would be housed here. Though the team operated under the auspices of the Pitkin County Sheriff's department, Walt Messina pretty much ran things the way he wanted to, it seemed, without any flak. Jayne was second in command in spite of being female and younger than most of the other members. No one appeared to resent her position. A couple of other women were affiliated with the team but worked in a support capacity only.

It took guts and strength, physical as well as mental, to do what these folks did. Heath had worked, in his capacity as a member of law enforcement, with a mountain rescue team once. A long time ago…before the accident. As an experienced climber he'd fit right in with the other adrenaline junkies, but at least those guys had had a cause.

Heath's gut twisted with remembered dread and regret and he had to look away. He'd had no cause other than utter self-indulgence. Climbing had been a hazardous hobby, an ego pump. He'd sworn he would never be a part of anything like that again. And here he was, playing along, as if he hadn't failed…as if he hadn't let someone die.

His gaze moved back to rest on Jayne.

He could handle this. His teeth clenched to hold back the instant denial. Holding the uncertainty at bay had been fairly easy until now. This meeting, seeing this team together and listening to them discuss rescues, hit him a lot harder than he'd anticipated. But he would get past it. There was no way around it. His assignment depended upon his ability to fit in with this group.

"I got the latest word on the avalanche advisory first thing this morning," Walt said, drawing Heath's attention back to the conversation around the table. "If the weather cooperates today and tonight as forecasted the advisory will be lifted tomorrow."

A dagger of ice cut through Heath. That would mean all hiking and climbing operations would be back in business. Not everyone closed up shop for an advisory of this magnitude but some did, Happy Trails being one of them. Jayne would go back to her day job, leading visiting nature and thrill seekers through valleys and over peaks. And it was Heath's job to stay right on her heels, to keep watch for the target's appearance. The bitter dread that had coagulated in his gut evolved into heart-pumping fear. A line of sweat beaded on his brow.

He could do this. He knew the drill, had all the right experience.

But after over three years had he lost the feel? Should he be up front with Jayne and avoid the risk altogether?

"I'd like to run a hut check," Jayne announced, jarring Heath back from his troubling thoughts.

Walt frowned. "The hut associations are responsible for spot checks. They rent them out. They do the maintenance."

"I know," Jayne returned, "but you said there had been a couple of break-ins reported. Supplies stolen. It wouldn't hurt for me to take a look, make sure all is as it should be before the advisory is lifted." She shrugged. "Even if the association does the same a second set of eyes can't hurt. I'm sure the sheriff's office would be interested in any additional detail I might pick up on."

Walt mulled over her suggestion just long enough to finish cranking Heath's tension to the breaking point. If the huts she spoke of were anything like the ones he'd encountered before, the small structures would be at higher elevations, nine or ten thousand feet at least. The huts were generally equipped with bunks, wood-burning or propane stoves and heaters and other basic supplies for survival during backcountry trips. Associations, owners rented them out for use during cross-country hauls for those who didn't care for sleeping on the snow-covered ground. Not to mention that anytime a climber or skier got into trouble, if he could make it to the nearest hut, his chances of survival until help arrived were greatly increased.

"Sounds like you've got cabin fever," Walt suggested with an I've-got-your-number grin. "Hut check if you want, just be careful out there and watch out for any of those snow shelves that might be about to deliver. Might be better if you took someone with you if you're going today."

"I'll do that," she assured her friend and boss. She jerked her head in Heath's direction. "Mr. Murphy over there wants to see firsthand what my life is like, I thought I'd give him a little preview. That competence test I mentioned."

Curious gazes shifted in his direction. He managed a negligible nod to Walt and the others before his gaze collided with Jayne's and the blatant challenge there. This was payback. He wasn't quite sure for what just yet, but he could read the triumph in her eyes.

"You sure he's up to the physical requirements?" Paul Rice, an EMT, wanted to know.

Her gaze never deviated from Heath's as she provided a confident response. "He can handle it." She laughed and glanced around at her teammates. "If not I'll drag him out. In any case, he'll get his story, right? Without getting in the way of a real rescue."

Laughter tittered around the group but Heath didn't find her smart-ass remark funny at all. Giving her grace, she had no way of knowing the impact of what she'd suggested and if he survived the trip he'd make sure she never found out. Knowledge was power and he had to make sure she didn't outmaneuver him when things got dirty.

He had to stay in control of this asset, which equated to one thing: all the best cards had to be in his hand.

JAYNE WATCHED HEATH with a critical eye as he readied for the trek to the Alpine Hut on one of her favorite peaks. She knew the trail well, could basically make the journey with her eyes closed, so she wasn't worried. The snow cornices along her chosen path weren't nearly as worrisome as in some of the more traveled areas. If you stayed in the business long enough around here, you figured out the best routes or made some of your own. They'd check out this one hut and head back. Walt was right on that score. The huts were well maintained. But it had been as good an excuse as any to put her journalist shadow here in the hot seat.

Heath's efficiency at the task of prepping for the cold surprised her. She didn't have to give him the first instruction. He abided by one law any climber worth his salt did, always wear synthetics, absolutely no cotton. Cotton didn't repel water. He even picked the best brands when it came to outerwear, including gloves and snowshoes. Maybe he just had good instincts, but her own instincts were humming a different tune.

This guy had done this before.

Her gaze narrowed with suspicion. He'd certainly left out that pertinent detail of his background. Not that she'd asked that many questions, but one would think that when in Aspen following around a mountain rescue team member a guy would mention winter hiking and/ or climbing experience.

"I'm ready," he announced when he'd pulled on the new parka that looked nothing like the elegant leather coat he'd had on when he arrived on her doorstep.

Very interesting turn of events.

"Let's do this, then."

Jayne clipped her pager at her waist and led the way to her four-wheel-drive clunker. She should have washed it at some point during her downtime but then, what was the point? It would only get dirty again. Snow might look good on the mountains and in the yards of the lovely homes around town, but it turned ugly and muddy on the streets and side roads. They never showed that part in movies, she'd noticed.

Neither of them spoke as she drove along Highway 82 until they reached the turnoff that would lead to the trailhead. The county road had been plowed recently, which made the going a hell of a lot easier. As she parked on the roadside, choosing to walk the rest of the way to their destination, the sun shone between the majestic peaks in the distance. It was going to be a beautiful day and yet the tension continued to thicken between her and her companion.

Jayne had the sudden uneasy feeling that she'd made a mistake. She covertly studied Heath Murphy, wishing she could read his mind. Why would an investigative journalist come here to do a story on the life of a trail guide and mountain rescue team member if he didn't care for the subject? Or apparently felt uncomfortable with some aspect of it? It didn't make sense.

Besides, she couldn't see this guy being afraid of anything. He was strong, confident, even a little arrogant at times. She shouldered into her emergency pack and considered again how he'd seemed to know just the right items to buy for his own pack. A real paradox, this guy.

With the pack and other necessary accessories draped on his back he looked even bigger and she was no petite gal. She stood five-seven, but he had to be six-two or -three. He weighed, she estimated, a hundred eighty pounds, most of which looked to be muscle if his chest and shoulders were any indication. Add to that a face with angles and planes that the sexiest man of the year would be jealous of and you had a hell of a great-looking guy. Even his nose was the perfect cut for balancing that classic square jaw.

Her gaze drifted down to his left hand. Why wasn't he married? Why didn't he get phone calls from a girl-friend? Of course, she supposed he could get all kinds of calls at night, but she hadn't heard his cell phone ring once and she hadn't noticed him making any calls.

Definitely strange.

Maybe he was a loner, she considered as she bent down and strapped on her snowshoes. He did the same. Again, his proficiency at pulling on and securing those time- and energy-saving accessories surprised her.

He looked upward abruptly, his fingers stilling in their work, his gaze colliding with hers.

"Something wrong?" he asked, his tone telling her he'd been aware that she was staring at him for some time now.

"Actually—" she dragged out the word long enough to recover her mental balance "—I was wondering if you'd done this before. You seem to know the routine though I kind of got the distinct impression you weren't looking forward to floundering around in the snow."

He straightened, smoothly shifting his gaze to the rustic beauty ahead of them, all around them really.

"I'm no virgin," he deadpanned, his attention moving back to her, "but it's been a really long time."

"Should I be concerned?" She had to ask though part of her wanted him to suffer, especially after that smart-alecky comment. God, where had that come from? She wasn't usually so heartless. But he made her angry...or something. Still, she couldn't let her annoyance at him get in the way of safety.

"I'll be fine."

His expression closed like steel doors slamming on a vault and she knew that the discussion was over.

Towering firs dotted the white landscape, their branches loaded with day-old snow. With several feet of compacted snow covering the plant life, the going should have been easier, but the fresh layer of fine powder made trail-breaking necessary. Every step she took sank in a foot or so—even with state-of-the-art snowshoes—ensuring maximum physical effort was involved.

To keep her mind off her companion, she mulled over the idea that tomorrow was her birthday and so far no one had mentioned a party. No one had mentioned her birthday at all. Her father hadn't even said anything. The possibility that maybe no one remembered that her birthday was less than twenty-four hours away only served to drive home the loneliness that gnawed at her from time to time. Usually she didn't let her lack of real family bother her. After all, she had Rafe and the guys.

But it wasn't the same. There were times when she had to admit that painful fact.

Admitting it and dwelling on it were very different animals and she refused to dwell on things she couldn't change. She forged forward, making a path in the deep, loose snow. Family was overrated anyway.

It was cold—around twenty degrees. But it didn't take long to warm up. Jayne paid close attention to her instincts. Even an experienced guide lost the trail from time to time. Definitely something she wanted to avoid. Losing the trail meant possibly going through deadfall from the surrounding firs and possibly crossing gullies shielded by the snow cover. There could be numerous other trip hazards hidden beneath the blanket of pristine white. Definitely something to avoid.

The farther they climbed the stiller the air became. The lack of breeze gave the peaceful environment a kind of surreal quality. The quiet was broken only by the breath that steamed in and out of their lungs. Heath hadn't lied about one thing—it had definitely been a while since he had done this. Though he'd stayed close on her heels when she took her early morning runs, this was an entirely different kind of workout. They had been moving at a good pace up this sharp ridge. She considered slowing down but knew they'd never make it to the hut and back before dark if she did.

"You okay back there?" She glanced back at him for the first time in almost an hour.

"Great," he insisted with a nod of his head.

But he didn't look great. Physically he appeared fine. Tough as the fresh powder made it, this wasn't the kind of climb that would endanger anyone who was in good physical condition and he met that qualification hands down. Not to mention she was the one doing the trail-breaking, all he had to do was follow in her compacted footsteps.

No, it wasn't his outward appearance that gave her

pause; it was something in his eyes. A dullness she hadn't seen before. That jarred her.

"We'll keep going then." Her instincts warring, she turned back to the trail and pushed forward. A couple more hours, tops, and they'd reach the false summit where the Alpine Hut stood. They'd replenish their fluids, eat, take a short break and then head back down.

Piece of cake.

HE WASN'T GOING TO make it.

By the time the hut came into view, after three and one half hours of steady climbing, Heath knew with dead certainty that he should have told her the truth up front.

Snowshoes and ski poles lashed to her pack, Jayne hustled up to the small, rustic cabin and unlocked the door. Heath made the final few steps a bit more slowly. He was in no hurry for her visual examination to confirm what she had clearly suspected two hours ago.

He was in real trouble here.

Panic had broken out in a cold, clammy sweat all over his body, in spite of, or maybe because of, the layers of synthetics he wore. Pants, shirt, parka, all of it was too familiar. Even the smell of the new fabric made his stomach churn. His heart pounded but it was more than the rigor of ascending several thousand feet…it was the whole package.

The vast whiteness. The mountains jutting toward the sky. The occasional scrub brush and spot of ground that defied the snow by remaining visible after a bona fide blizzard. He had tried to talk himself down from the anxiety. Blamed the physical symptoms on the altitude and the fact that he hadn't climbed in more than three years.

But it was none of those things.

It was the memories.

The way she'd looked at him before she'd fallen... before he'd failed her.

His fault.

He'd dragged her to Utah, insisted that there was this one peak he just had to climb. He wanted her there with him. She'd relented, though climbing was far from her favorite leisure time activity.

Only one of them had climbed back down that mountain.

It had taken days to recover her body.

No one had blamed him. It was an accident.

But he knew then and he knew now that it was his fault. She only went to please him.

Heath stalled just inside the door of the cabin, tore off his pack, gloves and parka and started to pace the small main room. But the anxiety only escalated. Being inside...this place... It made things worse. The smell of something burning jerked his attention across the room.

Jayne had built a fire.

He blinked, tried to steady himself. She already suspected something wasn't right. He had to get back in control of the situation. He'd known this would happen. No one else at the Colby Agency had possessed his climbing skills. His selection had been necessary. There had been no time to prepare another investigator for this assignment. Not to mention the I.A. investigation had dictated that he be the one. He'd thought that maybe he could handle it. But he'd been wrong.

A new realization made Heath go stone cold. Right now, at this precise moment, she was not safe with him. He wasn't at all sure he could protect her if the need arose. He hoped like hell Howard Stephens didn't choose this particular moment to show up. He'd managed to keep his guard up fairly well on the way up, surveying the area, watching for any sign of movement, though he doubted if he'd been at his best.

Heath's eyes closed and for the first time since the morning began he let the climate's bitter cold invade his senses. He was freezing. His fingers were numb in spite of the high-tech gloves he'd worn. His leg muscles ached and he felt more exhausted than—

"Okay, enough of this."

Jayne's firm tone ushered his eyes open. She stared at him as if she feared he might make a run for it any second. And, truthfully, that's exactly how he felt, as if he needed to run all the way back down this damned mountain and not look back. He clenched his fists, set his jaw hard. Anything to keep himself from flying apart.

Deep in his gut he'd known this was a bad idea. But not once had he considered that it would be quite this bad. He'd thought he had put the past behind him. He'd been wrong.

"What's going on?" Jayne demanded, drawing his attention back to the here and now. "You look terrified. What the hell are you doing following me around, Murphy, if you're scared of heights?"

"I'm not afraid of heights," he growled, too frustrated to keep the savage sound out of his tone.

She glanced at the pack, parka and gloves he'd discarded so carelessly. Whatever she thought of that she kept to herself. Instead of pounding him with more questions, she pulled the food from her own pack as well as his and warmed it over the flames. He stood back, unable to participate, and watched her methodical, familiar movements. His mind immediately conjured flashes of memory of him doing that very thing. He'd been there…done that…one time too many already. He had to be insane to be here now.

The room started to heat up and Heath unbuttoned the Gore-Tex shirt he wore over two layers of full-length underclothes. The floor glistened with the snow that had melted from their boots. He wet his lips and swallowed back another surge of panic. Control, he had to grab back control. They were safe. There was no need to panic. And, yet, he couldn't slow the adrenaline soaring through his veins.

He curled and uncurled his fingers and looked around the room for something to focus on or something to do.

"The woodpile looks a little low," he muttered, more to himself than to the only other human being within a few thousand feet of him.

She set the grub on the table and looked from him to the woodpile in the corner and back. "There's probably more out back. I'll bring some in to replace what we use after we eat. *You* need to eat and calm down."

He shook his head and reached for his parka and gloves. "I'll take care of the wood."

Before Jayne could say more he'd tramped out the door. What the hell was the deal here?

She went to the window, forgetting the food that would get cold a hell of a lot faster than it had gotten warm, and watched as he checked a couple of snowdrifts before he found the woodpile. He gathered an armful of chopped wood and hauled it into the hut.

When he'd stacked it in the corner he turned back to her. "That's the last of what's been prepared for the stove." He gestured to the wood-burning stove she had going at maximum capacity. "If there's an ax around here I'll chop some more."

He couldn't be serious. "Of course there's an ax in the hall storage closet, but you don't need to do that. The owner or the renters take care of that, it's—"

He cut her off, those dark brown eyes going from a listless deadness to a glittering granite glare. "It's like you said, it doesn't hurt to make sure all is as it should be before the avalanche advisory is lifted."

Well, he had her there. Before she could even attempt to argue with her own words, he'd stormed back out into the frigid air.

Not so foolish as to ignore her own needs, Jayne nibbled at her food as she observed his maniac episode and that's all she knew to call it. He'd exposed a pile of larger sticks of wood and was now hefting the ax to chop them into smaller, stove-size pieces. It was insane. Though she doubted she had to worry about him freezing to death. It just wasn't right.

After thirty minutes of grueling labor, including stacking the newly chopped wood into a neat pile, he came inside again. This time he stomped most of the snow off his boots first. He put the ax away and came back into the main room where she stood, flabbergasted.

"Anything else you'd like to do around here?" She waved her arms in punctuation of the question. "I don't know, maybe like clear the snow off the roof?"

He didn't answer, just grabbed up his cold food and ravenously devoured it.

When he'd finished fueling his body and cleaned up the remains her patience slipped again. "Okay, Murphy, let's have it," she demanded, hands planted on her Gore-Tex–clad hips. There was nothing attractive about cold weather gear for climbers. The thick layers of protective clothing probably made her hips several inches wider. She shook herself and refused to even speculate on why that thought had never once occurred to her before. This *thing* going on between her and him was too bizarre. They were strangers. She didn't even like him. Especially right now.

"Have what?" He avoided her eyes, pretending to be concerned with something outside the front window.

"You're not fooling me for a second." She marched up to him and poked him in the chest, not that the move did much good with all those heavy clothes in the way. But it did get his attention. "I know a panic attack when I see one. I've dealt with plenty when overzealous climbers underestimate their fears. You almost lost it on the way up here. Why?"

They didn't have time for this. The daylight was wasting away while she played twenty questions with a virtual stranger. She had to be losing it, too. But there was something in his eyes…an emotion that compelled her to ask…to understand. Every instinct told her that this man was far too strong and capable to be turned inside out by a moderate climb. There was more…a lot more.

His answer was so long in coming she'd wondered if he intended to answer at all. Finally he did, but not before wiping his face and eyes clean of emotion. "I told you I'd done this a few times before."

She nodded once, afraid to speak or make any sudden moves for fear of stopping him.

One shoulder jerked in what was likely intended as a shrug. "There was an accident." His gaze connected with hers on a level that took her breath. She could feel his agony. "I don't want to talk about it." She blinked, he didn't. "I haven't climbed since."

She wanted to curl up and die. What a jerk she'd been.

"I'm sorry." She let go a heavy breath. "I shouldn't have dragged you up here like this." He didn't respond, just stared at her. "But I wanted to get back at you for…" Man, her motivation sounded so lame now. But she owed him the truth. "You walked out on me last night and I was supposed to walk out on you," she said in a rush.

He didn't look completely surprised at her silly admission, but then he didn't look happy about it either.

He blew out a weary breath of his own and shoved his hands into the pockets of his cold-weather pants. "Well, if it makes you feel any better," he offered, those dark eyes soft and sexy as hell once more, "it wasn't easy."

A moment of awkward silence hung in the air. Jayne wasn't sure whether she should demand to know what his statement meant or run for her life.

She decided on the latter.

"We should go. Walt was right, this was totally unnecessary."

She didn't give him an opportunity to debate the assessment. She put out the fire she'd built, carried out the ash and locked up the hut, safe and sound.

Just under four hours later they were back at the trailhead and climbing into her old clunker. She drove straight to town as quickly as the slick road allowed, parked and immediately headed up to her apartment.

All without exchanging a word or glance with Heath Murphy.

CHAPTER SEVEN

Jayne soaked in the tub for nearly an hour. She'd had to keep adding hot water in an effort to ward off the chill that seemed to come from her very bones. It was scarcely six o'clock and already she felt like midnight had come and gone.

She kept seeing his eyes…the agony.

There was an accident.

I haven't climbed since.

She squeezed her lids shut and tried to banish the memory but it simply would not go away.

She opened her eyes and looked at her hands, the small calluses there. The physical rigor of her work left its mark other places as well. She lifted her left leg from the water and studied the jagged line on her calf where she'd taken her first fifty-yard tumble down into a gulley a few years ago. Twenty-eight stitches had been required to sew her up. Bruises and other aches and pains came with the territory on a regular basis.

But there were other marks, the kind that scarred a person's heart and soul. The ones like Heath bore. She moved her head slowly from side to side in confusion. She hadn't noticed when they first met. She should have. Anyone who'd ever watched someone fall to their death or who had dragged a body out of a river a few thousand feet below where the victim had fallen had a look about them. It wasn't pretty. She should know. She stared into that haunted expression every day in the mirror.

Her worst nightmares came from the rescues. Not the ones who survived but the ones who didn't. Those times when a rescue became a body recovery. Kids were the worst. God, she didn't know how parents dealt with the loss. Expert climbers fell occasionally. Not often, but once in a great while. She remembered one retrieval where a man with thirty years' climbing experience behind him disappeared. It had taken days to find him. He'd fallen but hadn't died immediately. Before beginning what would be his final journey he'd opted not to carry a transmitter, commonly known as an avalanche beacon. He had carried his cell phone. But the vicious cold got the battery and then it got him. He'd left a journal of sorts down to the bitter end. His last entry spoke of feeling splendidly warm.

The phenomena was kind of like a mirage in the desert, a person suffering from the final stages of hypothermia would feel incredibly warm and even start shedding the very garments keeping him alive.

An experience like that had left its mark on Heath. She'd known people who lost friends and relatives but it didn't keep them away from the challenge of climbing. It was like an addiction, got in your blood. You couldn't deny the rush. That's what kept people like her going back out there bringing back the lost even after scraping up body parts from rocky gullies.

But Heath hadn't gone back. Today had been tough on him. She'd watched him almost come apart right in front of her. Sheer determination had held him together enough to walk off that mountain. A new kind of respect for this man sprouted inside her. Mixed with that respect was guilt for putting him through the pain. But she hadn't known. She should have, but she hadn't. His courage had won out, though. He was every bit as strong mentally as he was physically.

The dreamy smile that pushed across her face fell just as quickly. But that didn't explain or excuse his final remark in that hut. *Well, if it makes you feel any better…it wasn't easy.*

What wasn't easy? Walking away? That didn't make sense…unless he was attracted to her and suffered the same malady of need as she did.

"Don't be ridiculous," she grumbled under her breath. He liked teasing her, that was clear. Definitely liked watching her, but that was part of the reporter gig, right? He couldn't do his job without getting to know her and observing her routine.

Oh well. She was probably better off not knowing what he'd meant. In a couple of days he would be gone anyway. She was pretty sure he was only hanging around in hopes of having the opportunity to observe an actual rescue.

A new line of confusion worried her brow. That didn't make sense. If he didn't climb anymore, how was he supposed to observe anything? She had a strong suspicion she wasn't supposed to have seen what she saw today. Just how the heck had he expected to get through the ordeal anyway? He'd be a liability. He had to know that.

She sighed and relaxed more deeply into the water. She was too tired to figure this out. But there was definitely something out of sync here. If he hadn't come to write about a rescue, then why here, why her?

Her father's warning exploded inside her brain, evaporating the oxygen in her lungs.

Killers didn't have panic attacks, she reasoned. This

guy had a full-fledged anxiety episode. She'd witnessed it with her own eyes. Spies and assassins didn't succumb to mere human frailties...did they?

"Just give it up, girl," she muttered as she reluctantly dragged herself from the water. A few more minutes and she'd be a prune. Tomorrow was her birthday. She wanted to look good even if no one noticed.

She wrapped a towel around her hair and then another around her body. She'd eat in tonight. Didn't feel like company and there would be a crowd in the bar. The outdoor enthusiasts would be in full swing, celebrating the lifting of the avalanche advisory.

That scene would just have to happen without her. She had a bottle of wine somewhere in her tiny kitchen, cheese, crackers. Hey, sounded like a party to her.

She stared at her reflection in the mirror. She'd be twenty-five in a few hours. No boyfriend. Not even any prospects. That was truly sad.

And then an old, too-familiar companion crept in. Loneliness.

HEATH WALKED THE perimeter once more before going back inside. He glanced at the display on his phone occasionally, quickly looking away when he noted Jayne's exact position. He drew in a deep breath of cold air. For the last hour she'd been in the tub. He'd known he couldn't hang around his room and *not* look at that monitor.

No problem. He needed to check the area anyway. Uneasiness nagged at him. He'd accessed the system with his cell phone, picking up the monitor's feed. The image was small enough to lack detail but sufficient to set him at ease as to her every move.

He stopped and turned around. The sidewalk wasn't

crowded just yet. In another hour the streets would be jam-packed, but for now, it was pretty deserted. But the hair standing on the back of his neck warned him that he wasn't the only one watching the Altitude Bar and Grill.

He was here.

Not just in the area, but *here*.

Heath surveyed the street, then the building before him. Its one-hundred-year-old facade was right in keeping with the old mining-town look still present around Aspen, as was the rustic interior. Even he couldn't deny that this was a lovely town. Picturesque most certainly. The snow-covered roofs and streets lit with holiday lights made the new as well as the old look cozy and welcoming. But it was the snow-capped peaks in the distance that drew folks from all around the country.

Not the kind of place one would generally expect to find a man like Howard Stephens lurking. But he was here all the same. Heath could feel the anticipation building and this time it had nothing to do with altitude.

He glanced right once more then headed toward the entrance of the bar. He'd lost a lot of ground today. Had allowed Jayne to see his weakness. She would have questions. Those questions would lead to more questions. Soon she would realize that two and two, in this case, did not equal four. And then the situation would spiral completely out of control.

Somehow he had to stop that from happening.

He hesitated at the door. His old psychologist would say that he'd faced his demons today. And he had. But he wasn't sure the challenge had accomplished anything other than distracting and exposing him.

He'd been distracted when they arrived back into

town this evening but not so much so as not to notice the change. His old, reliable cop instincts had surfaced in the nick of time. He'd felt someone watching Jayne, watching him, as they'd exited her vehicle and headed into the bar. With each passing second since, that well-honed instinct he'd depended upon more than once had been sending him a warning with escalating urgency.

Jayne might not have the opportunity to figure out who he really was and why he was here. He had a bad feeling that learning who and what her father was might just take precedence sooner than he'd hoped.

One good thing had come of today's loss of control. Jayne had connected with him on at least one level. Even if she only felt sorry for him, it was a starting point. He'd need all the help he could get before this was over.

He checked the screen on his cell phone once more before going inside. Jayne was busily drying her hair, still clad in that damned towel. His throat went instantly and fiercely dry. This was the first time since…in a long time that he'd wanted a woman the way he wanted Jayne. He respected her, was awed by her determination. Maybe it was that she so effortlessly achieved what he'd once loved. To stand on some fourteen-thousand-foot summit and peer out over the world had once completed something inside him. That, he realized then, might just be the unexplainable connection he shared with her.

She moved with nature, not against it. He felt reasonably sure that watching her was all that had prevented today from turning out far worse. She'd kept him grounded to a degree.

Needing her, however, would be a liability for both of them in the end.

"Hey, Murphy! Come over here!"

Rafe gestured wildly for Heath to join him at the

end of the bar. A small crowd had already gathered around the tables and the music whined and coiled its way around the room.

"What's up?" He paused at the bar, anxious to get to his room…to a better, larger image of the woman upstairs. He groaned inwardly at his inability to keep his head on straight. Oh, hell, what was one more admission today?

"Listen, Murphy," Rafe said in a stage whisper, "you gotta help me out here."

"Rafe, I don't—"

"There isn't much time, you've got to take care of this for me," the old man insisted.

Heath held up his hands in the classic surrender gesture. "Tell me what you need me to do."

Rafe edged closer as if his instructions were top secret. "Go upstairs and keep my girl occupied until I tell you to bring 'er down."

A frown furrowed a path across Heath's brow. "How's that?" The music was loud, maybe he'd misunderstood.

"It's her birthday, man," Rafe urged. "Keep her busy until I get everything in order down here."

Heath surveyed the crowd more closely and recognized the other mountain rescue team members and several people he'd noted Jayne chatting with when she'd waited tables.

"Look back here." Rafe grabbed him by the arm and hauled him to the kitchen door. He grinned like a new grandfather when he pointed out the enormous cake holding a place of honor on the island.

"I see." Heath nodded. "I'll go up now." His entire body tightened at the prospect. Rafe had no way of knowing that sending him to her room was not a good idea.

"Give me the number of that slick cell phone you carry," Rafe said, grabbing a napkin and the pen from his shirt pocket.

Heath rattled off the number and headed toward the back stairs. He hesitated at the short corridor that led past the public rest rooms long enough to give the old guy a two-fingered salute. Rafe grinned and rubbed his hands together in anticipation.

At the end of the corridor was a door marked "Employees Only" that led to the storeroom where the stairs were located. A smile tugged at Heath's lips as he double-timed it up the ancient steps. He should have known her friends wouldn't let her down. He was glad. He'd seen her eyes after that call from her father. As contented as Jayne liked to pretend she was, she was lonely. She would love this.

He stood outside her door for several seconds before he knocked. His hesitation wasn't about courage, it was about that other "c" word. He was having a hell of a time with control where she was concerned. Where this whole case was concerned. She'd likely figured out that walking away from her without doing something stupid like kissing her last night was what he'd meant about it not being easy.

Just another admission he should have kept to himself. Already regret weighed heavily on his shoulders. He didn't want to be the one to do this to her…to show her the truth.

Her door opened and she stood there, now wearing that ragged terry cloth robe and still clutching a hairbrush. She blinked away the surprise at seeing him and asked, "What's up?"

Whether she'd intended the next move or not, he couldn't say, but the one thing he could predict was its effect. Her gaze slid down his body, from the V neck of the lightweight sweater he wore beneath the jacket that concealed his shoulder holster and weapon to the wellworn jeans he preferred over any other trousers. Muscles already taut with tension turned rock hard with want.

Definitely a bad sign of how this day could ultimately end.

"Can I come in?" he asked, drawing her gaze out of dangerous territory and back to his face.

Big mistake.

That wide-eyed innocent stare glowed with desire. She blinked. "Sure."

He waited for her to step back and open the door wider. Keeping physical distance was imperative right now if he was to have any hope whatsoever of keeping this on a professional level. In his wildest dreams he would never have imagined it would be this difficult. The concept that he might not be cut out for this kind of work nudged him for the second time since he had left Chicago.

He'd done a little undercover work back in his cop days, but he'd never had this much trouble keeping perspective.

"Is something wrong?" she asked, eyeing him speculatively. Not that he could blame her, he'd pretty much lost it on that mountain today. She had good reason to doubt his sanity.

He tried not to look at the shoulder bared by the loose fitting robe when she inclined her head to the right like that. "Ah...maybe you'd be more comfortable if you got dressed. I don't mind waiting." He gestured to the closest chair. "I'd like to get some more background information. If that's okay?" The house of lies he was building felt shakier with each one he added.

Confusion skittered across her makeup-free face. "Okay. Good." She shrugged, which bared more of that gorgeous shoulder. "I'll...ah...get dressed."

When she'd left the room Heath breathed a little easier. He took advantage of the moment and looked around to see if anything had changed since he was here before. He wondered if her father had come into the room. He'd had the perfect opportunity while they were climbing today. Heath slipped a palm-size electronics detector from his jacket pocket and scanned the room and the tiny, adjoining kitchen nook. The only bugs he found were the ones Cole's people had installed, but that left the bedroom and bathroom. That opportunity might not present itself unless he could slip away from the party for a few moments tonight.

Heath paused to study a framed photograph of a much-younger Jayne and another woman who he suspected was her mother. The resemblance was there, too dramatic not to notice. He hadn't found any pictures of her father, didn't see any now. Stephens had probably warned her not to keep any around, a sacrifice of the job. Jayne was a smart lady; he wondered if she blindly accepted his explanations for his long absences and stealthy behavior. It seemed unlikely to Heath, but then a kid would do most anything for a parent's approval.

He thought of his own parents and how he rarely got down to see them anymore. He'd blamed his negligence on the accident, like he did everything else, but maybe it was more related to the idea that he didn't want to see the accusation in their eyes. Or, like his psychologist had suggested, maybe it was merely his own self-guilt that made him see and feel only what he expected to see. Either way, he couldn't deal with it.

"That's me and my mom when I turned eighteen," Jayne said from behind him. "Less than a year before she died."

Heath turned to face her. "You look a lot like her."

She smiled, her eyes distant with memories. "Thanks. We were very close."

"Staying in tonight?" he asked, changing the subject.

She looked down self-consciously at her attire, faded jeans and an equally fatigued Altitude T-shirt. He hadn't meant to make her feel self-conscious. It's just that he knew what was in store. He couldn't help grinning at those bare feet. Pink nail polish gleamed on her toes. Cute. Sexy as hell. Something else for him to think about when he should be concentrating on his job.

"Yeah." She shrugged. "I'm spending the night with a bottle of wine."

He'd noticed the bottle on the kitchen counter…and the single stemmed glass.

"It's my birthday," she explained as she padded over to the counter. "At least it will be in about four and a half hours." She uncorked the wine and reached for the glass. "Would you like to join me?"

The voice of reason told him to say no, but he just couldn't turn her down. She looked so vulnerable and needy. Where was the strong, determined young woman he'd first met some forty-eight hours ago? Apparently he wasn't the only one baring weaknesses today.

He took the glass from her. Their fingers brushed, the resulting sizzle chasing away the last of his good sense.

She prowled in the cupboard for another glass and

came out with a plastic one sporting the logo of a local Mexican restaurant. That blush of self-consciousness tinted her cheeks again. "I don't have guests often," she explained.

"Here." He exchanged glasses with her. "It's your birthday."

The gesture brought another of those sweet smiles to her lips stealing Heath's ability to take a breath.

When she'd poured his wine he offered a toast, "To you, may this be the best birthday ever."

She touched her glass to his. "To me," she murmured before taking a sip of the amber liquid.

But this wouldn't be her best birthday ever. That's why he was here, to rip away the fantasy. To make her see the worst in the man whose shadow she'd clung to all these years.

Heath drank deeply in hopes of drowning the guilt, but it wouldn't work. He'd tried that before. That he'd gone into this with his eyes wide open only made him more of a monster and he had to live with that. Even if what he was about to do was for her own good.

Or was it?

Why couldn't Danes have found some other way to lure her father? Then the man would simply have stopped calling, stopped making those rare visits. She would never have had to know the truth. She could have made up a dozen different romantic and heroic scenarios for his disappearance.

Damn Cole Danes.

Heath clutched his drink so hard it was a miracle the plastic didn't crack.

"Murphy, I was wondering—"

"Heath," he interjected, his voice stilted. "You were going to call me Heath, remember?" She should at least be on a first-name basis with the man who was about to turn her world upside down.

"Heath," she relented. "I know you wanted to ask me some questions, but, if you're up to it, I'd like to talk about that accident you mentioned. What happened to you today…" She looked away for a moment. "I'd like to help."

To his supreme gratitude his cell phone rang just then. "Excuse me." He set his glass aside and turned away from her expectant expression to answer the call just in case it wasn't Rafe. "Murphy."

"We're ready down here," Rafe whispered.

"I understand." Heath closed the phone, scarcely suppressing the smile that tickled his lips. Rafe was something. He would be here for her. As would the others on her rescue team. They would help Jayne through the devastation to come. That assuaged his conscience a fraction, but it didn't relieve him of responsibility.

He dropped the phone back into his jacket pocket and faced the woman who seriously messed with his objectivity. "I have to pick up an incoming fax at the Mail Boxes Etc., across the street," he said without hesitation. "Would you walk over with me? We can talk on the way." That last comment was purposely misleading. He wouldn't be talking about the accident. Couldn't. But he needed her to go with him, for that she needed motivation. More lies. Funny thing was, each one pinged his conscience a little harder.

She glanced at the clock. "Are they still open?"

He shrugged, dismissing her concern. "Must be, they called."

She set her wineglass on the counter. "A walk would be good."

She grabbed her ever-present pager then tugged on

her ankle boots and he helped her into her coat, relishing the feel of her hair against his hand. This was the first time she'd worn it down. He liked it that way. The image of the silky stuff gliding over his skin as they made love loomed large in his overactive imagination before he could stop it.

Another bad omen.

IT WAS A GOOD THING Jayne knew the stairs down to the ground floor by heart because she couldn't take her eyes off the man at her side.

The stark contrast between what she'd witnessed on that mountain and the man with her right now totally blew her away. So polished, so damned good-looking. Perfect composure, radiating strength and confidence.

Whatever had happened to him was too horrible to talk about. Too horrible to relive and yet he made that climb with her today as if his life had depended upon it.

The two extremes didn't mesh, made no sense at all. Why would he put himself through that kind of mental anguish to get a story? Did his job depend upon this one story? He'd said he worked for a number of publications. Maybe his career had taken a downward spiral and he hoped for *the* story that would put him back on top.

Whatever the case, she had to respect that kind of grit. She'd known he was strong from the beginning but that glimpse of vulnerability today had shaken her to the core. She'd never met a man confident enough in his masculinity to risk such a display.

God almighty, she was falling for this guy.

A soft sigh ached out of her. And he was only here temporarily.

How could this happen?

She'd sworn never to let this happen. Okay, it hadn't yet. At least not completely. Firming her resolve as they reached the door that led out into the corridor, she promised herself not to let this relationship progress any further into personal terrain. From now on this would be a purely professional relationship of interviewee and interviewer. Nothing more.

"Jayne." He stopped shy of opening the door.

She looked up at him and every speck of willpower she'd gathered scattered like snowflakes on a windy day. "Yes?"

If he hadn't looked at her that way, hadn't let his gaze drop to her lips, she might have had a chance, but he did look at her that way…as if he wanted to kiss her more than he'd ever wanted to do anything in his life.

"Happy birthday," he said softly. He kissed her cheek and her heart stumbled. In that infinitesimal moment before he drew away—that throbbing pause that turned one's knees to mush—he whispered two words that sent uncertainty rushing through her veins. "Forgive me."

She stared at his profile as he opened the door and ushered her into the corridor. Before she could demand an explanation hundreds of arms were reaching for her, voices crying out, "Happy birthday, Jayne!"

Her friends dragged her toward the center of the room, away from Heath, where a huge birthday cake awaited.

As Rafe draped an arm around her shoulders the entire crowd broke into a seriously pathetic rendition of the birthday song. Jayne couldn't help herself, she had to cry. Foolish tears rolled down her cheeks and the members of her team all had a good laugh.

"Well, now Jayne," Walt said, pushing his way to her other side, "we didn't mean to make you cry like a baby, but since we did, we'll need a picture for future corroboration."

Cameras flashed as she swiped her eyes and struggled not to laugh. This would ruin her tough-as-nails reputation. "Just wait," she threatened, "I know your birthdays, too." She looked from Walt to Rafe. "I'll make sure the funeral director's hearse is parked out front."

"Let's get this party started before the little lady gets to any of the rest of us," Chad, her team partner, suggested.

Cheers of approval went up as someone pumped up the music's volume. Chad gave her a hug, then Paul. She lost count of the number of people who wrapped their arms around her and pointed to gifts piled on one end of the bar. She hadn't even noticed the gifts.

She looked for Heath but couldn't find him in the crowd. Had he meant that she should forgive him for being in on this surprise? The words, his tone, felt too somber for something as happy as this.

Forget it. This was her birthday party and she could do anything she wanted, including letting her hair all the way down for the first time in a very long time.

HEATH KNEW STEPHENS was out here. His weapon palmed, he moved around the building once more, watching for any movement between the parked cars.

He'd seen someone at the bar's main entrance. He'd gotten only a glimpse of the man's profile, but he was ninety-nine percent certain it was him.

Daddy had come to see his little girl on her birthday.

Fury pounding in his skull, Heath searched the entire parking lot, looked inside every car before accepting that the area was clear. He had to be sure Stephens was gone for now.

Heath clenched his jaw hard when he found no sign of the man. *Bastard.*

How could he do this to his own daughter?

Heath went back inside and quickly scanned the crowd to ensure all was as it should be.

Jayne's friends toasted her over and over and the many famous Altitude concoctions were loaded onto tray after tray, never allowing anyone to go thirsty. She'd shed her coat. The simple T-shirt clung to the soft swells and lean valleys of her torso. The jeans complemented her lower anatomy with every bit as much natural sensuality. She had an amazing body. His throat parched sending him in search of a bottle of water behind the bar. There'd be nothing else alcoholic for him tonight.

He kept his distance from Jayne for the remainder of the party. He wanted this night to be filled with good, with no significant memories of him. No one's birthday should be tainted with the kind of hurt his name would be forever associated with in her mind. She deserved better than that. Had already been let down, big-time, by the bastard who'd sired her.

And then there was that other bastard. The one who'd sent Heath here, who'd used Jayne as nothing more than human bait to lure in her evil father.

Men like Cole Danes were barely a cut above the lowlifes they hunted down.

This—Heath's gaze followed Jayne across the dance floor in another man's arms—should never have happened.

But it was too late for regrets now.

The game had already started.

CHAPTER EIGHT

"I've had visual contact."

Heath had waited until dawn to contact Danes. He'd hoped his anger would have diminished to some extent by morning but it hadn't. His attention remained fixed on the monitor's image of a sleeping Jayne as he paced his small room. He wanted to reach across this telephone line and punch Danes for setting this stage.

"Excellent. I knew he would be close."

Heath held his breath in an effort to slow the avalanche of fury rushing through him, but the move was futile.

"Tell me why it had to be this way."

His words were bitter, cold, filled with animosity for the man in charge. He didn't need to spell it out. Danes would understand.

"It's the *only* way."

Heath shook his head, his fingers clutching the cell phone with white-knuckled intensity. "I won't accept that."

An unexpected silence followed.

When it dragged on Heath was suddenly certain he'd crossed some unseen line with Danes. His new career might very well be over before it had much of a chance to get started…but he didn't care. This was wrong. He couldn't imagine Cole Danes having any kind of explanation that would make it right.

"The information that would clarify the situation for you is highly classified."

Heath rolled his eyes. "Screw that crap. I'm not buying it."

Another prolonged silence.

"Since this mission depends solely upon your complete focus and cooperation I'll make a judgment call and take the position that you *need* to know."

Anticipation surged, momentarily slowing Heath's mounting fury. "Don't yank my chain, Danes," he warned. He'd had enough of this guy's games. If he knew more about Stephens he should have told Heath up front. He didn't like going in blind on any level. He damned sure didn't want any half truths now.

"I will give you the justification your conscience needs," Danes allowed, "but know this, Mr. Murphy, I find insubordination on any level unacceptable."

Heath choked out a laugh. "If you think a threat is going to do the trick, Danes, you're sadly mistaken. I didn't sign on for these head games. You tell me why this is going down this way. Tell me now or I'll take charge of the situation myself."

"You mean," Danes suggested, "the way you took charge of the situation when your partner used your distraction to get away with murder?"

The words had the desired effect. The rug jerked right out from under Heath's feet.

"Or perhaps you mean the way you took charge of the situation when your girlfriend found herself on a slippery ledge and fell to her death."

"You son of a bitch." Heath slammed his cell phone closed. His fingers curled around it as if he could somehow prevent more of the truth from spilling out of it. He closed his eyes and shook with the effort of holding his emotions together. A part of him wanted to beat the hell out of Danes. But another part of him, the part that recognized the truth in the bastard's words, wanted to cry out with the agony that still lived in the furthest recesses of his brain. Never completely going away.

He'd left a vital piece of himself on that damned ledge three years ago and nothing was ever going to bring it back. He'd screwed up and she had paid. His inability to pull himself back together had allowed his new partner to hurt innocent people...and almost get away with it.

But, by God, he wouldn't screw up this time. Jayne's safety depended upon him. She might never forgive him for his part in all this, but he had to protect her.

Heath flipped open his phone and stabbed the necessary numbers. He didn't wait for a hello. "Tell me what you know," he demanded. He could imagine the look of satisfaction on Danes's face.

"Twenty years ago Howard Stephens was more or less a two-bit hood for hire. It's true he spent a couple of years on the military's payroll in a capacity much like a Central Intelligence asset under the curiously vague network of Special Forces shadow operations. But his value was greatly reduced when his superiors discovered his fetish for selling secrets."

"I'm not interested in ancient history, Danes. Save it for the textbooks."

A hum of amusement vibrated across the line. "Where is your patience, Mr. Murphy?"

Heath opted not to answer what he presumed to be a rhetorical question.

"Our Mr. Stephens joined forces with a man named Errol Leberman, the arch nemesis of James Colby."

James Colby was Victoria's first husband. Heath was

aware that the Colby Agency had been plagued by an enemy named Leberman who was responsible for the kidnapping of Victoria's son, Jim Colby. But Jim was back now, after years of brutal persecution by Leberman.

"And you think Stephens is the one who kept the information flow between someone at the Colby Agency and Leberman," Heath finished for Danes. "I've heard all that before. And as sorry as I am for what happened to the Colby family, what does this have to do with Jayne Stephens? Why does she have to suffer for her father's sins?"

"Relax, Murphy, we're only now getting to the good part."

His condescending tone set Heath on edge all over again.

"Leberman was so preoccupied with revenge he more or less allowed Stephens to do as he pleased with the little mercenary operation he'd started. A grievous error in judgment. Stephens decided that the occasional foray into third world countries to murder and steal weren't lucrative enough. So he started another kind of service right here in this country."

Dread twisted in Heath's gut.

"His team specialized in assassinating those most killers for hire preferred to avoid. Cops, members of the military, even the occasional politician, always making the murder look like an accident. A shoot-out with a drug dealer, a helicopter crash or simple car accident. Most of his clients are foreigners. Persons from countries who, shall we say, have a distaste for our way of life. Few things happen by accident, Murphy. A man like Stephens could, for example, perpetrate an uprising of Iraqi rebels against American peacekeeping troops and it would be blamed on the terrorists or the fallen regime. People believe what they want to. They need an explanation for why things happen. Men like Stephens prey upon that need. He has no conscience, is loyal only to himself."

The whirlwind of emotions Heath had tangled with all night gave way to astonishment. "Why hasn't someone stopped him before now?" He shook his head in disbelief.

"No one knew who he was until recently. You see, according to the military's records, Howard Stephens died eighteen years ago, about the same time the Colby child went missing."

That didn't make sense. "But he's kept in touch with his daughter."

"A daughter who protects him, does she not? What did she tell you about her father?"

A chill leeched into Heath's bones. *There's no one but me.*

"But he's made contact with her," Heath argued. "Has surfaced more than once?"

Danes hissed a breath of impatience. "No one knew to look for him. There was no reason. He was dead. He has operated under a number of aliases all these years. It was only discovered recently that he was still alive."

An epiphany struck Heath fast and furiously. "You found him," he said, almost to himself. He could see that. Cole Danes would find the truth when no one else could. He was relentless like that.

"Lucas Camp hired me to look into this case. I traced the connection to Stephens."

Heath felt stunned all over again. This was entirely too much to digest.

"We have to stop him, Murphy. He knows we've done

what no one else ever could. We're on to him. And we've locked on to the one person who can prove he's still alive."

Jayne.

"There has to be another way." A sinking sensation dragged at Heath's conviction that he could make this right somehow. This was way over his head.

"There is no other way. If you fail, finding him again will likely be impossible."

"Why me? Why don't you send a whole team of government agents down here if all you say is true?" How the hell was he supposed to stop a guy like that? How could he protect Jayne if Stephens brought in his team of mercenaries? Heath didn't have that kind of training. He was no secret agent. He was just an ex-cop.

"If Stephens suspects for one moment that I'm involved or that any government agency is aware of his existence, he'll bolt. He has to think this is low level, revenge for his involvement with Leberman. If he believes that he's only going up against a P.I., one who doesn't even have a proven track record, he'll feel free to expose himself. It's the only way."

Heath had known there was more to his selection for this case than his climbing skill and lack of involvement in the agency's past. "But what makes you so certain he won't bring a half-dozen mercenaries with him?"

"He won't take the risk. For nearly twenty years he's kept his daughter out of what he does, anonymity protected him as well as her. A group of mercenaries wreaking havoc in Aspen, Colorado, would draw far too much unwanted attention. Stephens's dirty little world depends upon complete secrecy. He needs it. He plans to keep it by taking care of this business personally and quietly."

"How can you be so damned sure?" Heath wasn't afraid for himself, his concern was for Jayne's welfare. She was totally innocent in all this.

"Trust me, Murphy. I am dead certain and I'm relying on you not to let me down. If you fail, there will be no hope for Jayne. There's no turning back now. The damage is already done."

Heath's gaze settled on the monitor as the call ended.

That was the one thing he and Danes agreed upon without reservation. The damage was already done.

THE SOUND OF THE telephone ringing crashed into Jayne's skull.

She groaned and rolled over.

She didn't dare open her eyes. The throb in her skull warned that it would not be a good thing.

Another ring and her head exploded once more.

She groped blindly over the bedside table, desperate to put an end to the torture. She gripped the receiver and dragged it to her ear with her eyes squeezed shut in hopes of warding off additional pain.

"Hello," she muttered, then licked her lips. Her mouth felt like cotton. If she ever even thought about drinking again she wanted someone to shoot her and put her out of her misery in advance.

"Jayne, you up yet?"

Walt.

She suffered a twinge of disappointment that it wasn't her father calling to wish her a happy birthday.

"Jayne?"

What did Walt want this early in the morning? She popped one eye open and was shocked to discover that it was seven o'clock already. Not so early by her usual standards.

"Yeah, sure...I'm up." She pushed the hair out of her face and considered sitting up but wasn't sure she could trust herself not to howl with the pain that would surely accompany the move.

"Good. I was afraid after the party last night you might forget that the avalanche advisory had been lifted so today's schedule is good to go."

Today's schedule? Oh, no. Ten o'clock prep class and then a three-and-a-half-mile jaunt on snowshoes at one. It was a beginner-level trek. But that gave her no comfort. She groaned again, certain she would not survive rolling out of the bed much less a dozen enthusiastic tourists.

"That didn't sound too good, Jayne," Walt commented, worry tingeing his tone. "Should I try and find a replacement guide?"

"No, no." She pushed up from the pillows, biting her lip to hold back another groan. This wasn't her usual fare. She led the more difficult ventures into the mountains and backcountry. But she'd promised one of her friends she'd cover this one for her. "I'll be there. Just let me get in the shower and make a pot of coffee."

"All rightie then. See you at ten."

His chipper voice echoed in her ears for a full minute after she'd hung up the phone. How could anyone feel that good after last night?

Jayne scrubbed a hand over her face and dropped it to her lap. Confused, she looked down at herself. To her surprise she still wore the jeans and T-shirt from the party. Why hadn't she changed?

And then she remembered.

Heath had practically carried her to her room. She'd had way too much to drink.

Jayne dropped her head in her hands and wished she could crawl into a hole somewhere.

She sat up suddenly. The idea that he'd put her to bed without undressing her, other than tugging off her boots, didn't bode well. What guy wouldn't have used the opportunity to get a look at her hidden assets?

She groaned again. The answer was simple. The kind of guy who had a job to do, a story to write. One who wasn't really interested in pursuing a relationship. Oh, she almost forgot, and one who wouldn't compromise his principles.

But he'd kissed her. On the cheek, but it was a kiss just the same. She'd felt the pull of desire, the heat simmering between them.

Obviously she'd been the only one feeling it. She'd noticed the way he'd studiously avoided her last night at the party. Whenever she'd looked he'd been across the room or talking to someone else. Her every dance had been with someone else.

Dammit.

She pushed to her feet and trudged to the bathroom. She'd known better than to fall for the guy. At least it was only a superficial prick to her ego. She liked him well enough, but that was all. It wasn't like she'd really gotten attached to him.

She turned on the shower and stared at her reflection in the mirror. That haunted look that always lurked just beneath the surface, the one that had seen too much on the job, was there as always. But there was another emotion, an unfamiliar one, hiding behind the mask of contentment she always wore as well. This one was hope.

For the first time in a very long time she'd hoped

for something more. Verged on the point of real trust. Thank God reality had opened her eyes before she'd made that mistake.

Jayne took a deep breath and prayed today's class and winter outing would be enough for Heath. Maybe he'd write his story and move on. Surely he wouldn't wait out a rescue?

One silly little detail that had been nagging at her from the beginning surfaced once more. Why did she never see him taking notes? Or taping interviews with her? For that matter, they hadn't actually had what she would call an official interview. Every reporter she'd ever met took notes. Maybe she'd asked him.

Or maybe she'd just let it go and hope he left soon. The longer he stayed the more likely she was to really get hurt.

And she'd have no one to blame but herself.

TWELVE EXPECTANT gazes watched Jayne's every move as she demonstrated the proper way to prepare for a cross-country snowshoe trek during winter weather.

There were actually only eleven students; the twelfth person present in the Happy Trails orientation room was Heath. He sat at the rear of the classroom, those dark eyes never leaving her.

At least the blush on her cheeks at the idea that she'd practically passed out on him last night gave her some color. Then there was that kiss. How could she be in the same room with him without thinking about that simple kiss on the cheek or the way he'd pinned her against the counter that first night in Rafe's kitchen. Those foolish thoughts inspired a warmth inside her over which she had no control, thus the blush.

Admittedly, she could use all the help she could get

this morning since she looked and felt like death warmed over. She had elected not to bother with a morning run since she would need every ounce of energy she could summon for this outing.

Each class participant had received a list of appropriate clothing for the trip as well as the necessary supplies for unforeseen occurrences. All appeared to be prepared. The forecast called for a sunny day with temperatures hovering in the midtwenties. The snow in the area had been groomed ensuring undemanding mobility. This was a level one trip; it didn't get any easier.

"Careful packing is essential," she told the attentive class of mostly older men and women. One couple looked to be in their forties, but most appeared more in the fifty to sixty range.

She covered the proper way to organize a backpack in a few simple steps. As she glanced around the classroom to see if everyone was listening her gaze unexpectedly tangled with Heath's. Something about the way he looked at her made the bottom drop out of her stomach and she totally lost her train of thought.

"Where's the nearest bathroom?"

Jayne blinked. "Excuse me?"

"The bathroom?" the woman repeated.

"Down the hall and to the left," Jayne explained, dredging up a patient smile.

"Not the bathroom here," the lady smirked, "the one on the trail."

The whole group burst into laughter. Jayne couldn't help but laugh as well. The sole person in the room not laughing out loud was Heath, but the amusement in that relentless gaze told her he'd gotten a kick out of the old lady as well. But there was an underlying seriousness in his expression that made Jayne uneasy. Today's schedule afforded little time to consider his odd behavior. Maybe tonight they would have time to talk.

He'd said he had more questions for her...but that had been a ruse to get her to the surprise party. Still, how much of a story could he write when he knew so little about her?

HEATH WATCHED JAYNE chat over lunch with the group of novice snowshoers. He'd selected a table at the rear of the nostalgic restaurant so that he could keep an eye on her as well as the main entrance and the kitchen door.

He wondered about her work at Happy Trails. The variety of trip offerings ranged from easy hikes, like today's, to difficult cross-country routes, backpacking and various degrees of climbing. He couldn't help thinking how boring an itinerary such as this one must be. Such a monumental waste of her extensive talent.

But she didn't appear bored at all. In fact, she seemed to enjoy the group's flamboyance and humor, all of which was so unlike her usual demeanor. Quiet, reserved. A loner to a large degree. Yet there was an energy about her that drew him. What made a vibrant young woman content with the status quo? Why not grab all the gusto while she was young? She certainly was fearless enough. It didn't add up.

There's no one but me.

Self-protection. Survival.

The impact of that realization hit him head-on. She was protecting her father and herself. If she never got close to anyone she didn't have to lie. Not outright anyway. It was the easiest way. No risk. No threat to the last person on this planet who shared her DNA.

Did she even realize that's what she was doing? Pushing the world away for those rare moments with her phantom father? The idea made him sick to his stomach. What had the bastard told her? Had he brainwashed her into thinking the enemy could be anyone, anywhere, anytime?

But she had gotten involved at least once before. Rafe had said something about some guy. A stranger to town like Heath. The memory of that kiss…of tucking her into bed after the party. As tough as she wanted to play, she was still vulnerable. Had some other guy taken advantage of that vulnerability? Heath had an uneasy feeling it wasn't as simple as that.

Forgetting his lunch, he pushed up from the table and sought a more private place to make a call.

The corridor outside the main dining room offered the only privacy from the lunch crowd and an unobstructed view of Jayne's table.

"Altitude Bar and Grill," blasted across the line along with deafening music.

"Rafe, this is Heath Murphy."

"I can't talk now," Rafe fairly shouted into the phone over the loud music and chatter in the background.

"Wait!" Heath urged. "I need you to answer one question."

"All right. All right. Let me go to the kitchen."

Heath waited, his impatience pounding in his temples, while Rafe made his way to the quieter setting of the kitchen.

"Shoot," Rafe snapped. "And make it fast. I got customers waiting."

"You remember telling me about some stranger who hurt Jayne a couple of years ago…maybe last year." Damn. He couldn't remember.

Dead air filled the void that went on for three beats.

"Why do you ask, Murphy?" Rafe's suspicious tone was to be expected. He loved Jayne, wanted to protect her.

"You have to trust me, Rafe, I need to know." Heath held his breath, hoping like hell the old man would cooperate.

"His name was Richie or Richard Rydner. I don't know. I've tried to forget the bastard."

"Thanks, Rafe."

Heath ended the call, not waiting for whatever warning the guy would surely have issued. His next call was to Cole Danes.

"Danes."

"I need you to check something out," Heath said quickly, not wanting to be distracted any longer than necessary.

"I'm ready."

"Richie or Richard Rydner." Heath could hear the scratch of a pen on the other end. "He and Jayne had a thing for a little while a year or so ago."

"This would impact the case in what way?"

"Just a hunch I've got," Heath admitted. "This guy suddenly disappeared when things turned serious."

Danes hummed a note of disinterest. "Nothing original about that but I'll check it out."

"Could you do it now?"

"It could take some time."

Heath shifted his weight impatiently. "With your connections you should be able to reach out and touch someone and get instant feedback."

"Stand by."

Heath leaned against the wall next to the door, his full attention on the woman under his watch. Hell, he would have loved watching her even if it wasn't his job.

Her hair was pulled back in that long braid again. She looked painfully young and completely innocent. His biggest regret was that he wouldn't be able to protect that innocence.

She smiled at the woman speaking to her and then held up one hand as if to halt the conversation. The reason became clear as she reached for her cell phone. A look of surprise brightened her face and she grasped the phone with both hands as if the call was both unexpected and thrilling.

Her father.

Heath's mouth formed a grim line. He knew it was him. Damn him.

A little late to be calling and wishing her a happy birthday. A decent father would have called her first thing this morning. Heath watched the happiness dance across her face just as it had the night before last. Late or not, she'd needed it…hoped for it.

"Richard Rydner," Danes said, jerking his attention back to the phone. "Twenty-six, software engineer from Phoenix. He was found dead in his own apartment. Murdered. The police ruled it as a robbery/homicide. The case stands unsolved." The date Danes provided coincided with the time frame of Rydner's involvement with Jayne.

"Bingo," Heath muttered.

"Would you like to share where you think this is going?"

"The bastard killed Rydner to protect himself."

"What?" Danes asked, skepticism in his voice.

"See if you can find any other men in her life who died an untimely death." He was on to something here, Heath was certain.

"She told me she was all alone," he went on. "What

better way to ensure she never shared the truth with another human being? Anyone who got too close went away. Giving her all the more reason not to trust men," Heath concluded, more certain than ever of his assessment.

Danes assured that he would do a thorough search of her background as far back as age twelve, but Heath was only half listening.

Someone talking in the room across the hall had distracted him. One of the private dining rooms, he assumed. He forced his attention back to watching Jayne and paying attention to the conversation with Danes.

His instincts wouldn't relent. The voice...*won't be long now. Love you.* The words were barely audible.

I love you.

This time he didn't hear the words, he saw them as Jayne uttered them to her caller.

He was here.

"I'll get back to you." Heath slammed his phone shut and dropped it back into his pocket while simultaneously whirling toward the door across the hall. By the time he burst through he had his weapon in his hand.

One large window on the far side of the room stood open, its sheer curtains flapping in the frigid air.

Heath swore hotly. He'd missed him. He knew it had been him. The hair on the back of his neck suddenly stood on end.

"Give me the weapon." The cold, hard tone was accompanied by the nudge of a steel barrel to the back of Heath's skull.

He bit back another curse. "No way," he ground out.

"Then die."

The cocking of the weapon echoed in the room.

"Go ahead, kill me," Heath taunted, in an effort to buy himself some time. "You're a dead man already, you just don't know it yet."

The barrel jammed harder into his scalp. "You think so? Tell me who the Colby Agency hired to find me and maybe I'll give you a fifty-fifty chance at survival. A gut shot instead of a bullet to the brain."

Heath laughed and told him what he could do with himself, which would be physically impossible in the literal sense.

"What's his name?" Stephens roared. "I want to know who managed what even Lucas Camp could not."

It was now or never. Heath knew he had to make a move. He was dead for sure if he didn't.

A scream and a loud crash near the door provided an abrupt but blessed distraction. Heath whipped around, leveled his weapon. Stephens had anticipated just such a move. He'd already grabbed the waitress who'd entered the room and shielded himself with her.

"Back off," he growled at Heath.

Heath ignored the order and moved in unison with him and his hostage as he closed in on the window.

"Let her go." Heath kept a bead on the bastard but the woman was in the way.

Stephens laughed. "Still too much of a cop to risk the hostage, I see."

Heath resisted the urge to lunge at him. His trigger finger itched to pull back.

Running footsteps pounded in the corridor.

Stephens shoved the waitress at Heath and dived out the window.

Heath stumbled back, catching the woman, but losing his aim on Stephens.

He steadied the lady then rushed to the window but it was too late.

Stephens was gone.

CHAPTER NINE

Convincing the restaurant manager that he was fine took Heath longer than he would have preferred. Thankfully the waitress had only seen the other man's gun. She hadn't noticed Heath's since her eyes had been squeezed shut in fear as Stephens used her for a human shield.

The manager had assumed the incident was an attempted mugging and insisted on calling the police. Heath barely talked him out of it, doing a little insisting of his own. He'd come to Aspen for a good time, not to deal with a mugging and the police. The mugging attempt had failed, no real harm done. In the end, Heath had won out.

The customer was always right. Wasn't that the motto in the restaurant industry?

Apparently the noise level had been high enough in the dining room that Jayne and her group had been spared the excitement.

As the group gathered their coats and readied to depart for the trailhead, Heath's cell vibrated in his pocket. He'd set it on vibrate before going into Jayne's class this morning.

"Murphy."

"What the hell happened?"

Heath swore. He should have called Danes back immediately but the manager had taken up valuable time and then there was Jayne and her group. He swore again.

This was not a one-man operation. A guy as experienced in this business as Danes should have considered that little detail.

"Our man had a question for me," Heath said flatly, then offered a smile for Jayne as she herded the geriatric group toward the exit.

"What was the question?"

Heath shook his head, still surprised by the audacity of his target. "I can't believe this guy," he muttered, turning away from the folks loading on the tour bus. "He set me up to walk in on him. He wanted me to know he was there. I'd probably be dead now if that waitress hadn't screamed and dropped a tray of glassware."

"The question," Danes repeated. "What was his question?"

Heath stilled. Danes had known this would be coming. He knew this guy's M.O. "He…" Heath swallowed, a new kind of uneasiness making his gut tighten. "He wanted to know your name. Wanted to know who had done what no one else appeared able to do."

Nothing.

Not a single word.

Silence.

"Oh, hell," Heath accused from between clenched teeth. "You *know* this maniac." He moved a few more feet away from the bus, scarcely able to keep his voice down. If Danes was playing games with him, Heath would—

"I don't *know* him," Danes allowed, taking some of the force out of the storm brewing inside Heath. "I know his kind," he added.

"Whatever. I have to go." Heath was sick of both Danes and Stephens. Both had clearly spent too much time in the spook business playing kill or be killed games.

"There's been a change in plans," Danes said, disregarding Heath's comment.

"What kind of change?" Heath couldn't hold up the group any longer. He climbed aboard the bus and claimed a seat at the very back.

"You must know, Mr. Murphy, that the final confrontation is near."

"No kidding," Heath muttered. Jayne glanced back at him and he pushed a smile into place for her benefit.

"I had hoped we could perhaps detain him, question him regarding a number of exploits in his past. I'm sure he knows things this government would very much like to learn."

"I'll do what I can." Heath couldn't make any promises. Stephens was not the kind of prey a mere cop usually went after, especially not alone. And Jayne's safety was Heath's number one priority.

"Don't trouble yourself. I want you to eliminate him. He represents far too great a threat to risk allowing him to escape."

Shock radiated all the way to the soles of Heath's feet. "Are you saying what I think you're saying?" he asked carefully. No way could he have understood right.

"Your orders are clear, Mr. Murphy. If you get Howard Stephens back in your sights, shoot to kill."

"I can't do that." No way in hell could he simply shoot a man without provocation. "Not unless he forces my hand."

"Take my word for it, Mr. Murphy, he will provide all the provocation you require. Make no mistake. Only one of you will survive the confrontation. The only decision you have to make is whether it will be you or him."

The conversation ended on that note.

Heath closed his phone and dropped it back into his pocket. Funny thing was, he didn't recall any of this being in the vague briefing he'd received prior to taking this assignment.

"Is everything all right?"

Heath looked up just as Jayne took the seat next to him. He smiled, unable to help himself. With her this close he didn't have to fake it. "Everything's fine."

She looked away for a moment. "I thought maybe that was your girlfriend or your wife."

Heath shook his head. "No girlfriend, no wife."

"Good." She started to stand but hesitated and leaned toward him instead. "I would have hated to punch you in front of all these people for kissing me last night if you were already taken."

He watched her go back to the front seat, pausing to chat with one person after another in her group. Damn her father and damn Cole Danes. They'd put him in this position. What the hell was he supposed to do? Shoot her own father right in front of her?

There would be no happy ending to this story.

Only shattered lives.

JAYNE SURVEYED THE group, ensuring everyone was properly suited up for the trek. Just over three miles with a gentle incline of about six hundred feet would be no problem for anyone in this group. As long as no one had fibbed about his or her general health and physical activity level. That was her only real concern in her line of work, especially when dealing with a slightly older crowd. No one wanted to admit they were old.

The driver would come back in four hours to pick them up, unless she called in and specified otherwise.

She made her way to where Heath waited, watching the bus leave the trailhead behind. "No need to worry, Murphy," she teased. "The bus will be back and this one's real easy, a baby slope."

When his gaze connected with hers she saw worry there. Maybe he just wasn't going to be able to deal with this environment at all. She suddenly wished she knew how to make the old hurt he carried around go away.

But she didn't. They barely knew each other, were still strangers really.

No, she amended, not strangers. *Friends.*

He pasted on a smile that didn't reach his eyes. "I'm okay. Don't worry, I won't freak out on you or anything." He reached down and secured his snowshoes, taking a good deal more time than necessary.

She braced her hands on her hips and watched his confident if prolonged movements. "I hope not. You'd be really embarrassed if any of this group had to carry you back to the trailhead."

Straightening to his full height, he laughed and this time the smile was genuine. "You have my word that I'm good to go," he promised on a more serious note.

"Let's get this show on the road then."

He nodded and gestured for her to go first.

"Okay, folks," she called out. "Let's go tramp some snow."

Since all of the participants had been in Aspen for more than twenty-four hours, altitude problems wouldn't be an issue.

Jayne described the terrain as she took the lead, explaining that this trail offered a pleasant and scenic hike, even in the snow.

The trail hugged the wide, swiftly running creek that cut across the ridge. The edges of the water were frozen, the blanket of snow pushing onto those icy ledges like a winter coat. If they were lucky they would see some of the local wildlife, maybe an elk or deer. Preferably no black bears or mountain lions. Though she carried a defibrillator she didn't want to have to use it.

For the next two hours Jayne did what she did best, talked about the beautiful landscape and pointed out the little things most first-time visitors missed. Like the way the sun peeked through the trees and dropped behind the summits of distant mountain ranges.

Today's generous sun had boosted the temperature to a pleasant thirty degrees Fahrenheit. To compensate for the unexpected warm spell, Jayne loosened her parka. She tried not to get caught up in thoughts of Heath. Each time she looked in his direction he was preoccupied with the terrain. She couldn't help wondering if he'd made a game of it, like counting trees or looking for faces in the clouds, anything to keep his mind off whatever ghosts haunted him.

Tonight they had to talk. She wanted to know why he took no notes for his story. Why he hadn't spent more time asking her about her work. He didn't strike her as the type to procrastinate where his work was concerned.

No girlfriend, no wife.

Excitement bubbled inside her at the prospect that he was, indeed, a free man. She reminded that foolish part of herself that he would be leaving and that falling any further for him would be a huge mistake.

Twice she'd fallen hard and lived to regret it.

She should be smarter than this, at least be more romance savvy.

But, in reality, was there anything practical or strategic about love? It just happened—came out of nowhere the same as Heath had.

Maybe the third time would be the charm. Wasn't that how that old saying went?

No, no, no. She gave herself a mental shake. She would not use the word love in the same thought as Heath Murphy. Not safe. Not safe at all.

Besides, how could she possibly ever trust him or any other man with her heart…with the truth about her father? His enemies would go to any extent to eliminate him. He'd told her that dozens of times.

Whatever she shared with Heath or any other man would always be overshadowed by that lie. The same way her mother's life had been. She had died an unhappy, lonely woman.

Apparently, Jayne was doomed to that same fate.

But her father was all she had. How could she risk causing him harm?

She couldn't. It was too much to sacrifice.

Jayne paused and pointed out a deer in the tree line ahead. While cameras were whipped out and amazed whispers rumbled, her thoughts returned to her nonexistent love life. Why did she worry about any of this? If she was to be alone forever as her mother had been, why not take her happiness wherever she could.

Like now.

With Heath.

Her gaze drifted back to him.

He was looking directly at her. A jolt of need roared through her. She hoped he could read in her eyes just how much she wanted him. She was tired of denying herself. He would leave anyway. What were one or two nights of stolen pleasure? The only person who would be hurt was her and maybe it would be worth it. She remembered the way his bare chest had looked, the strength his body radiated and she knew damn well it would be worth it.

No one could accuse her of being promiscuous, but she couldn't be expected to live out her life with no sexual interests. She was a woman, needed to feel like one from time to time. Most of her male friends treated her like one of the guys and that was fine, great in fact, but she didn't want Heath to treat her like a guy. She wanted him to bring out the woman in her.

What was wrong with that?

Nothing, she decided, as she visually measured him once more. Not a darn thing. She could keep her sex life and her personal life separate...just for as long as Heath was in town. That wasn't too much to ask.

HEATH COULDN'T SAY for sure whether it was the fact that the snowshoeing venture was scarcely more than an uphill walk in the snow or that he was fiercely focused on keeping a watch out for Stephens, but he didn't feel the first prick of panic related to the past.

The only urgency he felt was for Jayne's safety.

It felt strange that he would experience such a strong compulsion to protect her from her own father. He needed to stop Stephens, no question. Clearly the man represented a threat to more than just the Colby Agency. But how did he represent a threat to Jayne, other than via the fallout from his chosen occupation?

He'd gone to extremes to protect his daughter, ultimately, of course, protecting himself. But he could have disappeared from her life all those years ago and never returned. That he did at all, taking even that minimal risk, told Heath that he loved his daughter in whatever way a monster like him was capable.

This same man who loved his daughter had been fully prepared to kill Heath today. He'd wanted the answer to his question and then he would have carried out his threat. Heath had no doubt there.

The one thing he didn't understand when he rationalized all else was why the man cared who'd discovered his existence. What difference did it make? A matter of pride? Heath couldn't get past the idea that there was a connection between Stephens and Danes. Why the hell else would Danes order Heath to eliminate the target? Sure, he deserved nothing better, but it wasn't Heath's decision to make.

And so what if he did stop Stephens. There was a whole posse of his followers out there somewhere. Who was to say those guys wouldn't come after Heath and the agency?

He pushed the puzzling questions aside. This was all personal—from Victoria's son to Cole Danes. None of it was coincidence. Heath might not be a trained secret agent but his instincts were honed by eight years of being a cop.

He'd walked into a setup. Gotten trapped in a war that went way back and in which he didn't know the players or the stakes…except for one.

Jayne.

"Ms. McFarland! Stay away from the water's edge!"

The words were no sooner out of Jayne's mouth than she lunged for the woman who'd moved too close to the creek's edge.

His feet were taking him in that direction before his brain assimilated the magnitude of the situation.

The creek wouldn't be deep.

But the water would be killing cold.

With that thought the splash of bodies hitting the water echoed in his ears.

"Get back!" he yelled at two of the men who rushed to the creek's slippery bank.

The men pulled back, discouraging the others from making the same mistake.

Heath hit the water running.

Jayne was up, tugging with all her strength to get the older woman out of the water.

"Help me," Jayne pleaded. Her hair was soaked. He knew without asking that water would have seeped in around her collar and anywhere else where synthetic fabric ended in skin.

Ms. McFarland gasped for air and wailed, "Oh, God. Oh, God."

Heath hefted her out of the water and managed to get back onto solid, snow-covered ground before the woman's weight pulled him to his knees.

"Ms. McFarland—" Jayne knelt next to her "—tell me where the water got in."

The woman looked dazed. "Just my hair, I believe." She pawed her head with one gloved hand. "My hat came off."

Jayne nodded. "Yes, ma'am. We both lost our headgear."

Water trailed down Jayne's face as she spoke but she ignored it. She dug into her backpack and pulled out a solar blanket. Heath helped her wrap it around the trembling woman.

"This will help keep you warm," Jayne explained. "Your hair is wet so you're going to get colder than I'd like, but the blanket will help." She surveyed the woman closely, likely looking for signs of shock. "Are you sure you don't feel wet beneath your outerwear anywhere else?"

Ms. McFarland shook her head. "No, I'm fine. I think," she added shakily.

"Let's get you on your feet."

The rest of the group, who had, thankfully, remained silent despite having moved in close so as not to miss anything, stepped back to make room.

"I'm okay," the woman assured. "Thank God." She looked at Jayne then. "I'm so sorry. I didn't mean to get so close." She shook her head. "These old eyes aren't what they used to be."

Since a Mr. McFarland didn't come forward, Heath had to assume this lady was the one single on the trip. "How about I walk with you from here," he offered.

"That would be very kind of you."

Jayne mouthed a thank-you.

Heath glanced back at the creek and the headgear that had floated off somewhere downstream. He pulled off his own and offered it to Jayne. "I'm not wet," he reminded when she would have protested. "I'll be fine."

She nodded, too smart to argue.

Upon Jayne's radioed request the bus would be waiting for them at the trailhead a few minutes early. The trip back, she warned the group, would be covered at a bit of a faster pace to ensure Ms. McFarland's comfort.

Heath knew there was far more at stake than comfort. Both these ladies were going to be cold as hell before they reached that bus. He wanted to ensure that Jayne was okay, to keep her warm, but she needed him to do exactly what he was doing.

JAYNE IGNORED THE cold that had penetrated her skin, absorbed into her muscles, chilling her all the way to the bone. She couldn't let it show.

They reached the bus in record time. Ms. McFarland appeared to be doing fine. Heath's gaze kept shifting to Jayne. She knew he suspected what she couldn't hide from him.

He was no novice like the rest of this group.

He could read the pain on her face as hard as she tried to disguise it.

She'd twisted her ankle in her attempt to save Ms. McFarland from the water. Nothing was broken, she felt confident. It wasn't even a particularly bad strain, just a nuisance. Something she could definitely have done without.

When they settled in for the ride back to the hotel, Jayne sat down next to the other survivor of the dip in the creek. "Ms. McFarland, I've got an EMT standing by at the hotel to check you out. Is that okay?" Before the lady could answer, she added, "It would really make me feel a lot better."

The woman, who looked frail compared to a few hours ago, nodded. "That would be good." She grasped Jayne's hand when she would have moved away. "Will he be examining you as well, Miss Stephens?"

"I'm fine," Jayne insisted. "Don't worry about me. This isn't the first time I've taken a tumble."

Jayne moved to the back of the bus to sit next to Heath. She sat there for a moment, not sure if she wanted to open this can of worms. He saw through her too easily.

"Thanks for taking care of her," she said softly.

"You're welcome." He turned his head then and looked directly at her. "How bad's the ankle?"

Dammit. She'd known he could read her too well. "Not too bad. A mild sprain. No real damage."

"Why don't we let your EMT have the final say on that?" he suggested quietly.

She pulled off his headgear and relaxed in the seat. She was still freezing but damned if she had the energy to do anything about it. She'd shivered until her teeth rattled. The heat on the bus was slowly doing its job, but not nearly fast enough to suit her.

"Men." She laughed softly. "You always want the final say."

As Jayne suspected her ankle was fine, just a mild sprain. Though she still felt chilled, her body temperature was back to normal and, thankfully, Ms. McFarland checked out A-okay as well.

Jayne couldn't imagine what made the woman wander so close to the edge of the creek. She'd said she hadn't realized she'd gotten that close and maybe she hadn't. No point in overanalyzing it. No one really got hurt and the whole group, including Ms. McFarland, had been abuzz about their adventure the entire trip back to town. There was no telling how many times and different ways this story would be told.

"There is a little swelling," Paul Rice, the rescue team's EMT, noted on his second look at Jayne's ankle.

"I'm fine," Jayne asserted. She wished Heath hadn't insisted that she do this. She knew what would come next.

"Okay, okay," Paul relented as he let go of her foot.

Jayne glowered at him, then she gave Heath the same treatment. She'd managed to get away from the hotel without Paul's knowing she'd been injured. When he showed up at her door only minutes later with Heath she'd known she'd been ratted out by her new friend.

He stood on the other side of her living room trying to look humble. Impossible. She doubted there was a humble bone in his cover-model-quality body. Despite her annoyance at the moment she desperately wanted to find out.

She looked away from him and took a mental step back. Having a one- or two-night stand with him had sounded great in theory but this was real life. She wasn't so sure it was such a good idea. She had too much emotional baggage to be carefree and casual about intimate relationships. The last thing she needed to do was let her lust override her reason.

"Sorry, Jayne," Paul said, dragging her attention back to his big, burly frame. "I'm going to have to recommend that you go on light duty for a few days as far as search and rescue goes."

"I told you I'm fine," she countered as calmly as her irritation would allow. "A hot soak in the tub and a good night's sleep and I'll be as good as new." She had changed clothes and dried her hair but hadn't made it to the tub yet. She needed that soak. Despite the pleasantly warm temperature in her cozy apartment, she was still cold inside. It would take at least an hour of hot, hot water to cure that.

Paul stood, hauling his medic bag up with him. "Don't give me any grief, Little Boss," he said with a pointed look at her. "I could tell Walt that you need a week or two of R and R."

Her mouth dropped open in dismay. "You wouldn't dare."

"Don't tempt me." He grinned. "Keep up your Happy Trails schedule if you feel up to it, but no rescues for two full weeks." He looked from her to Heath and back. "Relax a little. Didn't you just have a birthday?" he asked her, then turned to Heath once more, "And what about you, don't you have a story to write?"

That reminded her.

"Get out of here, Paul," she groused. "I don't need any orders from you. You tell Walt anything about this and I'll make you wish you hadn't."

The EMT's eyes rounded in mock fear. "I'm shaking in my boots." He hee-hawed at his own humor. She merely rolled her eyes. Heath kept out of it.

"I'd better get going," Paul said, apparently knowing he'd worn out his welcome.

"Thanks," she muttered as she drew her knees up to her chest. Damn, she just couldn't get warm. As soon as Heath gave her some privacy, she intended to do something about that. She had some brandy around here somewhere. Maybe she'd start a little fire inside, as well.

Heath closed the door behind Paul and locked it. She didn't know why he bothered with the lock. He would be leaving next.

"Thanks again," she said when he walked toward the sofa. She hugged her legs tighter when another chill shivered through her, but she was reasonably sure this one had more to do with the man watching her than with her recent icy swim.

"Why don't I draw you a bath," he offered, his voice far too soft, too intense.

This was not a good idea. If she was smart she'd give him an unequivocal no.

She looked him dead in the eye and said exactly what she felt. "I'd love it."

CHAPTER TEN

Jayne shivered at the sound of the water running in her tub. Was she really going to do this?

"How about a glass of wine?"

The sound of his voice as he moved back into the room sent more goose bumps over her skin. "I…" She took a deep breath. "I have brandy somewhere over there."

"Brandy will be even better."

As he prowled through her cabinets, she tried to reason out the whole issue, but too much of her brain was focused on analyzing the way he moved. He'd stripped off his Gore-Tex and Nomex synthetic wear, but he hadn't bothered to go back to his room and change. The cold-weather pants gloved his strong body in such an enticing manner that she could scarcely bear to look. He'd pushed up the sleeves of his oatmeal-colored long-sleeved undershirt.

His hair was windblown and so damned sexy. She swallowed to ease her parched throat. How could she say no to all that? She closed her eyes and chastised herself. Okay, okay, it wasn't just about the great packaging.

Heath was kind and generous. She liked the way he interacted with her friends, especially Rafe. He'd gone right to Ms. McFarland's rescue. No matter how little she knew about him, he was simply a nice guy.

And she wanted so to be with him.

Maybe it was a foolish mistake.

Her father was probably right. She should steer clear of strangers…should protect herself. But she was so tired of doing the right thing.

She wanted to indulge herself just this once.

To be foolhardy and self-absorbed.

Just for tonight.

"Here ya go."

She looked up to find him watching her with those intense brown eyes. She would never forget the pain she'd seen there that day on the mountain. Like her, he had baggage, too. Maybe that was one of the things that attracted her to him.

Her fingers brushed his as she accepted the cup of brandy. She didn't own any fancy stemware other than the one wineglass and it was in the dishwasher. "Thank you."

He nodded. "I should check on your bath."

She watched him walk out of the room, unable to resist that additional pleasure. She wanted this far too much. It had to be a mistake. Nothing this good had ever turned out right in her life.

A sigh pushed past her lips. Well, that wasn't true. She had her work and the mountain rescue team. She loved living here, enjoyed her friends tremendously. Those were all wonderful things. But those things didn't keep her warm at night, didn't make her feel like a woman.

She needed intimacy, too. She'd gone far too long without it as it was. She'd been so afraid to go out on that limb again…after Richard.

Her college days and that one other big fiasco didn't count, she told herself. Everybody made mistakes at that age. It was a rule of some sort. How else would a person ever learn anything? Risks were necessary.

This was necessary.

She thought about the other girls, some friends, some not, from her high school and college days. Most of them likely had big-time careers or husbands and kids, maybe both by now. She'd shrugged off a graduate degree in favor of being a trail guide. Had all but given up a sex life to be a part of mountain rescue.

It felt safer on those kinds of cliffs and ledges.

But there was something wrong with that picture on the most basic level.

Don't overanalyze, Jayne. This isn't rocket science. It's sex.

She closed her eyes to the count of three and banished all thoughts of rights and wrongs and what-ifs. Then she promptly downed the brandy, cringing at the burn and waiting for the courage it would instill with its warmth.

"Why don't you get in the tub and I'll get you a refill?"

Jayne gasped and looked up at the half-dozen feet of lust-arousing male towering over her. He was too gorgeous. "Sure," she croaked.

He offered his hand for support. She clasped it, feeling the electricity even before their palms touched. He helped her to her feet when she could certainly have managed the feat on her own. She must be drunk already, she mused. Otherwise having a man help her in this way couldn't possibly be so much fun. She usually preferred taking care of herself, being strong.

Tonight she wanted to be vulnerable…weak. She wanted to be needy. She wanted that need filled.

To her credit she walked out of the room without hobbling once. She couldn't deny more than a little discomfort but she wasn't going to own up to it. It annoyed her immensely that Paul had put her on light duty for a few days. She hated when he did stuff like that. When she'd taken her first tumble, garnering herself all those stitches in her leg, he'd put her on six weeks of light duty. Way more than she'd needed. She might be enjoying Heath's attention, but she hated the idea of any sort of weakness on her part getting in the way of her work. But then, setting her injured ego aside, rescues often involved life-and-death situations. Time was always the enemy. Even a mild sprain could waste precious time.

When she opened the bathroom door the steam wafted out to greet her. She liked that. She'd have to remember to keep the door closed that way. Her clothes came off in nothing flat and landed in a pile on the floor. Her hair went up with a handy claw clip. The steam settled on her flesh like a lover's whisper.

Shivering, she eased carefully into the water, moaned with the incredible ecstasy it sent cascading through her body. Any lingering chill in her bones dissipated as she relaxed into the massive claw-footed tub. That was the best thing about this tiny apartment. She wouldn't trade this place and its tub for one of the fanciest condos in town.

The steam continued to hang in the air like fog, adding the perfect ambience to the faint light glowing from the ancient wall sconces that hung next to the mirror. She'd have to thank Heath for this. She smiled. Really, really thank him. She thought of at least a half-dozen ways to show her gratitude.

He tapped on the door. "Would you like that brandy now?"

Her smile stretched into a wicked grin. "Yes, please."

The door opened and he stepped inside. She drank in the sight of him, but couldn't quite quench that particular thirst by merely looking. He set the cup on the little wrought-iron table next to her tub, the one she used for shampoo and body wash.

"Thank you." She reached for the brandy and sipped it, braced her fledgling courage.

"I'll call you later tonight. Let me know if you need anything else."

Her heart bucked against her sternum. He was going to leave. She couldn't let him go…she had to do something or say something.

"Can you stay a while longer?"

God, the request came out all whiny instead of sultry. Couldn't she do anything right?

He hesitated at the door, allowed his gaze to search hers for a time before he spoke. "I'm not sure you really mean that the way it feels like you do."

Dammit. He obviously knew a pathetic job at seduction when he had one thrown at him.

She moistened her lips and summoned her bravado. "What does it feel like I mean?" She downed the rest of the liquid courage, suppressing the need to cough.

He sighed. She held her breath.

"You're beautiful, Jayne, and I'd like nothing better than to climb into that tub with you, but it would be a mistake. I, for one, have already made enough of those for one lifetime."

If she let him go after a confession like that she really was crazy.

She set the cup aside and pushed up from the steaming water. For a second she thought he might bolt, but when she stepped out of the tub he just stood there, staring at her as if…as if he felt torn in some way she couldn't fully understand. *No girlfriend, no wife.* No need to be torn in her opinion.

She walked right up to him and took his face in her damp hands. Before she dragged his mouth down to hers she took a long, slow look…first into those smoldering eyes, then at the planes and angles of that face she'd come to see in her dreams…and then those full lips. Her mouth watered the same way it did when she anticipated the first bite of a delectable hot-fudge sundae.

Her pulse pounded, her heart raced, but she'd never done anything this bold before and she wanted to experience every single moment and detail of it. She tiptoed, moving closer, parting her lips slightly. He held absolutely still, as if he'd read her mind and knew exactly what she intended.

The ache of need was more than she could bear…she had to touch him. She pressed her lips to his, keeping the pressure light, enjoying the sensation of his mouth against her. Warm…firm and smooth. His lips felt good. Heat seared through her, took her breath. She had to have more. She drew his bottom lip between hers, sucked it like candy, tasted the man and the lingering flavor of coffee. She moaned with the flood of sensations that washed over her.

Her hands began to move, to feel, to seek new discoveries. She loved the varying textures of man and material. Her breath came in rapid bursts…his did the same but he held completely still, waiting.

She wanted to feel his naked flesh. As she drew more deeply on his lips, sucking, enveloping, then licking, she tore at his soft undershirt. When her palms found his hot skin the urgency inside her increased to a fever pitch. Her arms went up around his neck and she closed her mouth fully over his, out of patience…needing more.

She'd wanted to make this moment last, to feel it evolve to the next level, but she couldn't slow down the pace. She wanted to experience more of him. She lavished him with fervent kisses—his face, his mouth—allowed her lips to drag over those planes and angles she'd admired for days now.

Just when she was certain he wasn't going to respond at all, his arms went around her. Those long-fingered hands glided over her wet skin, tracing, teasing. He took control of the kiss. Touched his tongue to hers, then suckled gently, drawing it into his mouth. She moaned. Buried her fingers into his thick hair. He learned her mouth with his tongue, tasted and sucked until she thought her heart would hammer right out of her chest. The lure and heat of that wicked tongue made her hungry for more.

He lifted her bottom, pressed her hips against his. He was hard. A responding desire coiled tighter inside her. He wanted her. She wanted him. Why had she waited this long? She should have kissed him the first moment she laid eyes on him.

She wanted him naked. Right now.

Pulling away from his mouth took all her willpower. They peeled off his undershirt together, tossed it aside. He yanked off one boot. Impatient, she dropped to her knees and removed the other. And then she reached for his fly, her gaze fixed firmly on his.

He didn't try to stop her, just watched as she tugged off the pants and then the long underwear the day's adventure had required. She hesitated at the snug fitting boxer briefs remaining. Her hands trembled just a little as she fingered the waistband, unable to take her eyes off the way they formed to his body, giving her a heady preview of what waited beneath that soft fabric.

She took her time, leaned closer, heard his sharp intake of breath as she kissed his lean hip. Once she'd started she couldn't stop. Her fingers curled into the waistband of that final barrier and dragged the soft fabric down his long, muscled legs. She touched him and he shuddered, balled his fingers into fists and pressed his head back against the closed door. She liked this feeling of power over him.

With more sexual daring than she'd realized she possessed she licked his entire length. The earthy taste of him, the tormented groan he exhaled fueling her confidence. The feel of his hardened length against her bare shoulder made her shiver with anticipation as she kissed her way over his ridged abdomen. Slowly, painstakingly, she licked and kissed, teased his male nipples, then stretched upward, seeking that hot, carnal mouth.

This was no slow, sweet kiss. This time it was urgent, needy and pushed her over some edge that she hadn't anticipated this quickly. He lifted her into his arms and carried her back to the tub. The water had cooled but did nothing to slow the sizzling passion building between them. Water sloshed onto the tile floor as he pulled her down on top of him beneath the water's enveloping embrace. She could feel that hard ridge of flesh beneath her, throbbing, pulsating with need. He pulled her to him, trailed a finger over her breast. She gasped. Wanted more.

He tilted her lips up to his and his hands moved over her now with renewed urgency, making her body mindlessly arch and undulate in search of the fulfillment only he could give. But she couldn't bear to leave his mouth and those mind-blowing kisses, couldn't stop touching his face long enough to do what needed to be done. His hands curled around her waist and lifted her upward, drawing her greedy mouth from his, at the same time, bringing her breast to his mouth. She braced her hands against the rim of the tub and gasped at the feel of his seeking mouth on her breast.

While he pleasured one breast with those skilled lips, he satisfied the other with his hand, plucking her tender nipple, cradling her roundness. Her thighs squeezed on either side of his hips. She couldn't stop that instinctive back and forth movement of her own hips. Every move pushed her closer and closer to release. The feel of his sex pressing against her, hard and smooth, was driving her mad. She wanted him inside her.

As if anticipating her desperation, his free hand slid between her legs, touched her. She cried out, unable to contain the wanton sound.

He shifted his tip into position but stopped her when she would have sunk onto him. She searched his eyes, a question in her own. He cupped her face in his hands and pulled her to him for one more of those slow, easy kisses. Every emotional barrier she kept locked so securely crumbled helplessly.

As precious as that kiss was, her body ached to be filled by him. To complete this mating. He didn't make her wait any longer. He settled his hands on her hips and ushered her downward.

Climax came in a landslide of sensation…of pure pleasure.

He wrapped his arms around her and rolled her onto her back sending more water cascading over the rim of the tub. He held still until she could breathe again… think again and then he started the whole process over again. He thrust long and deep, taking his time, kissing her like she'd never been kissed before. And then she knew why he'd waited until she recovered. He didn't want her to miss anything...wanted her to feel every inch of him, every thrust, until she flew apart in his arms once more and he came with every bit as much force as she did.

HEATH HAD NEVER shampooed a woman's hair before. He liked it. He liked it a lot.

"That was amazing," she said, sitting upright, her legs still wrapped around his waist. He'd lost count of the number of times they'd added more hot water to the tub. They had taken their sweet time washing each other's body, relishing the simple act of touching.

"If you think that was amazing, wait till I do this." He took her hand in his and kissed each fingertip and then the palm of her hand. She sighed dreamily. He was certain he'd kissed every part of her at least twice and still she responded like it was the first time.

"You know," she said drawing his gaze up to hers, "I'd planned to spend this night questioning you."

He leaned back in the tub, loving the hell out of the view. She had a gorgeous body. But that was no surprise. The size and tilt of her breasts were every man's fantasy. He couldn't help reaching out to touch one.

"I'm serious." She batted his hand away.

"Okay. I'll behave." He clasped his hands across his chest and gave her his undivided attention...well most of it anyway. There wasn't a damned thing he could do about the reaction of his sex to her round bottom.

"Why don't you take notes?"

He frowned in confusion. "What notes?"

She folded her arms over her chest, hiding those luscious breasts from his view. "Notes. You are writing a story, right?"

He gave himself a mental kick. "Oh, yes." He shook his head. "I don't need notes." He grappled for some explanation. "I'd rather observe and then tell the story in my own words."

That appeared to satisfy her on that score. "But what about questions? Don't you have more questions for me? Additional background information for your story?"

Now she was worried about whether he was legit. She was running scared. He had to do something about that. A deliberate smile kicked up the corners of his mouth. "I've been asking questions. Just check with your friends, like Rafe."

Her serious expression rearranged into surprise. "Oh." Then she fired off another question. "What did you mean last night when you said forgive me?"

He carefully schooled any reaction to her reminder of his one slip in composure. Forgiveness was something he did not expect…not when she learned the truth.

Dodging her question, he threaded the fingers of one hand into her hair and pulled her close. "Don't do this, Jayne. Just let me make love to you."

She hesitated, then surrendered without a fight. He made it worth her while. He kissed her until they both had to come up for air. With that done, he lifted her out of the tub careful of the numerous towels they'd scattered about to soak up the water.

He settled her on her feet and took his time smoothing a towel over her skin, kissing her shoulder, her elbow… every part of her the terry cloth touched. When her breathing grew as choppy as his own, he swung her off her feet and carried her to the bed. He lowered her to the sheets, his eyes never leaving hers. He wanted her to see how much this meant to him. How much *she* meant to him.

He kissed his way down her satiny skin, pausing to pay special attention to her breasts, something he'd just learned she loved. He traced a scar on her leg with his tongue and made a mental note to ask about that later, then licked and suckled until she quivered beneath his touch…until she begged for him to finish it.

And still he tortured her…tortured himself with the most intimate of acts. He spread her legs wide and tasted her. She arched upward, her fingers knotting in the sheets. He didn't want her to forget the way he'd loved her…had to imprint his touch on her memory. He had to have her until he exhausted himself. He wanted her so much…had thought himself incapable of feeling this way again. It was a blessing and a curse.

He couldn't think about that tonight.

Nothing else mattered…not the future or the past. There was only here and now. He couldn't let it go.

"Please." She reached for him and he could not deny her.

He moved up over her with the knowledge that she was right on the verge of going over the edge. Her body writhed with needy impatience under his. She couldn't catch her breath.

He kissed her cheek. Just like the first time he'd kissed her…before her birthday party.

"No more," she pleaded. Her legs wrapped around his and pulled his hips toward hers.

He pushed inside her in slow, agonizing increments. His entire body shook with the effort of restraint. She clawed his back, surged upward and the control he'd held on to for so long snapped. He pounded into her until she screamed his name…until he followed her over that emotional cliff and altered the landscape of his heart forever.

CHAPTER ELEVEN

Inside the Colby Agency

Cole Danes turned off the portable remote observation monitor and pushed away from the desk.

He moved to the wall of windows overlooking the city of Chicago. Lights glittered in the darkness for miles all around him like fallen stars. Maybe there was a single sentimental cell left inside him after all, but he doubted it. More likely his mental waxing was a result of boredom.

He'd underestimated Heath Murphy's self-discipline. He'd expected this physical bonding twenty-four hours ago.

Cole crossed his arms over his chest and tapped his chin. There would be no more waiting, however. Stephens would act at once as he'd done in the past.

Murphy was no fool. Even with next to no facts on the case, he'd figured out the target's motivation as well as his M.O. That definitely merited high marks.

Cole smiled. He'd made the right choice.

Stephens would have no recourse but to reach out to any and all contacts. He would *need* to know who'd breached his carefully constructed security.

Tonight had given Cole the reassurance he'd needed. Murphy would not fail, nor would he require backup. He would eliminate the target without hesitation. Stephens would provide the necessary motivation…it was his one fatal flaw. His emotions where his daughter was concerned were unerringly predictable. And that would be the death of him.

Then justice would be served on all counts.

Cole turned out the lights and walked out of Victoria Colby-Camp's office.

The next move was the target's.

CHAPTER TWELVE

Jayne lay still for long minutes, watching the morning sun creep into her bedroom. Fingers of golden light reached across the bed, highlighting the masculine planes and ridges of Heath's muscular body. A smile played around the corners of her mouth as she considered how warm and secure she felt in bed with this man. The feeling was so unfamiliar, surreal almost…like a fantasy come to life. He made her feel complete. Complete on some level she'd never known existed before now. She'd felt a kind of bond the two other times she'd fallen for a guy, but nothing to compare with this.

She didn't want to think, she just wanted to enjoy this moment. Overanalyzing was a bad habit of hers. Searching for the hidden agenda behind everything good in her life was growing tiresome. *This* was good. *Heath* was good. Being with him made her feel fulfilled, something she'd been lacking for a very long time.

A soft sigh whispered past her lips. She could look at him like this forever. Shadows still obscured his face but she knew every angle and curve by heart. A day's growth of beard gave him a rugged, almost dangerous air. That smile nudged at her lips once more. She liked his strength, even that hint of mystery that shrouded him.

A reporter who asked few questions. By his own admission he preferred diving into a subject and then writing the story in his own words. After last night, she decided that she liked that strategy herself. Diving in was very, very good, she mused.

Memories of the water sloshing over the sides of the tub, and Heath pulling her down on top of him filtered through her mind like a movie in slow motion. The way he'd kissed her. Her smile widened to a grin. The way she'd kissed him. Boldly, wantonly. Now that was a first. She'd liked that power. Had loved the feel of his skin against hers, of his body mated fully with hers. Soft moans, savage groans, urgent pleas combined with the sounds of their bodies coming together in those final frantic moments. And the sweet, earthy fragrance of their lovemaking.

Heat simmered inside her, making her wet and restless with anticipation, making her want to push him onto his back and climb aboard.

And why not do just that?

She'd decided to go for it. To put aside her usual inhibitions and defenses. There was no rule that said this had to be a one-time thing. They could make love at every opportunity for as long as Heath was in town.

An ache pierced her. Because she was certain that when he was gone she'd never be able to feel like this with anyone else.

No more thinking.

She smoothed her hand over that awesome chest. His lids fluttered open and those dark brown eyes instantly cleared of sleep and focused on her. He smiled, the sexiest damned smile she'd ever laid eyes on.

"Good morning," he murmured, his voice husky with sleep and with the desire that promptly shimmered in his eyes.

She had done that. Her touch had set him off the same as merely looking at him had done her.

He didn't resist as she pushed him onto his back. To the contrary, he relaxed into the pillow, his arms thrown over his head, those corded limbs resting on either side.

"Don't move," she ordered.

He licked his lips, his gaze settling intently on hers. "Not even if you put a gun to my head."

Raising up on all fours, she straddled him, braced one hand next to his face and leaned down to taste those tempting lips as she simultaneously rubbed her moist heat along his smooth, hard length. "I woke up wanting you," she whispered breathlessly, her voice reflecting the wondrous glow she felt inside at the memory.

He kissed her lips lightly, the same way one tasted wine. A single sip, but with a thoroughness and concentration that involved all five senses. "I woke up dreaming of you," he murmured, each word punctuated with another tender meeting of lips. His hands skimmed her body, leaving a path of fiery sensations wherever he touched. "And here you are."

His words only added to the urgency and it would not be denied any longer. Giving him one last kiss, she shifted her weight to her knees and reached down to guide him to just the right spot. He watched her, the fierce need in his eyes emboldening her all the more. She sank slowly, until her body sealed completely against his and they cried out together. Long moments passed before she could move. Her body pulsed with the sensation of being filled so completely by Heath. *Heath Murphy.* She never wanted to forget his name, his face… or the way he made her feel. She felt his fingers tighten on her thighs as he struggled to do as she'd ordered. She was in charge. He wasn't to move.

When her senses had recovered from the overload of pleasure the deliciously deep penetration had wrought, she began to move, undulating her hips in that age-old rhythm that came as naturally as breathing.

She wouldn't be able to hold out long. The drag of her soft, swollen flesh along that generous, hard length quickly took her to the very edge of climax. She fought it with every ounce of determination she possessed, wanted to hold out, to make him writhe beneath her as she had beneath him last night. She wanted him to beg for her to hurry…to plead for mercy. But release came before she could slow its desperate rush. The sounds of her pleasure burst from her throat as spasm after spasm gripped her. She wanted to curl up against him and revel in the cascading sensations that followed. She refused. Kept moving at that slow, steady pace though her heart thundered and her body shuddered with the aftereffects of release.

He groaned deep in his throat. With monumental effort her eyes opened to watch. His fingers gripped her thighs to the point of pain and his body trembled and shuddered as hers had.

Her name came from his lips in a savage gasp.

She knew what he wanted, but she didn't give in. Slow, back and forth, over and over. Her skin slickened with sweat, as did his. She could feel him throbbing inside her, his control almost gone. Like her, he resisted, wanted to make it last for as long as possible.

She panted, unable to drag oxygen into her lungs fast enough. It was all she could do to keep this unhurried pace. She wanted to…oh…she felt herself coming again.

Too soon.

She squeezed her fingers into fists. No. Not yet.

He murmured something inaudible. Tried to urge her into a faster rhythm with his hands but she refused to surrender.

Color flared behind her closed lids. Every muscle in her body contracted, then shuddered as the ultimate moment of pure physical gratification shivered through her, starting at her center and moving outward like the shockwaves of an explosion.

She couldn't move anymore...the intense pleasure was too overwhelming. Heath pulled her down to his chest and rolled her onto her back. He withdrew to the very tip and thrust deep, driving into her with such force that she lost her breath...couldn't think, couldn't speak. He pumped harder and faster until his own release roared through him.

He thrust again and again, slower this time, allowing the final waves to wash over them, melting every muscle.

Their breathing ragged, they collapsed together, a tangle of trembling arms and legs.

She traced a path on his chest, unable to look him in the eye just yet. "That was like climbing to the very top of the highest, most rugged peak you can find for the first time."

He lifted her chin and smiled down at her. "No." He shook his head. "It was better."

Those three words took her breath away all over again. He kissed her before she could recover. Any possibility of resistance, of going on with her life as before, disappeared like an early morning fog beneath the rising sun.

"Do you have plans for the day?"

She nodded, her smile dragging into a worried frown. "Unfortunately I have to take a small group to the Maroon Bells. Rescues might be off-limits but I can pace myself on this one."

The change in his eyes was instantaneous. He knew precisely what that meant. High elevation, level five, difficult climbing. Definitely not for amateurs. Considerably more arduous than the trek they'd made up to the Alpine Hut. Regret squeezed her heart. "You shouldn't go," she said quickly. "It'll be—"

He pressed his finger to her lips. "If you go, I'm going."

She took his hand in hers. "I don't get that about you, Heath. Why did they send you to cover this kind of story? It doesn't make sense."

There was something new in his eyes when he spoke. Something she couldn't quite read, but it filled her with an emotion akin to dread.

"It had to be me."

Jayne sat up and fished for something to put on. A shirt, anything. "You know, I could use some coffee. How about you?" She tried hard to inject lightness into her tone but failed miserably. He was leaving out some pertinent information and she didn't understand that.

"Sounds great."

She tugged on her tattered robe and shimmied into a pair of panties. She tossed him his cold-weather pants, which had been hung across a chair after getting wet on the bathroom floor last night. "Guess that means you get the shower first."

She wiggled her fingers at him in a goodbye and rushed out of the room. The real world was suddenly pressing in around her, reminding her that her time with Heath was short, temporary. And that something wasn't quite right. Lead filled her tummy. She didn't want to feel either of those things…she definitely didn't want him to see her get all emotional.

Ten minutes. That's all she needed to pull herself back together. She'd be fine. She'd gotten over far worse in the past. Her heart launched an immediate objection.

This time—she had an awful feeling—would be the worst by far.

HEATH DRAGGED ON THE cold-weather pants and several realizations slammed into him at once.

He'd made love to Jayne.

He zipped his fly and closed his eyes in despair. He'd lost all sight of objectivity, had shirked any pretense of professionalism.

But the worst of his transgressions was what he had done to her. She trusted him. Finally. And he was, basically, her enemy. Their lovemaking would only add insult to injury when she learned the truth about him and her father.

Not to mention—he swore hotly—that he'd been so caught up in the intensity of their coming together that he'd forgotten about the camera monitoring her room. He gritted his teeth to hold back the words he wanted to hurl at Danes, who was no doubt watching. Instead, he stormed over to the tiny electronic eye, gave his temporary boss a universal hand gesture he'd have no trouble deciphering, then switched the damned thing off.

So much for his new career.

Heath ran a hand through his hair. How the hell had he let things get this far out of control? Had all those years as a cop taught him nothing? You don't get personally involved with a suspect or a witness. Anyone associated with a case was off-limits.

But he'd screwed up. Let his emotions rule him. Maybe he should have given up any sort of investigative work after the accident.

He headed into the bathroom for that shower but stopped shy of the tub.

A quick inventory of his emotions gave him a start. He mulled over his findings as he cleaned up the mess of wet towels from the floor, his movements on autopilot. He piled them near the door and searched the tiny linen closet in hopes of finding at least one last dry towel. Thankfully he found two. He took one, draped it over the rod that circled the big old claw-footed tub then drew the shower curtain around and turned on the water.

It was the strangest thing. He shucked off his pants and tossed them aside.

Moments ago, when he'd thought about the accident, he'd done so without the usual plunge into bad memories. He shook off the idea, not wanting to press his luck.

Damned strange.

He stepped into the tub and pulled the shower curtain closed. His eyes drifted shut as the spray of hot water sluiced over him. Jayne's image filled his mind. Flashbacks from last night as well as this morning tightened his muscles, made him want to call out to her and drag her into this shower with him. Then the fear intruded, twisting his gut in agony. Not that old familiar fear from his past, but a new one, razor sharp in its own right.

The fear of losing her.

CRADLING A STEAMING cup of coffee, Jayne curled up in the chair in front of her computer. She hadn't checked her e-mail in days. Not that she got any that often. She mostly used the Internet for checking the weather advisories and the news around the nation. She didn't spend a lot of time in front of the television. Somehow she got more out of it when she read it. Or maybe the news anchors just annoyed her.

Her telephone rang and she hissed a curse. Setting her hot coffee aside, she reached for the cordless receiver next to the computer with her free hand. She hated having her first cup of coffee interrupted.

She thought of Heath in the shower and considered that he was one interruption she would have happily tolerated. But she'd needed these few moments of space to get her act back together. She was okay now. She could handle this morning-after thing.

Hell, she was twenty-five. Not a kid anymore. If she couldn't do it now, there wasn't much hope. She'd wanted to be with Heath, facing the consequences was part of the deal.

"Hello." She reached for her coffee and stole a sip that scorched her lips and tongue.

"Jayne."

Her heart rocketed into her throat and she nearly dropped the suddenly too heavy cup. She set it aside just to be safe.

"Dad?"

He'd never called her three times in the space of one week. She prayed nothing was wrong.

"We have to talk, Jayne. It's important."

"Is something wrong?" She held the receiver with both hands, her pulse pounding. His voice sounded so... so flat. This had to be bad news.

"Remember I warned you to be careful of strangers."

She nodded stiffly then blurted, "Yes, I remember. What's wrong? Has something happened?" She ignored the concept that attempted to trickle into her awareness. She would not go there…would not think that.

"It's the reporter, Jayne. Heath Murphy."

Her hands started to shake as ice slid through her veins. At first she couldn't respond, but then she blurted, "No, Dad, you're wrong." She felt so cold. This wasn't possible. No way. He'd made a mistake.

"I knew this would be hard for you. He's…gotten close to you. I've sent you an e-mail containing all the evidence necessary to prove that I'm right. Don't believe anything he tells you. I'm coming for you and then I'll explain everything."

The line went dead but Jayne couldn't move.

Her father had to be wrong.

She pressed the Off button and stuck the receiver back onto its base, her actions automatic. Her entire being had gone from cold to numb.

Her father had to be wrong.

But he'd sounded so…certain. So afraid for her.

She reached for the mouse and clicked to open her inbox.

Her hand trembling she opened the message marked "Heath Murphy." An image filled the screen. A picture of Heath. She scrolled down to the next image. A copy of a Salt Lake City newspaper article: *Woman Falls to Death*. The story described in gory detail how climbing enthusiast Heath Murphy, a homicide detective from Gatlinburg, Tennessee, had lost his fiancée in a devastating accident. The two had set out to scale the Moses Tower, an infamously difficult climb, only one had returned alive.

Tears spilled down Jayne's cheeks by the time she reached the end of the article. This was the accident he wouldn't talk about. The woman had been his fiancée. No wonder he didn't climb anymore.

There was more. Just over two years later. Several articles on an internal affairs investigation involving a Gatlinburg, Tennessee, homicide department. Detective Heath Murphy had been cleared of wrongdoing but had resigned, walking away from a stellar eight-year career.

A frown nagged at Jayne's brow. Was that when he'd decided to go into journalism? It didn't seem likely to her. Lots of guys in law enforcement turned to writing, she argued, mentally ticking off several she'd read about over the years. She recalled at least one homicide detective who had turned to writing after a high profile Beverly Hills murder. But this was different. Heath had represented himself as an investigative journalist, not a novelist. Why hadn't he mentioned that he'd been a cop? She could understand him not wanting to talk about the accident, but his career as a detective shouldn't have been off-limits.

Then she reached the final part of the e-mail. A current dossier on Heath Murphy.

Colby Agency investigator.

The Colby Agency was a private investigations firm in Chicago. He wasn't a writer. Had nothing to do with any newspapers or magazines.

Jayne's hand fell away from the mouse.

Heath wasn't here for a story on mountain rescue.

He was here for her…to learn about her father.

But he'd never asked anything about her father. She blinked. Well, he had asked about family, but just that once. If he wanted to know more about her father why didn't he ask questions?

It didn't make sense.

She closed the confusing document and read the sub-ject line of the new e-mail she'd just received.

Physical evidence.

Renewed dread gelled in her stomach.

She clicked on the message.

Look in his jacket. He carries a weapon. The newest message from her father listed five areas in her apart-ment that she should check for what he called surveil-lance bugs. The final part of his message proved the most unsettling of all. *I won't be able to contact you again. With these two e-mails my enemy will know I'm on to them.*

Her heart started to beat faster. Fear tangled with the dread expanding inside her. He couldn't be right. He just couldn't be.

But she had to know for sure.

She got up from the chair, her now cold coffee for-gotten. She moved to the built-in bookshelves against the far wall. The books she considered keepers were there. Her small thirteen-inch television and a CD player. She tiptoed and felt along the top of the books on the shelf above her head, the one her father had told her to check.

Her heart stumbled painfully when her fingers en-countered a tiny object.

She didn't want this to be true.

Oh, please, she didn't want this...

The object was small and black but even she recog-nized it as a sort of camera. The eye or lens, whatever it was called, was unmistakable.

She threw it against the floor.

Her fury exploding inside her, one by one she found the surveillance bugs and threw them as hard as she could against the hundred-year-old hardwood.

The water in the shower had just stopped. He would be coming out any moment.

But she didn't care. She shook with the pain of his betrayal. She waffled between wanting to scream and cry and throw up. Her stomach twisted and her eyes filled with tears despite all her attempts to keep them at bay.

She found his jacket, sat down on the foot of the bed and held it for a few moments before she reached inside. Touching the weapon wasn't actually necessary. She'd already deduced from the weight of the jacket that there was something heavy in one of the pockets.

Still, she wanted to see.

A sob ripped out of her throat.

To know without doubt that her father's words were true.

Her fingers curled around cold steel. She withdrew the weapon and stared at it. Black. Similar to something she'd seen on television or in a movie. That's all she could determine. She knew nothing of weapons.

It surprised her that her tears abruptly dried upon making this final discovery. There would be more, she knew, when the numbness wore off.

Her father had warned her.

But she hadn't listened.

He'd told her to beware of strangers. He'd known trouble was headed her way. Had even cautioned her that he feared as much.

Still she hadn't listened.

She'd had every warning, every reason to see Heath Murphy coming.

He'd skated right into her life.

Another pang of hurt ached through her, twisted in her chest.

She had to tell Walt that they'd both been fooled. His

friend had lied to him. Heath had lied to her. How had she missed all the signs?

Her eyes closed and the hand holding the weapon fell to her lap. Because she'd needed him to be real. She'd needed him. For months—no years—she had denied that need. To keep her father safe, to protect her heart.

Somehow Heath had undermined her defenses. Had known all the right things to say and do.

Because he'd known who she was before he came.

Fury whipped through her and her eyes opened wide.

He'd likely studied her. Had devised the perfect plan to get to her. To make her vulnerable. So he could get to her father.

Her fingers tightened around the butt of the gun.

She would not let him do this. She had to protect her father.

Private investigators worked for clients, didn't they? Heath's client was no doubt her father's enemy.

A cell phone rang.

It wasn't hers.

She stared at the jacket on the bed next to her.

Heath's.

The bathroom door opened just then. Heath, clad in nothing but a towel, took two steps before the gravity of the situation struck him.

He looked from her to the weapon in her hand and back to her. She watched the muscles of his throat work as he swallowed with considerable difficulty.

"Let me explain."

She shook so hard it was all she could do to stand, but she managed. She pointed the gun at him just like she'd seen in the movies. "Tell me the truth. *Now.*"

CHAPTER THIRTEEN

Aboard the Colby Agency jet

Cole Danes closed the now useless handheld monitor. He glanced out the window and considered whether or not making this journey to Colorado was of any real consequence. The target would be eliminated before dark, he felt confident. All the key elements had been set in motion.

And yet, his own need for absolute certainty required that he take no chances.

Howard Stephens had played right into his hands. His every move had been choreographed from the very beginning by Cole himself.

Cole had spent his adult life doing this kind of work. He never failed. Once he outlined a scenario, things never failed to fall into place. Heath Murphy's resistance to accept the assignment, his very past had been factored into the profile.

Then there was Jayne, the daughter. She too had reacted exactly as Cole had estimated.

He smiled.

The game was over.

CHAPTER FOURTEEN

Heath didn't move a muscle.

"Put the gun down, Jayne," he suggested quietly.

"Tell me," she demanded, her voice quavering, "the truth."

Her hand shook and Heath swallowed hard. He couldn't be sure the weapon's safety was still engaged. To his knowledge Jayne had no experience with handguns, but he wasn't absolutely certain. Some of her mountain rescue buddies could have shown her the basics.

He drew in a steadying breath and held out his hands in a let's-stay-calm gesture. "I don't know what's happened since we made love in that bed this morning," he inclined his head in the direction of the tangled sheets "but whatever it is, it's wrong."

"I know who you are." She blinked rapidly. God, she was going to cry. Regret sliced through him. "But I want to hear the truth from you," she added tightly. "Why did you come here?"

The way Heath saw it he had two choices. He could keep lying to her and take his chances with her marksmanship or he could tell her the truth and…well, basically risk the same. He was screwed either way.

But none of that mattered.

The only thing that mattered was the way she looked at him right now. The way her eyes glittered with tears.

He'd hurt her and nothing he said or did would change that. But he had to try. The idea that this was only the tip of the iceberg banded around his chest making a deep breath impossible.

Obviously they were still in the apartment alone since her father had not put in an appearance. Still, the son of a bitch had contacted her somehow.

"I am Heath Murphy," he told her, letting his hands fall to his sides.

Anger tightened her lips into a bitter line.

"I'm an investigator for the Colby Agency, a private investigations firm in Chicago."

"Why are you here?" she repeated, her voice a little stronger now. But her hands still visibly shook.

Damn, he had to talk her into putting down that weapon or someone was going to get hurt. "Look, Jayne, I know you want answers, but I really need you to put the gun down. You know I won't hurt you."

Her eyes widened with a mixture of fear and fury. "That's just it," she shouted, all semblance of calm evaporating. "I don't know anything. Now, tell me the real truth! All of it," she added before taking a deep, halting breath.

To his extreme relief she lowered the weapon's barrel slightly. At least now if it went off it wasn't as likely to be lethal.

That could very well change with his next statement.

"I'm investigating your father, Howard Stephens."

She flinched but didn't actually look startled. "Why?"

He closed his eyes and blew out a heavy breath. Whatever her father's side of this had been, Heath knew with complete certainty that she was not prepared for what he was about to share with her. "Let me get dressed and I'll tell you everything."

She shook her head. "Don't move, just talk."

Now or never. He had to know just how serious she was. He couldn't risk that she was simply buying time until her father showed up. If he was lucky Danes would be watching via the monitors and would take some sort of action if Stephens made an appearance with Heath in a vulnerable position.

He leveled his gaze on hers. She flinched again. The reaction was like a sucker punch to the gut, because this time it was about him...not her father or the investigation. She didn't want him to look at her. That hurt more than he could have estimated. This situation was totally out of control. His objectivity had gone into the toilet. What the hell. He was standing here naked and disarmed. He had nothing else to lose.

"Do what you have to do, Jayne, but I'm getting dressed. We'll talk then."

Heath turned his back on her and walked into the bathroom. He didn't close the door, just pulled on his clothes and boots without looking back. He ran his fingers through his hair, drew in a fortifying breath and deliberately returned to the bedroom where she waited. The look of devastation that had now claimed her face twisted in his chest, made him want to beat the hell out of Cole Danes and put a bullet in her father's head.

Her father had done this to her.

Cole Danes had added salt to the wound.

Leaving Heath with no way to make it right.

She sat on the edge of the bed now, still clutching the weapon like a rock pick on a slippery ledge.

He sat down in a chair next to her dresser. "I'll tell you the truth but you're not going to like it."

She lifted her chin in defiance of his statement and those big green eyes stared expectantly at him but he could see the hurt quivering just beneath the surface. She'd trusted him and he'd let her down.

Damn his job.

Damn him for letting this get personal.

He was as guilty as Danes or her father.

"Your father isn't in the CIA as you believe. He never was."

A flicker of uncertainty moved across her expression, but she quickly banished it.

When she didn't comment, he continued, "He did work for the military about twenty years ago but he faked his own death so he could disappear."

"That's insane," she countered. Her fingers tightened on the butt of the weapon. "My mother told me about the money the government deposited in her bank account each month. If he wasn't in the military or CIA all those years then why did they pay him? How could he call home or visit if he was pretending to be dead. That's just crazy."

She would cling to any thread of hope as long as possible, but time was running out. If her father showed up…Heath couldn't take that risk.

"Death benefits," he explained. "The government thought he died in the line of duty. They still believe he's dead. Why do you think you're not allowed to talk about him? This is why he wants you to tell anyone who asks that he's dead. Because, to the rest of the world, he is. You're the only one who knew…until a few days ago."

"That's to protect him against people like you," she argued, her words accusing. A lone tear streaked down her cheek. She scrubbed it away, her lips trembling with renewed fury. "People who want to hurt him."

"Your father faked his death and went to work for a man named Leberman."

She went abruptly still. "Leberman?" she repeated.

"Do you recognize that name?"

She blinked then glared at him. "I…No."

Heath tensed. Something about the name was familiar to her whether she wanted to admit it or not. "Leberman operated a team of mercenaries, your father was one of them. Still is, only now he's the one in charge. They get paid to assassinate people. People whose only crime is being targeted by some scumbag who wants to profit somehow from their death. The list of crimes is long, Jayne. Including kidnapping and torturing a child."

She shook her head, her whole body shuddering at his words. "I don't believe you," she argued vehemently.

"His name was Jim Colby. He was taken from his family home eighteen years ago." Heath leaned forward and pressed her with his gaze, needing this next part to hit home particularly hard. He had to get through to her. "This seven-year-old child was kept in a house in Oak Park, in the basement. The torture was relentless."

The color of rage drained from her face. "You're making this up." Some of the conviction had gone out of her voice this time.

Heath straightened. "Why would I do that?"

"To get to my father."

He nodded. "That part's true. My goal *is* to get to your father. He has to pay for his crimes and he may have additional information about what happened to the Colby child."

"Is…" She licked her lips. "Is the boy dead?"

Heath shook his head slowly and moved a step in her

direction. "No. He's alive. But he's badly scarred, mentally and physically. Your father helped Leberman destroy his life." He stole another step toward her. "There were many, many others who didn't survive. There will be more unless he's stopped."

She lowered the weapon. Dropped her hand to her lap and stared down at it.

He couldn't bear the despair shrouding her. He had to go to her. He crouched in front of her and reached for her hand. She drew it away. "Jayne, I'm sorry you had to find out this way. I know he's your father and that you love him, but you have to believe me."

Her gaze jerked to his. "Why should I believe anything you say?"

"There's no way I would hurt you with these kinds of accusations if they weren't true." He tucked a wisp of hair behind her ear and she recoiled from his touch. He refused to give up. He had to make her believe him. "Last night meant something to me. You have to trust me. I'm trying to help you. I'm afraid of what your father might do when he learns that you know the truth."

She offered the gun to him and stood. "Get out." She pointed to the door. "I don't ever want to see you again." She pivoted away from him before he could stop her and escaped to the bathroom.

"Wait. Jayne, please."

She hesitated at the door and glared back at him, then moved her head firmly from side to side. "Go. The only thing I want to do right now is wash the lies off my skin."

She slammed the door, shutting him out. He heard the lock slide into place.

He tucked the weapon into his waistband at the small

of his back and reached for his jacket. He had to call Danes. A small object in his peripheral vision snagged his attention. He crossed the room to take a closer look.

The surveillance camera.

Within seconds he'd discovered that she had destroyed all five devices. Her father had contacted her and told her exactly what to look for and where to look.

He'd been here—inside this apartment—since Heath's arrival.

Why the hell hadn't Danes warned him?

JAYNE HUNKERED IN THE shower, the tears would not stop. Her body shook so hard she could scarcely breathe.

None of this could be true. Her father wouldn't have done those things.

Heath…oh, God. How could he do this to her?

She'd scrubbed her skin until it felt raw.

She drew in a shuddering breath but couldn't manage to get enough air into her lungs.

She pressed her forehead to her knees and inhaled slowly, deeply, once, twice, three times. She couldn't hide in here forever. She had to get dressed and get to work, had to pull herself together.

That was the one thing she could count on. Her work. Her friends here in Aspen—Rafe and Walt and the others—they were all she needed. She didn't need Heath or her father.

Her father was never around anyway. Fury tightened her lips.

Memories of the way her mother had grieved tumbled one over the other into her mind. She'd talked of his desertion. Of how he had loved his work more than her or Jayne.

But Jayne had always pretended that he loved them too much and that that was why he'd stayed away.

She thought of her childhood home in Oak Park. Of the terrifying basement she'd only dared to visit once. Her father had taken her down there and told her never, ever to go down there again. That it wasn't safe.

Leberman.

She didn't know why the name felt familiar to her, but somehow it did. She shut off the cooling water and concentrated hard. Had she heard her father talking to someone named Leberman? Had her father mentioned the name? Or maybe she'd encountered someone at college or in her work with that name. She just couldn't remember.

But one memory stood out in her mind so vivid that it took her breath every time she dared let it creep into her consciousness.

The little boy.

She remembered a boy, maybe the same age as her at the time…six or seven.

Her father had gone away after she'd seen him with the boy. Her life had changed forever. She and her mother had abruptly moved from their home and never looked back. All the way to California.

Why had she never thought of that boy again… until now?

Leberman.

A cold hard fist of panic slammed into her stomach.

Her father had said the boy was Leberman's son. She remembered that now.

Wait.

Her heart fluttered, sending a new rush of emotion to her stinging eyes.

She shook her head.

She wasn't sure about that.

Maybe she was confusing her vague memories. Maybe part of her wanted so desperately for Heath to be the real thing that she was turning her father into a monster.

Wouldn't her mother have told her about any of this? Jayne had been just a child, but her mother would have recognized the lies…wouldn't she?

Or maybe, like Jayne, she hadn't wanted to see.

Jayne jerked the shower curtain back and climbed out of the tub. She didn't want to think about this anymore. Heath was a stranger. One who had lied to her repeatedly. Had used her. How could she possibly believe anything he told her? What kind of fool did he think she was? Her father couldn't be the monster he portrayed him to be. That simply wasn't possible. She squeezed her eyes shut and forced away the nagging voices that suggested otherwise.

She had a life. She had to get back to it.

Maybe she would be better off if she never heard from Heath or her father ever again.

Forcing a calm she didn't feel, she dressed for work and gathered her gear. She hissed a curse when she glanced at the clock. There was no more time to dawdle. Walt would likely be wondering where she was. None of this was about her. She had to remember that, shove it away. To hell with Heath Murphy and to hell with her father. Let them figure out this insanity.

Her arms loaded with her gear she moved to the living room in search of her boots.

Heath sat on the sofa.

A new blast of anger bolted through her. "I thought I told you to leave."

"I can't."

She rolled her eyes and threw her gear, onto the floor. Dammit she'd had enough. "Get out now before I call the sheriff."

Heath stood but made no move toward the door. "Finding your father isn't the only reason I was sent here," he said firmly. "I'm here to protect you from him. I'm not letting you out of my sight."

Her mouth dropped open and she made a sound of disbelief. "What's your game now, Murphy? Do you think you can frighten me and I'll pretend you didn't lie to me? That you didn't have sex with me just to get close to me so you could find my father? You keep talking about the truth, well I know the truth. The truth is you started flirting with me right from the beginning, I was just too stupid to see it." She flung her arms outward. "This whole thing was just a game—a ploy—to help you get what you wanted! Well, I don't want any part of it."

Heath closed his eyes for a moment before he responded. She wanted to hit him. The urge was very nearly irresistible. She hugged her arms around herself and fought off another wave of knee-buckling emotion. Dammit. How could he still make her feel this way? Make her feel drawn to him? After all he'd done.

"I didn't have sex with you to get close to your father," he said softly. "I made love to you because I wanted you more than anything I've ever wanted in my life."

Her pager sounded, the ominous tones jerking her attention down to her waist.

She turned away from Heath and grabbed the phone,

automatically punching in the numbers. "What's up?" she asked crisply.

"Jayne." Walt's voice. "We need everyone to come in ASAP. It's a bad one."

"I'm on my way." She depressed the Off button and pitched the phone onto the nearest chair.

"What's going on?"

She leveled her gaze on Heath. "Mountain rescue's been called out. I have to go." She held up her hand when he would have moved toward her. "I told you to go. Don't come near me again."

She jerked on her parka and boots and gathered her gear.

Heath still stood there, watching her, when she'd finished.

"I'm not letting you out of my sight," he warned. "I told you that I came here to protect you and that's what I'm going to do."

"Get out of my way."

He stepped aside but followed when she walked out the door. She ignored him, just kept moving forward. If she'd hesitated for a single second she might...she just might have let herself be stupid enough to believe him.

"Be careful out there, Jayne," Rafe called to her as she passed through the bar. Rafe's scanner had likely already warned him of whatever incident had occurred.

"I always am," she tossed back without looking his way. If he got a look at her face he would know something was going on and she just didn't have time to deal with that right now.

Lives were at stake.

She had to focus.

THE MOUNTAIN RESCUE headquarters on Main Street was crawling with activity when they arrived. Heath had followed Jayne in his rental since she refused to let him ride with her. Not that he could blame her.

Two county sheriff's deputies and more than a dozen mountain rescue volunteers were already on site. Walt Messina was outlining the search area on a topographic map.

Capitol Peak.

Not good.

Heath had never climbed, other than his little trek with Jayne, in this area, but he'd heard of that peak. It meant several things to him. High elevation, rugged terrain, tough going even in summer months. Those most likely to attempt such a climb would be skilled; if they couldn't get back down there were injuries or worse. The situation would be dire.

"Why can't the chopper just drop us in on this ridge?" Jayne pointed to a place on the map.

Paul Rice spoke up, "*Us* would not include you, Jayne," he said flatly. "You're on light duty."

She wheeled on him. "My ankle doesn't even hurt," she protested.

"That may be," he allowed, "but that doesn't mean it'll hold up under this kind of physical strain."

Heath watched the tension escalate several notches. All other eyes were on the two, as well, waiting to see how this would play out. Heath knew that Jayne was one of the best climbers the team had. To leave her out was a major call.

"You're out, Jayne," Walt seconded.

"Walt, you can't do that!"

"It's done," he said, his tone final. "Now, let's not waste any more time."

Jayne backed off. She wouldn't let her own ego get in the way of saving lives.

"The call came in about an hour ago," one of the deputies said. "One of the climbers, a fellow by the name of Carter, managed to make it out, found his way to Tom Barker's dude ranch and called for help from there. Apparently the cold got the batteries in the cell phones the group carried."

"Any of them wearing transmitters?" Walt asked.

The deputy, Lebron Littles, shook his head. "But the one who walked out gave us the location of his friends. He says a couple fell and the others got trapped trying to rescue them. He stayed back to go for help if necessary."

Heath understood that there was always room for doubt in any story, but Deputy Littles sounded less than sold on this particular one.

"Do we have any other information on this group?" Jayne asked, determined to be a part of the operation. "Anything that would indicate trouble?"

"Four males, two females. All worked together. This was some kind of business retreat," Littles told her. "But..." He inhaled a heavy breath. "This guy seems a little jumpy to me. His story has changed two or three times." He shook his head. "I don't like it."

"All right," Walt said. "To answer Jayne's original question, we can't use the chopper because of the storm brewing around those peaks. We may get as much as fifteen to twenty inches of snowfall in the next two hours." He shot Jayne a look that said he'd expected her to know that. "The weather advisory was issued early this morning."

Jayne felt the bottom drop out of her stomach for the third time this morning. She always, always checked the advisories…but this morning she'd been distracted. She pressed her lips together as anger, as much at herself as at Heath, swelled inside her once more. She'd let him… let this whole situation affect her work.

Lives depended upon her and she'd messed up.

She shot him a scathing look.

To his credit he didn't look away but that only made her angrier.

Walt laid out the plan in his usual thorough manner. The hasty team would leave immediately. Paul Rice, Chad Wade and four others would lead. The support team would follow. The one climber who'd walked out this morning wouldn't be able to assist since he was suffering from moderate hypothermia. He'd been taken straight to the hospital for treatment. The deputy's suspicions about his explanation of how these events had played out would have to wait.

"Jayne, you'll run the operation from here," Walt told her. "Mason and Snyder will stay behind as well in case anything comes up."

"Yes, sir."

She hated like hell to see the team go without her. Especially Walt. He was good. Damn good, but he was fifty-two. This kind of rescue would be hard on him. She should be leading. It had nothing to do with ego and everything to do with worry about the man.

"Walt?" she called, stalling him at the door. "Be careful. I've got a feeling this one isn't going to be easy."

He nodded and then he was gone.

Deputy Littles patted Jayne on the shoulder. "I'm gonna update the sheriff. He wanted me to keep him posted."

She nodded and dragged her attention back to the task at hand. In fifteen minutes she would conduct a communications check. When Walt and the team reached the trailhead, he'd make contact once more before setting off. Adrenaline surged. She hoped like hell the storm would hold off until this was over.

"Mason, get an update on the storm. I want to know if there's any chance it's going to blow over."

"Gotcha, Little Boss."

She smiled. Dammit. She didn't know why. She didn't have a single thing to smile about. But something about the ordinariness of him calling her that or maybe it was simply the realization that she was needed here made her lips lift into that stupid smile.

"How about some fresh coffee?" Snyder offered.

She sighed. "That'd be great." She hadn't finished even one cup this morning. She could definitely use some caffeine about now.

A phone rang and she turned just in time to see Heath pulling his cell from his pocket. She remembered it ringing earlier. He moved to the other side of the room to answer and she turned away.

Why didn't he just go? Having him here was nothing but a constant reminder of the mistake she'd made. Something deep inside her went very still.

No. His presence meant a great deal more than that. He was here to apprehend her father, if anything he said could be believed. Her father had told her he was coming. What would happen then?

Heath would do his best to bring him down and her father would likely do the same.

Someone would be hurt…or worse.

Jayne closed her eyes and braced against the worktable for support. She'd let Heath inside her, physically and emotionally. They hadn't used protection, which presented numerous problems of its own. Problems she couldn't even bring herself to consider right now. She'd trusted him, fallen for him. And he'd used her.

But was he the bad guy here?

How could she believe that her father, the man she'd worshiped from afar since she was old enough to look up to him, was such a hideous villain?

Her mother's haunted image kept nudging into her thoughts. Her father had destroyed her mother. She'd always known that, had held that against him in a sort of way, still did. But he was her father. All she had left in the world and she'd forgiven him that grievous error for the most part. He'd had a job to do. She'd told herself that he was some sort of hero out saving the world all those times he'd left her and her mother behind.

How could all that she'd believed in, all that she'd clung to, be a lie? Hurt squeezed her heart, knotted in her stomach.

She opened her eyes and settled her gaze on Heath.

Every man she'd ever trusted had let her down. Lied to her.

Could she possibly, as much as her heart yearned to, trust this man for even a second?

CHAPTER FIFTEEN

The snow had started to fall, gently, innocuously. Estimates went as high as two to three feet over the next twenty-four hours. But there would be nothing gentle or innocuous about the winds combined with that snow at the higher elevations. Visibility could drop to nothing.

For Jayne and her mountaineer comrades left behind, the advisory meant that they could be living at this cabin headquarters for the next few days.

Heath had every intention of staying put wherever she was, whether she liked it or not.

These kinds of weather conditions could lead to more hikers and climbers becoming disoriented and lost. Mutual aid calls would be required, summoning rescue support, volunteer and otherwise, from surrounding communities. Heath knew the drill. All too well.

He'd spent the last hour fighting the panic trying to take root. It was as if he had no control over his own body.

He'd been here before. Watched the flurry of activity that could prove futile. Nothing anyone could have done had saved *her*...and it had been entirely his fault.

His palms started to sweat and he sucked in another deep breath. He knew what he had to do at times like this, knew all the steps for fighting this kind of inside attack. But none of it appeared to work at the moment.

He had to find a way to focus.

Howard Stephens could show up at any time. Jayne was in a public place, one over which Heath held no dominion. He was an outsider, here merely as an observer. Under present circumstances he knew with utter certainty that if he got in Jayne's way she would have him taken away by the sheriff's deputy standing by as incident commander liaison. Heath had to tread carefully here.

A damned panic attack was the last thing he needed.

Heath kept his respiration slow and deep and his attention centered on the woman in control of the moment.

Jayne Stephens was a natural born crisis manager. As report after report of worsening conditions squawked over the radio she grew calmer and calmer, fully focused, completely committed. Not the first sign of panic.

He couldn't help admiring her. Despite the worst kind of father, she'd turned into a true champion, a heroine. She had every right to be bitter and cynical and yet she was neither of those things.

Until Heath's arrival, her life had been content. He'd noted that before. He'd taken that from her. No matter how this turned out, she wouldn't be able to escape the cynicism this time. She would be left hurt and bitter. But she was a survivor. That was quite clear. If her devil of a father didn't get her killed, she would carry on. Heath was dead certain about that. She would not let down her friends or her community. Only her feelings would be damaged…her heart. And Heath was neck deep in guilt for having taken part in that travesty.

He pushed the thought away and counted heads again. He had to stay on top of the situation, had to remember what he was here to do. He had his orders. Stephens had to be stopped. And he would be coming. It would have been nice to believe the man cared about his daughter, but Heath doubted that. More likely he would want her out of the way so that no one could reach him via that route again. Oh, she wouldn't like that one little bit. He wondered how her father would react when she told him to forget it. That she wasn't going anywhere.

She had a life here…one Heath's assignment had turned upside down.

He'd tried to reach Danes twice this morning with no luck. He glanced at his watch. He hadn't been able to reach anyone. It was past time someone had come into the office at the Colby Agency. He'd gotten a call back from the answering service but nothing else.

Trying again, he took a step back from the group monitoring the ongoing rescue, pulled out his cell phone and punched the appropriate speed dial number. The call was answered on the first ring.

"Elaine, this is Heath Murphy. I need to speak with Mr. Danes."

"I'm sorry, Mr. Murphy, but Mr. Danes is not in the office as of yet."

Heath definitely hadn't expected that response. "How about Ian or Simon then?" He had to update someone on the situation here since Danes hadn't called him last night or this morning and Heath hadn't been able to reach him. Where the hell was everybody?

"Ah…Mr. Murphy, there isn't anyone else here except me."

Uneasiness trickled through Heath. "What do you mean? What about Mildred?"

"Mildred left a message for me that she had to go out of town on a family emergency. That's all I know."

"Fine." Heath considered what he should do. "Just have Ian or Simon call me if Mr. Danes doesn't come in. I need to talk to one of them." What were the odds that reaching both men would prove impossible? Sounded like Danes's work to him.

"I will, sir."

Heath closed his phone and dropped it back into his pocket. It seemed impossible. Though it was Saturday, Danes had put the entire staff on a seven-day workweek until further notice. Another of his interrogation tactics. Yet, there was no one at the Colby Agency. Not even Mildred. Mildred was always the first to arrive and the last to go…it didn't make sense.

"If the storm hits as hard as expected," Snyder said, his voice somber, tugging Heath's attention back to the here and now "we'll have to call 'em back."

Jayne shrugged. "Maybe. But it's not like we don't know where these people are." She studied the map again. "If Walt and his team can make it in they can provide emergency medical care and dig in for the duration. Walt knows how to sit out a storm." She studied the incoming weather reports once more. "At least that way maybe these folks will have a chance of surviving."

"Have we heard anything from the request for backup from Fort Carson?" Mason, another of Jayne's mountain rescue teammates, wanted to know. "With those all-weather helicopters they could fly these people out no matter what the storm does."

"The base is already supporting a couple of other rescues," Jayne said thoughtfully. She rubbed at her forehead, the first indication of stress Heath had seen. "I'm hoping they'll get to us soon," she added.

"Walt can lie low if need be until then," Mason allowed. "Like you said, Jayne, he knows how to handle this."

"I just hope it doesn't come to that." Jayne chewed her lip. "I think maybe I'll give the base liaison a call and get the latest on their ongoing ops."

All three were restless, wanted to be out there in the field helping instead of stuck in this cabin coordinating. But the job they carried out was essential. Walt and his teams would be helpless out there without proper support on this end. What Jayne did in here was every bit as important as those making the trek up to that peak.

More rescue volunteers wandered in as the time crept past. Unfortunately for Heath they weren't alone. The media had discovered the drama and converged upon the rescue headquarters. Dozens of cars were parked along the sidewalk outside. From what Heath could determine the Denver company that employed the injured and trapped climbers was of more than casual interest to the statewide media circus, especially considering one of the victims was the CEO. Snyder and Mason kept the growing crowd apprised of the situation. Heath's primary concern was not only to keep an eye on Jayne but also to monitor every new face that bobbed into the scene.

Not so easy with reporters swarming like bees in search of the nearest hive.

"Jayne."

Jayne looked up at the sound of her name, time and place slowly coming into focus. She'd been studying the maps and weather radar screen so closely for so long she'd lost track of the goings on around her. She'd been vaguely aware of the arrival of the media. Perfect.

"Yeah, Lebron, what's up?"

Deputy Littles sidled up to her, closer than necessary, sending her on instant alert. "I've got the sheriff on the line."

She noted the cell phone in his hand then. "Is something wrong?" Her first thought was that there'd been a slide somewhere close to Walt that she hadn't heard about yet. She hated when ICS, the incident command system, worked against her like that. Base operations here needed the information first, not the sheriff's office.

The deputy offered her the phone. "I'll let him explain so there's no confusion."

Jayne took the phone. "Sheriff, this is Jayne Stephens. Do you have information that affects my team in the field?" She walked away from the buzz of ongoing speculations and calculations, more to gain some privacy than to hear better.

"Jayne, I have a situation that I'm not comfortable putting through normal channels."

"Okay," she said slowly. Jayne wasn't sure how the sheriff expected her to respond to that comment. In her three years as a part of mountain rescue she'd never encountered a situation not appropriate for normal channels.

"Dispatch received a 9-1-1 call ten minutes ago regarding an injured climber."

A frown worked its way across her forehead. "Why wouldn't you want that call to come through normal channels?" If they had another victim out there they needed to know. "Is this one related to the ongoing rescue?"

A heavy breath hissed over the line. "No." The sheriff swore softly, surprising her. That wasn't like him. "Just as quickly as I clear one heap of trouble another one drops in my lap," he explained. "Our man, Carter, has come clean and finally admitted that he and the CEO had fought. The CEO slipped over the edge and the rest pretty much went down as Carter had reported. He knows this is his fault and he left the group with the intentions of running. By the time he'd made it to Barker's dude ranch guilt had changed his mind and he called in."

Jayne couldn't help wondering why that mattered just now. She had a rescue to oversee and this was nothing more than a waste of her time, but she didn't see any reason to tell the sheriff that. He had to know it. Clearly he was under a lot of stress here, but who wasn't?

"I'll let you know as soon as Walt reports in," she said for lack of anything else to say. "They probably won't make contact for a while yet." If the CEO was dead, Carter would be up on manslaughter charges, she estimated. Between now and then she imagined the guy would be sweating bullets.

"That's not why I called," the sheriff said, surprising her all over again.

Now she was really lost and she definitely didn't have time for this.

"The other call, the one that came in about ten minutes ago."

Damn. She'd forgotten he even mentioned another call. She massaged her temple and forced herself to pay attention to the conversation for a few minutes more, but her mind was on Walt. She should be the one out there, not him. "An injured climber?" she asked. This could mean sending another group out into the field. Just what she needed.

"The caller said he had fallen and broken his leg. The connection was bad. I've played the tape twice and I scarcely made it out myself."

"What's the location?" Jayne hurried back over to the map as the sheriff called off the information. Not such a bad place to be stuck even in weather like this. The retrieval wouldn't be that difficult, but it would require expertise and a strong knowledge of the area since visibility would be seriously limited.

"I'll get a team right on it," Jayne told him. This was easy compared to what Walt was going through. She didn't understand the sheriff's strange behavior on this one.

"I guess the thing that strikes me as odd," the sheriff said at last, "is that the guy asked for you by name and the call registered as having come from Thurman McGill's cell phone."

Now that got Jayne's attention. Victims didn't usually ask for rescuers by name. Even stranger, Thurman McGill was a local resident they called upon quite often for air support. Thurman owned two helicopters, used them for giving tourists aerial tours. She supposed Thurman could have asked for her but more likely he would have asked for Walt.

"Did he crash?" That didn't seem reasonable to Jayne. Why would he have been out in this weather? Unless the storm came on more quickly than he'd expected.

"That's just it, Jayne. The voice didn't belong to Thurman McGill. I've tried calling the number back, in case it was a mistake. That happens once in a while, a number will show up as one thing when it's really something else. No system is perfect. There was no answer and I didn't get an answer at Thurman's place either. I sent a deputy over there and nobody's home."

"I'll get a team headed up to that location right now, Sheriff. Keep me posted."

"Jayne," he said, waylaying her, "I don't like this. Maybe you'd better send Littles along, too. I'll send another of my men to cover things there."

She glanced at Lebron. He was a pretty good mountaineer. She didn't have a problem with that. "All right. Thanks, Sheriff." She passed the phone back to the deputy.

"Mason, Snyder." Jayne gestured for the two senior team members present to join her.

"Walt just checked in," Snyder informed her. "They've made contact with the fallen climbers. And Fort Carson called, they've got a Chinook headed Walt's way. He had a time getting over the Continental Divide, but he thinks he can rendezvous with Walt's team within the hour."

"Excellent." That was definitely good news. The Chinook was a large enough helicopter to turn this hazardous rescue into a walk in the park. "Did you pass that along to Walt?"

He shook his head. "Just got the call. I'll do that now."

"In a minute." Jayne took a breath. "I'm leaving you two in charge here." She looked from Snyder to Mason. "You've done this before with me and Walt. You know the steps. Deputy Littles and I are going to follow up on a 9-1-1 the sheriff received." She quickly outlined the location on the map and filled in the sketchy details the sheriff had provided.

"You sure you can handle this with only the deputy?" Mason glanced toward the officer in question.

Jayne nodded. "I've worked with Lebron before. It won't be a problem. He and I should be able to secure this guy. If we can't get him out you can send that Chinook for us when Walt's team is taken care of." She grinned. Mason and Snyder were well aware that the route she would need to take was child's play for her and she had the proper emergency medical training to secure the victim.

"Wait a minute," Snyder said, his expression turning wary. "Rice said you were on light duty. As simple as this rescue sounds, it isn't light duty."

"I'm fine." She gave each of them a stern look. "There's no time for this. Take care of things here, Lebron and I will handle this one. If anything else comes up have the sheriff's office call for mutual aid. Two other mountain rescue units are already on alert status. You've got a few more good volunteers here but I want you or Snyder manning this base. No one else." On second thought, she added, "Keep this second rescue under wraps for now. I don't think the sheriff wanted the media to get wind of it just yet."

Snyder and Mason assured her they would handle things here. Jayne had known Thurman McGill since she'd arrived in Aspen. As a widower, he lived alone. She didn't want to consider whether he might have run upon foul play. It wasn't impossible that he would ask for her rather than Walt. She'd coordinated the use of his helicopters before.

"What's going on?"

She and Deputy Littles had started for the equipment room when Heath's voice reminded her that he was still there.

All that had happened that morning came rushing in on her at once. Jayne closed her eyes and blocked the emotional landslide. She didn't want to feel this, couldn't deal with it right now.

She opened her eyes and looked straight into his. "I have a job to do. Just stay out of my way."

Heath stepped close, intimidatingly so. "I told you that I'm not letting you out of my sight."

Deputy Littles laid a hand on Heath's shoulder. "Back off, sir," he ordered sternly.

Heath stared at the man's hand and then at the man. "That's not happening."

When the deputy's other hand moved toward his holstered weapon Jayne knew she had to do something. "It's okay, Lebron. Mr. Murphy might be of assistance to us." Her gaze leveled on Heath's. "We're headed up to do another rescue. If you're up to it, we could use you." A line of fury burned through her despite her best efforts to keep her mind away from personal issues. "But if you're not, stay out of the way because I'm not letting anyone die today because of you."

Heath didn't have to answer, she saw the hesitation in his eyes a split second before he banished it. "Wherever you go, I go."

"Fine, just don't get in the way."

Jayne had to admit, this was the most unlikely rescue team she'd ever led but there was no time for overanalyzing. She couldn't leave Mason and Snyder shorthanded. The remaining volunteers were needed here. Another call could come in. Walt's team might need additional backup though she doubted it with the Chinook en route.

This injured climber was her problem. She could drag him out alone if necessary. Deputy Littles was more for that other unknown element than for anything else. On that same note, she had to confess that having Heath come along wasn't such a bad idea. No one attempted a rescue alone. Not even a climber as confident and, at times, as cocky as her. It was the first rule of rescue.

Create no new victims.

CLAD FOR THE WORST winter weather and wearing emergency packs loaded with the necessary supplies, Jayne led the procession from the trailhead. Deputy Littles had driven his SUV, updating the sheriff as to their plan en route.

The weather worked its will as they set out, the wind howled and the snow drove hard into their faces. Goggles protected their eyes. Mere humans, who had any common sense, acceded to the weather's demands on days like this. But Jayne knew that plenty of folks would venture out just the same. They had paid for a holiday in winter's paradise, and they intended to have it. So, with little experience in the mountains those cocky few would venture into the twilight zone made accessible by bravado and Gore-Tex. If they were lucky they survived their stupidity. For others, mountain rescue volunteers such as herself would forge out into the deadly weather and drag them back to civilization.

Jayne had insisted on breaking trail, tromping through the fresh layer of snow, each step plunging all the way up to her knees, slowing her forward movement. But she'd be damned if she'd do this any differently just because the man she'd slept with last night wanted to play the big bad protector.

Heath stayed right behind her, forcing the deputy to bring up the rear. Littles didn't like it and Jayne didn't have time to care.

She kept thinking about Thurman McGill and wondering why he'd asked for her and why the hell he'd gone out on a day like today. Maybe he'd heard that Walt and the others were already out on a rescue and had hoped to help, but that didn't make sense either since he would have taken a different route for that purpose. And he, of all people, was well aware of his equipment's limitations. She'd know soon enough.

It took barely more than an hour to reach their destination. Heath stopped her when she would have continued up onto the ridge. "I'll take the lead from here," he said, his tone brooking no argument.

In spite of her determination not to, Jayne had spent the last hour working hard not to think about the things Heath had accused her father of. She'd come up with a dozen different scenarios and excuses that explained every little thing his accusations had caused her to remember. She'd found no solace. As much as she cared for her father, she would have some answers. If he had done these things…she shuddered and pushed the horrible possibility aside. Not now. She couldn't go there.

Another thing she'd done in the past hour was to talk herself out of love with Heath Murphy.

Love.

God, how could she let that word even wiggle its way into this crazy mixture?

She couldn't…wouldn't. Whatever they'd shared was over.

"I told you to stay out of my way," she snapped, unable to keep the hurt twisting inside her out of her voice. The wind had died down and the snow had diminished to nothing more than a flake or two swirling through the air from time to time. Snyder had radioed her with the word that the Chinook was in the process of hauling Walt's people to safety. All she wanted to do was get this rescue over with and go home.

She didn't want to think anymore.

Heath unzipped his parka with a jerk. His goggles dangled around his neck, as did hers and Littles's. "Just let me do this, Jayne. It's not a big deal."

He seemed damned steady for someone who'd almost freaked out on her during their last climb. "Not unless you panic," she retorted. Around this bend and over this little ridge would be a straight drop. Their rescue was most likely on that ledge. Maybe Heath hadn't figured that out yet, but she knew this terrain like the back of her hand.

"I've got it under control," he growled.

"Right," she quipped, smirking.

If he hadn't grabbed her by the arm she might have believed him. He'd spoken with fierce confidence. But she felt the tremble in his hands before his fingers tightened solidly around her.

Their gazes collided but he blinked away any fear before she could make it out.

"I'll lead," Littles butted in. "I'm the one with the badge and the weapon."

Jayne swore softly.

"What did he mean by that?" Heath demanded as the deputy moved past them.

She hadn't wanted to go into this with Heath. She knew he'd make something of it. "The sheriff had a bad feeling about this call." That's all she intended to say. She yanked her arm free of his grip. "Stop wasting my time."

Heath insisted on staying in front of her, but didn't slow her progress. "Tell me exactly what he said."

Jayne ignored him. If this man was injured—if it was Thurman McGill—she didn't want to waste any more time talking.

"Jayne, tell me—"

Heath froze.

It wasn't a particular sound or movement that stopped him in his tracks, rather it was the total lack of either.

Nothing.

The sound of the deputy's plunge through the fresh snow had been silenced. Nothing moved. If the deputy had encountered the victim, why didn't he say anything? Heath drew his weapon.

"Dammit!"

Jayne scrambled over the rock outcropping before Heath could grab her. She'd apparently sensed the same thing he had. He resisted the urge to call out to her. They rounded the slight dip and bend in the ridge at the same time.

Jayne abruptly stalled. "Dad?"

The word echoed in the air at the same time Heath's gaze landed on the man. He stood on the ledge as if he'd been dropped on that particular spot to wait for them. Deputy Littles lay at his feet.

Jayne would have rushed to aid her friend if Heath hadn't held her back.

Howard Stephens lifted one booted foot and pushed the deputy's too-still body over the edge. Jayne screamed, tried to tear away from Heath's hold.

"Don't move!" Heath commanded.

Stephens looked at him and laughed. "You must be kidding."

"Don't make me do this," Heath warned. Somewhere deep inside him he'd known all along that it would come to this. Danes had put him in this position. Had ordered the man's execution.

Stephens shook his head. "Do you really think I'm worried about you shooting me in front of my own daughter? No. I don't think so. I know what the two of you have been up to."

"Don't you do this, Heath," Jayne cried. "Don't." Devastation echoed in her voice, she shook violently.

Heath couldn't look at her, had to keep his full attention on Stephens. But he didn't have to look. He knew that her eyes would be wide with terror, bright with emotion. And this son of a bitch didn't care.

"Come to me, Jayne."

"No way." Heath tightened his grip on her arm. "She's not coming near you."

"It's over now, Murphy," Stephens said. "I already have the answer I wanted. It's Cole Danes. But don't worry, he won't get away with this. Sending you here did nothing but sign his own death warrant."

Heath kept his expression carefully schooled. "This is over, Stephens. Throw down your weapon."

Stephens snorted. "Oh, that's right. You're not going to give away anything, are you? It's all about the assignment, right? You don't want to screw this up like you have everything else in your life."

Heath clenched his jaw hard to fight the impact of the words…the truth. He fought fire with fire. "Why don't you tell your daughter how you screwed up her life? Maybe tell her about what you helped do to the Colby family or maybe show her your most recent kill list. I'm sure she'd find the names interesting reading."

Stephens took a bead right between Heath's eyes. "She'll never believe you over me. I'm still her father."

"You…you killed Deputy Littles," Jayne said, as if the realization had only just then penetrated.

"Come to me, Jayne," Stephens ordered. "I have a helicopter standing by. Let me take you away from this man. He only used you. He doesn't care about you."

Helicopter?

Jayne stared at her father. He stood on that ledge dressed much as she was, in full climbing gear. At first, she'd been confused. Lebron Littles was dead. Her father had pushed his body off the ledge. She squeezed her eyes shut, trying to blot out the image of him falling that bloomed in her mind's eye.

Her father had killed him. She hadn't heard the gunshot. Hadn't seen him do it, but it was true. Her mind just didn't want to accept it. Deputy Littles wouldn't have attempted to harm her father. There was no reason he would have represented a threat to her father...

Helicopter. Thurman McGill. Her father standing there with a gun. All the fragments coalesced in that instant.

"Did you hurt Mr. McGill? Did you use one of his helicopters to get up here and set this up?" Her eyes widened with her next thought. "It was you who called in the 9-1-1."

"Come to me now!" he commanded cruelly.

Jayne jerked at the sound. She hadn't heard her father shout like that since...memories flooded her. Long buried memories of a time when her father had done a lot of that. Shouting at her mother. Name calling. Cruel behavior. Her breath caught in a ragged gasp. How could she not have remembered?

"Drop your weapon, Stephens," Heath cautioned. "I don't want to have to shoot you, but I will."

"So shoot me," her father said, "and I'll shoot her. You think you can get a direct enough hit to stop me before I get one off? Trust me, Murphy, I won't miss."

Jayne went still. Heath felt the change.

"She's your daughter," Heath said, the words bitter on his tongue.

"I brought her into this world, I can take her out."

Jayne shuddered then abruptly wrenched away from Heath before he could stop her.

"Stay back, Jayne!"

She'd rushed straight up to her father before the warning stopped ringing in the air.

"Why are you doing this?" she asked as she peered up at the man she'd loved and made excuses for all these years. "I thought you loved me."

Heath readied his grip on his weapon at the sound of hurt in her voice. Killing this bastard was far too simple a fate for his heinous acts.

"I do love you," her father said, careful to keep his eye and his aim on Heath. "That's why I have to do this." He pulled Jayne close to his side, his full attention never leaving Heath. "You see, sweetheart, as long as you're alive they won't stop coming. Now that they know about us, they'll want to use you to get to me. I can't take that chance."

Heath snugged his finger around the trigger but couldn't risk the shot with her in her father's hold.

"Move away from him, Jayne," he urged, not completely successful at keeping the desperation out of his voice.

Jayne blinked, her brain still struggling with the harsh reality. The weapon in her father's hand twitched twice.

An almost inaudible hiss sliced the air after each twitch.

It took several seconds for Jayne to assimilate what her eyes saw. Heath fell to the ground. Her entire being went numb as her father released his hold on her long enough to kick Heath's weapon out of his reach.

She swayed but caught herself.

This couldn't be real.

She shook her head. Not real.

The hard clutch of her father's hands on her shoulders tore her from the dizziness of shock dragging at her consciousness.

"You understand why I have to do this, don't you, Jayne?"

Her gaze connected with his and for the first time in her life she did understand. He was her father. He loved her. But he was willing to sacrifice her or anyone else to save himself

"Yes," she whispered, unable to push the words past her lips with any more force than that. "I understand."

The wind whipped up a little, swirling snowflakes between them.

"Good." He released her. "Then I'll let you do the honors." He gestured to the precipice of the snow-covered ledge. "You're a good daughter, Jayne. I know you won't let me down."

He was right. Not once in her life had she ever let him down. She'd trusted him, believed in him despite all that he'd done to her mother...to her.

She thought of Heath lying there, unmoving on the ground. Was he dead? If not he would be soon. He'd come here to warn her...to protect her. She hadn't believed him, had been taught not to trust. She'd never been allowed to have anyone, not really...because of her father. She went very still inside as the haze of years of lying to herself cleared.

"There's just one thing," she said, looking deeply into her father's eyes.

"Be quick," he suggested, certain of his destiny. "My enemies are too close for comfort."

"You go first!" Jayne plowed into him with all her weight…with all the rage bursting inside her.

He went down, the lower part of his body dangling over the edge. She stumbled back, fear pounding in her chest. He clawed at the ledge, grabbed onto her leg. She hit the ground—tried to reach the weapon he'd dropped. He pulled her farther away…she couldn't reach it!

"You little bitch!" he screamed.

She felt herself sliding, moving over the ledge.

Jayne grappled for a handhold. Couldn't grab on.

Her hips followed her legs over the precipice.

She screamed. Tried to kick him loose.

He hung on.

The sound of a gunshot shattered the frigid air.

The weight dragging her downward fell free.

The sudden shift loosened her grip on the snowy ledge.

She cried out.

A hand clutched her forearm.

Halted her fall with a jerk.

Dangling in thin air, Jayne stared upward.

Heath's grip on her left arm was all that kept her from following her father's descent.

Her heart thundered in her throat, the ache of it swelling against her brain. If his grasp slipped… "God, don't let me fall."

Heath lay on his stomach flat against the ledge. He strained to grab on to Jayne with his left hand. If he could just get a hold of her with both hands he could pull her up.

"Please, Heath," she begged, "pull me up."

The panic hit him like a runaway train. Slammed into his gut. Paralyzed him. He'd been here before. His grip the only thing standing between the woman he loved and certain death.

The understanding in Jayne's eyes told him she knew what was happening. That he was helpless.

"You can do this, Heath. I know you can."

She swung her right hand up and snagged a handful of his parka sleeve.

Sweat beaded on his forehead. He couldn't move. If he moved a single muscle she would fall…he was certain, he'd done this before. He'd reached with his other hand and *she* had fallen.

A rush of weakness swept over him and he shuddered. Stephens had hit him in the side and in the thigh. He'd lost a lot of blood, wouldn't be able to hold out long. He couldn't save her.

"Reach for me, Heath," Jayne urged. "Reach with your left hand, too. Pull me up."

"You'll fall." Nausea churned in his gut.

"I trust you, Heath," Jayne whispered. "I know you can do this."

She hadn't listened…wouldn't reach up to him when he'd begged her to. That's why she'd fallen. God…that's why he hadn't been able to save her. Heath clenched his teeth hard, pushed past the fear and memories, reached toward Jayne with his left arm. His right arm trembled with the strain. He fastened onto her with both hands and pulled with all his might.

He howled with the pain and effort, his body trembling with the fatigue sucking at his ability to stay conscious. He didn't stop…didn't let go.

Suddenly she was up and over…falling onto the snow with him.

"Thank you." She gasped the words over and over.

He hugged her close, relief gushing through his veins. "If I'd lost you," he murmured against her cheek.

She drew back, touched his jaw. "You're not going to lose me."

"I'm sorry."

She shook her head. "You were right. I…" She let go a heavy breath, the ragged sound tearing at his heart. "I should have seen the truth before now."

Before he could respond, pain screamed through him on the heels of the receding adrenaline. "You're going… to—to be okay." He closed his eyes against the burn in his side. His leg had already gone numb.

She scrambled up and grabbed the radio clipped to her parka.

Heath closed his eyes and struggled to relax…to ignore the pain. In the background he heard her telling Snyder to send the Chinook but the sound kept fading and then coming back. He didn't want to pass out. She might need him. Stephens hadn't gotten here by himself. His buddies might show up.

"Heath." Jayne moved down next to him. He tried to open his eyes but couldn't manage. "Heath, help is on the way. I'm going to try and stop the bleeding. Stay with me, okay?"

He moved his lips but wasn't sure he actually spoke.

"Stay with me, Heath."

She sounded far away…in a tunnel or a cave.

"Heath…"

CHAPTER SIXTEEN

Heath gasped.

He opened his eyes. The room tilted, went blurry, then came back into focus.

White walls.

He moved his head slightly to the left—IV pole and bag.

Hospital.

Then Heath remembered. He had been shot. Stephens was dead.

"Jayne." His voice sounded rusty. His mouth and lips felt dry. He licked his lips and tried to sit up. A stab of pain sliced through him, forcing him back down. He groaned, his senses becoming suddenly aware of intense pain radiating through his entire body.

"You're out of surgery and stable, Murphy."

He opened his eyes to find Cole Danes standing over him.

"Where's Jayne?" He licked his lips again.

"She's just outside the door. I have a few questions and then you can see her."

"Stephens is dead. What else do you want?" If Heath hadn't been in such extreme pain he would have climbed out of the bed and beat the hell out of the guy.

"Correct. His body was identified one hour ago. The Chinook from Fort Carson that brought you and Miss Stephens off that mountain encountered a civilian helicopter en route to your position. I'm assuming the two men inside were Stephens's cohorts."

Heath bit back a groan. He'd be damned if he'd let Danes see his agony. "That's probably right. He mentioned something about them picking him up. We think he stole a helicopter from a local."

"Yes, a Thurman McGill. The sheriff found his body shortly after you arrived at the hospital."

"I want to see Jayne now," Heath insisted, uncertain how long he could handle this level of pain without passing out. He balled his hands into fists and struggled with the urge to just let go and pass out. Damn. Was it supposed to be like this?

"I need to know exactly what Stephens said to you," Danes instructed. "Don't leave anything out."

A realization somehow skirted its way through the fog of pain. Heath focused his weary gaze on Danes. "I was right. Something about this was personal between you and Stephens."

"Answer the question, Murphy." Danes's intent expression never wavered. He had his agenda and nothing was going to stop him. "I know you're in pain. Don't waste energy pretending otherwise."

A hiss of pain slipped past Heath's tightly clenched teeth. "He knew it was you," he growled. "He…" Heath clenched his teeth again as a new wave of pain crashed through him.

"Tell me the rest, Murphy," Danes urged.

"He…" Heath swallowed as best he could. "He said you'd signed your own death warrant. That you wouldn't get away with it."

"Thank you, Murphy. You did well."

Heath clutched the bed rail with his free hand and lifted his head, defying the pain. "You risked too much,

Danes," he accused. "Jayne could have been killed. How could you take that kind of chance?"

Danes paused at the door and looked back at him. "It was the only way."

He walked out without further explanation.

Heath collapsed, gasping to get air into his lungs.

When he got out of here he intended to tell Victoria just exactly what kind of man the Colby Agency had hired to conduct this internal affairs investigation.

If anyone could get this situation back under control, Victoria could.

"Heath?"

He knew an instant's relief at the sound of Jayne's voice. She rushed to his side and took his hand in hers.

"He wouldn't let me see you." Her eyes were red from crying.

For him, Heath thought, then he remembered she'd just lost her father.

"I'm sorry it had to happen this way, Jayne." She would hate him when the excitement had faded. When she'd had time to think. She would never want to see him again.

She squeezed his hand. "Let's not talk about that right now." She stared down at their hands a moment. "I'm still torn about my…about him." Her gaze settled back on Heath's. "I have to come to terms with that. It'll take time, I know." She smiled, but as sweet as it was, Heath saw the sadness just beneath the surface. "Right now all I'm worried about is you." She blinked uncertainly. "And us."

He rubbed his thumb over the back of her hand, ignoring the pain vying for his attention once more. "We're good," he assured her. There was so much more he could tell her that might help her get over her father faster. Like the fact that he'd killed at least one other man she'd cared about in the past, but what would be the point? She'd heard and seen more than enough. He wouldn't add anything else.

She shrugged, then swiped at her eyes. "I'm not sure I could ever leave this place."

He reached up, gritting his teeth against the pain knifing through his side, down his leg, and touched her cheek. "You don't have to worry about that. I don't think I'm cut out for investigative work anymore. Maybe Walt can use another guide."

The hope that sprang to life in her eyes almost undid him completely. "You're sure you're up for this kind of life? I know being here has been especially hard on you. I know about what happened on the Moses Tower."

That was a part of Heath's past that he would never forget, but the past few days had taught him that he couldn't go back. Couldn't change anything. He was only human, had made a terrible mistake. He had to try and move past it. The past belonged exactly there, in the past.

"I'll work it out." He cupped her soft cheek. "We both will. Time is all we need."

She bent down and brushed her lips against his, giving him another moment's reprieve from the agony. "I care very much for you, Heath." She swept the hair back from his forehead. "I think I might be in love with you." Her lips trembled.

He smiled, his heart brimming with emotion. Thank God he wasn't in this alone. "Remember, I said you weren't going anywhere without me?"

"I remember."

"That's a promise I intend to keep."

COLE DANES STOPPED at the nurses' station a few steps from Murphy's room. The head nurse glared at him as she rose from her chair like a warrior ready to do battle. Though they'd clashed once already, she still took the time to take in the length of his hair and the earring with a blatant look of distaste.

"I assume I can administer Mr. Murphy's pain meds now," she snapped, her expression furious, her voice scathing.

"You may."

She pivoted on her heel and hurried to do her duty. He respected vigilance even when it was at odds with his own.

Cole turned to the elevators directly across the corridor and depressed the call button. There was no point in explaining to the good nurse that he'd needed Murphy alert to answer his questions. Had he had his way he would have questioned him before surgery but Jayne Stephens had won that battle.

Only because Cole had allowed it, however. Even he wasn't without a respectable amount of compassion.

The cell phone in his jacket pocket vibrated. He moved slightly away from the area of the nurses' station as he took the call. "Danes."

"I want an update on Heath," Victoria Colby-Camp demanded with as much decorum as one could expect after all she'd heard this Sunday morning.

"His condition is stable," Cole told her without bothering with small talk since she hadn't. Small talk, polite conversation, that wasn't his style in any event. "The surgeon expects a full recovery."

"Thank God." The enormous relief she felt echoed across the line as clearly as her words.

A beat of weighty silence filled the air.

"What happens now, Mr. Danes?"

Her question was just shy of curt. Cole smiled. She didn't like him. Understandable.

"Now I return to Chicago to finish this."

"You're certain you've made no mistake."

The hesitancy in her tone was no surprise.

"Ask Lucas. He'll tell you. I never make mistakes." He moved back to the elevator as the doors glided open. "Trust me, *Victoria*, this investigation will be over soon and you will know why your most trusted employee betrayed you."

Cole dropped the cell back into his pocket and depressed the button for the lobby.

That was the thing about his line of work, he simply couldn't make it clear that there were no happy endings, only solved cases.

When he was finished there would be no more unanswered questions.

There would only be truth.

* * * * *

FULL EXPOSURE

This book is dedicated to a young man
who is tall, dark and handsome—the epitome
of a romance hero. The woman who captures him
one day will be a very lucky lady indeed.
This one is for you, Robby, nephew extraordinaire.

Love, Aunt Deb.

CHAPTER ONE

Winnetka, Illinois, Monday, 10:15 a.m.

"Give me one good reason why I shouldn't kill you right now."

The tip of the gun barrel bored into her skull. She shuddered at the harsh words. *Dear God, please help me! Don't let him kill me until I know she's safe.*

"I don't know what else you want from me." The words echoed hollowly from her throat. A defeated sob tore loose from her trembling lips before she could stop it. "I've done everything you asked."

"You're pathetic," the evil man hovering above her hissed. "The least you could have done was fight, but you just dropped to your knees like a spineless puppet." He laughed, the sound cruel, mocking. "Don't you know it's people like you who make the few and strong like us so powerful?" The cold steel drilled harder into her head.

She didn't have to look up to know he stared down at her, the truth in his words glaring like a humiliating spotlight. He would kill her, she didn't doubt her fate for a single moment. And he was right, she was worse than pathetic...less than nothing. She closed her eyes and pictured her sweet baby in her mind. Who would take care of her now? There was no one else.

And it was entirely her own fault.

"Maybe…" the hateful voice offered slowly as the pressure on her skull lessened ever so slightly. "There might be one last use for you."

For the first time since she'd fallen to her knees, pleading for mercy, she looked up at him. "Anything." She moistened her brutally dry lips. "I'll do anything. Just—" she swallowed hard "—just don't hurt her."

"You gave us a name." One side of the man's vile mouth lifted in the barest hint of a smile. "We want him."

Dread expanded in her chest once more. "I don't know what else I can do." She'd done everything they had asked already. He'd promised to leave her alone. But the man who'd made that promise didn't appear to be in charge anymore. Another, even more evil man apparently had control. She couldn't trust this one. Though she'd never met him before today, somehow she knew with complete certainty.

This man would kill her.

She didn't even care anymore. If only he wouldn't hurt—

"Bring him to us," he ordered, a new kind of chill in his tone. "We want him to pay for what he has done."

Confusion spiraled into her already fragmented thoughts. "I—I'm not sure—"

"We want to teach him a lesson first, then he'll pay," he explained, an eerie look of anticipation in those icy gray eyes. "Yes." He nodded succinctly as if having weighed the merit of his suggestion he found it worthy. "Perhaps if you did this for us, we could spare her."

A glint of faltering hope sent a new wave of emotion brimming against her lashes. "Please." She lifted her hands in supplication. "Please don't hurt her." She struggled to draw in an agonizing breath. "I want to help you. I swear I do, just don't—"

"You have forty-eight hours. I'll be in touch with specific instructions. Bring him to us or she dies."

Terror squeezed her heart. "Please." *God, please don't let him do this...* "How can I bring this man to you when I don't even know him? How am I supposed to find him?"

The man wielding the ultimate power of life and death over her world snickered. "Don't worry, Cole Danes will find you."

CHAPTER TWO

Inside the Colby Agency, Monday, 10:30 a.m.

Cole Danes watched Lucas Camp enter the office of Victoria Colby-Camp, head of the Colby Agency. Cole had anticipated this meeting. He'd known when he turned in his final report that his conclusions would not sit well with his employers on this assignment.

No one liked the truth when it hit too close to home.

He'd been summoned to Victoria's office this morning, however, she had insisted on waiting for Lucas's arrival before starting the meeting. Cole hadn't argued. His findings were conclusive. Whether she wanted to believe him or not was strictly her decision. Lucas, however, would surely look upon the situation with a bit more objectivity. He, after all, had been the one to hire Cole. Lucas Camp would not second-guess Cole's work.

Lucas, his trademark limp scarcely noticeable to anyone unaware of his past, moved to the wing chair adjacent to Cole's and nodded once to his lovely wife as he sat down. He propped his distinctive cane against the chair and leaned back, his full attention settling onto Cole.

"Mr. Danes," Victoria began, her voice stern yet with an underlying fragility that Cole found intensely curious, "I have reviewed your report very thoroughly and I must say that your documentation of evidence is rock solid."

Cole inclined his head in agreement with her assessment. "I'm certain you expected nothing less."

He studied her during the moment of uncomfortable stillness that followed. Strong, capable. Victoria was both of those things. He knew from the dossier he'd compiled upon Lucas's request that he consider this assignment, that she had suffered greatly in her life, had every reason to falter, and yet she had not.

Until now.

The uncertainty—the utter vulnerability—he saw now surprised him. Had his findings somehow served as the final blow that would crumble her already heavily burdened emotional fortress?

"Having recognized that undeniable fact," she continued, surprising him once more with the sudden burst of strength in her tone, "I will, without reservation, stand behind this member of my staff in unconditional rejection of your charges."

Impatience trickled through Cole. His record was irrefutable. He never failed to complete an investigation and his findings were always infallible.

Her denial, he admitted, was not completely unexpected. Though strong and capable, Victoria Colby-Camp operated with one weakness that Cole had long ago conquered, human compassion. A crippling emotion at best.

She cared deeply for her agency and those she employed there. Too deeply, it seemed, to see the truth now.

"I understand your hesitation, Mrs.—"

"No you don't." She leaned forward, braced her arms

on her polished mahogany desk. "I've spoken at length with Heath Murphy since his surgery barely thirty-six hours ago. Some of his accusations against you were corroborated by the medical staff at Aspen Valley Hospital. So don't pretend to understand how I feel, Mr. Danes. I'm of the opinion that *feeling* is something you're quite incapable of."

Well, she had him there. He had done what he deemed necessary to complete the mission. He refused to apologize for it.

"Let's not get off track," Lucas offered gently.

Cole turned his attention to the man who'd brought him into this situation. Lucas Camp, deputy director of Mission Recovery, a shadow operation that scarcely anyone was aware of, had hired Cole to perform an internal-affairs investigation to find a leak in the Colby Agency that appeared to go back at least two years.

Victoria and her agency had been plagued by a man named Errol Leberman for nearly two decades. He had kidnapped her son, tortured and brainwashed him, ultimately sending him to assassinate his own mother some eighteen years later. Leberman had spent many of those years, while waiting for the son she thought dead to become the killing machine he needed for his coup de grâce, playing head games with both Victoria and Lucas. There were times when his moves could only have been made with skilled help. And, more recently, with the use of inside information. Lucas had recognized that cold hard fact even when Victoria had not wanted to see it.

One week ago when Cole assumed control of the Colby Agency to begin his internal-affairs investigation he already knew the name of the primary man who had helped Leberman. Cole had needed only two things to complete his work, the identity of the agency employee who had leaked information and the elimination of Leberman's associate.

He had accomplished both. The first he had quickly ascertained through his interrogations and extensive background investigations. The second had taken a bit more time and the help of one of the Colby Agency's investigators. The newest investigator on staff, one who would have no ties to Leberman and the leak. Heath Murphy.

Heath had not failed him, though he had been royally P.O.ed at what he recognized as a setup early in the game. But that was his problem. Cole's single goal was to see that the elimination occurred.

Leberman's associate, Howard Stephens, was dead, and Victoria had her name. The Colby Agency's involvement in the matter was over. Cole had his own agenda from here. Nor would he apologize for using Stephens's own daughter, Jayne, to bring him down.

"Danes," Lucas addressed Cole now, "I brought you into this investigation because you're the best."

He was. Lucas and his team of Specialists were superior, as well. However, Cole had possessed one piece of information they hadn't. That was part of what made him the best in this particular situation. Lucas and his lovely wife had no need to know certain details.

"Thank you, Lucas." Cole looked directly at the man when he spoke, allowed him to visually inspect his eyes and expression. Cole knew he watched for any sign of deceit. "I have yet to fail."

"There's always a first time," Victoria accused.

Cole offered her a patient smile. She responded with a furious glare. "I appreciate that this is a delicate situation, but I can assure you that my assessment is correct."

Lucas held up a hand when she would have argued otherwise. "Let's just say that I agree," he ventured.

Cole knew it was a front to spare his wife from feeling further injury. Lucas knew he was right. He was no fool, nor was he blinded by overpowering emotion on the subject.

"If you have any doubts," Cole suggested with little attempt to keep the smugness out of his tone, "why don't you speak with the employee yourself? I'm familiar with your interrogation techniques, Lucas, a few questions is all it would take and my conclusion would be corroborated."

Lucas's expression turned hard. "You know the answer to that, Danes."

Oh, yes. He knew why the employee couldn't be questioned. This meeting wasted precious time. Perhaps he was the only one present who truly understood just how little of that valuable commodity remained within grasp.

Mildred Parker, Victoria's longtime secretary and personal assistant. A woman who had started at the Colby Agency with its inception. *She* was the leak. She'd gone missing in action two days ago, at basically the same time the final piece of evidence had confirmed his suspicions.

Victoria stood. Her chair banged against the credenza behind her desk. "I will not listen to another word of this." She glowered at Cole. "Mildred has dedicated her life to this agency. She would never do anything to harm me or anyone else here, much less my son."

She was right about one part. Mildred's involvement in leaked information only went back two years. Prior to that Leberman had used guesswork and an uncanny knowledge of his prey's method of operation to go about his nasty business. No one at the Colby Agency had helped Leberman take the Colby child. He'd merely waited for the right opportunity and utilized a skilled accomplice. Revenge was a strong motivator and as misplaced as his had been, Leberman had been out for the ultimate revenge.

Victoria stormed out of the office. The door slammed, punctuating her determined exit with a firm thwack.

Lucas expelled a heavy breath. "There's more you're not telling me, Danes."

Cole redirected his attention to Lucas. He hadn't expected anything less of the man. Lucas Camp had spent a lifetime reading between the lines. "There is."

"Why haven't you shared this additional information?" Lucas kept his temper carefully contained though Cole knew for a certainty that he felt supremely annoyed by this admission.

"Your wife has no need to know this part," Cole said bluntly. "It would only add to her discomfort." He propped his elbows on the chair's arms and steepled his fingers thoughtfully. "Contrary to popular thinking I do suffer a measure of compassion."

Lucas chuckled but the sound held little humor and his expression exhibited even less. "Perhaps we'll debate that issue another time." The older man's gaze pushed hard against Cole's. "I know you, Danes. You're forty years old. You've spent the past dozen years of your life making other people's lives miserable. You're the best interrogator in the business. Since moving into internal affairs at NSA ten years ago you've proven your ability time and time again. Nothing gets past you. Tell me what it is you're leaving out."

Cole rarely worked directly for the National Security

Agency these days. His skills were too highly sought after to remain attached to one agency.

"Fair enough," Cole permitted. But Lucas would only know what he wanted him to know. As good as this longtime superspy was, he wasn't quite as good at deception as Cole.

"If my calculations are correct," he said, choosing his words carefully, "only two men remain of the original group Leberman started some twenty years ago."

Leberman had also been in the military at one time. Trained by a Special Forces type unit, Leberman had left the military on bad terms and then he'd proceeded to start his own little mercenary miniarmy. He and Stephens had organized a team of six men, all tops in their field. Together this group, of what Cole considered terrorists, had made a fortune in blood. Kidnappings, assassinations, just to name a couple of their offered services.

Now only two of that original six remained. A muscle in Cole's jaw ticked despite his efforts to maintain an impassive exterior.

"Go on," Lucas prompted, his expression clearly suspect.

"Those last two want revenge for the elimination of their leader."

"Howard Stephens," Lucas filled in.

Cole nodded. "He basically took over years ago, even before Leberman's death. Leberman was too caught up in revenge against the Colbys to keep up the pace required of a true leader. Though the team still respected him and used him from time to time, he was more a planner than a practitioner."

Lucas shrugged. "No surprise there. I knew Leberman was the brains behind whatever exploits he and his minions executed." He looked directly at Cole once more. "So those last two want you."

"Precisely."

"And you," Lucas added, "believe they're holding Mildred and her niece, Angel, hostage to that end?"

"I do."

That wasn't entirely accurate, but it was close enough. Angel Parker, Mildred's beloved niece, had been the one to actually leak the information. Cole didn't know yet what they'd used against her to get the information. A thorough investigation of her finances had not indicated that she'd done it for money. As a single mother of a three-year-old and a full-time nurse at Winnetka General Hospital, the young woman scarcely eked out a living. Without her aunt's generosity, unmarried and pregnant, Angel likely would have crashed and burned long ago.

Since Mildred had never married or had children of her own and Angel's mother had died years ago, Angel had been like a daughter to Mildred. Angel's child, Mildred's pseudograndchild, wanted for nothing.

"For now," Lucas allowed, "we'll operate under that assumption. Since we haven't been able to contact or locate either Mildred or Angel, my hands are tied to do otherwise. What plan of action do you plan to take?" Lucas cocked an eyebrow. "I, of course, am assuming that you consider this next step part of completing your task here."

Lucas read him rather well even if he slightly missed the mark. Cole couldn't prevent another tiny smile. "Of course."

"Details, Danes," Lucas pressed, his expression as ferocious as a lion protecting his den.

"I will offer myself in trade since it was my investigation that landed Ms. Parker and her niece in harm's way." Cole flared his hands humbly. "I should have anticipated this move but I didn't. As Mrs. Colby-Camp said, perhaps there is a first time for failure even for me."

Lucas didn't look convinced. "I'll call in two of my Specialists to provide backup."

"No," Cole said sharply, allowing his composure to slip for one fraction of a second before locking down the momentary weakness. "This is something I must do alone. Any outside involvement could trigger an undesirable result."

The level of suspicion in Lucas's gaze increased by several degrees. "Do you have substantiated intelligence to confirm that assessment?"

"All I have is gut instinct." Cole angled his head and surveyed the man analyzing him so closely. "Isn't that the reason you hired me? For my instincts?"

Lucas backed off marginally. "I will expect to be kept up to speed on every step you take. I understood and tolerated your need for secrecy as you conducted this investigation into the employees of this agency. But I will not permit you to proceed under those terms now."

Cole stood. "I'll keep you abreast of the situation."

Lucas pushed to his feet with less effort than one would think considering he wore a prosthesis for a right leg. "See that you do."

Cole nodded once before moving toward the door. Lucas Camp would soon learn that Cole Danes shared only what he needed to share. Not even a man as powerful and experienced as Lucas could intimidate him. No one could.

"Just one thing, Danes," Lucas called to his back.

Cole paused at the door and turned to face him.

Again, he indulged himself and allowed a smile to steal past his careful control. "Don't waste your time, Lucas. I know what I have to do. Nothing you say is going to change my methods."

Lucas smiled then, broadly, openly. "I'm well aware of that, Danes. Well aware." His smile vanished as abruptly as it had appeared. "But know this, if anything you do or say causes harm to come to Mildred Parker or her niece, you will answer to me."

For three beats the two men stood there staring at each other, decades of untold secrets and power over life and death pulsing between them.

"Make no mistake," Lucas went on, "I am fully aware that you're keeping something more from me. We all have our secrets." The depth of knowing in that statement glinted in his eyes. "But if yours hurts someone I care about there won't be anyplace on this planet you can hide."

Cole didn't hesitate. "Understood."

With that said he walked out of the office.

He ignored the angry glances from the agency staff members he encountered in the corridor. They had all seen more than enough of him, would likely never forget his name or face.

Few ever did.

But it was all part of the job he was paid to do.

If it were an easy task anyone could do it. Clearly that was not the case.

In the elegant lobby Victoria Colby-Camp stood near the receptionist's desk. Despite the devastations of her past she had surrounded herself with the best, both in material possessions and in staff and associates. But she, as well as her loyal staff, were mere humans. The finery glittering about them man-made. Just like eighteen years ago, Victoria Colby-Camp could not stop this bad thing from coming home to her. Errol Leberman had started it, but Cole Danes would finish it. For that reason she would never forget or forgive him.

Their gazes collided as if he'd somehow telegraphed that last thought.

She said nothing.

Cole depressed the call button and waited for the car to arrive on the fourth floor. Her silence made no difference to him one way or another.

Words weren't necessary in any event.

He already understood how she felt. She despised him for shedding light on a dark corner of her existence she'd rather not have seen.

She, too, would never forget his name or his face.

Few ever did.

CHAPTER THREE

Winnetka, Illinois, 1:00 p.m.

Nearly three hours and nothing.

Only forty-five hours left.

Fear crammed into her throat, twisted in her stomach.

Angel Parker hadn't left her living room, afraid she might somehow miss her next instructions. What was she supposed to do now?

She moistened her lips and wrung her shaky hands together. How could she save her aunt if no one told her what to do next?

How long was she expected to wait?

Where would she find Cole Danes?

Think, she commanded. She had to think past the fear and confusion. What had the man said?

Don't worry...Cole Danes will find you.

But he hadn't found her.

Angel pushed up from her sofa and started to pace. Her legs felt weak and rubbery after sitting so long. Or maybe it was the lingering effects of the fear. Fear did that—made you weak. She knew that better than most and still she couldn't slow the terror throbbing through her veins. As a nurse she'd watched otherwise calm and knowledgeable patients suffer near panic attacks when faced with the unknown—some unexpected surgery or medical procedure.

No one wanted to face their mortality. Not even the strongest and most intelligent of the human race.

But it wasn't her own death Angel feared.

Her knees buckled and she grabbed for the nearest wall to catch herself. A wave of emotion washed over her, ushering a sob from her dry throat.

She'd done this.

Her aunt could die and it would be her fault.

Angel sagged against the wall and slid down to the floor, the hurt overwhelming her ability to stay vertical.

She'd done everything they'd asked.

For two years she'd lived in fear. She'd changed her work schedule as well as her route to and from work so often she felt certain her superiors considered her a mental case. She'd moved Mia to a different childcare provider every few months, as well.

And still she'd failed.

For a while she'd even foolishly thought herself free of the evil. She laughed bitterly. They hadn't bothered her in four months.

Not since Victoria Colby had gotten her son back.

It was then that Angel had known the magnitude of her sins.

The man who had come to her two years ago, the one who'd held her baby hostage for twenty-four hours just to prove he could, had worked for another even more sinister man named Leberman. Four months ago Mildred had cried and told Angel how thankful she was that Victoria finally had her son back. She'd told Angel about Leberman's death and all he'd done to the Colbys as well as Lucas Camp. As Mildred related the events of the past two years, each one had tied in with the simple, seemingly innocuous, information Angel had secretly passed along.

Each time that telephone had rung, the caller asking only one question, always something so trivial, the call had preceded some evil Leberman had orchestrated.

She'd wanted so desperately to tell her aunt then and there that she'd done this horrible thing. That she had helped make these terrible, terrible things happen to the Colbys. But she couldn't. They had taken her daughter once and had promised that next time Angel would never see her again. All she had to do was give them the information they asked for from time to time and her baby would remain safe. If she ever let them down or told that she'd been contacted, her child would die. She would never forget the look in the man's eyes—a man whose name she didn't even know

Tell anyone about this and the little girl dies. Nothing you or anyone could do will save her. Believe that if you believe nothing else.

To demonstrate his point he'd taken her to Lincoln Park in broad daylight. Right before her eyes he'd killed a homeless man sitting on a park bench and then he'd simply walked away...with the parting advice that she should run like hell and that she was to remember his warning.

She had remembered.

And she'd believed. He'd killed a man for no reason without caring who saw him.

He would have taken her baby and killed her just as easily had Angel not cooperated. This kind of man feared no one...not the authorities, certainly not the Colby Agency.

Angel curled her arms around her knees and tried to stop the quaking that rocked her body.

She would carry the guilt of what she'd done to Victoria Colby to her grave. For these past few months she had told herself that she had to put it behind her, that things had worked out despite her part in Leberman's sinister plans. She'd made a mistake. She had to get past it. She'd thought it was all over. Nothing she could do would change what was done any more than she could resurrect that poor homeless man who'd died to prove some madman's point.

Then one week ago she'd gotten a visit rather than a call. He'd wanted one thing—another seemingly simple bit of inconsequential information. Just a name. The name of whoever was conducting an internal-affairs investigation at the Colby Agency.

Angel had agreed to get the information and he'd left. She'd known what she had to do. In those few months of reprieve she'd learned a few things…had wondered at what perhaps she could have done to make all this turn out differently. Armed with that knowledge, she had made a decision. She would not let this bastard use her again. She would tell her aunt everything. But first she had to hide her child.

It had taken her four days to make contact with the right people. An underground community of sorts for abused women and children. These people would protect her child until the danger had passed. They had begged her to go into hiding, as well, but she refused. She had to do the right thing this time, had to make this right as best she could.

Once Mia was safely tucked away by people who had the resources to move her from household to household if need be, she had called her aunt. Night before last Angel had gone to her aunt and told her everything.

They had cried together and then they'd decided upon the best way to handle the situation. Angel let her aunt make the final decision. They would see Lucas Camp together. He could take care of the man threatening Angel, her aunt insisted.

But that man had shown up just then. He and one of his henchmen. They'd taken Mildred and her to an empty warehouse. They wanted only one thing, the name. Angel hadn't known…but Mildred had. When the man threatened to kill Angel, Mildred had surrendered and given the name.

Cole Danes.

They'd let Angel go with the warning that if the information proved wrong or if she went to the authorities Mildred would die.

Angel hadn't seen her aunt since.

This morning she had learned why. She had just over forty hours before the woman who'd been more like a second mother than an aunt would be killed if Angel didn't come through.

…*you're pathetic.*

The bastard who'd visited her today was right. She was pathetic. Her aunt's life was on the line and she sat there sobbing like a child.

Angel's fingers balled into fists.

She had to be stronger than this.

Her aunt's life depended upon her.

She thought about her options and in a moment of utter clarity, Angel knew just what she had to do.

Suburban Sportsman, Melrose Park, 2:30 p.m.

ANGEL TIGHTENED HER FINGERS around her purse strap and mustered the courage to approach the clerk behind the counter. She'd surveyed the entire upscale sporting-goods store and selected the youngest male clerk on duty.

"Good afternoon." He smiled widely, his gaze instantly doing a head-to-toe sweep as she approached. "May I help you?"

She prayed the nonbusiness interest she saw in his eyes would help her. Angel produced what she hoped would prove a flirtatious smile. "I hope so." She glanced around quickly to make sure no other customers were nearby. "I need to purchase a handgun."

He looked surprised but swiftly recovered. "O...kay. Follow me."

Angel guessed this guy to be no more than twenty-one or two. Cute. Innocent—something she would never again be.

The clerk paused at a display case. "What size weapon were you thinking about?" he asked, his smile not quite so wide now.

Angel scanned the array of offerings behind the glass. Confusion frayed her already frazzled nerves. She didn't know where to begin. Had never so much as touched a gun.

"Something small?" he suggested in a helpful tone.

She nodded. "Yes."

"Very good."

He started behind the counter but she stopped him with a hand on his arm. "What do I have to do to purchase one?"

She'd startled him again. Angel released his arm and tried to look calm and apologetic regarding her behavior. It wasn't working. She could see the uneasiness in his eyes now. "I'm just a little nervous," she offered.

"Ma'am," he said quietly, his gaze darting around to see if anyone had wandered near, "there's a three-day waiting period. Even if you buy one, you can't take it with you today."

The words sent terror slamming against her rib cage. "But I have to have one today." She poured every ounce of desperation she felt into her expression. Prayed he would see…that he would somehow help her. "Please, if you can help me…"

He looked away a moment, spoke under his breath as if he feared being overheard. "Go to Lake Street on the West Side. Try Tito's Pawnshop."

"I can get one today there?" Hope swelled, pushing away some of the paralyzing fear.

He cast a look side to side again. "Maybe." His gaze settled back on her desperate one. "Probably."

"Thank you." Her voice wavered and tears brimmed. She battled the emotions back down. "Thank you."

He touched her arm when she would have walked away "Listen, lady." His hesitation sent a new trickle of dread snaking through her veins. "I don't know what kind of trouble you're in, but don't go to Lake Street after dark. Go right now. Get your business done and get out of there. Okay?"

She nodded stiffly and turned away.

"Good luck."

She didn't look back. She had to do this. It was the only way.

Lake Street, Chicago's West Side, 2:30 p.m.

FORTY-THREE HOURS.

She had to hurry.

Angel parked at the curb between two SUVs.

No wonder the clerk had warned her about coming here. Though she'd lived in the Chicago area her whole life she couldn't recall ever having been to this particular street.

Young guys huddled in groups called out their wares to slowly passing motorists. *Rocks, blows, weed!*

Drugs. They were selling drugs right on the street in the middle of the afternoon.

Of course she had known things like this happened in all urban areas, but knowing it and seeing it were two different things. Her protected, suburban life hadn't adequately prepared her for this reality. She'd watched scenes on the news channel, but there'd always been police involved handling the situation. There was no sign of policemen here.

Teens, high-school or college types, cruising slowly down the street in their expensive, late-model sedans and SUVs appeared to be the customers the hawkers called to. Other throngs of what looked like older men huddled on the sidewalk tossing dice. Angel saw a couple of women sitting on their stoops, their preschoolers at their feet, watching the rawest form of capitalism play out.

Angel shook off the troubling thoughts and focused on her mission. She had to purchase a weapon. She refused to be vulnerable, refused to let these evil bastards rule her life a moment longer. She should have done this long ago. Giving herself grace, she hadn't known then how to protect her daughter. Now she did.

Tito's Pawnshop wasn't very large. A glass door and display window, both clad with iron bars, fronted the store. A beggar sat on the sidewalk beneath the window, a used foam cup in his extended hand.

Angel braced herself and entered the shop. Four men loitered inside, two sitting, two leaning on the counter. All four illustrated the term unsavory to its fullest meaning. She moistened her fiercely dry lips and held on tightly to her purse strap as she forged her way toward the counter at the back of the shop. Display case after display case flanked both sides of the narrow aisle. Shelves stocked with pawned merchandise lined the walls behind the display cases. The place smelled like old shoes and sweaty flesh... or maybe it was the men now eyeing her so closely.

The two men leaning on the counter stepped aside as she approached. Each sized her up and snickered but she didn't make eye contact, kept her attention focused on the man behind the counter.

"You lost, lady?" the shopkeeper asked.

"I need to buy a weapon."

The room burst into laughter.

Angel swallowed hard and fought to keep a grip on her thin composure. "I have money." She pulled the wad of twenties out of her purse. She had withdrawn one thousand dollars from her savings account. Surely that would be enough.

Silence abruptly replaced the laughter.

The guy behind the counter looked a little nervous now. "Put your money away, lady." He held up a hand as if trying to avert disaster.

Angel sucked in a shuddering breath and did as he told her. "I...I just need to buy a gun."

Any sign of uneasiness the man had shown morphed instantly into fury. "I don't know what you're doing in this neighborhood, honey, but take my advice and go home." He leaned intimidatingly nearer. "You don't belong here and you damn sure don't want to be caught on this street after dark." He looked at her purse then back at her face. "Now get out of here. Go buy your firearms on the North Side like the rest of your friends."

Every instinct screamed at her to run like hell, but desperation kept her rooted to the spot.

"Come on, baby," one of the guys on her side of the counter said, moving in close. "Let me walk you to your car."

Angel recoiled. "Stay away from me," she ordered, but the quiver in her voice left the threat hollow.

Another round of laughter broke out.

Anger sizzled inside her, burning away the last of her fear. She glared at the man behind the counter. "I said I needed to buy a gun. I was told you could help me. Now, are you here to do business or what?"

He bracketed his waist with his hands. "Just what the hell are you gonna do with a gun?"

Angel flinched. "I...I need protection."

"Honey, you should of thought of that before you came in here," the guy on her left said as he surveyed her backside.

She pushed as close to the counter as possible and let the shopkeeper see the desperation in her eyes. "Please. I need a gun."

Something in his eyes changed, she couldn't say what, maybe the single shred of decency he possessed made an unexpected appearance. He held up a hand for the others to quiet. Angel's heart beat so hard she felt certain everyone in the shop could hear it.

He jerked his head toward the end of the counter. "This way."

Her pulse tripping, Angel followed the man into a dark room behind the counter. The voice of reason screamed again, warning her to run, but she ignored it.

He flipped a switch and the blink of fluorescent lighting filled the graveyard-quiet, warehouse-grim space.

Boxes in a variety of sizes and stages of deterioration lined the walls. A grimy, cluttered desk held center stage.

The man propped on the edge of the desk and looked at her long and hard before he spoke. "What kind of trouble you in, lady?"

"I can't tell you that," she answered sharply. "Just sell me a gun."

He smirked. "All right. What you looking for?"

She hadn't actually considered what kind of gun. She shrugged. "Something small." Her hand moved down to her shoulder bag. "Something I can carry in my purse."

He shook his head slowly from side to side. "Have you ever even fired a weapon?"

"That's none of your business," she snapped. "Stop wasting my time." The vulnerability in that last statement made her cringe.

He threw his hands up. "Whatever." He retrieved a box and set it on the desk. Inside packing materials surrounded the contents. He dug out a smaller box and opened it.

"This—" he exhibited a small black gun "—is a Smith & Wesson 9mm. It's small, less than seven inches in length, and only weighs about a pound and a half. Very light." He depressed something on the weapon and a cartridge slipped out of the handle. "Eight plus one rounds." He pulled back a mechanism on the top. "That action puts one in the chamber." He flipped a small lever. "That's the safety. Turn it off and you're ready to fire." He offered the weapon to her.

It felt heavy in her hands but not as heavy as she'd expected. The cold of the black metal penetrated her skin.

"Hold it like this." He showed her how to grip the weapon. "Feet wide apart for balance. Look down the barrel here."

She did as he instructed.

"Then squeeze the trigger and that's it."

She looked at him and hoped it would be that simple.

He sighed and scrubbed a hand over his face. "Look, if you've never fired a weapon before take some advice."

Angel nodded expectantly.

"Wait till he's close. The closer your target the less likely you'll miss. Aim for the chest."

She licked her lips and tried to swallow back the bile in her throat. "If I hit him in the chest, that's enough right?"

He lifted one shoulder in an indifferent shrug. "Maybe, depends on if you hit anything important."

Okay, she knew that. She was a nurse for God's sake. "So, technically I could hit him in the chest and miss anything vital and he could still hurt me."

"Technically," he said in a mocking tone, "that's right. So shoot him more than once. Twice at least. If he keeps moving, shoot him until he stops."

The images his words evoked made her tremble. How could she possibly do this? Her aunt's face loomed large in her mind. Because she had no other choice. She nodded. "Got it. Shoot until he stops moving."

He put the weapon back on safety and retrieved two more cartridges from the box and offered them to her. "When you empty a clip, shove in another one and keep firing if you need to."

"Okay." She chewed her lower lip a second, giving

a wave of nausea time to pass, then asked, "How much do I owe you?"

He cocked his head and looked at her with the kind of belligerence she would expect from a man like him. "How much you got?"

"One thousand." Her palms started to sweat as reason tried once more to intrude.

His gaze drifted down her body. She shuddered. Even with a conservative sweater, jeans and a suede coat she felt naked somehow. When his attention settled back on her face she didn't miss the sexual hunger there. She held her ground, didn't run—*had* to do this. Whatever it took.

"Eight hundred," he said flatly, sexual interest clearing from his eyes with one downward swoop of his dark lashes.

She counted out the twenties onto the desk and shoved the goods she'd purchased into her purse. "Thank you."

He moved in close…so close she could smell the spicy scent of the Mexican food he'd had for lunch. "Just remember," he said, his tone menacing, "if you kill someone with that weapon you didn't get it from me. Got that?"

She nodded jerkily. "You don't have to worry, sir," she assured him, a kind of defeat she'd rather not have exposed in her voice. "If I have to use this, I probably won't live to tell anyone anything."

Confusion cluttered his features and then he laughed. He swore softly. "I can't believe I'm saying this…" He looked directly into her eyes. "Lady, why don't you go to the cops for help?"

"Because they can't help me." It seemed incredible. The system she'd believed in her entire life couldn't help her. For that one instant she suddenly knew how people on this side of the tracks felt—totally alone…desperate to survive. She swallowed back a rush of emotion. "No one can help me."

And then she did the only thing she could.

She drove back to her small cottage in the safe, cozy suburb of Winnetka where nothing bad was ever supposed to happen and waited.

There was nothing else she could do until she received further instructions.

Or until Cole Danes showed up.

The man holding her aunt hostage had assured her that Cole Danes would find her, but every minute that passed made her more uncertain of that possibility.

Except there was no alternative.

She had no option but to wait.

A framed photograph of her and her daughter together tugged at her heart. She reached for it, held it close to her chest. At least her baby was safe. She had done that right if nothing else.

High-pitched, melodious notes abruptly shattered the silence, sending her pulse into another erratic rhythm.

It took a few moments for her to catch her breath and to allow her heart to slide back down into her chest and start beating normally again.

Her cell phone!

She laid the picture and her gun down then snatched up her purse. The zipper hung and she tugged frantically as another ring chimed. Where the hell was it? Finally her fingers wrapped around the cool metal.

"Hello." The two syllables were more a rush of shaky breath than a word.

"When Danes arrives you follow his lead."

It was him. The man holding her aunt.

"What?" She clutched the phone harder. "He's coming now? How do you know? How is my aunt? Let me speak to her."

"No questions. Just follow my instructions. When he arrives, do exactly as he says. We've set a trap for him."

She nodded then realized he couldn't see her. "All right."

"Don't make any mistakes, Angel," he warned. "Time is running out. Don't think we'll stop with your aunt. You may believe you've hidden your daughter from us, but, trust me, we can find her if we need to."

The connection went dead.

Angel's hand fell to her lap, her fingers automatically depressing the end button and then the two others necessary to lock the keypad. Her gaze drifted down to the photograph on the sofa cushion next to her.

For the first time since this nightmare began she realized the full ramifications of her situation. It didn't matter what she did at this point, she was dead. She and her aunt. Tears welled in her eyes. They were both dead.

The only thing she could hope for was that if they got Danes they wouldn't bother her child. If they had what they wanted and she was dead—of no further use to them—why would they need to harm her child? They wouldn't. Her three-year-old was far too young to remember what the men who'd held her looked like. She was no threat to anyone.

Her baby would be safe then. The people harboring Mia would see to it that she was well cared for if Angel never returned. Her baby would be safe.

She had to do this right.

No mistakes.

She thought of Cole Danes. A man she'd never met. Who might even have a family of his own. But she couldn't think about that.

There was no room for sentiment or sympathy.

She had to turn off her feelings...deny the single most significant emotion that had led her into the field of nursing.

There could be no compassion in this equation.

She would feel nothing—except determination to do the unthinkable...to lead Cole Danes to his execution.

CHAPTER FOUR

The residence of Angel Parker,
Winnetka, 6:28 p.m.

Cole watched the house for some time from his rental car and the cover of the dark winter evening. Halfway up the block a street lamp struggled to illuminate the night but failed miserably. No one stirred. The evening rush hour had passed. Dinner and television would be on the agenda for most of the residents of this quiet neighborhood.

Inside the small home he monitored there were no lights, no sound. But her car sat in the driveway. He checked his thermal scanner once more. There was definitely a warm body inside.

He deposited the scanner back into his pocket and withdrew his cell phone. When he'd entered the necessary numbers, he waited as the telephone inside Angel Parker's house rang three times.

"Hello."

A moment passed before he depressed the end call button.

From that single word of greeting he'd concluded three significant factors. Angel was inside. She felt defeated. But she wasn't afraid.

The latter intrigued him.

She should be afraid.

He unsheathed his weapon and exited the vehicle, the interior lamps set to the off position to ensure no interruption in his cloak of darkness. He wore black, always did, as much for intimidation as for camouflage. In any interrogation setting the tone proved every bit as crucial as the interrogator's skill.

No textbook or classroom exercise offered by the traditional means had taught him those essential elements. He had learned the unvarnished truth about interrogation the hard way, as a prisoner and hostage. His work had allowed him to hone his methods. Wisdom earned from a decade of experience in the field had boiled all he'd gleaned down to one basic fact, fear proved a far more advantageous weapon than pain.

He needed Angel Parker to feel fear.

Before this night ended she would know its true meaning. That fear would ultimately save her.

Cole paused outside the front entrance to the quiet house. He considered the owner for a moment, then the layout of the property. Small, well-groomed front yard with a postage-stamp-size lawn. Neat sidewalk lined with clay pots he imagined would be filled to brimming with flowers in the spring and summer. A tiny stoop, a welcoming wreath on the front door. The backyard looked much the same with a bit more grass and a child's swing set.

He estimated that his target sat approximately five yards from the front door. He listened intently for ten seconds. Still no sound. That she hadn't moved since his arrival forty-five minutes ago warned that she waited for something or someone.

His steps silent, he moved around to the back of the house. He curled his fingers around the knob of the rear entry and discovered the door unlocked. A red flag went up. The defeat he'd heard in her voice nudged at him. She thought she'd lost this battle already. Her child had been unaccounted for during the past three days. That would certainly defeat any caring parent.

The door opened noiselessly. Cole entered in the same way, every step carefully calculated for optimum stealth. He moved slowly through a tiny kitchen and into a short hall, giving his eyes time to adjust to the lack of moon and starlight he'd used outside. A subtle fragrance lingered in the air, apples and cinnamon. Some sort of potpourri, he surmised. The interior temperature felt too cool as if she hadn't bothered to turn on the heat on this cold winter day.

He waited at the doorway leading into the living room until he'd determined her exact location and gauged her posture using the sparse moonlight that filtered in through the window.

Cole leveled his weapon and moved toward her. She sat on a sofa, very dark in color, navy or forest-green perhaps. She wore dark slacks but the light color of her sweater or blouse kept her from totally disappearing into the opaque furniture. And there was her hair. Very blond, white almost. It fit with her name. She had the pale complexion and translucent blue eyes often associated with heavenly creatures. But this woman was not only very much from this earth, she definitely was not innocent. He paused in front of the coffee table, less than six feet from her position.

"Turn on the light."

She gasped at the sound of his voice.

As long as she'd been sitting there in the dark her reaction surprised him somewhat. Her eyes had surely adjusted to the near darkness. She should have noticed his presence when he'd entered the room, should have felt the shift in the atmosphere around her. But she hadn't. Clearly she'd been preoccupied with her thoughts.

"Please just tell me that my aunt's okay," she pleaded, assuming he was one of the men involved with Howard Stephens, Errol Leberman's murdering partner.

"Slowly reach for the lamp on the table next to you," he instructed firmly, ignoring her plea.

She obeyed, using her left hand. She was right-handed. His grip tightened on his weapon.

A *click* sounded and light spilled from the lamp.

The gun in her hand registered in that same instant, visually confirming his suspicion.

"Who the hell are you?" she demanded.

Maybe she hadn't lost all hope. She stared up at him with pure hatred, both hands now firmly locked around the 9mm. She'd purchased herself some protection recently. Illegally no doubt. There was no weapon registered in either her name or her aunt's.

"Lower your weapon," he countered, "and we'll talk."

She made a scoffing sound. "You lower yours," she tossed right back. "I'm not stupid."

No. She wasn't stupid. Just not wise in the ways of kill or be killed. He could have squeezed off a round and ended her life several times since the conversation began, while she still contemplated what would happen next.

"If I wanted you dead, Miss Parker, you would already be dead." He nodded to the table that stood between them. "Put it there. Use your left hand."

She blinked, long lashes momentarily hiding the fear in those pale eyes. "No."

"Then you leave me no choice."

Before she could comprehend his intent he had snaked

out his left hand, snagged the weapon and twisted it out of her grasp. She rocketed to her feet but froze when the barrel of his weapon leveled back on her chest.

"Sit."

"What else do you want from me?" she demanded. She started to shake. Panic…adrenaline. She was on the edge, but not quite where he needed her.

"I think you have me confused with some of your longtime associates."

Her expression turned bewildered but only for a moment, realization dawned. "You're…," She moistened her lips as if buying time to marshal the additional effort required to utter his name. "You're Cole Danes."

"Sit down, Miss Parker."

She eased down onto the navy slipcovered sofa. From what he knew of her finances the old sofa had likely been covered out of necessity rather than design.

"Three days ago your daughter disappeared, then twenty-four hours later your aunt vanished. I know you were involved with Howard Stephens as far back as two years ago. I also know that the disappearances of the people you care about are connected to him and certain information involving the Colby Agency." The first glitter of true terror appeared in her eyes. "I already know the worst of what you've done, Miss Parker, so start talking and don't leave anything out."

Angel had no idea what Cole Danes looked like. But, whoever this man was, he had her gun. Fear knotted in her stomach. Why hadn't she just shot him?

Because she couldn't.

The men holding her aunt hostage wanted Cole Danes. If she killed him…God she didn't even want to think about what they would do to her aunt. What was she thinking? She couldn't kill anyone.

She clasped her hands in her lap in an effort to disguise their trembling and took a deep breath. The man on the phone had told her to follow Danes's lead.

Her gaze moved back up to the man standing over her. "If you know so much why do I have to tell you anything?" She didn't have to make this easy for him. He was her enemy just as much as the other two were. She couldn't trust anyone. Not even the people Mildred trusted at the Colby Agency. They had sent *this man* after her.

The Colby Agency couldn't help her. Not that she could blame Victoria for hating her now. The idea of what her actions had put the woman through…Angel shuddered.

The police couldn't help her, either.

She was on her own.

"Don't try my patience, Miss Parker."

What she saw in his eyes more than the sound of his voice warned her that he was not a man who liked games. The intensity in those blue eyes unnerved her completely. It didn't help that he had long hair secured in a ponytail and a silver hoop in one earlobe. She shivered. He looked as if he belonged on a seventeenth-century pirate ship rather than in her living room. But she'd seen guys like him in contemporary movies. Always ruthless, always ignoring laws other than their own.

"All right." She closed her eyes briefly and prayed that those other men wouldn't storm her house just now and kill them both before she could at least attempt to find her aunt. She had no way of knowing their intentions. She could only do as she was told.

She didn't know why she bothered, but she decided

to tell Mr. Danes the truth to the extent she could. Why add one more transgression to her rising tally of sins to answer for? she reasoned. Right now, she considered morosely, going to hell was the least of her worries.

"Two years ago a man approached me at work and asked for scheduling information regarding Victoria Colby." She shrugged. "I thought it was some sort of joke until he told me that he had my daughter and that I wouldn't get her back until he had the information. I argued that I had no way of getting what he wanted and he countered that all I had to do was access the agency's system through my aunt's ID."

God it seemed so long ago now. She shook her head slowly from side to side. "I went to my aunt's office for lunch that same day and while she was in Victoria's office, I looked at her computer. Got what they asked for." She swallowed back a lump of remembered emotion. "They gave me my daughter back and threatened that if I ever told anyone that they would kill her next time."

"So you told no one," Danes prompted. "You didn't trust your aunt enough to tell her."

Angel glared at him. "Do you think I'd risk my child's life? I couldn't take the chance." She'd done the right thing. Like now, what other choice was there?

"Howard Stephens was the man who came to you for information from time to time?" he asked.

She nodded. "I didn't know his name for a long time. It was all done anonymously. Once in a while he or one of his men would be waiting at the child-care center where I took my daughter just to prove they could get to her. They even came in my house in the middle of the night. I'd find my baby's crib empty." Tears burned her eyes. "I'd search the house frantically only to find her sleeping in her playpen." She looked up at the man no doubt passing judgment on her at that very moment. "They would do this just to prove they could. To keep me aware of who held all the power."

"How did you manage to hide your daughter this time?"

A new kind of fear froze in her veins. "I won't tell you where she is. Even if you torture me, I won't say."

Apparently he believed her since he moved on. "Something tipped you off, gave you the opportunity to get one step ahead."

"Aunt Mildred told me about Victoria Colby's son." Colby-Camp, she reminded herself. Victoria was now married to Lucas Camp. "When she explained all that this evil man Leberman had done I realized that his actions in the past two years coincided with information I had given Stephens." A heavy breath pushed past her lips. She would never forgive herself for what she'd had to do. She certainly didn't expect God or anyone else to. "I hoped that since Leberman was dead that it was over. I couldn't imagine any reason his men would continue to haunt my life or Victoria's."

She let go a weary breath. "But about a week ago Aunt Mildred told me about the investigation and that there might be a leak at the agency. I knew then it wasn't over."

"Get up."

His command startled her. "What?"

"Get up."

She pushed to her feet, uncertain whether he intended to kill her or…some part of her brain wondered if Stephens's men had anticipated this move. Did Victoria Colby-Camp want revenge for what Angel had done? Angel could scarcely blame her. But she hadn't known

Victoria's missing child was related to those evil men… hadn't been able to do anything else.

"You have five minutes to pack whatever you think you need."

She blinked, confused all over again. So he wasn't going to kill her?

But where was he taking her? Would those men be watching? Was this part of their plan?

She shoved her hair behind her ears and reached for some semblance of composure. Didn't matter. She had her instructions.

She grabbed her purse from the floor and made her way to the bedroom. Cole Danes stayed right behind her, his weapon carefully trained on her back. She didn't have to look to know, she could feel it.

Somewhere she had an overnight bag. She prowled through the closet until she found it. A nightshirt, a couple of changes of undergarments, sweaters and jeans. Oh, yeah, and socks. Too cold to go without them. Toothbrush, toothpaste. Antiperspirant. She couldn't think of anything else.

"Get your coat and let's go."

She faced him, the weight of her bag dragging at her right shoulder. "Where are we going?" Surely he wouldn't turn her in to the police. Lord, she hadn't thought of that until that very second. What she had done was criminal. She could go to prison. Her aunt would die and her child would be raised by strangers. All of which, she admitted, a new flood of oppression washing over her, would likely happen anyway.

"No questions."

She resisted when he took her arm and would have ushered her from the room. The other man, the one who worked for Howard Stephens, had said those same words. *No questions.*

How could she be sure this was Cole Danes? What if she went with this man and it was a mistake?

"I need to see some ID." She tugged her arm free of his firm grasp, knowing she couldn't have done so had he not allowed it. He was strong. Tall, broad shouldered, but lean and powerful like a panther.

He reached into his jacket with his free hand and withdrew a leather case. "Be my guest."

She took the case from him and opened it. The picture on the credentials was this man all right. Six-two, one hundred seventy pounds. Forty. That surprised her. He didn't look more than thirty-five. Lived in Washington D.C. She handed the case back to him. She didn't want to know anything else.

"Convinced?"

"I suppose." Credentials could be forged. She didn't see the point in bringing that to his attention. He would likely know.

He slipped the case back into his interior pocket then motioned to the door with his gun. She reached for a jacket in her closet and tugged it on.

"Back door," he said when she would have turned toward the living room.

Angel drew in a long, deep breath of cool night air as Danes hustled her across her neighbor's backyard. The moon did little to light their path but he apparently knew where he wanted to go. He moved in the night like most people did in the daylight, without hesitation or conscious thought. Even she didn't know her neighbor's yard so well.

When they'd crossed to the opposite side of the street,

he waited beneath the shadow of a copse of trees before resuming the journey to wherever he'd parked.

A dark sedan eased up to the curb in front of her house. Angel peered through the darkness and tried to see who got out. Two people. Tall. Male, she decided, after surveying their bulky frames.

Stephens's men.

One moved stealthily toward her front door while the other crossed the street and searched a car parked there.

More lights came on inside her house.

The guy at the car swore hotly then moved quickly to join his friend in her house.

"What—"

The rest of her query died in her throat as Danes's hand closed over her mouth. When she struggled his arm clamped around her waist and hauled her against him. His body felt hard against her backside. His arm a band of unyielding steel.

The two men suddenly burst out through her front door and rushed to the car they had arrived in. She couldn't make out their gruff dialogues before they'd piled into the vehicle and sped away.

The man who'd called had told her to follow Danes's lead. Was she supposed to have kept him at her house until they arrived? Had she somehow made a mistake?

Fear exploded inside her. Would they kill her aunt now? Start the search for her child? No. No! Please, God. No.

Danes released her. Her knees gave way beneath her.

All that kept her from an up-close encounter with the ground was his swift reaction. He had her back in his

powerful arms in the nick of time. Her mind whirled
with more questions…mounting fear. What did she do
now?

"Can you walk?" He shook her when she didn't respond. "I said, can you walk?"

She nodded and grappled to regain her equilibrium.
"Yes."

He took her bag, draped it over his own shoulder and then she was suddenly moving forward…
through the dark, through more yards that weren't her
own. His punishing grip on her wrist lugging her in
his path.

"Where are we going?"

"Shut up."

He had to know something she didn't, knew those
men would be out looking for them. "Are they searching
for us now?"

He halted abruptly and his face was suddenly right
in front of hers. His grip had somehow relocated from
her wrist to her chin. "If you want to live, *shut up*."

She trembled. Bit down on her lower lip to hold back a
pained yelp. His fingers tightened. "No more talking."

He started forward again, his viselike grip on her wrist
once more. She thought about the gun she'd bought. The
advice the man at the pawnshop had given her. Why
hadn't she shot him when he told her to turn on the light?
Why had she let him take her gun away?

Those men wanted him. They were angry that they'd
missed him. Somehow she had made a mistake, was supposed to have kept him occupied until they arrived.

Wait.

Her frantic thoughts jarred to a stop.

They wanted to teach Danes a lesson first. He'd said
that. She remembered now. Maybe this was part of the

lesson—a sick game of some sort. But how was that possible? It felt wrong. As if Danes was in control. She'd heard the man who'd checked the car swear. He'd been furious. If things had gone as he'd planned why would he be angry?

Danes suddenly stopped.

He opened the passenger-side door of a black SUV. Did it belong to him? If so, why had the other man thought the car parked across the street from her house belonged to Danes? Had he thought that at all? She couldn't be sure. She'd assumed. None of this made sense now.

"Get in."

"Is this your car?" She shook her head. "What about the car parked across the street from my house?"

"Pay attention," he growled as he pulled her intimidatingly near. "Get in."

He'd told her to shut up. Her skin still burned where he'd held her chin. She nodded and climbed into the seat. He leaned in over her. She sank as far into the leather seat as possible, but it wasn't enough. His scent, something too subtle to distinguish, invaded her senses. The hard feel of his shoulder as she braced her hand against it in an effort to push him away, but he was far too strong. He withdrew something from his pocket and moved it over her purse. Small, black. A red light flashed on the small object.

He opened her purse and rifled through the contents.

"What're you doing?" she demanded when he pulled out the lipstick she carried. She didn't know why she bothered carrying it, she never used it.

He tossed the lipstick then moved his hand down the length of her legs, over her torso. Even in the sparse moonlight the intensity in his eyes unsettled her all the more. He checked her overnight bag in the same manner.

When he was satisfied he closed her door, swiftly skirted the hood, tossed her bag into the back seat and slid behind the steering wheel.

He'd driven to the end of the block and turned onto the main thoroughfare before he switched on the headlights. Angel tugged her seat belt into place and bit back the questions that rushed into her throat. She'd watched movies where devices were used to track the movement of vehicles and people. Is that why that red light had flashed on her purse and then he'd tossed her lipstick? She didn't dare ask.

This couldn't be happening. She rubbed at her eyes. Tried to think. Her hands shook so badly. She clasped them together and reached for a calm she knew she would not find.

Pay attention.

He'd told her to pay attention. That's what she needed to do. Where were they going? He took one turn after the other. Taking his time, moving forward a few blocks and then to the left. A right, then forward through a couple of intersections. He made it difficult to follow but she finally decided that the interstate was his destination though she couldn't be absolutely certain until he'd taken the turn.

I-94 South.

Chicago.

Fear crashed into her. Was he taking her to the Colby Agency? Maybe he did intend to turn her over to the authorities.

To her surprise, once on the interstate, he took the first exit that came into view. Her heart pounded hard against her sternum. Where was he going now? She tried to think what was on this exit. He wheeled into the parking lot of a small motel and drove all the way to the back of the parking lot. Her fear mounted.

He got out, reached in the back seat for her bag then flashed her a look that told her in no uncertain terms to get out. At the front of the vehicle he latched on to her arm again and led her to a lower-level room. When he jammed the keycard into the lock she couldn't keep quiet any longer.

"What are we doing here?"

He ushered her inside and locked the door.

After a survey of the room with the same device he'd used on her purse he dropped her bag on the floor and shouldered out of his jacket. He tossed it onto the foot of the bed as if he intended to stay awhile.

"Enough." She'd had it. "What the hell are you doing? Why did you bring me here?"

He simply stared at her.

She hugged her arms around her middle. "They're going to kill my aunt," she said, her voice lacking enough strength to actually call her words a successful plea. It was too late…she knew it. She'd screwed up somehow.

He moved closer, that intense gaze searching her face. Maybe he would feel sorry for her and help her. She didn't care if he saved her…if he would only help her aunt, protect her child.

"Please," she murmured, desperation urging her to act. "You have to help her."

He moved so suddenly, so lightning fast that he'd pinned her against the wall before she'd realized he'd moved at all. The air rushed out of her lungs more from the intensity of his eyes than the impact. "Don't presume that we're on the same side," he whispered fiercely, his face so close to hers she could feel his breath on her lips.

A new kind of fear synapsed in her brain, igniting every cell in its path with sheer terror.

"When I told you to talk, I wanted everything. Clearly, you left out a few details."

He knew.

How could he know?

Oh, dear God. He'd tapped her phone. He had to have heard the conversation…but then why ask?

"I know they contacted you earlier this evening."

Was it her imagination or had the pressure of his touch eased slightly? The fear throbbing inside her made it difficult to judge.

"Yes," she relented. She had to breathe, once, twice. "One of them called."

His hold relaxed. "What were his instructions?"

He didn't know. Relief trickled into the mix of churning emotions. He might have been listening but somehow he hadn't been able to hear…to understand… Something.

She still had a chance here. This had to be part of whatever they'd planned for Danes. *Some kind of crazy game.* But why would they want to play games? So much didn't make sense. He'd said he wanted to teach Danes a lesson. For what?

Danes waited for her to answer. He hadn't drawn his weapon yet but she knew he would if she didn't tell him more. She had to be careful. She couldn't reveal too much.

"They…" She tried to slow her respiration. The quick, shallow breaths would only make her hyperventilate. "They told me to wait for you. That you would be coming." She looked into those analyzing eyes and prayed he wouldn't see the lie in hers. "That's what I did. That's why I went out and bought a gun today." She relaxed a fraction when his expression didn't change. "I didn't know what would happen."

His stare...the silence...went on for so long that she felt a line of sweat bead on her forehead. *Please, please, let him believe me.* She knew it was wrong to pray for that kind of deception, but she was desperate. God knew just how desperate.

He drew slightly back, his gaze never leaving hers. "You're lying."

Her pulse jumped as his hold grew brutal once more. "No... No. I'm not lying." She shook her head adamantly. "All they want is you." Was that too much? She had to say something more. He'd seen through her deception. "You're all they want," she insisted. "If I stayed put and let you come after me they would release my aunt unharmed."

There was something about the way he looked at her then that sent a chill straight to the marrow of her bones.

"How valiant of you." The words were barely more than a whisper but even then she heard in his silky voice just how much he despised her.

She closed her eyes and fought back the humiliating tears. He was right to feel that way. All of this was because of her. Her child was living with strangers, her aunt being held hostage, this man's life on the line because of what she'd done.

Because of her mistake.

"I'm sorry." She moistened her lips and tried to take a breath but her chest felt too tight. "This isn't about you. This is my fault." She looked directly into those accusing eyes. "He told me my aunt would be safe if I did exactly as he said."

"The chances that your aunt is still alive are slim to none," he said bluntly. Her heart wrenched at the cold words. "If you're leaving anything out to protect her, don't waste my time. Think about your daughter, Miss Parker. These are not the kind of men who leave loose ends. Your aunt is likely already dead. They will kill you, that's a given. Then they'll kill your little girl just for the sport of it. It's what they do."

Despite her best efforts hot tears streamed down her cheeks. "Then what am I supposed to do?" How could she trust this man? If she told him the rest…she couldn't do that.

"I'm the only chance you've got of surviving. You can either trust me or we'll both end up dead."

He backed off physically but that penetrating stare never deviated. "Get some sleep. Think about what I said. Let me know what you decide."

Sleep. She frowned.

Her gaze flew to the digital clock on the bedside table.

7:56 p.m.

Panic broadsided her. "But we don't have time."

He moved in close again, his size, his scent, the way he studied her, terrified her all over again. "What's the hurry, Miss Parker? We're safe for the moment."

"He said I had forty-eight hours," she confessed, defeated. She couldn't do this anymore. "Forty-eight hours or she would die."

"Forty-eight hours for what?"

Every debilitating emotion she'd felt…every horrible moment she'd lived through these past few days crowded in on her at once. Her mistakes. Those awful men taking her aunt away. The call. The waiting.

Cole Danes.

The sudden, foolish desire to trust him…to believe in anything even remotely right in this insane situation.

"To make sure you walked into their trap." There. She'd said it. "To teach you a lesson," she explained. "They plan to play some sort of game with you first. Someone will contact me with the next step. That's all I know."

For the space of three excruciating heartbeats he didn't react…Just kept up that relentless stare.

"Very good, Miss Parker." A grim smile lifted the corners of his hard mouth. "Now we're on the same side."

CHAPTER FIVE

9:15 p.m.
37 hours remaining…

"Why do they want you?"

Perched on the edge of the mattress, Angel Parker had considered him at length before asking her question. Cole felt reasonably certain that she'd spent that time working up the courage to do so.

He wondered if a woman so young, barely twenty-five, and inexperienced in the ways of his world could even begin to comprehend the actual answer to that question.

Cole dismissed the possibility without further deliberation. He'd achieved his goal, prodded her fear factor until she reached a vulnerable zone in order for him to obtain the required information. She knew nothing else of value at this time. Her continued participation in this matter was merely a technicality to ensure the link between him and his target.

"Do…" She dropped her gaze to her hands briefly before meeting his once more. "Do you know these men?"

"Do you?" He increased the intensity of his stare several degrees. She looked away again. Didn't like the way he analyzed her. Not a particularly burdensome task from his vantage. Angel Parker was quite attractive.

Slender, maybe too much so, medium height. Her white blond hair and clear blue eyes made him think of far-away places. But her lips were her most distracting asset by far. Overly full, incredibly lush. The kind of lips women with the means sought from skilled surgeons.

She licked those lush lips genetics had provided, the movement sparked by discomfort at his presence. Angel Parker was not an overtly sexual creature. Not that he doubted her ability to be infinitely sexual, she simply concealed her appeal. Or perhaps she was not aware of that power. No, he amended. That conclusion gave her more credit than he was prepared to give at this time. She was no innocent.

"I know Howard Stephens," she said in answer to his question. "But I don't know this new man…the one who gave me the instructions this time. I'd never met him before." She stared at her hands once more. "Mr. Stephens is the one who wanted to know your name. He took my aunt."

"Howard Stephens is dead."

Slowly, as if afraid of what she might see, she lifted her gaze to his. "Did you kill him? Is that why these men are after you now?"

He watched her eyes grow wider, saw the fear tighten its noose.

"In a manner of speaking," he allowed, uncertain why he bothered to tell her anything. He had set things in motion. His intricate planning had ensured the outcome.

"I don't understand." She sucked in an unsteady breath. "Why are they doing this to me? They got what they wanted from my aunt." She searched his face. "Why don't they let her go? Why are they using us to get to you? My aunt had no part in any of this."

Cole leaned forward and braced his forearms on his widespread knees. "Because they can."

"So you do know who these men are?"

"Yes."

She dropped her hands to the mattress on either side of her. Her fingers curled in the covers as if she needed to hang on. "What do we do now? We can't just keep waiting. Time is running out." Her voice grew more frantic with each word. Pumping up her fear had been necessary, but he didn't need her hysterical.

"He'll call."

"How can you be sure?" She trembled but quickly stanched the telling reaction. "We've been sitting here for over an hour. They might not call. Maybe I did something wrong. Maybe they know you're on to their plan."

"He will call. I'm well aware of how these men operate. Waiting is our only option."

She lunged to her feet and started to pace the small room. He monitored her escalating apprehension but made no move to interfere. Let her walk off the adrenaline. Fatigue would do its work in time.

"I bought that weapon to protect myself." She whirled to face him, anger fueling, renewing her determination. "I convinced myself I could kill that man if I had to." A visible shudder went through her, testing her hold on composure. "Told myself I could kill you if that's what it took." She scrubbed at her forehead with a shaky hand. "But I couldn't. I couldn't do it." Her watery gaze found his once more. "And now my aunt is going to die because I'm too weak to help her."

She rushed to where he sat and dropped to her knees. "I have a three-year-old daughter. She needs me. Isn't there something you can do to help us? I have to get through this for my daughter," she urged, then her face fell. "But I don't think I'll be able to live with myself if my aunt dies because of my mistake."

She had no idea how dangerous this game really was. Not a clue. As guilty as she was for succumbing to Stephens's ploy in the first place, there was no denying the lack of malice and calculation in her personality, though he wanted to do just that. Her only crime, he realized, was a lack of intelligent reasoning and foresight triggered by extreme fear.

She lifted her gaze to his, only inches separating them. "Please help me. Don't you have any children of your own? A wife? Family somewhere? You must know how this feels. How it could end."

She was right about one thing, he already knew how this would likely end. "Don't waste your time attempting to play on my sympathies," he warned, purposely adding an air of danger to his tone. "I've never felt the need for a wife or children. And empathy is not one of my strong points."

She sat back on her heels and studied him, surprisingly not put off by his strategy. Her gaze moved over his every feature, his eyes, across his forehead, along the bridge of his nose, and the line of his jaw, then to his mouth. A frown disturbed her smooth forehead as she assessed his hard features. The sudden, almost irresistible urge to touch that troubled skin caught him off guard. He refrained from touching her but refused to draw away, instead he remained perfectly still, allowed her to look at her leisure. She would only see what he wanted her to see. Nothing more.

"You think you don't need anyone, don't you?" Those translucent eyes met his with a kind of knowing that sent a chord of uneasiness through him. "You think you've got everything figured out and that you're above it all. You're wrong."

He seized her wrist and held her close when she would have moved away. "I'm never wrong, Miss Parker."

Any lingering fear had vanished from her eyes. There was only a certainty that infuriated him.

"This time you are."

Angel wasn't sure how she'd worked up the nerve to argue with him on that particular point but the realization that she'd broken through some barrier was palpable. She'd gotten to him somehow. The burst of fury that darkened his eyes made her shiver. She should be afraid. Every instinct warned her that she should be seriously afraid and, yet, she wasn't. She felt calmer than she had in days.

He smiled then, widely, an intimate awareness in his eyes that stole her calm as abruptly as if he'd jerked a rug out from under her feet.

"Need is a very misunderstood element of the human psyche, Miss Parker." His voice was like silk, smooth, rich, but there was no mistaking an underlying lethal quality. "One either attends to it or denies it. When I experience a need, I satisfy it and walk away." His fingers tightened around her wrist. "What I need right now is for you to do exactly as I say and nothing more. Do you understand?"

She nodded, the movement uncoordinated.

"Get some rest." He released her. "There's nothing more we can do until he calls."

Angel pushed to her feet and backed away from him. She bumped into the mattress and let gravity drag her down to it. She closed her eyes to block him from her sight. There would be no reaching this man. She'd been stupid to try. He was as ruthless as the men holding her aunt hostage.

A medley of musical notes cracked the thick tension, yanking her from her disturbing thoughts. *Her cell phone.* She scrambled across the bed and grabbed her purse.

Danes manacled her wrist before she could depress the button to accept the call. "Be very careful what you say. Let him hear your fear. Show your eagerness to do whatever he asks."

His words elicited a powerful bolt of both emotions. "What if he asks about you?" What was she supposed to say then? The second cluster of notes pealed. Anticipation urged her to answer the call.

"Tell him the truth, that I'm holding you hostage."

She blinked. Was she a hostage? The idea startled her though it shouldn't have.

"Answer the call *now.*"

Her pulse jumped at the savage sound of his voice. *Wait. Hurry. We're on the same side now.* All of it was too confusing.

Stay calm. Think rationally.

She depressed the necessary button and held her breath. "Hello." She refused to consider how fragile she sounded. Blocked out the image of Cole Danes towering over her.

"Is he with you?"

Him. The man. She recognized him instantly. "Yes."

"Good."

His response caused a hitch in the breath she finally released.

"What am I supposed to do?" Sound eager. Was that eager enough? God, she didn't know.

"Is he listening?"

She nodded then caught herself. "Yes. He's right here."

The sinister rasp of a ruthless chuckle vibrated across the line. "Excellent. Tell him to take you to Lincoln Park at dawn. I'll be waiting."

"What about my aunt?" *Please, please, let my aunt be safe,* she prayed.

"I'll release her as soon as Cole Danes is dead."

Angel squeezed her eyes shut and pressed the heel of her hand against her forehead. She wanted to cry... wanted to demand that this bastard let her aunt go. None of this was Mildred's fault. *She* had caused all of this. She was the guilty one.

"Take me," she murmured. "You can have me instead. Please. Just let her go. And stay away from my daughter."

"Oh, but I need you right where you are, *Angel*," he cajoled hatefully. "You see, I want Cole Danes dead and you're going to help me make that happen."

She started to shake with something besides fear and anticipation. Rage blazed through her. "There's nothing I can do! Don't you see that?"

"The only thing I need to see is you *and Danes* at dawn."

He disconnected.

She wanted to scream.

Danes took the phone from her hand and turned it off.

"What're you doing?" She vaulted off the bed to put herself on more even ground with him. "He might try to call back." Was he out of his mind? She needed that connection!

"He won't. He's given you your instructions."

"Leave it on just in case." Why risk it? She reached for her phone but he held it away.

"That call established a link," he told her. "If we leave on the phone he can track our location."

Defeat sagged at her shoulders. "Why would he do that? He wants us to meet him at Lincoln Park at dawn. Why bother setting up a location if he planned to come after us now?"

"Insurance," he insisted calmly, too damn calmly. "He would prefer to track our movements. That's why we're going to stay one step ahead of him."

She sliced her arms through the air, sick of his persistent calm. "This is crazy. The two of you are playing games and my aunt is in danger." An epiphany flashed in her brain, the possibility so disarming she trembled at the idea. "Do you know more than you're telling me?"

"Give me the rest of what he said and then get some sleep otherwise you'll be useless come dawn."

She grabbed his arm in an attempt to make him understand that she needed to know. The hard muscle beneath her fingers brutally drove home the point she did not want to face. How was she supposed to contend with this kind of strength and determination? But she had to try.

"What is it you're not telling me? You know something." She was operating in the dark here. Didn't he know that? If he had more information, he needed to share it with her. Surely he wouldn't stand back and risk her aunt's life…surely he didn't know the worst already…. Had he said something to that effect?

"What else did he say to you?"

She let go of him and pressed her fingertips to her temples. She felt confused…afraid. She didn't know what to do. The gun had been her only means of fighting back. She had nothing. She looked straight at Cole Danes. Only this man. A man void of emotion. Defeat settled heavily onto her shoulders.

"Start at the beginning."

Well, he was her only chance. She had no choice but to work with him.

"He wanted to know if you were here," she told him wearily. "I said yes. Then he wanted to know if you were listening. I said yes again. He wants you to take me to Lincoln Park at dawn."

"What did he tell you about Mildred Parker? What was his response to your offer of trading yourself for your aunt?"

She glared up at him. "He wouldn't tell me anything. Said he needed me here, that I was going to help him kill you and that my aunt wouldn't be released until you were dead." She flung the words at him like missiles intended to wound, but his emotions were impenetrable.

Danes inclined his head. "Interesting."

His reaction made her more certain than ever. "There's something more going on here. What is it you're not telling me?"

A new kind of tension thickened between them, the silence wholly unnerving, his unwavering gaze adding yet another layer of relentless strain.

"I know these men," he confessed though clearly he didn't want to tell her anything. "They're the final two members of the death squad Errol Leberman and Howard Stephens created. Both will die before this is over. *If* you get in my way, you'll die, too."

5:15 a.m.
29 hours remaining

COLE WATCHED the woman sleep. She'd tossed and turned for most of the night, but she'd finally surrendered to her body's need to shut down at 2:00 a.m.

He'd taken a few minutes of rest here and there, never indulging in more than that at any one time.

Dawn would arrive within the hour. It was time to wake her. Yet he hesitated. Preferred not to bother her, she slept so peacefully now. Even in the uncharitable glow of the cheap bedside lamp, she looked agonizingly young. And innocent, he admitted. Leberman and Stephens had used her. She'd been afraid and had acted accordingly.

But her innocence or guilt were of no consequence. His mission could not be accomplished without her and for that reason it was necessary to keep her unbalanced, fearful. She was determined, he had to give her that. Her aunt's safety, as well as that of her child, appeared to be primary. Another unforeseen turn. He'd expected the child to hold precedence but not the aunt. Whether Angel fully realized it or not, her aunt's survival of this ordeal was not likely. Yet she would not give up on finding her unharmed. He had not anticipated that level of selflessness in one so young and seemingly focused on her own life.

Cole dismissed the surge of respect he experienced on the heels of those deductions. However selfless Angel Parker might be, she had brought this war down on herself. He had to bear that in mind. She was not completely innocent.

He refused to acknowledge the other nagging instinct. Something he hadn't felt for a very long time—ten years actually. A foolish part of him wanted to protect her from further damage. He stood, shook it off.

Hadn't he learned long ago that those with whom he dealt rarely deserved such a costly commodity?

The urge to protect, like compassion, served only one purpose: to make you weak. To steal crucial attention and energy.

He never made mistakes. He would not make one now.

Time to go. No more dwelling on a subject best left alone.

He moved to the bed where she lay and shook her, none too gently. "Wake up. It's time to go."

She sat up instantly, her heavy, long-lashed lids fluttering open. Her breath caught when memory identified him and reminded her of time and place.

She climbed out of bed without responding. Her hair was tousled, her clothes rumpled, but she didn't appear to care. She went directly to the bathroom and closed the door. Two minutes later she exited, her hair finger combed and her clothes straightened somewhat.

"I'm ready."

One look in her eyes told the truth of the matter. She wasn't ready, but she would do what she had to in an effort to help her aunt. To rid their lives of this curse once and for all.

He sent a pointed look at her bare feet.

"Oh." Her cheeks flushed. "I forgot." She quickly tugged on her sneakers without bothering to untie them.

"The jacket, too." He indicated the jacket lying on the end of the bed.

Angel shouldered into her well-worn denim jacket and let go a grave breath. Now or never.

"Get your purse," Danes said. "We won't be coming

back here." He picked up her overnight bag and slung it over one broad shoulder.

She nodded and snagged her purse. "Can I turn on my cell phone now?"

"No."

She muttered an unflattering adjective under her breath.

He walked out the door ahead of her, surveyed the parking lot then motioned for her to follow. For a man who seemed to care about no one she couldn't help wondering why he bothered. Maybe he wasn't quite so ruthless as he wanted her to believe.

Streaks of gold-and-purple light had started to cut through the night, lending an ominous ambience to the cold, wet morning. She shivered as the frigid air penetrated her thin jacket.

Pull it together. Stay alert, she ordered. Wet from the rain that had fallen sometime during the night while she slept like the dead, the pavement looked inky black. A perfect morning for this sort of excursion, she supposed. Cold and ugly. Threatening.

Glass shattered next to her.

It took several seconds for Angel to realize the car window on her right, less than two feet back had burst as she passed it.

Suddenly she slammed downward…onto the damp pavement. The impact knocked the air out of her lungs.

Danes was on top of her, firing his weapon rapidly, the sounds exploding in the air, deafening her.

"Get under the car."

She tried to comprehend his barked order but somehow she couldn't.

He shoved her toward the vehicle on her left. "Get under there now!"

She scooted on her belly. Didn't stop until she'd reached the middle. Her breath came in ragged spurts. The smell of oil and gasoline caused her to gag.

The loud thunder of Danes's gun echoed, the explosions followed by odd pings and more shattering glass. She saw a clip hit the ground near where he crouched. It looked much like the ones she'd purchased with her gun…only bigger.

Why was he shooting?

Her mind suddenly wrapped around the other strange sounds and the broken glass.

Silencers. Whoever was shooting at them had sound suppressors on their weapons.

Who would be shooting at them?

One step ahead. Danes had said they were one step ahead. He didn't want them to know this location. He'd been wrong. Who else could this be? They had to know. It had to be *them.*

Tires squealed.

Three, four, five more shots from Danes's weapon.

Silence.

She forced her thoughts to slow. Tried to gulp in a deep breath to steady her respiration.

Silence.

She could see Danes's leather shoes where he still crouched. She squeezed her eyes shut for a moment just to be sure the shadow of the image wasn't somehow burned on her retinas.

She looked again.

He was gone.

She jolted into action, sliding quickly from under the car. Sirens wailed in the distance. Faces peered from between the narrow gaps in drapes. No one moved between the parked vehicles. Broken glass. A car alarm throbbing.

Where was Danes?

She saw the man on the ground and was moving in that direction before the identity of the other man bent over him registered.

"Don't you die on me just yet, you son of a bitch," Danes snarled. He'd torn the man's shirt open. Blood seeped between his fingers where he attempted to stanch the flow from midtorso.

"We need an ambulance," Angel shouted back at the faces in the windows. Her purse...cell phone. The sirens. Someone had already called. She dropped to her knees on the other side of the man and checked his respiration and heart rate. Still breathing. Pulse thready. *Damn.*

"Tell me what I want to know," Danes growled.

The man tried to talk, his words too choked to understand.

"Don't try to talk," Angel told him before shooting Danes a glare. She surveyed the man again. "The ambulance is here," she told the man on the ground. "Hang on." Thank God someone had asked for an ambulance as well as the police. She could only assume that the call was made as soon as shots were fired for this kind of rapid response. The man's pulse rate was dropping.

Angel tried to assess the damage based on what she saw. She only knew that it was critical. Massive hemorrhaging. She couldn't do any more than Danes was already doing for that. Had the bullet exited? Turning him over was too risky.

Suddenly an EMT appeared next to her. She stood and immediately stepped back. This was EMT territory. They had the equipment. The second EMT moved into place next to Danes and initiated the IV while the other assessed the now unconscious patient's condition. She tried not to think about the fact that this man, though not the one who had shown up at her house yesterday, was likely involved in her aunt's kidnapping.

"I need this man alive," Danes said sharply.

The EMTs ignored the comment, conversed quickly about the man's worsening condition, but Angel didn't really absorb their words; she couldn't get past what Danes had said. This couldn't be good. Where was the other man? Why had they shown up here? In her peripheral vision she caught a glimpse of two or three police officers headed their way.

"We have to get him to the hospital," the EMT said. "He needs surgery. *Now*." The last he directed at Danes.

"Ma'am, can you tell me what happened here?"

The officer's voice tugged her attention from the scene on the ground. "I'm really not sure," she said hesitantly. "We came out of our room and this man—" she gestured to the ground but the EMTs had already loaded the patient onto a gurney and had headed to the waiting ambulance "—he…he started shooting at us." Sometime during the hail of bullets sunrise had lightened the sky. It seemed impossible that only moments ago she'd been hiding in the dark beneath that car.

The officer asked something else but Danes's climbing into the ambulance behind the two EMTs distracted her. "I'll be happy to answer your questions," she assured the officer. "Just let me check on…" She gestured to the ambulance.

"Of course, ma'am." Apparently he assumed she

meant Danes. "But I'll need a statement from both you and your husband."

Maybe in some remote part of her brain she did need to check on Danes. Had he been injured? She smiled faintly as the officer let her pass. She hurried toward the ambulance.

He thought she and Danes were a couple. The idea almost made her laugh. If her heart hadn't been beating so fast and her stomach hadn't been twisted around her esophagus she might have done just that.

She slowed at the rear doors of the vehicle, stunned somewhat that they hadn't rushed away before now. Was the man dead already? Was Danes hurt?

"Here are my credentials." Using one bloody hand Danes thrust the leather case he'd shown her last night in the man's face. He turned to the other EMT. "Now wake him up."

"Look man," the EMT with the credentials said. "I don't know anything about—"

"Who the hell is this guy?" the other one demanded of his partner, clearly not happy with Danes's orders.

His partner shrugged. "NSA."

"You know as well as I do that this man will not make it to the hospital," Danes said quietly, the intensity in the softer tone wholly unnerving. "He's dying. Now wake him up so I can question him."

The first EMT shoved the credentials case at Danes and looked at his partner. "We could try to bring him around with some epinephrine."

"Are you crazy?" his partner demanded. "We gotta roll with this guy."

Danes braced his hands on his hips, pushing the lapels of his jacket out of the way just far enough to display his shoulder holster and gun. "I don't care what you have to do. But do it here and now. *Wake him up.*"

Angel wanted to back away, didn't want to see this, but morbid fascination paralyzed her. She couldn't move… she could only watch as the eppie was administered, giving the man's heart rate and blood pressure a jolt to draw him back to consciousness.

Whatever his sins he was about to pay the ultimate price.

Her gaze settled on Danes.

She'd been wrong.

Cole Danes was far more ruthless than she'd even suspected.

CHAPTER SIX

7:25 a.m.
26 hours, 50 minutes remaining…

"Why are we coming back here?" Angel demanded as Danes ushered her back into the motel room. "I thought you said—"

He secured the door then surveyed the parking area before pulling the drapes together more tightly. "We'll be safe here as long as those squad cars remain in the lot."

The blood on his hands, on hers, had dried, but the smell still haunted her. She'd never get used to that. Never. Her stomach roiled and she closed her eyes against the images and sounds. The gunfire…the blood. That man had died. What did that mean? A part of her couldn't help regretting the loss of human life, criminal or not.

"Take off your clothes."

She jerked to attention. Blinked twice. "What?"

"Take off all your clothes. Now."

He stared at her with that usual intensity, his words perfectly clear, uttered in that brisk, cold tone, but she still didn't understand.

"Why do you want me to take off my clothes?" The idea seemed ludicrous given the current situation.

"Do it."

He strode into the bathroom and turned on the basin faucet. Dumbfounded, Angel watched as he scrubbed the blood from his hands. The nurse in her mentally ticked off the numerous diseases both of them would need to worry about. She stared at her own hands. They'd had to at least attempt to give the man aid until the ambulance arrived. For the good it had done. There had been so much blood. He most likely would not have survived... *Wake him up now.* She shuddered at the memory. Danes hadn't appeared to care if the man died, he'd wanted answers.

Had he gotten them? She'd turned away from the scene, hadn't been able to watch. The police officer had eventually wandered over and started his questioning again. Strangely, only minutes after the ambulance had left for the hospital with their patient who would be dead on arrival, the police had given them the go-ahead to leave, as well. Just another thing she didn't understand in any of this.

Who was Cole Danes that he could have a shoot-out in a public place, kill a man—in self-defense admittedly—and walk away with scarcely a comment to local law enforcement?

"I said take off your clothes."

She jumped at the sound of his voice. She had to get a hold of herself here. "Let me wash my hands." Another shudder rocked through her.

"In a moment."

He was serious. Dammit, she wasn't taking off her clothes without a good reason. "No." She shook her head adamantly. "Not until you tell me why."

"They knew to come here. We walked right into their trap. Maybe they locked in on our location during the call, but I don't think so. Tracking down a cell phone takes time. Either way, I'm not taking the chance that there's a bug I don't know about."

"But you checked me for bugs already." She remembered quite well the little thingie he'd used to scan her and her bags.

"New technology comes on the market every day. It's not impossible that he used something undetectable by the usual means."

She gestured to the bathroom. "I'll toss my clothes out to you."

He moved his head side to side. "It's not really your clothes I'm worried about. I need to inspect every square inch of your body."

Cole knew he'd shaken her with that request but it was necessary. "Now," he reiterated.

She hesitated a moment longer, likely grappling to find another excuse to argue the point with him. But, in the end, she was too smart not to see the obvious. Taking her slow, sweet time she shouldered out of her jacket and draped it on the foot of the bed.

He didn't like it when the target one-upped him and he'd definitely been one-upped this morning. But he had what he needed now. He would finish this, whatever the cost. The local police hadn't appreciated his refusal to cooperate. Nor had they been pleased at his ability to shift jurisdiction with a single phone call. And they definitely didn't like cleaning up someone else's mess. Cole didn't see the big deal. No civilians were harmed. Insurance would pay for any damage done to the vehicles in the lot. The only casualty was a man who'd overstayed his welcome on this planet years ago.

One left to go.

When that final piece of scum had ceased to share the same airspace as Cole he would at last be satisfied.

He'd waited ten long years to finish this.

She toed off her sneakers, rolled off the socks, then carefully placed the items next to her jacket.

In a show of his impatience, he folded his arms over his chest. The move sent pain slicing through his side. He gritted his teeth and ignored it. He'd endured much worse for far less. He would endure this. Time was short. The next move needed to be his.

The one remaining man was one he had studied well, knew almost as well as he knew himself. Not that finishing the matter would be simple, there were a number of complications, including Mildred Parker. But it would be an enjoyable task.

Angel's fingers moved to the buttons on her sweater. His gaze followed the release of each of three buttons at her throat. Stealing a quick glance in his direction, she crossed her arms in front of her and took hold of the hem of the sweater. The fabric slid up and over her head, landing on the bed with a good deal less care than the other items.

She looked directly into his eyes. "I'm not taking off my…" She cradled her arms in front of her breasts.

"I'll work around it," he allowed. Relief flooded her expression. "Stop stalling."

She turned her back and unfastened her jeans. The soft denim slid over her hips, revealing delicate bikini panties, the light pink color a perfect match to her bra. She lifted first one leg then the other to tug off the jeans. They plopped onto the bed. Timidly, her arms went up to shield as much of her torso as possible.

"What now?" she asked looking back over her shoulder at him.

Cole stood very still, his attention oddly distracted by her skin. It looked incredibly smooth, like porcelain. Her white-blond hair draped halfway to her narrow waist. The silky tresses looked even softer against the sleek shell of her skin.

The idea that touching her would be a mistake flitted through his mind but he dismissed it. This inspection was essential to his success. Not sexual…not pleasurable in any way.

He closed the distance between them in two long strides. Using both hands he scooped up her hair and fingered slowly through it, searching for any kind of device. Something organic likely, perhaps even a device that deteriorated in time, maintaining its shape and function only long enough to provide location.

Her hair felt every bit as silky as he'd anticipated. Then his fingers moved to her skin. She gasped. He recoiled abruptly at the warm feel beneath his fingertips. The smooth texture he'd anticipated, but not the warmth. Her flesh had looked too pale and sleek to be this warm. Bracing himself, he lowered his fingers there once more. Slid the tips over her shoulders, closely searched the flawless surface with his eyes as well as his touch.

"When they took your aunt away," he began, his voice strained somehow, "did either of the men touch you in any way? Brush against you?"

She shook her head, the movement sending long tendrils of pure silk swaying across her shoulders. "Not that I can recall. They…" She inhaled an unsteady breath. "They mostly just grabbed my arm."

Cole was surprised to see his hands shaking slightly as he moved toward the closure of her bra. He squeezed them into fists then relaxed. He clenched his jaw and focused. He had a job to do. He reached for the closure and unfastened it. She shivered, he did the same. The reaction annoyed him.

"Wait."

She turned slightly, staring up at him over her bare shoulder. The image tugged at something inside him which only made him angrier at himself.

"I almost forgot," she rushed to say. "They took our coats. I remember now that I forgot mine when they took me away afterward." A frown marred her smooth forehead. "Those two men, the one who died this morning and the other one who came to my house yesterday, drove my aunt and me to some place to question us. We were blindfolded so I don't know where."

"How long was the drive? Did you stay on paved streets?" Irrationally, Cole was thankful for the reprieve. At least he had time to regroup before touching her again.

"I…I'm not sure. I was so upset. Maybe thirty minutes."

Thirty minutes from her aunt's condo in Chicago. Angel had already told him that she'd gone to her aunt's place to tell her everything when the men arrived.

Angel pushed her hair back from her face and turned more fully toward him. "That man, the one who died this morning—" her gaze drifted to the window "—he searched us thoroughly. Made us open our blouses so he could see if we were wearing a wire or something like that."

Cole swore softly. "He knew you weren't wearing a wire," he snapped. "It was an excuse to get you to strip for him."

She looked mortified. "No…"

"Show me how he touched you," Cole ordered.

Angel tried to remember exactly what happened that

night, but so much had happened...think! She had to think. She clutched her bra to her breasts with one arm and reached down to show him with the other.

"I remember he ran his hands over my sides." She focused hard on that horrifying moment. "All the way around to my spine. But he didn't have anything in his hand." She'd been so terrified, could she really say that with any real accuracy?

"Like this?" Danes flatted his palms against her abdomen, then slowly slid them around her waist.

Her breath trapped in her throat. Those wide, strong hands created a blaze wherever they touched. That intent blue gaze connected with hers and, knowing he wanted an answer, she nodded as best she could.

As he'd warned at the outset, he inspected every square inch of her torso from the sensitive area beneath her breasts to the rim of her panties. She couldn't look at him, though she knew he was looking at her. She could feel his eyes on her, watching, analyzing. She didn't want him to see the way his touch affected her. It was crazy. He was ruthless...uncaring...

"Don't move."

She opened her eyes in time to see him crouch down in front of her. He turned her slightly and inspected her left hip. She could feel his breath on her skin. Goose bumps skittered. Her fingers itched to touch his hair. To see if it felt as thick and silky as it looked. Despite the uncharacteristic length, the man had great hair. She closed her eyes and banished the crazy thought.

He lifted something from her skin and peered at it for a time before looking up at her. As startled as she was to see that he'd found something, for one moment she couldn't get past the vision of his face so close to her quivering belly.

"This is how they found us."

He stood and showed her the tiny transparent disk that had been stuck to her skin.

A line formed between her eyebrows as she stared at the near-invisible object. "I should have felt that?"

"You wouldn't. Certainly not under the circumstances."

He walked to the bathroom and flushed the disk down the toilet.

She looked at the dried blood on her hands and shuddered. "Can I wash up now?"

"You're certain he didn't touch you anywhere else?"

"I'm certain."

He nodded. "Clean up."

Angel couldn't say for sure right now since her own emotions were in a tailspin, but she got the distinct impression that Mr. Cold-As-Ice was uncomfortable.

Unbelievable.

10:00 a.m.
24 hours, 15 minutes remaining...

COLE WAITED in a parking garage downtown until the shops opened. He'd allowed Angel to take a shower, during which time he'd closely inspected the clothing she intended to wear. No more silent bugs. It annoyed him to no end that he hadn't considered that possibility. He should have.

"What're we doing?"

To her credit she hadn't asked any questions since they left the motel. He assumed that his seeing her undressed had unsettled her. Unfortunately it had rattled him to some degree. He didn't know what to make of that. Perhaps it was his proximity to finally achieving his goal that made him susceptible. Whatever the case, he was back on track now.

"We're going to make a few purchases and find a place to lie low until dark."

"Until dark?" Leather crinkled as she turned more fully toward him. "I only have twenty-four more hours. They're going to kill my aunt! I can't sit around waiting."

"He," Cole corrected.

She cut her hands through the air. "How the hell do you know there's only one guy left? He could have a dozen friends in on this with him."

"There's only one to be concerned with."

She plowed her fingers through her hair and heaved a sigh. "You can't be certain."

He leveled his gaze on hers. "I am certain."

"Whatever," she snapped. "We can't just sit here."

"What do you propose we do?" He injected a good measure of condescension in his tone to put her in her place. He doubted the strategy would be entirely successful but he had to try.

Her mouth dropped open but no words came out. From her frustrated expression he could see that she frantically searched for an option. One she wouldn't find.

"So we just wait for him to call again?"

"No." He removed the keys from the ignition. "We wait for nightfall."

He emerged from the SUV, which he had also swept thoroughly for alien electronic devices, and moved around to the passenger side.

He opened her door. "Get out."

"Didn't anyone ever teach you any manners, Mr. Danes?"

She climbed out to stand next to him. She waited, staring expectantly up at him. Apparently the question wasn't meant as a rhetorical one.

If he hadn't been so damn tired he might have been able to come up with a scathing reply that would shut her up but he lacked the energy to waste.

"Miss Parker, in case you've forgotten, I saved your life this morning. Try and show a little gratitude."

"Not so fast." She snagged his arm when he turned away.

He produced the kind of stare that generally sent anyone of the species, male or female, into retreat. "What is it now?"

Her face turned grim. "What was it you asked the man you shot? What did he tell you?"

He'd expected her to get around to that eventually. She'd been too traumatized to inquire before now. Obviously, the shock had worn off to an extent.

"I asked him where they were keeping your aunt," he told her, seeing no point in hiding that fact from her.

She blinked, startled. "Did...did he tell you?"

"No."

A brutal blow of defeat punched Angel, making her sway. She was running out of time. In twenty-four hours her aunt would be dead. She wasn't any closer to finding her now than she had been when that bastard issued his ultimatum. What was she supposed to do?

The feel of Danes's hands on her arms, holding her steady, tugged her from the troubling thoughts.

"Sorry...I—" Why the hell was she apologizing to him? She pulled free of his hold. "Let's get this over with."

He escorted her to the major department store next door to the parking garage. With an economy of time and effort he purchased a change of clothes for himself as well as for her. Apparently he wasn't taking any chances on more bugs.

Her suspicion was confirmed when he picked up another rental car at the airport, leaving his SUV in the short-term parking area. The only items she was allowed to keep were her purse and cell phone, which he had disassembled and reassembled in under a minute.

He pointed the new rental in the direction of town and drove for half an hour without saying anything.

"What are we doing now?" she asked as he finally parked midway along a crowded city block. She hated being left in the dark. He'd scarcely said a word since the exchange regarding the day's agenda in the parking garage nearly two hours ago.

He didn't bother responding, just got out and came around to her door. What was the point in arguing? He had the guns, hers included, he was in charge.

She followed him into the large corner drugstore, her mind drifting to her daughter. She tried not to think how long it had been since she'd seen her…held her. If she closed her eyes she could call to mind her daughter's sweet baby scent. Oh how she missed her. If she could just get through this and get back to her little girl…if her aunt was safe. She'd never ask God for anything else as long as she lived.

By the time her mind shifted back to the present, Danes had filled a small shopping basket with several items. She frowned as she attempted to identify the various goods. Gauze. Antibiotic ointment. Peroxide. A travel-size sewing kit. Gauze tape. A few male essentials, like a disposable razor and shaving cream. Two toothbrushes. Toothpaste.

Some of the items she could understand but what was with all the medical supplies?

Before she could question his selections he strode up to the counter and paid. Moments later they were in the car again. She didn't ask any questions because she sensed that he had no desire to talk. Instead, she studied his stony profile. As unyielding as the angular lines of his face, as hard-hearted as he clearly was, she had to admit that he was a handsome man.

Nothing about his hard, determined demeanor had really changed. She inclined her head and considered him again. No, maybe it had. She sensed another kind of distance about him, a new sort of remoteness. He felt even more unapproachable. And there was a decidedly weary edge about his posture.

She prayed that man hadn't told him more than he would say. If Danes already knew that her aunt was… hurt…

"Are you certain there isn't something you need to tell me?" she ventured.

"I've told you all there is to know."

He sounded tired rather than annoyed or impatient.

"I still don't like the idea of wasting the rest of the day. Shouldn't we be out looking? Isn't there something we can do?" It just felt wrong to wait while her aunt remained in the hands of a killer. She suppressed a shudder. What if the other man never called? How would she find her aunt then? She could be anywhere. Fear twisted inside her.

Danes pulled into the lot of a hotel, this one more upscale than the last. After parking in front of the lobby he sat silently for so long that Angel worried she'd pushed him too far. Anxiety sent her heart thumping against her rib cage. She should have kept her mouth shut. Another mistake. Would she never learn?

"Go in, get us a room." He handed her a credit card and driver's license. "Use that name."

"What?" He wanted her to go in alone? She had to have heard wrong.

"Just do it."

If the ferocity behind those three words hadn't been enough, the lethal look he pointed in her direction definitely did the trick. Angel wrenched the door open and hurried into the hotel lobby without hesitating. She glanced at the name on the credit card, then verified it with the name on the license before reaching the desk.

Damon Rodale. Cincinnati, Ohio.

"May I help you, ma'am?" The clerk gifted her with a practiced smile from behind his gleaming counter.

"Yes, I need a room." She placed the credit card and driver's license on the counter. "Just for one night," she added, producing a smile of her own.

The credit card was approved with a single swipe. No questions other than the usual, smoking or nonsmoking, king or two double beds. Incredible. He recited the directions for the easiest access to the room and passed the key card along with the credit card and license across the counter.

"Thank you." She gathered the cards and fake ID but hesitated before leaving. "Do you have room service?" she asked, certain a hotel this size would.

"The kitchen is open until midnight," he assured with another gracious smile.

"Thank you."

Food entered the chaos in her head for the first time in

more than twenty-four hours. She couldn't even remember the last time she'd eaten. Before she and Mildred had been descended upon by madmen? She was pretty sure that was correct. After she'd gotten her daughter safely tucked away she'd forced herself to eat in order to keep up her energy.

She wondered then when Danes had eaten last. She couldn't imagine him confessing to any sort of physiological need.

The sight of him sitting, his forehead braced against the steering wheel, struck her hard as she approached the vehicle.

She rushed to his door. "Are you all right?"

His head snapped upward at the same time his hand flew to his weapon with phenomenal speed. "Did you get the room?"

She nodded. "We can drive around back and park there. There's a rear exit near our room." It wasn't until she told him those details that she realized she should likely have asked for those very accommodations.

"Good."

As soon as she'd gotten in he pulled away from the parking slot and followed her instructions. She watched him closely as he walked to the hotel's rear entrance. His movements seemed steady but something was clearly wrong here. It wasn't until they were safely behind the locked door of their room that she knew just how wrong.

He winced as he removed his jacket. The tear in his black shirt and the slight variation in fabric color in the surrounding area loudly telegraphed the problem.

"You've been shot." She breathed the words.

He staggered but regained his balance with the aid

of the nearest table. "I think I'm going to need your assistance."

"How bad is it?" She rushed to him and started to unbutton his shirt.

He manacled her hands in his. "No matter what happens," he warned, his voice taut, "don't take me to a hospital. We have to stay out of sight."

"But what if—"

He fell against her, his weight dragging them both down to the floor.

This time he didn't try to catch himself.

This time he didn't speak.

CHAPTER SEVEN

Inside the Colby Agency, 11:45 a.m.
22 hours, 30 minutes remaining...

Lucas Camp sat down at the long conference table, alongside his wife. He didn't like the worry etched across her lovely face. He hadn't seen her this upset since before they'd discovered her son was alive.

When would this end?

"Still no word from Cole Danes?" she asked, her voice hollow from lack of sleep.

Lucas shook his head. "Nothing. I haven't been able to contact him since he left the office yesterday."

Victoria pressed her hands to her mouth.

"I know this is difficult, Victoria, but I still believe he will pull this off. He's never failed before. He won't this time."

She turned to him, anguish clouding her eyes. "How could this happen? Mildred..." She shook her head. "He may not be able to save Mildred and her niece. And, dear God, what about the child? Has anyone figured out where the child is?"

This hit far too close to home. Lucas hated to see her go through this kind of torment again. He'd sworn to protect her and he hadn't been able to. Leberman, the devil, still had his cronies. Lucas had a bad feeling that it wouldn't really be over until every last one of them was dead.

"I've got people working on it," he assured her gently. Never one to take chances, Lucas had two of his Specialists working the case. Unfortunately, Cole Danes had proven every bit as capable as his Specialists. He'd given them the slip as if they were mere recruits fresh out of training. But they would pick up his trail again. For now, Victoria didn't need to be bothered with any of that. "Casey believes Angel hid the child. That's why they've taken Mildred. It was the only other way they knew to get at Angel."

"What else does Casey have to say?"

Thomas Casey was Lucas's boss. The director of Mission Recovery and a good friend. He'd gone through this nightmare with Lucas, had provided unrelenting support. He had called this morning with an update he didn't want to discuss via the airwaves. His plane had arrived in Chicago thirty minutes ago. Lucas had sent a car to bring him to the office. Meanwhile, he and Victoria could only speculate as to what Casey had uncovered.

The door opened and Thomas Casey stepped inside the conference room. Lucas stood to greet him. Though nearly twenty years Lucas's junior, Thomas Casey had amassed a wealth of experience in the world of covert operations. He was a top-notch director. But no one, not even Lucas, would ever know the man behind the job.

Thomas Casey didn't let anyone close.

"I apologize for being so vague when we spoke this morning," Casey said by way of greeting as he shook Lucas's outstretched hand. He nodded to Victoria. "Good to see you, Victoria."

"Thank you for coming. I hope you have some news that can help us, Thomas."

No one else in the world called Director Casey by his first name. Lucas suppressed a tiny smile. He doubted anyone other than Victoria would get away with it.

"I believe I have some insight that might be of use," he allowed.

"Why don't we sit." Lucas gestured to the chair directly across the table from where he and Victoria sat. "Coffee?"

"None for me, thanks." Casey settled into his chair.

Victoria shook her head when Lucas looked to her.

"Well then, let's get this thing started."

Casey set his briefcase on the table and opened it. He removed a manila folder marked classified and passed it to Lucas.

"I've looked a little more deeply into Cole Danes's past."

That news surprised Lucas. "His record is outstanding."

"That's true. Not a single failure." Casey leaned back in his chair. "Graduated from Yale with a law degree, went on to achieve his doctorate in foreign affairs. The man speaks a dozen different languages, even trained with Special Forces just to get the physical logistics right in case he needed them. He has negotiation and intimidation tactics down to a science. I'd like nothing better than to recruit him for my unit."

"So what else is new?" Lucas already knew all that. That's why he'd selected Danes for this assignment.

"Professionally he's something of a superhero," Casey agreed. "It's his personal life where things get complicated."

Lucas shrugged. "His father was an ambassador to an African country. He and his wife have since retired to

Florida. One brother, six years older, who also worked for the State Department."

"Died in a car bombing in Libya fifteen years ago," Casey interjected.

"Not surprising," Lucas countered. "Libya's not exactly the place to be if you're American, not then, not now." Even with the new, so-called cooperation the Libyan government had shown lately, the country was still an unstable environment for Americans.

"One would think," Casey said mysteriously. "But when I considered Danes's handling of the Howard Stephens case and then this latest turn of events, I took a closer look at his activities in the past ten or so years."

Lucas leaned forward to flip through the pages of the file Casey had brought.

"We know Errol Leberman and Howard Stephens formed an alliance. With a team of six men they carried out death warrants all over the world."

Again Lucas wondered what was new with that. "Go on," he prompted knowing Casey would not have come all this way without good reason which would include new information.

"I formulated a number of simulations," Casey explained. "I considered the deceased Danes son's work in international terrorism and the time frame. The man had quite a handle on the homeland terrorist situation even then. He made statements that our own worst enemies might come from within.

"If Cole Danes's beloved brother, his only sibling, had been murdered by homeland terrorists rather than foreigners that would make for excellent motivation for Danes to go after the culprits."

Lucas narrowed his gaze. "You're saying someone commissioned Leberman and Stephens to do the job and make it look 'work' related, as if his visit to Libya had been the reason he'd died."

"Right."

"But that's only speculation." Lucas flared his hands skeptically. "I'll admit that after what's happened I considered the possibility that Danes had a personal stake in this, but there's no evidence to back it up."

"Maybe there is." Casey pointed to the file. "Check the dates. Until today, four of the six men Leberman and Stephens had recruited have been executed. We know this from what Victoria's son has related during the past few months."

Victoria shifted in her chair. "He hasn't remembered everything," she reminded. "There are a lot of holes in his memory."

"I understand that. But in each instance when one of Leberman's team was executed, there is documentation that Cole Danes was traveling in the area."

That got Lucas's attention. He shuffled through the pages. "You're certain." He didn't know why he asked. He knew Casey wouldn't introduce the scenario if he hadn't done his homework.

"Even when Leberman was here in Chicago, Danes was in the area. There's no evidence, of course, that he was involved in any way or made any sort of contact, but he was here."

Lucas sat back in his chair, a cold hard knot of apprehension forming in his gut. "So you think Danes is avenging his brother's death."

Casey nodded. "Not just his brother, his brother's wife and children, as well. Vengeance is the most likely scenario. Especially considering this morning's shoot-out. Another of the original six went down."

Lucas knew all about this morning's escapade.

Chicago PD had related the story to Victoria when she called to inquire. One officer insisted that the EMTs had stated that Danes had questioned the shooting victim extensively before allowing him to be transported. The man had been DOA. Both EMTs had admitted that he would likely have died anyway. He'd lost a massive amount of blood, had serious internal injuries.

"That leaves only one," Victoria said, the worst-case scenario obviously taking shape for her, as well. She turned to Lucas. "My God," she murmured. "Surely he won't put his need for revenge ahead of Mildred's life."

Lucas wanted to reassure her…but he couldn't.

Considering this latest data, there was no way to know what Cole Danes would do.

"I will say this," Casey offered, dragging Lucas's attention back to him. "Cole Danes has a reputation for being fair as well as ruthless. Despite the scenario I've presented, we have every reason to believe he'll do the right thing. He always has."

Lucas hoped like hell he would do the right thing this time. He set his jaw hard. If Cole Danes allowed Mildred or Angel Parker to be hurt, Lucas would have no one to blame but himself for bringing the man into this situation. There was nothing he could do to change that glaring fact, but he would make it right on one level. It would be Cole Danes's first and final mistake.

CHAPTER EIGHT

Renaissance Hotel, East Side of Chicago,
12:20 p.m.
21 hours, 55 minutes remaining...

There was no exit wound.

The bleeding had stopped but from what she could see Danes had already lost more blood than he should have. Too much for her comfort.

He lay on the bed now, a feat she would never have been able to accomplish alone. He'd roused enough to help, though she'd hated that his exerting any additional effort had been necessary.

"What're you waiting for?" His voice sounded sterner than it should for a man in his condition, but she didn't miss the thin quality. In the past twelve hours or so she'd come to know quite well the strong, rich sound.

She ordered her hands not to fidget and kept her gaze carefully away from his. "There's no exit wound."

"You'll find tweezers in the supplies I purchased. Dig it out."

Disregarding his suggestion, she looked around for any kind of distraction. "Have some ice chips." She'd called room service and ordered bottled water, crushed ice and coffee. She'd needed the caffeine, the rest had been for him. She'd cleansed the wound and surrounding area with bottled water and the peroxide he'd purchased.

She'd also gone into the bathroom and made one other call…he wouldn't like it.

As hard as she tried her fingers still shook as she held a few chips of ice to his lips. He sucked them from her fingertips, the feel of his lips even under present circumstances sent an unexpected tingle through her.

She bit down on her lower lip and studied the small wound in his side as if considering his suggestion. There could be internal hemorrhaging. Experience told her that if the internal injuries were massive he'd be in shock by this point, suffering from extreme blood loss. But she couldn't be certain. Each individual's tolerance for pain and ability to function beyond normal limits was always different. He could be hanging by a thread, but his vitals were damn good if that turned out to be the case. His pulse was still strong, his heart rate very good considering.

"What have you done?"

Her head came up. "What do you mean?"

A knock at the door confirmed his suspicions. Why was it her luck never held out?

The weapon was in his hand before she realized his hand had moved. "That better be room service again."

She stood quickly and backed away from the bed. "I had to call a friend."

He pushed up into a sitting position. The grim line of his mouth exposed plainly how much the move cost him but he didn't make a sound in protest. "Don't answer it," he ordered, fury flashing in those eyes. "I don't want to have to kill anyone else this morning."

His words shook her but she refused to be intimidated on the issue. He needed more help than she could give. She was only a nurse, not a surgeon. "You don't have a choice." She strode to the door and reached for the knob.

The sound of him chambering a round gave her only a second's pause; she twisted the knob and opened the door.

Keith Anderson smiled at her. "I was beginning to think you'd played some kind of joke on me," he said good-naturedly.

She pulled him into the room and quickly closed and locked the door. "Thanks for coming, Keith."

"Whoa! Who's the guy with the gun?"

Angel rolled her eyes and heaved a put-upon sigh. "Put the gun down, Danes. He's here to help."

Keith Anderson looked at her a little skeptically. "Are you in some kind of trouble?"

He'd asked that on the phone but she'd insisted that there was no time to explain. She'd only known Keith a few months. He was friendly and flirtatious and currently in his surgical rotation. She'd warded off his friendly advances from day one. As nice as he was, as cute as he was, she'd learned the hard way not to date the doctors, med students or interns.

She grabbed him by the arm and pulled him closer to the bed. His hesitation was understandable since Danes refused to put his gun away.

"You brought what we need?" She glanced at the large shopping bag in his hand. She'd warned him not to *look* like a doctor, hence the casual attire and big brown paper bag.

A mixture of confusion and apprehension had claimed his face. "I brought what you asked for."

"Who the hell is this guy?" Danes demanded. His hair was loose now, hanging around his shoulders, the silver earring glinting in his earlobe. His black shirt ripped open, the leather shoulder holster still in place. She could well imagine what Keith thought.

"Keith Anderson. He's an intern at the hospital. He's going to help."

She looked away from Keith's questioning expression. He would want to know later, assuming either of them survived to see a later, why she'd lied. She saw him most every day at the hospital rightly enough, but he was only a fourth-year medical student. Still, he had three things going for him, he was in the final weeks of his surgery rotation, he was friendly and Angel knew she could trust him.

Danes's furious gaze locked onto hers. "Did you warn him that I'd have to kill him when he's through?"

"Put the gun away. We're wasting time," she ordered in the sternest tone she could marshal.

"Look, Angel." Keith backed away a step. "This is a little intense."

She seized his arm with both hands and waited until he'd looked at her before she spoke. "Please, Keith, this is important. I won't let him hurt you. Just do this for me, would you?"

He looked from her to the gun still aimed in his direction and back. "All right, but it's going to cost you." A wicked grin slid across his handsome face, outshining any of the other emotions still lingering there. "I won't let you forget it, either."

"Whatever you want," she promised.

Keith passed the bag to her and sat down on the edge of the bed, ignoring Danes's glare as well as his weapon. That was another thing she'd known about Keith. He would risk his standing at the hospital as well as the university to bring the necessary items. She doubted anyone else would have done that for her.

"Let me have a pair of those gloves," he mumbled

to Angel, already distracted by the injury. He pulled a stethoscope from his jacket pocket.

Relief chased away the last of Angel's uncertainty. She handed him a pair of the gloves he'd brought and hurried to set up so she could assist him. She dragged the chair and table closer, then arranged the surgical equipment and medical supplies from the bag atop it.

"Let's get that IV going," Keith told her. His eyes told her he wasn't completely happy with the circumstances. She understood.

Angel donned a pair of gloves, took the necessary implements and moved to the other side of the bed. She draped the IV bag on the headboard and repeated, "Put the gun down, Danes."

He lowered the weapon to the mattress but didn't release it. When she pressed him with her gaze he said, "That's as good as it's going to get."

"Fine." She surveyed his forearm and decided on the best spot for the introduction of the IV catheter.

"What's in that?" He glanced toward the IV bag.

"Nothing to worry about," she assured, annoyed. The man needed help and all he could do was ask questions and complain. "You need the fluids, you've lost a lot of blood."

"No drugs?"

"No drugs yet, sir," Keith answered for her. "But you'll need something for this. It's going to be quite painful."

"No drugs." This time Danes directed his no-arguments order at Keith. "If I feel the first glimmer of an anesthetic you'll regret it."

Keith looked from Danes to Angel. "No way am I doing this without anesthesia."

Damn. "Did you bring a local?"

He shrugged. "Yeah, but—"

"Give him that."

"Angel, you—"

"Do it," Danes commanded. He repositioned the weapon on his right side, well within Keith's line of vision.

"Whatever."

Angel would not soon forget the next few minutes. The local helped somewhat, but not nearly enough. It was insane to do it this way, but Danes refused to allow any additional numbing drugs. To his credit, he didn't make a peep as Keith increased the size of the wound, then prodded with a pair of surgical retrieval forceps until he found the bullet lodged against a rib and removed it.

"Man, you were damn lucky," Keith said as he explored the area as best he could for any other damage. "A millimeter to the right and that sucker would have gone through your lung. As it is, you've got a fractured rib, but not a lot of other damage."

A fractured rib was no laughing matter. Angel scrubbed the back of a gloved hand over her forehead. She couldn't see how he'd withstood the pain for hours. They'd waited in that parking garage for what felt like forever, then purchased new clothes and come to this hotel. He'd driven, staying in complete control without so much as flinching. Amazing. She refused to consider that the bullet he'd taken had been as much to protect her as to help himself.

As far as she was concerned at this moment, he didn't deserve quite that much respect or gratitude just yet.

As any good nurse would do, she wiped his face with a cool cloth, his sweat the only outward indication of what he'd just endured.

"I'll get this sutured and then you'll need an injection of penicillin. That drug acceptable?" Keith inquired facetiously.

Danes lifted the corners of his mouth in a facsimile of a smile. "That and nothing else."

Angel rolled her eyes again. She had no desire to watch this part. The local was surely wearing off by now. She busied herself cleaning up the remnants of the crude procedure. Using a trash bag from one of the lined cans in the room she concealed the contents by tying the bag. She doubted Danes would want anyone to know surgery to remove a bullet had taken place in this room. There wasn't much she could do about the bloody towels except trash them, too.

"Looks like you'll live."

As she moved back into the room Keith stood and gathered the remainder of the items he'd brought. He'd bandaged the wound and injected the antibiotic.

"I suppose I'll allow you to do the same," Danes offered with something less than civility.

"I really appreciate your help, Keith." Angel followed him to the door. "I know this was…" She couldn't think of any words to put the situation into proper context.

Keith tugged her into the corridor and pulled the door closed behind them. "Look, are you sure you're okay? What's going on here?"

For a guy so young, with mostly medicine and sex on his mind, Keith looked dead serious and immensely worried.

"I can't tell you anything more now." She placed her hand over his. "I promise I'll explain everything later."

He shook his head. "But this guy. He's—"

"Helping me," she finished. "I can't do this without him. Trust me, Keith, I'm doing what I have to."

"All right." He brushed a kiss across her forehead. "Be safe. I plan to collect on this debt."

Angel couldn't say what possessed her at that moment, but she flung her arms around the handsome young doctor-to-be's neck and kissed him hard right on the mouth. She couldn't help herself. The desperation, the need to connect with another living human was too great to ignore. And the last thing she intended to do was let that need get out of control with no one around except Cole Danes.

Maybe this kiss really did belong to him, but he wasn't going to get it.

"Well now, that's what I call tangible appreciation," Keith murmured when at last they came up for air. He kissed the tip of her nose. "Be safe. I'd like to follow up on this procedure, nurse."

Trembling with the sudden drain of adrenaline, she watched him walk out the rear exit of the hotel. A part of her now certain that she'd lost her mind completely. She'd just kissed the cutest, sexiest, most available male medical student at Winnetka General. And she hadn't felt a thing—except desperation.

Maybe she was already dead.

Any woman who could kiss a guy like that and feel empty afterward had to be dead.

She trudged back into the room, certain her past experience with one particular doctor was surely the reason for her lack of physical reaction. One look at Cole Danes and she knew it was a lie.

"What the hell are you doing?"

He'd holstered his weapon and managed to get out

of bed. The grim, listless expression on his face served as irrefutable proof of the discomfort involved.

"Get your things. We're out of here."

He ripped off the tape and removed the IV catheter to reiterate his announcement.

"Now," he added, just in case she still didn't get it.

She flung her arms heavenward in disbelief. "Are you nuts? You should be in bed for at least twenty-four hours. There could be other problems. God forbid, an aneurysm related to the injury. Or infection."

And then it hit her. In less than twenty-four hours her aunt would be dead if they didn't find her. Her child might be lost to her forever. Danes wasn't willing to risk any outside interference, not that she believed Keith would call the authorities, but it was a risk. Not to mention, even she had already learned that staying in one place any longer than necessary was a risk in and of itself.

She wilted. Any strength and determination flowing out of her so fast she scarcely stayed on her feet.

"You'll drive."

Her hands trembling, she pushed the hair behind her ears and nodded. "Okay." She gathered the new clothes he'd purchased and the toiletries before heading for the door.

She hesitated there, had to ask the question that now burned like a wildfire in her brain. "Do you think he'll call?" If he didn't…what would they do? How would they find her aunt in time?

Danes looked tired, the pain no longer hidden. The lines drawn by the fatigue and pain added a new dimension to his face. Made her see more than the classically handsome angles good DNA had provided. Yet his eyes revealed the most. Despite the physical discomfort, this man was stronger than anyone she'd met in her life. He would not stop, would not give up…and that gave her hope in the midst of her mounting despair.

"He'll call."

Again some renegade brain cell took control of her determination to maintain distance, both physical and emotional, between them. "Thank you," she whispered, her emotions too raw to manage anything more than a murmur. She would never forget the way he'd thrown her to the ground and covered her with his own body, then ushered her beneath that car while the bullets hissed around him. "For saving my life this morning."

"Don't thank me yet."

Blue Moon Motel, outside Chicago, 4:15 p.m.
18 hours remaining…

ANGEL AWOKE WITH A START. The room was dark. She blinked. Where was she?

Then she remembered.

The shooting. The makeshift surgery.

Danes had instructed her to drive here. Too exhausted to fight the need then, she'd slept. She dreamed of her sweet little girl, of how their life used to be before evil had intruded. Then the nightmare had begun.

She sat up now and listened.

Where was Danes?

The sound of running water drew her gaze toward the bathroom. Light spilled from beneath the closed door. He must have decided to risk leaving her alone long enough for a shower himself. As if she would make a run for it? What would she do then? Her only option was to stay with him and pray he knew what he was doing.

Why hadn't the man called?

She switched on the bedside lamp and crawled off the bed. Curling up in a chair near the window, she fished around in her purse for her cell phone. He'd turned it off again.

She turned it on and checked her voice messages. Nothing.

How was the call supposed to come with the phone turned off? His cutting remark that the cell phone could be used to track their whereabouts flitted through her mind. But that was only after a call had actually connected, right?

She shoved the hair back from her face and tried to reason the best course of action. Leave it on or turn it back off?

The blast of chimes as it rang made her jump. She almost dropped the phone. It took a second for her to catch her breath as well as her wits to answer it.

"Don't answer it."

Her thumb froze on the button, the desire to press downward a near palpable force.

"It's him." She recognized the jumble of numbers and letters. Danes had explained that the untraceable characters meant nothing. The call couldn't be traced and couldn't be called back.

"Put the phone down."

He stood just outside the bathroom door. She could answer it before he reached her. He didn't have his gun or his holster. A loosely tied towel hung around his lean hips. A fresh, dry bandage covered his recent injury but his damp hair told her he'd only just emerged from the shower.

The burst of melodious notes crackled in the dead air between them, urging her to respond.

"We're running out of time," she pleaded. "Please, I have to answer."

"No."

There was no hesitation, not the slightest inkling of uncertainty in his expression or his voice.

What did she do?

Trust this man's judgment? A stranger who'd alternately treated her like a criminal and saved her life?

"He'll call again, then you'll answer."

A third ring rent the air.

"How can you be so sure?"

"I know what he wants. He won't stop until he has it."

Maybe it was the soft, however deadly quality of his voice, or maybe it was the sheer determination in those penetrating blue eyes. Whatever motivated her, Angel had to believe. Had to hang on to something…anything. And he was all she had.

She set the phone on the table next to her purse. Two more urgent rings and silence filled the room once more.

Her gaze moved to latch on to his. All signs of fatigue and pain had vanished along with the stubble on his jaw. He looked ready for anything, including her protests. He needn't worry, she had no energy to argue. She moved back to the bed and drew her knees up to her chest. She didn't want to be near the phone, wasn't sure she could resist answering it if it rang again.

She closed her eyes and fought a wave of fierce emotion. Defeat conquered any remaining determination. They were running out of time and she was completely lost as to what to do. Every fiber of her being screamed at her to do something, yet, in her heart she feared that nothing she did would matter. That this would not have a happy ending no matter what anyone did.

The scrape of fabric skimming flesh followed by the metal on metal grind of a fly closing registered his continued presence in the room. She could only hope that he had a plan and was getting dressed in preparation for carrying it out.

She felt the mattress shift, smelled the scent of soap, the one the motel provided, the same one she'd used. Instantly the image of him gliding that small bar over his skin evolved in her mind.

"This is difficult, I know."

She lifted her gaze to his. Her eyes stung with the tears she could no longer hold at bay. "I just want my life back. I want my baby back home. I want my aunt safe."

For the first time since he'd barged into this whole crazy mess he touched her in a way not meant to restrain. He tucked her hair behind her ear so gently her breath trapped in her chest. That he could be so gentle startled her. But it was his eyes that did the most damage to her already strained and raw emotions. The intensity she fully recognized, the feral determination as familiar as his face and name had become. It was the one alien element that shook her as nothing else could have.

Need.

Absolute, infinite.

"Tell me about your daughter."

The request surprised her all over again. Did he really want to know, or was this some method of distracting her so she wouldn't go off the deep end looming entirely too close?

"Her name is Mia." Angel smiled as she thought of her sweet baby. "After my mom."

"Where is she?"

Warning bells jangled in her brain. "Why do you want to know?"

He studied her closely for a moment before he answered. "Someone from the Colby Agency could see that she is safe."

Her hackles rose. "I already know she's safe. Months of research went into my decision," she said tightly. "Like you, I didn't want to take any chances."

"Fair enough."

The hint of amusement in his expression only made her more furious. "Just because you don't care about anyone that much doesn't mean everyone looks at life through those jaded lenses."

The amusement vanished. "I'm not jaded, Miss Parker. I'm simply focused."

She huffed a skeptical breath. "That's just an excuse not to let anyone close to you, *Mr. Danes*. There are lots of people who are focused without being so..." She frowned as she searched for the right word. "Untouchable. It's not natural to be so far removed from life. You have to trust someone sometime. Have to take a chance."

"Like the one you took four years ago?"

His barb had the intended effect. The old hurt twisted deeply through her. "Yeah," she admitted, though she'd have preferred to tell him where to go and how to get there. "Exactly like that. I trusted him. Even stupidly fell in love." She looked straight into those piecing eyes. "And I don't regret it. I have my daughter because of that relationship."

She'd been in her last year of nursing school. He'd been an intern at the hospital where she took her training. The relationship had been over as fast and furiously as it began, but she would never regret it. Sure the guy had been a jerk. He'd wanted no part of a child, had never called even once since moving away. But Angel didn't care. She loved her daughter.

"She looks like you."

Danes's comment drew her back to the present.

She nodded. Though she didn't hate the guy who'd fathered her child, she was thankful her daughter didn't look like him. Mia had the same blond hair and pale blue eyes as Angel. Not a speck of Dr. No-Strings showed through.

"But I'll have to tell her about him sometime," she said more to herself than to the man sitting next to her. She wasn't sure why she'd said it out loud but there it was.

"He has no interest in the child?"

She couldn't help smiling. What was with Danes tonight? He was full of surprises.

"I imagine you know the answer to that already." She felt confident he'd thoroughly investigated her past.

The barest hint of a smile twitched one corner of his mouth and her heart surged at the sight. She was hopeless. She'd been sure that kiss she'd laid on Keith and then the long hot shower and couple hours of sleep would clear her head. Evidently it hadn't.

Cole Danes might be totally ruthless but he was undeniably appealing on a wholly physical level. No way could she ignore that fact a moment longer. It had to be the stress. Had to be that crazy connection people shared when under extreme pressure.

Like now.

"You think you've got me all figured out," he proposed, that voice silky, sexy and way too deep and rich for comfort.

Why pretend? He'd read her already, knew exactly what was on her mind.

She shrugged, shook her head. "I wouldn't presume to understand a man as complicated as you," she admitted. "It's me that I'm having trouble with."

His gaze latched on to hers and for one mad moment she was certain he would kiss her. Crazy. The worst possible thing that could happen. And yet she wanted it more than she wanted to draw her next breath.

The tinny chime of her cell phone shattered the air.

Danes looked away first.

Angel didn't have to move…didn't have to look at the caller ID.

It would be *him*.

CHAPTER NINE

"What am I supposed to say?" Angel's heart pumped frantically. The passage of time abruptly pressed in on her once more. She'd lost track there for a moment. Foolishly. They should have been planning some sort of maneuver…some strategy.

Danes extended his hand toward her, the cell phone lying in his palm. "Start with hello."

Another barrage of musical notes punctured her composure. She moistened her lips, exhaled an unsteady breath and reached for the one connection between her and the man holding her aunt for ransom.

"Hello."

"Where is Danes?" the harsh voice demanded.

"He…he's right here." Her gaze locked with the one watching her so very intently.

"You tell that son of a bitch he's mine."

Danes snatched the phone away from her and severed the connection. Stunned, she at first thought he'd reacted to her mushrooming panic but that wasn't the case at all.

"What did you do that for? He didn't have time to tell me what to do next?"

"When he calls back," Danes began, "I want—"

"Are you crazy?" She grabbed for the phone. "Time is almost up. I have to know what he wants us to do next!"

"When he calls back," Danes repeated, his voice cool, calm, patient, "I want you to tell him I won't let you talk to him anymore. That I'm through playing games. Before I end the call again you shout out that the other man told me what I needed to know."

She blinked. "He told you what?" Why hadn't he said anything? Why hadn't they already rescued her aunt if he knew *everything?*

"It's imperative that you do exactly as I say."

"Wait a minute." She shot up off the bed, planted her hands on her hips and glared down at him. "You mean to tell me you know where my aunt is? If you've been keeping that from me—"

The telephone jingled, cutting off the rest of her intended threat.

"Do exactly as I said," he reminded before handing the phone back to her.

She wanted to hurt him. The need overwhelmed all other emotions. She punched the talk button. "He won't let me talk to you," she blurted.

"Then your aunt—"

Danes snatched the phone from her hand and gave her a prompting nod.

"He already knows everything!" she cried. "Your friend told him everything before—"

Danes ended the call. "Very good."

Angel sagged down onto the mattress, the barrage of emotion too heavy to bear. "Please, just tell me the truth. I need to know she's going to be all right."

She would not cry. Damn him. She looked at the clock and fought another wave of emotion. Only seventeen hours left. They had to do something.

Danes pushed to his feet and for a while she feared he wouldn't bother to answer. Would simply ignore her plea. Then he looked down at her with something like compassion in his eyes. But it couldn't have been that simple, she knew all too well. Cole Danes felt nothing for anyone. Yes, there might be a physical spark between them, but that was it.

He would never allow anything more.

"It's me he wants. As long as he needs your aunt to lure me in, she'll be safe."

"Is that supposed to make me feel better?" She lunged upward, matched his stance. "How is he supposed to lure you in when you won't let me talk to him?" God, she couldn't believe she was asking that. Now who lacked compassion?

"We should get started."

Angel rubbed her eyes and shook her head. This whole thing grew more and more insane with each passing moment. "You're hurt, you shouldn't be doing anything but resting." Her voice sounded as hollow as she felt. Nothing made sense anymore. She didn't know what to believe, or what to hope for. If she prayed for her aunt's survival, did that mean Danes was to die?

What did that make her?

What would Mildred do in her shoes?

And suddenly Angel knew. Mildred would be strong. She would do whatever necessary to accomplish her goal.

"The pain is tolerable," he stated matter-of-factly. "I'll be fine."

"Do you need me to drive?" She gathered her purse, dropped the cell phone into it.

"That would be helpful." He pulled on his jacket. From the corner of her eye she saw him wince.

She nodded and followed him out the door. However stoic he appeared, she knew he suffered. Though the injury mostly involved tissue, no major damage other than the cracked rib, there would be pain associated with that as well as the sutures. Since he refused to take any sort of pain reliever, he had to be working hard to tune out the pain. Weakness as a result of the blood loss was likely taking its toll. She'd have to keep an eye on him.

For the first time since she'd encountered Cole Danes she wondered what drove him? Why was he doing this? She knew full well how important Mildred was to Victoria Colby-Camp and the Colby Agency. Was Danes doing the job he'd been hired by Victoria to do or was there something more here? Something she didn't fully understand.

She sensed there was. But how in the world could she possibly hope to learn the secrets of a man like Cole Danes?

COLE DIRECTED HER to the temporary apartment he'd moved into while working on the Colby Agency investigation. Only a few blocks off the Magnificent Mile and from the Colby Agency offices, the luxurious high-rise had offered nothing more than a place to sleep and change clothes.

"Mr. Danes, how are you this evening?" the uniformed doorman asked as Cole approached the door.

"Fine, thank you, Metcalf."

The doorman, one of four employed by the building, nodded to Angel. She smiled awkwardly, hesitated as if not sure what to say or do. Cole ushered her into the lobby and toward the elevator.

"Where are we?" she whispered when they were out of earshot of the doorman.

"My place."

He almost smiled at her surprised look. He'd learned that about her in the past few hours. She wasn't very good at disguising her emotions, was a hideous liar. Just another of those little things that made her far too innocent to be involved with men like Leberman and Stephens and their cronies.

With men like him for that matter.

In the elevator he selected his floor, ten, and waited impatiently for the doors to close and the car to glide upward.

"I guess you make a lot of money in your line of work," she ventured. "Much more than a nurse." She smiled shyly.

That smile, though chock-full of trepidation, disturbed him somehow. He didn't understand it, didn't even try. He could only reason that lack of sleep and physical discomfort were playing havoc with his ability to think clearly. He had to focus.

"More than a nurse most likely," he agreed, though he kept his gaze focused anywhere but upon her. The clothes they'd purchased fit differently from the ones she'd been wearing before. Tighter perhaps, more form-fitting certainly. Under other circumstances he would have considered the possibility as a ploy to distract him, but the selections had been hurried at best. Perhaps he hadn't really noticed the finer details of her figure previously.

He shouldn't notice now.

That he did provided ample evidence of his inability to stay focused.

"Wow."

He'd scarcely opened the door and turned on the lights and already she moved around the living room, admiring the decorating and furnishings. None of which had anything to do with him. The place had come furnished.

There was no time to waste giving her a personal tour. He'd barely seen the place himself. In reality, elegance was something he'd come to take for granted. Money could buy most anything and that was a luxury he'd never been without.

The supplies he needed for tonight were stowed in the bedroom closet. He selected carefully and packed the items in a backpack. He straightened, hauling the heavy pack onto his shoulder, a stab of pain cut through his gut.

A line of sweat instantly popped out along his forehead. Getting shot hadn't been part of the plan, but it was a deviation he could deal with. In the en suite bathroom he swallowed a couple of over-the-counter pain relievers and washed them down with a gulp of water. That would have to get him through the night.

Time was too short to allow anything to slow down his responses.

He found Angel in the kitchen.

"Your cupboards are bare," she said jokingly, though he sensed that it wasn't actually a joke.

"You're hungry?"

"Starved. I hadn't even thought about it until a little while ago." She glanced at the digital clock on the microwave. "But the time is going by so fast." Her worried gaze bumped back into his. "What do we do now?"

"Now we get you some food."

They exited the building and, with her at the wheel of the rented car, he directed her to a drive-thru restaurant. Sub sandwiches and soft drinks were fast and easy. Food would help fuel him, as well. Though he rarely bothered to slow down long enough to eat when on an investigation. The injury added another demand on him physically. Food would be helpful.

In deference to the time, they ate en route. Occupied with the food and following his instructions, she didn't ask about the final destination until they'd parked in the quiet Chicago Heights neighborhood.

"Where are we?" she asked. She'd polished off her sandwich. The lady had definitely been famished.

"At the home of one of the EMTs."

"Why?"

"Because our friend will want to know what I learned from his fallen comrade."

Even in the dark, fear glittered visibly in her wide eyes. "What did you learn?"

"That's not important at the moment."

When she would have argued, he cut in smoothly, "We have to go inside his house and set up our surveillance."

"We're going to break into his house?"

Clearly the EMT wasn't home. The house was dark. And Cole already knew that the man volunteered at a local soup kitchen two nights per week, this being one of them.

"How do you know he'll come here? Weren't there two EMTs?"

Very good. He liked that she could think beyond the moment.

"The other EMT is pulling an extra shift tonight. He'll be the easiest to locate."

"How do you know that?"

"I made a few calls while you were sleeping." He'd asked after both EMTs and the dispatcher had happily given him all the information he requested. Of course, the fact that he'd introduced himself as a federal agent had helped. He theorized that their target would do the same.

"What if the first EMT tells him all he needs to know?"

"He can't, he wasn't close enough to hear."

She appeared to accept that explanation.

"I've never broken into anyone's house before," she admitted.

But then he knew that. Angel Parker had never been in trouble in her life until Howard Stephens appeared. She'd just been a typical single parent attempting to survive despite being overworked and underpaid.

She would never be typical again. Her life was forever changed.

For the first time in a very long time, Cole wished he possessed the power to right someone else's wrong. He'd been so focused the past ten years he hadn't taken the time to wonder or even to care what happened to anyone else. He had his own demons. But now, sitting in the dark, outside a stranger's house, he truly wished he could make all of this go away for this young woman.

But he couldn't.

He had to finish this.

And nothing, not even this innocent woman, would get in his way.

Angel followed Danes through the darkness. The last time she'd looked at the clock she'd had to fight off a tidal wave of fresh fear. Barely fourteen hours left. It felt as if they were no closer now than they'd been this time last night. It seemed impossible that she'd already spent more than twenty-four hours with Danes.

Strangely it felt like a lot longer. Like a minieternity. All the while bouncing from one extreme to the other.

One minute she hated him and the next she wanted to touch him as, apparently, no one else ever had.

She couldn't think about anything else right now. Her aunt's life hung in the balance. She hadn't seen her daughter in days. And she was so tired. Those few hours of sleep had done little to ward off her bone-deep fatigue.

She could only image how Danes felt. He hadn't slept at all as far as she could tell. The pain had to be a constant nag. But it didn't slow him. For that she was thankful. If he could help her aunt, she'd follow him most anywhere.

He withdrew a small tool from his shoulder pack and in seconds was inside the back door of the tiny cottage. The man could do anything it seemed.

She shivered at the thought of what kind of lover he would make. Would he be as brutal in bed as he was on the job? Why was she even thinking about that? Now of all times? The whole idea was far too ludicrous to even consider.

You are truly out of your mind, Angel.

Her cheeks flushed when she thought of how she'd kissed Keith Anderson today. He had to think she'd lost it completely. The guy had been after her for weeks—months—for a date. If she survived this, she would never keep him at bay now. Maybe it wouldn't be so awful if she hadn't been obsessing about Danes. He was the one she'd wanted to kiss. Stupid. Stupid.

How could she want to kiss a man who'd been nothing short of mean to her? Okay, he had saved her life. But he was…rude and grouchy. He barely showed any emotion. The whole concept was nuts.

But then, she could pick 'em, couldn't she? She'd fallen head over heels for the father of her child and what had that gotten her? The child she loved, yes, but a broken heart, too. She'd promised herself not to fall for another guy she couldn't read…couldn't trust.

Cole Danes was impossible to read and trusting him was emotional suicide.

But he was all she had in this.

She watched him move about the dark house with nothing but a flashlight to guide him. His movements were smooth, his gait as sleek as a cat's. Not once had he bumped into anything. She didn't dare move for fear of knocking something over. He was completely at home in the dark.

His clothes blended perfectly with the night. Black shirt, black slacks. He probably wore black briefs or boxers, as well.

She thought about the way he'd looked when he came out of the bathroom wearing only a towel. His skin was as smooth and sleek as his movements. Stretched tight over ridges of muscle that made her mouth dry just remembering them. As strong as he was, as well-defined as his muscles were, he looked lean and hard, not an ounce of fat or unnecessary bulge of muscle. She doubted anything about this man went to waste. Unlike other humans he didn't waste energy on emotion. That ability made him immune to the hurts of everyday life.

What kind of childhood environment or event in his life had made him that way? At forty, he should be married, should have kids. But he didn't. He claimed he didn't have anyone. What about parents, brothers or sisters? Surely he had loved his family.

He evidently had money, seemed accustomed to its availability. Had he been born to wealth or was he a self-made man?

"Now we wait."

She jerked at the sound of his voice right next to her. "You're through?"

"Yes."

She'd been lost in an imaginary episode of Cole Danes. Had lost all sense of the here and now. "We wait in here?"

"In the car. I'll monitor the house from there."

"Good." She didn't know what else to say. Still had no clue what he had planned.

Sensing that he didn't want anyone to hear them she kept her questions to herself until they were safely settled back into the car. He took the passenger seat so she slid back behind the steering wheel.

He placed a small black box on the dash and tinkered with it for a bit, all without the aid of light.

She couldn't wait to see if he could leap tall buildings in a single bound. He'd taken a bullet without much more than a blink.

So this was what action heroes were like. Extremely intelligent, relentless, but sadly lacking in the personality department.

Too bad.

She had to think about something else. She couldn't stand sitting here in the dark in shocking silence. Thinking about him…not thinking—obsessing.

She'd gotten up to the three digits when he asked, "Do you always count stars when you're nervous?"

She relaxed into the seat and folded her arms over her breasts. "I wasn't counting stars," she lied. "I was…" What? "Checking out the constellations."

He made a little sound, a kind of breathy chuckle. It surprised her so that she had to look at him.

"You have something to say?"

She couldn't believe she'd asked that...couldn't believe any of this was happening.

What had she done to anger the universe? Her aunt had been kidnapped. Her daughter in the care of strangers. And here she was chatting about the constellations with a man she'd only met twenty-four hours ago and who had threatened to kill her at least once.

But he did save your life, a little voice reminded.

"Tell me about you and Mr. Anderson."

His question startled her from her confusing thoughts.

"Keith?"

"Yes. The gentleman who kindly stitched me up."

"I see him at the hospital."

"I know that part. What about the rest?"

She frowned, irritation drawing a line between her eyebrows. "We're friends, if that's what you mean."

"Maybe from your perspective," he said off-handedly.

Why the hell were they talking about this?

"Excuse me, can you tell me what we're waiting for here?" She plopped her hands out in a what-the-hell gesture. "You haven't told me anything."

She had to get back on track. She closed her eyes and ordered herself to calm down.

"We're waiting for our EMT to come home. My guess is our target will soon follow."

"Then what?" He never told her everything. Never. He'd give her so much and then nothing!

"Then we take it from there. Our move depends upon what he says and does."

The epiphany struck her like an electrical charge from a cardiac defibrillator. "You don't know anything, do you? That dying man didn't...Oh God." He couldn't rescue her aunt because he didn't know anything. That's why they were sitting in the dark waiting for the EMT to show…hoping the target, as he called him, fell into the trap.

"I know enough," Danes said as he surveyed the still-dark house.

She grabbed his shirtsleeve, demanding his full attention. "Why didn't you let me talk to him? He would have told us what he wanted us to do next!"

If Danes played out this stupid scenario and her aunt was harmed in any way—

He manacled her wrist and jerked her close. "This isn't about what he wants," he growled savagely. "This is about staying one step ahead, leading the game instead of following."

"This isn't a game," she cried softly.

"It's been a game from the very beginning," he argued, some of the conviction seeping from his harsh tone. "That's what men like Howard Stephens and Errol Leberman do. They play games with life and death. It's who they are."

She swallowed at the panic crowding into her throat. "And is that who you are?" She blinked back the sting of tears. Dammit, she would not cry. Not now.

Her eyes had long ago adjusted to the dark night, allowing her to make out the details of his face in the light from the low-slung moon and brilliant stars. His gaze dropped to her lips and she trembled. Foolish, foolish, but she simply could not suppress the reaction.

"I don't play games, Angel," he murmured. The sound of her name on his lips sent another shiver racing through her.

"Just promise me that you won't let anything happen to my aunt. I need to know that this is going to be okay.

I don't think I can keep it together much longer without something to hang on to."

"I'll do everything I can to keep her safe, but I can't guarantee you that he hasn't hurt her already."

A sob quaked through her in spite of her best efforts to hold it back.

"But I can promise you that this nightmare will soon be over. He will die."

Again the idea that this was more than just a job prodded at her. This was personal somehow. She could feel it. Could feel his hatred. She had no idea where he'd come from or how he fit into this. All she knew was that the Colby Agency had hired him to find the leak. But there had to be more.

"Who are you?"

"It doesn't matter." He released her and turned his attention back to the house.

Angel thought about that for a time. She mulled over the mistakes she'd made in her own life. How she'd mourned the loss of her parents. They'd been ripped from her life in an instant by a drunk driver. She closed her eyes and pushed away the memories of that night. Her aunt had brought her the news in person, not wanting her to learn from anyone else or over the phone. She'd been there for Angel ever since.

A part of her would always be convinced that the sudden, unbearable loss had caused her to seek solace in all the wrong places. First by driving herself too hard in her studies. It sounded like a worthy cause, but she'd ended up run-down physically and with a case of the flu she'd had a hell of a time shaking. Then she'd turned to other interests, like her sorely lacking social life. The next thing she knew she'd fallen for the wrong guy and ended up pregnant.

Once again, her aunt had been there to pick up the pieces. Her daughter had become the center of her life as well as her aunt's. Life had felt pretty close to perfect for a little while.

Then that evil man had shown up at her door, had taken her child just to prove he could. He had forced her to do things that would ultimately hurt her aunt. There had been nothing else she could do. At least she'd thought so at the time.

Had she been wrong?

Could she have made different decisions?

She just couldn't risk her daughter's safety. That was the bottom line. She had done whatever necessary to keep her safe.

Isn't that what all parents did?

Once you had a child, everything changed. Nothing else in the world mattered as much.

Without reservation she knew that her aunt understood and would have made the same choices herself. That was the one part in all of this that she felt absolutely certain of.

Still, with all she'd learned in church all those Sundays as a child, with every fiber of her being, she knew that what she'd done was wrong.

And now she had to face the consequences. She had to do whatever it took to save her aunt.

Her gaze drifted back to Cole Danes.

His need to do this was every bit as strong as hers. She could feel the rightness of that conclusion in the deepest recesses of her soul. But why? What had driven him to this point? To this terrible place?

"Tell me," she said, her voice sounding stark after the long minutes of silence. Danes turned to look at her, his expression utterly void of emotion. But there was something there, something she just couldn't see. The intensity of it reached out to her on a level far beyond words. "What did he do to you?"

CHAPTER TEN

8:30 p.m.
13 hours, 45 minutes remaining

The question echoed in Cole's brain. *What did he do to you?*

He stared out into the night, torn by the woman more than the question. How was it that she had penetrated his defenses so easily? In more than a decade no one had held the power to make him feel uncertain...until now.

"I know there's something," she pressed. "This is as personal to you as it is to me. You know all there is to know about me. Why can't I at least know this about you?"

Such a simple question.

And yet more complicated than she could possibly fathom.

Years of pent-up emotions churned inside him, dwarfing the nagging pain in his side.

"What makes you think I know all there is to know about you?" he asked, changing the course of the conversation.

Soon the EMT would arrive and there would be no more time for talk.

"Wait a minute," she argued with a husky laugh. "The question was about you, not me."

The uproar inside him instantly began to settle at the sound of her voice, soft and fragile, yet immensely warm. This was the first time he'd heard her laugh. He liked it. Full, rich, not that silly tinkling sound most women made. Coming from such a slender, vulnerable-looking waif it took him entirely by surprise.

He swung his gaze to hers. "I didn't know about Dr. Anderson."

"Please," she protested with a dramatic roll of those lovely eyes. "I told you, we're friends. And, to be honest with you, he's not even a doctor. He's a med student." At his skeptical look she quickly added, "But he is in his surgery rotation. And we are only friends."

"Not from the gentleman's perspective." Keith Anderson wanted her. His interest was quite clear. Somehow that realization had disturbed Cole. Ridiculous, he knew, but true. He didn't like the way the young man looked at her. Admittedly, Anderson's age and occupation were more suitable. Cole was much too old, his work far too dangerous.

What the hell was he thinking?

"Cole..." A little hitch in her breathing, the one that unsettled him so unreasonably, disrupted her intake of breath. "I'm sorry. Danes," she amended.

The pause that followed went unanswered. He knew what she wanted. Proper etiquette insisted that he assure her that she could call him by his first name if she liked. But Cole had never been one to adhere to anyone's etiquette.

"I made it a rule a long time ago," she went on despite his flagrant snub, "not to get involved with anyone at work. I learned the hard way that things aren't always what they seem."

She didn't say more but she didn't have to. As she'd

alluded, he already knew most everything. She rarely dated and nothing came of the few efforts at socializing she'd attempted since her child came into her life. Cole suspected she either had a problem committing or hadn't met anyone interested in a ready-made family.

`"My daughter is the top priority in my life," she noted aloud, confirming his conclusions. "I can't imagine my life without her."

Something about the way she said that last statement drew his eyes back to her. So damn young, barely twenty-five. A three-year-old daughter and all alone, except for the aunt she adored.

Cole swallowed at the uncharacteristic lump of emotion clogging his throat. How was it a woman so seemingly fragile survived in such a tough world. Especially when faced with men like Howard Stephens and Errol Leberman. He couldn't imagine the fortitude and courage required coming from someone so young and inexperienced.

Angel Parker had no idea just how cruel the world could be. She had not and likely would not ever know the harsh realities he had looked dead in the eye. She could not possibly imagine what Stephens and Leberman were truly capable of. Her experiences had merely scratched the surface. And yet, here she sat fully prepared to do whatever it took, to face anything necessary to keep her aunt from harm.

"You have no idea the level of danger you are in at this very moment," he offered, unable to hold back the words.

She blinked those long lashes a couple of times to disguise the fear that flickered in her eyes, but he saw it just the same. "Yes, I do. That's why I bought the gun. I was afraid…I knew I couldn't do this without help." She stared down at her hands, her fingers twisted together nervously. "I don't want to be a victim anymore. I want this over."

That was just it. No one wanted to be a victim.

But every day, every hour, every damn second of each minute, someone became a victim in one way or another. The only way not to be a victim was to do as he had. No attachments. No close contact on a personal level at all. Complete focus on one's mission. Nothing else. Even basic human compassion was a weakness.

People like Angel Parker weren't built with the necessary equipment to turn everything and everyone off. For that very reason, she would always be susceptible.

Not like him.

If he died this second no one would care. He doubted if even his parents would mourn the loss of the son they'd actually lost ten years ago. They had grieved for one son. Cole had ensured that they would not grieve for another. He'd taken himself out of the equation, lived for only one purpose.

Revenge.

He had not confessed that truth to anyone, not even himself until now. His father had realized the task he'd taken on and that was part of what kept Cole away.

The irony was that here, in the darkness, a fragile woman he'd only just met, made him feel the one thing he'd sworn never again to suffer.

Need.

An error of monumental proportions.

Her life, the life of her aunt, depended upon his ability to do what he did best.

Forge ahead without distraction, without care for anyone or anything else.

Somehow, in the past few hours, a seemingly insignificant space in time, she'd taken that advantage away from him.

And he had no idea how to get it back.

For the first time in more than a decade, the vaguest glimmer of uncertainty crept into the cold, unfeeling pump that pulsed in his chest.

He almost laughed. His punishment, he concluded. God had taken his time, but the moment had finally come. Cole Danes would now stand in judgment for all his cruelties. For his lack of compassion, for his relentless determination to rid this world of scum like Stephens at any cost.

A hell of a time to reap what he'd sown.

The most amusing part was that he'd stopped believing in God about the same time a vital element had gone missing in his damaged heart. Accountability. Another human weakness he had triumphed over. Yet even he had to admit that his current predicament was far too ironic to be the result of mere fate.

Just his luck.

Cole reached into the glove box and withdrew the compact 9mm he'd taken from her that first night. "Keep the safety on until you're prepared to shoot."

She accepted the weight of the weapon into her small, delicate hands. A deep, ragged breath accompanied her visual inspection. "I've never shot a gun before." Her gaze locked onto his. "I'm not at all sure I can."

A self-deprecating smile stole across his lips. "You'll do what you have to when the need arises." He had little doubt in that department.

"Shouldn't he be here by now?" she asked, shifting her gaze to the house they'd come here to watch.

"Soon." The EMT's shift at the soup kitchen had

ended twenty minutes ago. Cole suspected his arrival was imminent.

"How can you be sure this man—" She stopped and turned back to Cole. "Do you know our target's name?"

Cole didn't see the harm in sharing that information. "The man who died yesterday was Anthony Rice. Our final target, the man who visited your home and who continues to call, is Wyman Clark."

"How do you know he's the final target? What if there are more?"

Clearly she hadn't thought of that until now. "There could be others working for him but he's in charge." Clark was Cole's final target. He was the last of the original team involved with…the murder of Cole's brother and his family. When Clark was dead he would be finished. "If we take him down, the entire organization will collapse."

"There's an organization?"

"In a manner of speaking," he allowed. The details were of no consequence—a waste of time to discuss. An explanation would only lead her back to the question he had no intention of answering.

"But how can you be sure Clark hasn't already tracked down the EMT? Maybe he went to the soup kitchen."

"Miss Parker," he used her surname in an effort to keep things on a formal level, "I didn't allow him that opportunity. By the time Clark tracked down and interviewed the first EMT who was on duty, which would be the first, most logical place for Clark to start looking, the other man would be leaving his volunteer work at the soup kitchen." Cole glanced at the digital clock. "He should arrive home any minute now." He placed a tiny wireless communications device in his right ear to ensure his uninterrupted surveillance when the need arose for him to exit the vehicle.

Angel's prolonged silence made him uneasy. She was smart. He didn't need her figuring out the things she wouldn't understand.

"Oh my God."

Too late.

"You planned all of this, didn't you?"

A hint of terror tinged the words uttered with a kind of disappointed disbelief.

"Now is not the time to discuss strategy," he said, infusing his tone with a cold, calculating brutality. He trained his gaze back on the house.

"The guy who died didn't tell you anything, you only want Clark to think that. All of this...every moment was choreographed by *you*."

Any sign of fear, disbelief or disappointment had vanished, only unadulterated fury remained.

"Keep your voice down."

"To hell with you," she snapped. "What are you going to do? Let Clark go in there and hurt this guy for information he doesn't even have?"

Any response he gave at this point would be unacceptable.

He did the only thing he could...the only thing that would settle the matter once and for all.

The barrel of his weapon came to rest against her forehead before she could launch her next tirade.

"Shut your mouth," he warned, wiping any emotion, real or imagined from his mind. "Don't say another word. I won't let anything get in my way."

Her fingers tightened around the weapon in her lap but he knew she wouldn't use it. She lacked the essential ingredient—a heart of stone. Unless provoked by what she presumed to be the true enemy she wouldn't pull the trigger. Even then he wasn't so sure she would overcome the deeply engrained instinct.

At that precise second he discovered an unexpected glitch in his perfect plan. A rip in his long-standing impervious armor. In light of what he recognized just then, he had to admit that maybe it would have been better if she had used the weapon. Anything would be preferable to what he saw in her eyes and the power that discovery wielded. The glow from the moon provided ample illumination for him to see her initial shock fade to a combination of extreme disgust and dislike.

Headlights in the distance shattered the tension-filled moment.

Cole turned his attention back to where it belonged. He clenched his jaw against the alien emotions that tightened in his chest. What she thought of him was of no consequence. It would be best for all involved if she hated him, which he imagined would be the final outcome of their association...assuming either of them survived the night.

The compact car advancing toward their position slowed for the turn into the driveway. Cole visually identified the make of the vehicle beneath the beam of the streetlight as it swung into the drive. The EMT.

Clark wouldn't be far behind.

Cole's anticipation moved to the next level.

Time to finish this.

Lights came on inside the EMT's house.

Angel's impulsive move was abrupt and swift, but not swift enough. Cole snagged the arm closest to him before she had managed to open her door.

"Let me go!"

"Don't move," he ordered softly. "Clark will be close."

"You going to shoot me?" She peered up at him in abject disdain. "Well, go ahead."

He moved his head slowly from side to side. "You don't want to force my hand, Miss Parker."

"I don't believe you'll do it."

With one flick of his thumb he disengaged the safety of the weapon. "Are you sure about that?"

For two excruciatingly long beats he thought he had her, but then she proved him wrong.

"Yes."

She jerked out of his hold. The door opened and she was out of the car in one fluid move.

"I'm not going to sit here and let this man die for you."

He'd set the interior lamps to off, but even in the near darkness her determination was crystal clear.

"Not even for your aunt?"

She shut the door without answering.

Cole swore as she hurried across the street.

He had no choice but to watch for Clark. He couldn't make a mistake…not even to protect her.

No matter how badly he wanted to.

Angel pounded on the front door until the EMT opened it. He looked startled to have someone at his door this time of night.

"I'm sorry to bother you," she said quickly, scared to death Clark would arrive before she got inside. If he did, she was likely dead…unless Danes intervened and she wasn't sure he would—not if it put his mission at risk.

"I remember you," the big, burly EMT said. For the life of her she couldn't remember his name. "You're the lady from the shoot-out." He frowned, peered past her shoulder, his posture going from confident to nervous. "Where's that guy who was with you?"

"Can I come in?" She had to get inside. Lock the door. Now! "Please," she urged when he didn't look compelled to offer the invitation.

He shrugged. "I guess so. What's this about?"

He closed the door behind her. "Do you mind locking it?" She could only imagine how that request struck him.

"Look, lady, I don't know what's going on with you, but I'm beat." He hitched his thumb over his shoulder. "I got the shower warming up. Whatever you and your friend are involved in, I don't want any part of it."

She heard the water running somewhere down the hall. He just wanted to be left alone. Boy, did she know how that felt. But it was too late, he was in this.

"I don't know how to explain." She hugged her arms around her middle. She'd tucked her gun into the waistband of her jeans at the small of her back. She hoped she wouldn't need it. "Anything I say is likely going to sound crazy, but you're going to have to trust me."

He lifted a skeptical eyebrow. "Lady, after what I saw your friend do, nothing would surprise me."

She moistened her lips and tried to smile, it didn't work. Her lips just wouldn't make the transition. "The man who was shooting at us—the one who got away," she explained, "is coming. Here."

His uneasiness hitched up a notch. "Why? What does he want?"

How would she ever control this guy if he didn't believe her? He was far bigger than her. No way could she strong-arm him.

"He wants to know what his friend said before he died."

The EMT choked out a laugh. "Well that's easy. He didn't say anything. His voice was all garbled."

She nodded. "I know, but you have to understand, the man coming doesn't know. He believes his friend said something that you can tell him."

The EMT held up both hands stop-sign fashion. "Lady, I'm calling the cops."

What should she do now?

"You know—" she followed him into the kitchen where his phone hung on the wall "—under normal circumstances I'd say that's a good idea. But, I'm afraid that won't help."

He hesitated, his hand halfway to the receiver. Just then, for some reason she probably would never understand, the whole scene hit her from a new perspective. Here she stood, in this man's kitchen, trying to make him believe a story no one in their right mind would believe. He was just a regular guy with a job that put him in contact with lowlifes from time to time. He lived alone it appeared. His house was cozy, decorated in an old-fashioned way, as if maybe he'd inherited the place from his grandmother. And he had no idea that in the next few minutes he could die...probably would.

"You tell me what the hell's going on here." He advanced on her.

Angel held her ground, hard as that proved. "This man is a killer. He wants anyone involved with the shooting dead," she told him, giving him the abbreviated version.

"Then we need the police," he urged, desperation rising in his voice.

"No," she said softly. *If only it were that simple.*

"What we need is a miracle." She thought of Danes. Tears burned in her eyes, but she blinked them away, leveled her gaze on the man standing before her in hopes he would see the desperation in hers. "But lately I've been having a little trouble believing in miracles. So, I think maybe it would be best if we got out of here."

His mouth opened but before he could speak a heavy knock rattled the front door.

She pressed her finger to her lips.

The terror that shot through her was reflected in the EMT's expression.

She grabbed him by the arm and moved silently into the hallway that adjoined the kitchen as well as the living room. The short corridor was dark but she followed the sound of the running water. A dim glow lit the small bathroom. Inside she closed the door and tried to lock it but the latch didn't work.

"It's broken," the EMT muttered.

Another pound on the front door.

"Look." She faced him. "He knows you're in here. Your car is in the drive and the lights are on."

"We shoulda called the cops," he whispered frantically.

A loud bang and the splintering of wood warned that Clark was coming in.

The EMT muttered a curse.

"Get in the shower." She shoved him toward the curtained tub.

"What?" he gasped.

"Get in. Hurry," she whispered.

He climbed into the tub. She climbed in right behind him and slowly pulled the curtain closed, painstakingly slowly so the metal rings glided across the chrome rod without making a sound.

She reached back and drew her weapon.

She spread her feet apart as best she could and held the weapon just the way the guy at the pawnshop had shown her. Hot water sprayed down on her but she ignored it. The EMT had moved to the far end of the tub, had pressed into the corner as far as he could. That was good.

She listened intently, trying to hear above the hiss of the water. If he opened the bathroom door did she fire then or wait until he drew back the curtain?

God, she didn't know.

Her heart surged into her throat. *Wait till he's close.* The pawnshop owner's advice rang in her ears.

She squeezed her eyes shut and did the only thing she could. She prayed for a miracle she feared would not come.

COLE WAITED UNTIL Clark entered the house before he moved. He moved in a dead run toward the vehicle Clark had driven. He hit the ground, ignoring the stabbing pain in his side. In less than ten seconds he had both tracking devices in place, along with a jam-buster. A man like Clark would definitely have one or more jammers on board to prevent anyone from tracking his location. But Cole owned the latest technology in rendering those annoying devices useless.

He rolled away from the vehicle, gritting his teeth against the pain. He moved into the shadow of the trees at the side of the house and pulled out his cell phone. If this didn't work he'd have no choice but to go in. If he went in Clark wouldn't go down without a bullet between his eyes so that had to be a last resort.

He had to make this work.

He depressed the necessary function key and waited

for the ring. He slowed his respiration, calmed his racing pulse.

Clark answered on the second ring.

"What the hell is it?" he growled, evidently believing the call came from one of his cronies.

"I'm waiting for you, Clark. Why don't you come and get me. Finishing this will be rather boring without your participation."

He ended the call.

Then he held his breath and waited for his target to take the bait.

ANGEL INCLINED HER HEAD, strained to hear.

A cell phone had rung. She recognized the sound.

She'd heard Clark's voice, recognized it, also, but couldn't make out his words.

He swore now, hotly, repeatedly.

That she comprehended perfectly.

Then nothing.

She held her breath…waited…listened.

Nothing.

Where the hell was he? Her pulse skittered into overdrive. Did she dare move?

The metal on metal grind of the doorknob turning split the air…cut right through the hiss of spraying water.

She heard the EMT's harsh intake of breath at the same instant that everything lapsed into slow motion.

Her grip tightened on the gun. She stared straight down the barrel and waited for the curtain to move.

The door creaked as it opened. Vaguely she noted that she hadn't noticed that before.

The distinct footfall on the floor. The whirr of metal gliding over metal.

Her finger twitched.

Her gaze collided with...

"Oh my God!" Her weapon clattered to the floor. "I almost shot you."

Danes lowered his weapon, glanced from her to the EMT and back. "We have to go. Now."

He assisted her out of the tub. "Stay someplace else for a couple of nights," he said to the EMT.

Angel glanced back at the poor guy. He'd huddled in the corner of the tub, his eyes wide. "Do you think he's okay?" she murmured shakily.

"He'll live."

Danes dragged her out the back door of the house and to the rented car.

"Where did Clark go?" she asked, suddenly realizing that she hadn't encountered his body. After the initial shock of seeing Danes on the other side of that shower curtain, she'd assumed he'd had to kill Clark.

"He's en route to your aunt's location."

Danes pushed her into the passenger seat. "What?" She couldn't have heard right.

He rounded the hood and slid behind the steering wheel before he answered. "He thinks we're there already." He started the engine and roared away from the curb, then tapped a keypad on what looked like a small, handheld computer. "We're tracking him."

Angel stared at the red dot moving on the map displayed on the screen. "Where is he now?"

"North on Highway 1."

She frowned, looked from him to the little computer and back. "How do you know that? You're not even looking at the screen."

He tapped his ear. "The route is being transmitted into my earpiece."

Mystified, she reached out and touched his hair. She should have known better, but she'd only wanted to pull it back and see the earpiece of which he spoke. He flinched. She drew back her hand in response.

He didn't want her to touch him.

Too bad.

Firming her resolve, she tucked his hair back so that she could see the tiny earpiece as they passed a street lamp. Wireless, she realized. She was aware that such technology existed.

"Neat." The single word sound stilted, but it was the best she could manage since the rest of her senses had zeroed in on the silky feel of his hair, the warm, smooth texture of his skin where she'd accidentally touched his jaw when she drew away.

She folded her hands in her lap, only then remembering that she'd dropped her gun in the EMT's bathroom. She stared down at herself and laughed tightly. She was soaked. The shower. God, she'd completely forgotten.

There was something else she'd forgotten. She turned toward Danes and said a silent thanks to God for sending her that miracle in spite of her lack of faith.

CHAPTER ELEVEN

The Port of Chicago, Midnight
10 hours, 15 minutes remaining...

Cole eased into an alley between two storage warehouses. The location made perfect sense. Clark and his men would have easy and immediate access to water or air transportation. A speedboat could be docked nearby for swift movement from the inland river system to the Great Lakes. A helicopter could be standing by on any number of helipads in the vicinity of the port. Every possible amenity had been added in recent years to lure in big business. Chicago liked being known as the "hub" of America's crossroads.

Operating 24/7, midnight comings and goings would not be considered suspicious. The sheer size and number of warehouses and facilities made the location a formidable maze, inadvertently, or perhaps not, allowing for a certain level of cover and anonymity. Getting lost amid the endless possibilities would be effortless for a man like Clark.

Were it not for Cole's state-of-the-art tracking devices and frequency bender that is. An antijam device, the bender, reconstructed twisted and broken frequencies, allowing the tracking devices to do their job.

He knew exactly where Clark was.

The warehouse looming to the left served as a

temporary storage facility, square footage for lease to the highest bidder. Stephens had no doubt claimed a section or perhaps the entire building for his base of operations. Or maybe Leberman had held the lease for all these years, under an alias of course, to carry out his sinister plans.

"What now?"

The tremble in Angel's voice tugged Cole from his study of the structure and those inside. She shivered uncontrollably. He frowned. The heat was off now that they were parked allowing the cold night air to invade the interior of the vehicle. But not so much as yet.

Her clothes were wet.

The shower.

He swore softly, cursing himself for forgetting all else but the chase. He shouldered out of his jacket, gritting his teeth against the nagging pain involved. "You have to get out of those wet clothes." He couldn't believe she'd sat there the entire trip across town and said nothing about being wet and cold.

"I don't think so," she fired back.

"You can put this on." He offered his jacket. The thick lining of the leather jacket would provide adequate protection. The length would likely hit midthigh on her considering her much shorter stature.

Still she hesitated.

"You're a nurse," he reminded, "you know what it takes to bring the body temperature back up."

She snatched the jacket from him. "Turn your head."

"Don't worry, I'm going in. You get those wet clothes off and stay put."

"No way." She seized his arm. "You're not going in without me."

He'd anticipated this reaction and still the ferocity of her determination surprised him. Considering her damp clothes and the idea that she was freezing, he would have thought getting out in the night air would be the last thing she wanted. Obviously, he had underestimated her true grit.

"Yes. I am going inside alone. No arguments."

"Fine." She folded her arms over her soggy chest. "I'll just follow you."

She would. Even if he locked her in the truck she'd likely kick and scream, leaving him no choice but to set her free.

"Clark will have others in there. The shoot-out you witnessed this morning was nothing compared to how this might end." There was no point in lying to her. She needed to understand what they were likely walking into.

"My aunt is in there, right?"

He bit back his fury, not wanting to waste the energy. Exhaustion clawed at him. The pain, it was steady.

"Yes. I would assume she is here, but I can't be certain." If she was in there and she'd been killed already, he didn't need a hysterical woman on his hands.

"Then I'm going in. Turn your head." She peeled off her sweater to leave no question as to her intent. He looked away, but he couldn't block the sounds. Wet denim dragging over slim feminine hips, down-soft skin. The drop of a damp bra against the carpeted floor. The whisper of his jacket's lining as she pulled it on, the rasp of the zipper as she closed the leather around her.

He closed his eyes and inhaled a deep, cleansing breath. He needed to clear his mind of all the static associated with this thing between them. And there was a thing. An attraction of sorts. Something else he'd never permitted to happen while on assignment.

He was slipping.

"I'm ready."

Indeed.

The real question remained. Was he?

Pushing all other thought aside, Cole emerged from the car, motioned for her to slide out on his side. He reached into the back and retrieved his bag of tricks, then closed the door as noiselessly as possible.

Clark had parked his vehicle in the next alley. The entrance he'd used for accessing the warehouse would be nearby. He wouldn't leave much distance between himself and his escape route.

With his scanner in hand, Cole pressed against the brick wall as he moved in that direction. The scanner would alert him to any electronic surveillance in time to avoid its net. Angel shadowed his every step and move. She listened well when she wanted to.

For the moment he was glad she hadn't thought to ask how he'd gotten Clark out of the house back there. She wouldn't be pleased when she learned he'd had the capability of contacting Clark since he'd disassembled her cell phone and installed a descrambling device. The number Clark used on the next call had been obtainable.

She didn't have the proper experience to draw upon to enable her to understand how a man like Clark worked. He had to believe he was in control until the end. It was the only way to keep him on track. If he'd gotten spooked he would have changed his method of operation, made some unexpected move. Cole needed him to react based on a well-planned strategy, not his equally well-honed instincts. Clark would merely have killed

Mildred Parker and disappeared until he regained the edge he'd had coming into this situation.

Patience was the only way to corner this kind of prey.

But Angel would never understand that.

She hadn't played this game. Cole had laid a trap and he'd waited.

In this game, the player with the most patience always, always won. No amount of strategizing or skill could outmaneuver a man with unending patience.

The element of surprise belonged to Cole.

The warehouse stood two stories and covered a sizable distance, perhaps a city block. The maze of alleyways and streets that surrounded the warehouses were lined with street lamps. The cover of darkness always worked as an ally. But not tonight. Tonight it was lacking.

He paused at the corner to the alley where Clark had left his four-door sedan.

Cautiously, he edged the scanner around the corner. It surprised him that no exterior electronic surveillance appeared to be in place. Whatever security Clark had in place, it would be inside.

Going in with Angel in tow would be risky at best. He turned to her and attempted once more to dissuade her from continuing.

"I need to go in alone," he told her bluntly. "There is no exterior surveillance which means it will all be inside. Moving around will be difficult."

"Forget it," she said in no uncertain terms. "I'm going in with or without you."

Cole braced against the rough brick wall, closed his eyes and fought a wave of vertigo. He couldn't waste energy arguing with her.

"I can't guarantee I can protect you in there," he said at last, admitting to his physical weakness. Another first. Bully for him. He felt like an alcoholic on the bottom three treads of the twelve-step plan. Going up was sure to be agonizing but going back down was out of the question.

"How bad is it?"

Well, now he hadn't expected that question. He opened his eyes and peered down at her. He'd anticipated her protests, even her denial that she needed his protection, but not this too knowing question.

"Not good."

She moved closer, searched his face. "The pain?"

He smiled but there was no humor in the gesture. "Nothing so simple as that. The pain I can deal with."

Her hand went to his forehead in the universal temperature-taking touch. "You don't feel overly warm. Tell me how you feel."

He drew her hand away, as comforting as her touch proved. "There's no time for this. The answer is, I felt like hell, but that's beside the point."

She shook off his hand and unbuttoned his shirt. She leaned down close to inspect the bandage. "No seepage. That's good."

"I shouldn't have brought it up." He pushed her hands away and buttoned his shirt. "I simply wanted to give you fair warning. I'm not exactly on my best game."

She harrumphed, an entirely rude sound. "Could have fooled me."

Then she walked right past him and into the alley.

Cole quickly caught up to her and pulled her back behind him. He put his face in hers. "We do this my way," he cautioned.

She backed away, offering her hands in a show of surrender.

He glared at her a second more, no longer trusting her seemingly shrinking ways. She'd grown herself a backbone a little too quickly.

The entrance was a steel door with a camera for identifying visitors. That avenue was out.

Cole walked the length of the building along the alleyway. Windows high above the ground, second-floor level he estimated, appeared to be the best possibility, but those would likely be wired to an internal alarm.

A roof access would be preferable.

At the end of the building the alley intersected with another. A ladder-type fire escape scaled the rear of the building's facade.

Excellent.

Still no detectable surveillance.

The iron ladder leading to the second floor and roof took its toll, but he managed. Once on the roof he slowed a bit to catch his breath.

A series of exhaust fans rose from the tarmaclike flat roof. Two doors, one on each end, offered access to the upper level of the building. Another architectural feature captured his attention and he moved toward it.

In the center of the mammoth roof was an enormous skylight. He approached it warily, uncertain what view would be provided. He kept Angel behind him. Obviously she hadn't realized his destination or what the pyramidlike structure offered.

A wide-angle, unobstructed view inside.

He crouched near the skylight to study the layout. Angel moved down next to him. The second level spanned the entire perimeter of the building like a narrow mezzanine. A number of doors on that level indicated offices and/or maintenance rooms. The lower level amounted to mostly wide-open space stacked three and four high with massive wooden crates. A shipping or main office claimed a portion of the warehouse floor on the far right.

Angel's gasp let him know she'd spotted Clark.

Clark stood, his back turned to their position, apparently arguing with another man who stood only a few feet away. The man clearly cowing to his boss's rampage was armed. Another man guarded the entrance Clark had used. No other comrades were readily visible.

Three, not such bad odds.

Clark suddenly stepped to the left and a woman, seated in a chair, her hands bound in front of her, came into view.

"Aunt Mildred."

Cole reached for Angel, pulled her against his chest. "Be very quiet, very still."

She nodded.

Clark ranted a while longer then gestured wildly toward the office.

The other man, the one who'd received the brunt of Clark's rage, pulled Mildred Parker to her feet and ushered her into what looked to be an office.

Clark entered a series of numbers into his cell phone and started to pace.

"Oh my God," Angel murmured. "He's probably trying to call us. I don't even know where the cell phone is."

Cole knew where it was. In the car. Turned off. But he had no intention of telling her that.

Clark closed his phone and rammed it back into his pocket. He strode toward the office, his movements filled with rage.

"We're going in now," Cole told her.

She held on to his shirt, her eyes wide with fear and brimming with tears. "Do you think he's going to hurt her now? He knows we've tricked him somehow."

"He won't hurt her until he knows he has us where he wants us."

She shook her head. "You told me you couldn't guarantee that."

He took her by the shoulders and held her firmly with his hands as well as his eyes. "I know how this man operates. I understand his methods. Trust me."

She nodded, swiped at her eyes. "Okay. What do we do first?"

He picked up the scanner and tucked it into his bag. "Let's see what kind of obstacle the door is going to present."

They moved quietly across the roof to the door at the front of the building. Cole hadn't had a clean view of what the second level had to offer on the back side. Better the known than the unknown. He checked the door and its locking mechanism for security devices.

Just as he'd thought. The door was tied into the building's security. Would have been truly stupid had it not been. He delved into his bag and placed the necessary electronic devices on the door, then picked the lock the old-fashioned way.

With that out of the way he slipped the pack onto his back, had to stifle a groan. The burn of the sutures as well as the soreness related to the cracked rib weren't easy to completely disregard. She noticed his discomfort.

"You're sure you're up to this?"

"I'm fine."

She didn't miss the edge to his voice but allowed it to

pass without comment. "What are those?" She pointed to the devices he'd installed.

"This door has sensors here and here." He indicated the locking mechanism and the top of the door. "Deactivating the lock won't be a problem, probably won't even show up on the security's monitoring system. But when the door moves away from its frame a fault message will trip the alarm."

"These little black boxes prevent that from happening?"

"Yes. They put off a signal that overrides the current one and remains constant regardless of the door's position. There's just one drawback."

Her gaze latched on to his. "What's that?"

"They only work for five seconds once the door is opened. We have to hurry."

She thought about that a moment, then nodded. "Okay. Let's do it."

He had to take a moment of his own. She stood on that roof, shivering from the cold air no doubt flying under the jacket which, as he suspected, hit about midthigh. She wore nothing else that he could see, except her socks and sneakers. She looked incredibly young and far too vulnerable to be involved with the likes of him.

He shook off the distracting thoughts. No time to think about that right now. He palmed his weapon, braced himself for a fight and opened the door.

The door closed silently behind them. If any alarm had been tripped it made no sound.

He surveyed the dimly lit stairs, scanning for electronics now as well as thermal images. He had no desire to run headlong into any of Clark's friends.

The stairs led down to the mezzanine. Fortunately the landing at the bottom of the last tread was tucked into a corner alcove. He waited, listening for a minute. A radio or television broadcasted somewhere in the building. The echo testimony to the lousy acoustics.

Staying out of sight in the alcove, he put his face close to Angel's, ensuring there would be no mistake in his words or his expression. The next few minutes would be crucial to their survival, as well as Mildred Parker's.

"I'm going to make a call," he told her, bracing for her reaction in much the same way he'd braced for moving in. "I'll give Clark a time and place. No bargaining. Dawn in Lincoln Park. The same ultimatum he gave us."

"Won't he know you're here? Trace the call or something?" As calm as she wanted the whispered words to be, he read the rising hysteria in her eyes.

"He won't know. My cell phone is secure, untraceable. He will probably rant and rave the way he did before, maybe worse. We'll have to ignore that. Eventually he'll calm down. When his guard has dropped enough, I'll make my move."

She chewed on her lower lip, the lushness making him ache to taste it…to soothe it with his own.

Finally she nodded. "Okay. I guess that's the best option."

Cole was not accustomed to waiting for anyone else's authorization or approval. Another crack in his armor.

"Trust me."

She searched his eyes, hers calm now. "I do."

He nodded. "Good."

Between their hiding place in the alcove and the radio or television, he felt confident his voice would not be overheard by the one man near the side door. There was at least a hundred yards between their locations.

DEBRA WEBB 371

Clark answered on the first ring. "Where the hell are you, you son of a bitch?"

Cole indulged in a smile. "Dawn, Lincoln Park," he told him casually. "Bring Ms. Parker unharmed and we'll finish this."

"I don't know what you think you're doing, Danes," he warned, "but I don't take orders from you. We'll do this my way or not at all. The game is over. I'm in charge."

"Not anymore. Lincoln Park. Dawn. My final offer. If you're not there, then you'll be looking over your shoulder for the rest of your life because I won't stop until one of us is dead."

"You smart-aleck bastard," he snarled. "If you knew where I was as you suggested in our last conversation, you'd be here. You don't know a damn thing."

"Perhaps. Are you willing to take that chance?"

Cole ended the called. Double-checked that his ringer was set to silent vibrate.

"What did he say?"

Cole didn't have to bother with a response. Clark stormed out of the office, sending the door banging against the wall.

"Am I surrounded by imbeciles?" he shouted. "You couldn't trace that call? Unbelievable! I thought you said we had the latest technology? How can some guy who works for NSA sneak under our net?"

"His signal bounced all over the country. Hell, even to Canada. I couldn't have locked in on his position if you'd kept him online an hour," his minion argued, albeit humbly.

Clark moved in on him, stabbed him in the chest with his forefinger. "What I want to know is how the hell he got my number."

Cole felt Angel tense next to him.

"We meet at Lincoln Park at dawn," Clark continued. "Assemble the rest of the team. I want them on-site well before dawn."

"Yes, sir."

Clark shouted to the man at the door. "Get your ass outside and start walking the perimeter. We've got things under control in here."

"Yes, sir." The man entered a code and slipped out the door to do as he'd been ordered.

Clark stood in the middle of the vast warehouse a second longer.

Cole tensed, drew farther into the shadows. The man's instincts were very good. He still felt that something wasn't as it should be.

Foolishly ignoring the instinct that had likely kept him alive many times in the past, Clark flipped open his phone once more, stabbed the necessary numbers.

He waited for an answer, apparently through three or four rings, then he said, "I want to meet."

Cole's tension moved to a new level. Who the hell had he just called?

"No." Clark shook his head. "Four o'clock this morning. I'll give you the directions en route." He provided a general direction for the caller. "Come alone or she dies. Is that clear?"

Satisfied with the response, he ended the call.

Clark glanced around the warehouse once more then disappeared into the office.

Cole waited ten minutes before making a move. During that time he considered who Clark could have called. Cole knew with complete certainty that Clark was the last of the original team. That he had at his disposal another team of mercenaries was no surprise.

But to have a contact, someone who would care one way or the other whether Mildred Parker lived or died, was another factor altogether.

He looked at his watch—12:45 a.m. Three hours and fifteen minutes until this unknown person arrived. As much as he wanted to kill Clark right now he had to wait.

He'd literally had the man in his sights during that last phone call. But his man had been in the office with Ms. Parker. If ambushed, Clark's men likely had orders to execute the hostage. SOP. Standard operating procedures for military and civilian operatives alike.

It was a risk he couldn't take…not with Angel right beside him. He couldn't do that to her.

Cole scrubbed a hand over his weary face. He'd waited so long to finish this. How could he let anything get in the way?

Fate had played a very bad joke on him, it seemed.

Whatever the case, he had no choice now.

And he definitely needed to know who Clark had contacted. It had to be someone with ties to the Colby Agency. As unlikely as that seemed considering Cole's thorough investigation, it was the only answer.

Come 4:00 a.m. he would know.

After ten minutes of no activity below, Cole decided to make his move to better cover. A place he could safely leave Angel when the time came.

He inched out of the alcove and surveyed the options to his right. The flat panel doors he presumed to be offices or smaller, private storage rooms. One door, about three doors down, was clearly marked maintenance. That would be the one least likely to be locked.

Angel moved up beside him and he gestured to the

door. "Stay low, move slowly and quietly, but wait for my signal."

She nodded but didn't meet his gaze.

There was no time to ask questions now. Besides, he had an idea what was on her mind.

He crept out of the alcove, then moved quickly, keeping low as he'd instructed Angel, until he reached the door. Hoping like hell he'd chosen well, he turned the knob. The door opened without resistance. He visually checked the area below, beyond the mezzanine's railing, then motioned for Angel to come.

She did just as he'd told her, moved quickly, without hesitation.

Cole didn't breathe easy until they were both securely ensconced in their new makeshift quarters. He'd stuck a small, wireless video-and-audio transmitter to the outside of the door near the knob to keep tabs on the goings-on below. He used his tools to lock the door from the inside. With the right tools and skills, keys weren't necessary.

After switching on a small flashlight to cut through the consuming darkness he quickly placed a series of six matchbox-size black boxes around the small maintenance closet. The room housed a basic cabinet with sink, another floor-to-ceiling cabinet marked Supplies, and a mop and bucket propped in the corner. The odor of cleaning products lingered in the air.

"What are those?"

"In the event," Cole explained as he made the last adjustment, "Clark decides to use a thermal scan to detect the presence of warm bodies in the warehouse, these devices will conceal our presence. They mask the actual temperature of the room, ensuring that it shows up at a temperature comparable to the other rooms around it."

"Oh."

He set the flashlight on the sink, directing its beam toward the supply cabinet, allowing for some illumination of the space without calling attention to the door and any light that might slip beneath it.

Her expression was closed, her lips drawn in a grim line. He wondered how long this eye of the storm would last. Not nearly long enough for his liking he felt certain.

Focusing on the other necessary tasks, he set his handheld monitor to the right frequency and adjusted the zoom of the lens on the electronic eye outside the door. He set the sound on the midrange since he wouldn't be able to adjust it until there was actual sound coming from the targeted area.

He placed the monitor next to the flashlight and relaxed against the opposite wall. Now all they had to do was wait for 4:00 a.m.

"When were you going to tell me?"

So it began.

He opened his eyes and looked at her. "Tell you what?" he asked, keeping his voice low in hopes she would do the same.

"That you could call Clark. That you had his number when you lied to me and said his call was impossible to trace."

"I told you what you needed to know, nothing more."

Fury gleamed in her eyes, giving the pale blue color a kind of iridescent quality. She closed the distance between them in two deliberate steps.

"I was worried sick that he wouldn't contact me again. You let me believe that."

"But he did," Cole countered, seeing no point in this exchange. "Your aunt is safe. In a few hours she'll be free and Clark will be dead."

"Why wait?" she demanded in a harsh whisper. "Why not just move in now. You've had a number of opportunities to shoot him."

"And the guy in the office would have executed your aunt. Don't think I didn't consider it."

A fraction of her anger diminished. "That still doesn't explain why you lied to me."

Ah, the proverbial "you lied to me" routine. They weren't lovers, they weren't even friends. His own anger sparked. He'd gotten her here. Her aunt was still alive. How the hell could she question his methods at this point? "I kept certain things from you because you weren't ready to hear the whole truth," he fired back, sealing his fate in her eyes.

He manacled her hand a split second before her palm made contact with his jaw. "Get some rest. We only have a few hours."

"I hate you," she whispered fiercely. "You're no better than they are."

He released her, lacking the energy or inclination to refute her claim.

She backed away, stopping only when she encountered the wall opposite him.

She was right anyway.

He knew what he was.

A man who left heavy collateral damage in the wake of each assignment. A man whose face and name few ever forgot.

No matter what happened this morning, she would not forget.

If only he could…just for a moment.

CHAPTER TWELVE

1:55 a.m.

Angel fought the exhaustion dragging at her. She'd spent the last hour thinking of her sweet baby and her aunt, reliving the happy times. Those days seemed so far away now. She desperately hoped their future together would not end tonight. Her aunt was still alive and safe for the moment. Emotions tore through her. She felt too many to label them all. Relief, profound relief. Some level of uncertainty still. The past forty or so hours had been like a nightmare or a bad movie about someone else's life.

How could she have gotten in this deep with madmen like Stephens and Leberman? Don't leave Clark out, she reminded sarcastically. Why did they keep coming back? Leberman, supposedly the leader, was dead. Stephens was dead. Why couldn't the last of his men just let this whole thing go? Because terrorists died for their causes. And these men were nothing more than terrorists.

The thought sickened her, but it was true. Relentless bastards who cared nothing for anyone who got in the way of their goal. How on earth had her quiet, ordinary life attracted the attention of such madmen? The Colby Agency. Her aunt's connection to the Colby Agency. In a moment of utter clarity, Angel realized that her family, as well as Victoria Colby-Camp's were victims of the same terrorist. It wasn't supposed to make sense, it was the idealism of a man both obsessed and insane. Leberman had started it, his men would finish it.

And somehow the conclusion had something to do with Cole Danes.

Her gaze drifted to the man. His eyes were closed. Like her, he leaned heavily against the wall. Fatigue lined his face, the one that had grown so familiar to her now. It didn't take any stretch of the imagination to know his injury added to the burden. The pain would nag at him still. She thought of the way he'd thrown his body over hers that morning, of how he'd come through again tonight and rescued her and the EMT by distracting Clark somehow. That part still wasn't clear, but whatever he'd done, it had worked. She shuddered when she considered that she'd almost shot him. Her finger had been so close to squeezing the trigger. The relief she'd felt at seeing his face when that shower curtain drew back was immeasurable... indescribable.

Each step he'd taken, every single move he'd made had been toward one end. Accomplishing his mission.

He'd found her aunt.

Now stood prepared to try and free her.

"Why can't we call for help?" she asked, voicing the next question that entered her mind. She cringed at how loud her words sounded in the cramped room when she knew she'd barely spoken above a whisper.

His eyes opened, the blue so dark it looked black in the dim lighting. "Any outside interference would motivate an attempt to escape. Your aunt would be executed. That's the way these men work."

She shivered at his words as well as the deep, rich sound of his voice. She shook herself. From the moment they'd met a war had started inside her. Part of her repulsed by his cold, relentless attitude, another drawn to him like a moth to the flame. "How can you be sure? If you told someone where we were, how many men they had and what their positions in the building were, it might work."

His eyes closed once more. "Don't believe everything you see on television, Miss Parker."

Fury whipped through her, shoving aside her fatigue. She wasn't that stupid. She abhorred his insistence on calling her *Miss Parker*. "It makes sense," she hissed, careful to keep her voice low in spite of her anger, "Anything's better than just standing here waiting." Claustrophobia had started to unravel her nerves or maybe it was merely the sound of his voice or even his words. She should have left well enough alone. She'd spent the last hour distracting herself with thoughts of her daughter and a happier past. Staying lost in the past had helped keep her calm. But now, reality was crashing back down around her.

Her aunt was in this warehouse. Angel's heart wrenched. There were only three men holding her just now. Surely a man like Cole Danes could take down those three. She said as much, laying down a challenge his arrogance would never allow him to disregard.

His eyes opened, and that laserlike gaze nailed her to the wall. "Yes, I could end this now. Even at three to one, the odds are in my favor. I have the element of surprise and I'm not afraid to die. The two men working for Clark are young, not nearly as experienced as he. They have no desire to die just yet. Taking them out would be a simple matter. Clark, however, would react on a wealth of experience in kill or be killed. He would take out the hostage first, then protect himself. He's not afraid to die, either."

Danes wasn't afraid to die. That was true. Not for a second did she doubt it. He'd covered her, pushed her to safety then lunged right into the hail of gunfire in that motel parking lot. Her heartbeat quickened at the terrifying memory. It seemed like a lifetime ago now. How could it have been just this morning? Well, technically, yesterday morning now. At any rate, he'd risked death to save her. He would do it soon to rescue her aunt. She didn't want him to die. No matter how ruthless he wanted her to think he was, somewhere behind that relentless armor was a man who cared more than he wanted the world to know.

"Will waiting make this easier for you? I mean, help you do what you have to do?" She cursed herself for letting him hear her worry. Why couldn't she stay angry at him? She hated him.

That was a lie.

She didn't hate him at all.

She hated what he did. But she didn't hate him.

"The meeting at Lincoln Park is a diversion. I want them focused on something besides the here and now. Their distraction is essential to our success. But that's not why I'm waiting."

He intended to tell her. Her senses rushed to full attention. Did he finally trust her? Believe she could comprehend his ultimate plan?

"I'm waiting until Clark's 4:00 a.m. meeting," Danes went on. "He called someone and demanded a meeting. Someone who would care whether or not your aunt lived or died. I need to know who that someone is before I proceed."

She vaguely remembered the call. Somehow she'd missed a crucial element of the conversation. Obviously.

If Danes were right, whoever Clark had called had some connection to her aunt.

The four o'clock appointment's identity would be important. For a number of reasons. Mainly to ensure that this was truly over. She wanted every connection to Leberman and Stephens exposed and squashed today. Her family would never be safe otherwise.

A weary sigh heaved past her lips. She should have trusted Danes to know what to do. Should have given him the benefit of the doubt. No matter how unconventional his means in her eyes, she should have trusted him from the moment he saved her life.

"Look." She hugged her arms around her middle and stepped toward him. "I owe you an apology," she said quietly. "I didn't mean to go off on you a little while ago." She stopped directly in front of him and met his wary gaze. "I don't hate you. I'm sorry I said that."

For several seconds she felt certain he wouldn't respond. He seemed to weigh his words as he searched her expression for some hidden motivation for the sudden about-face. She wasn't the only one around here who had difficulty with trust issues. Cole Danes had issues... lots of them. It didn't take a degree in psychology to recognize a man with a seriously screwed-up history.

"Don't give me too much credit, Miss Parker," he countered. "I'm not nearly as heroic as you believe. Saving your life was necessary to my endeavor."

She tamped down the automatic surge of anger at his indifferent attitude. He had an explanation for every damn thing. Nothing was left to chance, nothing motivated by mere emotion. His every move, every thought was a carefully calculated strategy.

A new and startling epiphany abruptly intruded. That was exactly what he wanted her to believe. It kept her, like all other humans, at a distance. The question she'd asked earlier tonight surfaced amid the other chaos in her mind. Within the answer lay the truth about the real Cole Danes. She felt more certain of that conclusion than ever.

"Tell me," she challenged, determined not to be put off, "what did these men do to you? Somehow you got here the same way I did. *By personal express.* I know it. Don't try to deny it, *Mr. Danes.*"

He moved far too quickly for her brain to absorb his intent. His fingers plunged into her hair and hauled her face up to his. "Enough talk," he whispered against her lips. She gasped; he kissed her hard, punishingly so, smothering the tiny sound before it escaped.

She flattened her palms against his chest to push away, she told herself, but her strength melted in a flash fire of heat as her entire body zeroed in on his kiss. She wilted into his arms, unable to resist.

His lips felt firm and yet soft somehow. Hot, urgent. His body was hard beneath her palms. His arms a powerful bond around her, holding her close… closer.

His kiss was uninvasive, involving only his lips. But that was more than enough. Shiver after shiver skittered over her skin, penetrating more deeply with each caress of his mouth. Then he touched her lower lip with his tongue, swept from side to side, tracing the seam that instantly parted for him. He thrust inside. An *mmm* resounded deep in her throat. He tasted vaguely of the spicy sauce they'd shared from their drive-thru meal earlier. But the physical passion he exuded overwhelmed all other thought. Made her squirm to get closer to him.

His fingers traced her face tenderly, thoroughly, as if he wanted to memorize every minute detail. He drew back just far enough to look into her eyes, the feel of his ragged breath fanning her trembling lips. "You are so beautiful," he murmured softly before nipping her lower lip with his teeth. "Far too sweet and innocent for a man like me."

She felt his withdrawal even before his hands set her away from him.

Fury erupted inside her again, but it did little to quell the riot of desire. Damn him. He was the master of distraction. He'd wanted her to stop talking. Well, he'd succeeded. Only this time he'd made a strategic error in judgment.

She moved in on him, closer than before. "You're not getting off that easy." She grabbed his face and pulled his mouth back to hers. This time she launched the attack, kissing him with all the emotion that had been building since they'd first met. With all the need exploding inside her. She needed him. He would not deny her. Her fingers threaded into his silky hair. Damn, she did love his hair.

His hands were suddenly under the jacket, latching on to her bottom. He pulled her hips against his. She moaned at the feel of his craving for her. He was rock hard. Want slid through her veins, fueling the flames already out of control inside her. She hadn't been held like this in so long…hadn't felt a man's hungry touch… tasted a greedy kiss in so, so long.

She needed this…needed him.

The zipper of her jacket lowered. Strong fingers closed around her breasts sending more delicious shivers over her skin. She wanted him to feel the same. Slowly, her lips never leaving his, she unbuttoned his shirt. Then she reached inside, reveled in the feel of his sculpted chest, taking care not to get too close to the bandage or the holstered weapon. She felt him tremble when her fingers encountered his flat, male nipples. She smiled against his lips. In a bold move of payback, he slid one hand into her panties. She tensed, her heart thundering with sudden trepidation, her entire body anticipating the streak of sensations that would follow.

He wrapped his free arm around her waist and leaned her back as he bent forward, at the same time as one long finger slid inside her quivering body. The position intensified the daring invasion. She gasped. Tried to kiss him but he evaded her, content to stare into her eyes as he plundered her drenched sex. His thumb pressed a hot button she'd almost forgotten existed, tightening her feminine muscles and sending a spiral of mind-numbing sensation cascading outward from the pulsing center. Her breath came in shallow little puffs as he drew response after response from her in this same manner, using nothing more than his magic fingers.

She fought the drugging effects of need. The urgent drive toward that precious pinnacle. Told herself not to let him do this. She wanted more than this. She wanted all of him. She wanted him to feel the pleasure, to reach this amazing peak. Too late. Her body went rigid, arched like a bow in his arms. Sensation after sensation rippled through her. Her muscles contracted greedily. She shuddered then felt her body go completely liquid.

He straightened, sagged into the wall, bringing her against his chest. His arms tightened around her, kept her vertical. She felt his heart pounding. Felt the hardness of his own flesh. She couldn't think clearly, couldn't understand why he'd satisfied her and not himself. The way he held her now…as if she mattered.

It didn't make sense.

Then she knew.

Distraction.

He didn't want to answer her questions. Didn't want her working herself into a frenzy with killers only yards away. Didn't want her dwelling on all that could happen in the next few hours.

So he'd done what he did best, distracted her.

She pulled away from him. Stared into those carefully shuttered eyes. Her body still throbbed with the lingering pleasure of the best climax she'd ever had. She ignored it. Summoned her determination, diverted the irritation building toward one goal: breaking him.

She backed away, until she bumped into the counter where he'd left the flashlight. She reached behind her, felt the cool counter, then the colder edge of the stainless-steel sink, moved beyond it until her fingers closed around the cylinder shape of the flashlight. She positioned the light on the edge of the counter where it met the wall. The glow formed a spotlight on her target who still leaned against the opposite wall. His black shirt gaped open, revealing that awesome chest. Her fingers had pulled his long, silky hair loose around his shoulders. He looked sexy, rumpled and entirely dangerous since he still wore his shoulder holster and gun. But she no longer feared him. His posture stiffened as she watched. Good. She wanted him on guard, wanted him to lose his cool. Her gaze dropped to the black trousers he wore. Some things just couldn't be hidden. That willing and ready hard-on definitely wouldn't be ignored. Not by her anyway.

A smug smile lifted the corners of her mouth. Maybe he was right, maybe she shouldn't believe everything she saw on television. But the one thing TV, movies and books alike had in common—at times like this the power of a determined woman could move mountains.

She hoisted herself up onto the counter, the chilly surface making her buttocks flinch. She opened the jacket wide and spread her legs in invitation. His intent gaze followed her every move.

She shouldered out of the jacket, let it fall onto the counter behind her. She watched that glittering gaze shift to her breasts. To further tempt him, she touched one taut peak. He'd made her that way. Had her breasts aching for more of his touch. His nostrils flared, his ragged breath audible in the otherwise silent room. She dropped her hand to her thigh, trailed her fingers toward the juncture there. Excitement rushed through her, settled in her sex. But it was his primal reaction that flooded her with the renewed heat of anticipation. He literally trembled. His jaw hardened. The effort to physically restrain the primitive need she had awakened undeniably visible.

Now for the final move to render him helpless, she mused. She waited for him to have his fill of staring at her body, then, when his gaze met hers, she laid down the true gauntlet. "I hope that wasn't the best you have to offer, *Mr. Danes.*"

He closed the distance between them in one fluid stride. Cradled her face in his hands and issued an ultimatum of his own. "Just remember," he warned, his deep voice as lethal as the savage gleam in his eyes, "you asked for this."

His mouth claimed hers in an open kiss so brutal she whimpered. But the pleasure of his touch...of her victory far outweighed the minor discomfort. The oxygen evaporated in her lungs like rain falling on a hot rock. His kiss proved every bit as relentless as the man, his hot tongue as masterful and bold as the pirate she'd likened him to on first sight. The feel of his trousers rasped against her wanton flesh. The counter held her at the perfect height for direct contact. Her trembling hands went to his fly. She wanted him now, wanted to feel him in her hands.

He pulled back, pushed away her searching hands. "Don't move," he ordered, his tone nothing short of barbaric.

That relentless gaze held her utterly paralyzed. The only muscle in her body able to move was her heart, it floundered helplessly. Her entire soul stilled, anticipating his next move.

The hiss of metal gliding over metal accompanied the lowering of his fly. She wanted to look, couldn't move… couldn't take her eyes off his. Not even the blood roaring in her ears could drown out the sound of rustling fabric as he reached in and freed himself. A muscle in the granite of his jaw flexed. She dragged in a jagged breath, her lungs begging for air. Felt the heat of his sex and he hadn't even touched her.

His fingers clutched her thighs and dragged her closer to the counter's edge. She rolled her pelvis in expectation, couldn't look away from those devastatingly intense eyes.

The first nudge made her gasp. Her eyes closed in ecstasy. His fingers threaded into her hair, cradled her head. "Look at me," he whispered, commanded.

Somehow she managed to open her eyes. Though she didn't know how. She couldn't think past the feel of him pressing into her. It had been so long since she'd felt this way, since she'd wanted anyone. And she'd never wanted anyone the way she wanted Cole Danes.

His fierce gaze holding her captive, he pushed beyond her opening, hesitated only a second. She cried out softly. Her body quivering, wanting. Then he thrust fully, didn't let up until he was deep inside her and even then he reached back with one hand and ushered her more firmly against him, completing the seal. The fingers of that same hand glided down her leg, lifted it around his waist.

"You feel that?" he whispered. "That's the *best* I have to offer."

She nodded. Her body throbbed, felt filled to capacity and then some. She trembled violently, but with pleasure not fear. Closed her eyes at the sheer sweetness of it. It felt so good.

He lowered his other hand, allowing her head to loll back as he trailed those long fingers along her other leg, lifted it, anchoring her completely around his waist.

The sensation of being filled, of stretching to accommodate his generous size, intensified.

"Look at me," he repeated.

Her lids fluttered open. Those dark eyes measured her expression, her reaction. The lines and angles of his face taut with restraint. That earring glinted in his ear reminding her again of a pirate on some ancient ship. He'd already rendered her utterly helpless. She could only wait for him to finish this. And here she thought she'd prove something. Not in this lifetime.

He took his time, flexed his hips maybe an inch, a slow in and out, just enough to shatter any semblance of control she grappled for.

"What do you want me to do, *Angel?*" One corner of that smug mouth lifted ever so slightly. "You wanted this, tell me what to do next."

Bastard. She tightened her legs around him, drawing him even deeper inside her. He didn't flinch, showed no outward reaction. "Don't pretend you don't feel this," she countered just as fiercely. "I know you do."

"You're wasting your time," he growled, putting his face closer to hers, teasing her lips with his own. "What do you want? Do you want me to make you come again? Just say it. Because that's all you're going to get from me."

She grabbed him by the shirt front and held on, determined not to let his uncaring words stop her. "Then shut up and do it."

Something changed in his eyes. A flash of surprise or maybe regret. He braced his hands on the counter and drew back, all the way to the tip, then drove into her with such force that she lost her breath. Again and again he withdrew, thrust deeply. She didn't want it to happen this way. Didn't want to let him do this... not like this. But she couldn't stop her body's plunge toward release once more.

Everything around her faded to insignificance. All his funny little electronic devices. The madmen below. The fear for her aunt's safety as well as her own. Nothing else mattered. She could only watch his unchanging face. Feel him sliding in and out of her. She wanted to resist...wanted to deny his power over her. But it was impossible.

She came. Forcefully. Couldn't hold out any longer, couldn't block the sensations.

His movements slowed.

She forced her eyes open. Saw the sweat on his forehead, the muscle pulsing rapidly in his jaw. Her hopes fell, her thrashing heart wrenched painfully.

But then she saw him tremble. Just a little.

She pulled his face near once more, kissed him with all the desperation screaming inside her. "Don't you dare stop," she murmured.

He made a sound that ripped through her emotions.

A guttural reverberation of helpless remorse, something intensely vulnerable. Something totally unDaneslike.

He thrust again. Shuddered visibly. She kept her arms around his neck, kept him close. Urged him on. He pumped in and out, his movements growing frantic. Not like before. Not controlled. Not brutal. Frantic and desperate. Needy.

Incredibly her utterly sated body reacted. Started to rush toward that peak of pure sensation all over again.

He didn't give in easily. He waited for her to catch up. Climaxes erupted simultaneously. This time it wiped her out. Every ounce of energy and emotion she possessed seeped from her as if she'd died in that final moment.

But she wasn't dead.

And neither was he.

He sagged against her. His weight making her tremble with relief. Making the tears stinging her eyes flow down her cheeks.

She'd conquered him for just that one moment.

Seen his vulnerability.

And like the man, it was overpowering—shook her as nothing else ever had.

Then she realized her mistake.

With his vulnerability had come her own. She'd let down all her defenses in an effort to break his, had sacrificed herself to reach him.

She'd fallen for him—fallen in love with a man incapable of loving her back.

CHAPTER THIRTEEN

Cole pulled out and quickly righted his trousers.

What the hell had he done?

He reached for the roll of paper hand towels mounted above the sink, pulled off a few and offered them to her. "Clean yourself up."

When she'd scooted off the counter he washed his hands and turned his back to give her some privacy.

How could he have been so stupid?

He'd been slowly losing it since laying eyes on her and now… Well, now he'd really screwed up.

He never made mistakes like this.

But she'd pushed him.

He closed his eyes and swore softly.

She'd pushed him until he couldn't do otherwise.

Yet, he couldn't blame her. He'd started it with that kiss. He'd made a mistake.

No condom. Nothing.

Stupid. Stupid!

Not that he feared disease from her. She didn't fool around—hadn't, as best he could ascertain, since the man who'd fathered her child. Pregnant women were tested for most anything a sexual partner would need to be concerned about.

"I don't usually have unprotected sex," he told her, in case she might be wondering the same thing. "You don't have to worry about that."

The water running in the sink was his only response.

"That shouldn't have happened," he added, more to himself than to her.

"Why?"

He faced her, saw the anger in her pale eyes.

"Because it proves you're human?" she tossed in for good measure.

Why lie? "Yes."

She'd zipped up the jacket, hiding the gorgeous body she'd so readily displayed minutes ago. She was so beautiful. His muscles contracted with want. The insistent ache in his side reminded him that he'd been shot recently. But he didn't care. He only cared that her sweet face showed signs of his aggression. There would likely be bruises on her arms tomorrow where he'd held her too tightly. There would be other aches, as well. He'd given her what she wanted, savagely so. All in an attempt to walk away unscathed.

It hadn't worked.

But she didn't have to know that.

She came toward him, her tousled hair making him want to touch it. His fingers itched to go there. Soft, like silk, like an angel's hair. He wondered if that's how she'd gotten the name. She looked like an angel. So pale and ethereal, like a vision. Her blue eyes so translucent they reminded him of light reflecting off water. All captured in a beautiful face that broke through his defenses with such ease.

"You still didn't answer my question." She lifted her chin in defiance of the emotions still glowing in her eyes. "What did Stephens and Leberman do to you?"

He took a moment to check the monitor. Nothing. Clark hadn't come out of the office, nor had the other man. The third man remained outside, likely freezing. Maybe he would freeze and that would be one less life to take to accomplish his mission.

"I won't stop asking until you tell me," she prodded. "You might as well get it over with."

He relaxed against the wall, took his time buttoning his shirt, then adjusted his shoulder holster. "What difference does it make?" A flagrant stall tactic.

She shrugged self-consciously. The answer would be more telling than she wanted but if she wanted him to spill his guts, then she would, as well.

"I want to understand you," she admitted. "I need to know what drives you. What makes you push the rest of the world away?"

This had gone too far already. He didn't like what he saw in her eyes. He wasn't the right kind of man for her and he didn't want to hurt her. The father of her child had done that rather well four years ago.

His own questions nagged at him. Things he suddenly wanted to find out when he knew with complete certainty that this impulse was utter foolishness, supreme stupidity.

"All right. I'll answer your question if you answer mine."

"Mine first," she interjected. "You already know a lot more about me."

"Fair enough." He folded his arms across his chest, gritting his teeth against a particularly nasty jab of pain. Overly aggressive sex wasn't exactly a smart move under the circumstances, but a long-buried flaw in his personality wouldn't let him regret the actual act. It was the consequences that bothered him.

"Where do you want me to start?"

He should never have asked that question.

"Where were you born?"

He glanced at his watch. "We only have two hours," he reminded—and that was assuming Clark didn't make any unexpected moves.

She looked at him expectantly.

He exhaled a heavy breath. "I was born in Louisville, Kentucky."

"Really?" Her expression brightened at the prospect of learning his secrets. "You don't sound Southern."

He laughed faintly. "Kentucky may or may not make me Southern but that was a long time ago."

"So you grew up in a city?"

He shook his head. "On a horse farm. City folks like you would call it a ranch."

"Horses? You ride and everything?"

"I used to. I actually spent a number of years in South Africa. My father was an ambassador."

"Incredible."

He rolled his eyes feigning impatience. "It's not that incredible."

"Keep going," she prompted.

"My mother and father have since retired from politics as well as horses to a vacation home in Florida. The farm still operates, breeding horses and the like but they rarely get back there."

"And what about you, do you ever go back there?"

"No."

Angel sensed the change in him instantly. He didn't want to talk about his life. The extraneous was acceptable, but not his actual connection to any of it.

"Any brothers or sisters?"

"One brother. He's dead."

Something about the way he said the last made her apprehensive. She wasn't sure she should pursue that avenue just now. His expression had closed completely. Time to take a page from his book of lessons. Distraction.

"So where did you go to college?"

"Yale."

"Wow. Yale, that's…" A frown furrowed its way across her forehead. "You must be really smart."

The shadow of a smile dimpled one jaw. "Not so smart."

"What does a smart guy who goes to Yale major in?" Her distraction had apparently worked.

"Law, with an emphasis on foreign affairs."

"You could have become a politician or gone on to become a lawyer," she teased, knowing he definitely lacked the necessary bedside manner, so to speak, for either.

"NSA recruited me my final year in law school."

"NSA?"

"The National Security Agency. They were looking for graduates trained in foreign languages. That I spoke several flagged my file. My studies in foreign affairs only added to my value in their eyes."

"What does a multilingual lawyer do at NSA?" Moving into hazardous territory again, she realized as his posture stiffened.

"I'm afraid that's classified."

She nodded, not doubting it for a second. "What happened to your brother?" She almost cringed, had hoped to slide that one in but he was far too fast for her.

He stared at her for a second that turned to ten, his gaze looking right through her, lost in some time and place in the past. When he finally spoke his words were hollow.

"He was murdered."

She sucked in a sharp breath. "How?" She hadn't meant to ask that. She should have left that subject alone.

"He worked for the State Department. He and his family went on a goodwill mission to Libya. The VIP vehicle that picked them up at the airport exploded. Everyone was killed."

He didn't have to say more. "Leberman and Stephens were involved," she guessed.

"I didn't know until several years later. I used my position at the NSA to do some investigating beyond where others had left off."

Her pulse accelerated at the horror he and his parents must have suffered. She wanted to reach out to him but knew her comfort, any kind of comfort, was unwanted.

"I'm sorry."

"So am I."

She stared at the floor unable to bring herself to look at him. He wouldn't want her to see any emotions he might not be able to hide. She understood that about him. He didn't like being vulnerable and that obsession became suddenly, agonizing clear. Being vulnerable had gotten his brother and his family killed. A man wouldn't find himself vulnerable if he kept the world pushed away.

"My father hounded me to let it go," he went on to her surprise. "He, apparently, didn't want to risk losing another son."

"How are your parents now?" Time was the great healer but she doubted any amount of time would be nearly enough to heal that kind of wound.

"I have no idea. We don't talk at all."

Disbelief pushed past all other emotion. "Because you're obsessed with vengeance?"

"Yes," he said succinctly. "And I will finish it."

Angel pressed a tremulous hand to her mouth as she absorbed completely the full impact of what she'd learned. "That's why you're here." She breathed the words, a new kind of fear making her voice falter.

"It has taken me eight years, but they're all dead now except one. Clark. He will die this day."

"You killed them all?" He'd led a one-man hunt, played judge, jury and executioner.

"All but one. Leberman. Someone else took care of him."

As he'd told her this awful truth she'd watched the cold, hard mask he'd worn when she first met him fall into place. She'd been wrong about him being afraid to be vulnerable. That wasn't it at all. The real reason he kept everyone at arm's length, even his own parents, was so that he could be an unfeeling, relentless machine. He'd closed out the world.

He inclined his head and studied her in that arrogant way he had of lending intimidation. "Now you know."

She nodded. "Now I know."

Her gaze drifted down to her hands. She thought about the way his skin had felt beneath her touch, hot and smooth. The way he'd held her after the first time she'd come apart at his touch.

"Cole." She approached him, uncertain how he would respond. It was the first time she'd called him by his first name without taking it back. "You did what you had to. If someone had done this to me, I would have reacted just as you did. I actually tried. I even bought a gun. You're punishing yourself for doing the right thing. You can't let it keep eating at you."

His gaze collided with hers, the fury there making her take a step back. "It has a name. Vigilantism. I killed those men in cold blood. Don't forget I know the law. Murder one. So don't try to pretty this up. I know what I've done. I don't regret it."

"But you knew they wouldn't stop." She reached out to him, let her hand come to rest on his arm. That he didn't flinch or draw away gave her courage to continue. "You did what you had to. What no one else had been able to do."

That fierce gaze wavered just a little. "Don't do this. Don't even bother." He laughed but the sound held no malice. "Don't try to save me, Angel. I know what I am. What I've done."

She lifted her chin in defiance of his summation. "You're right. I don't have to try and save you. I know you, better than you think. When you've finished this, you'll save yourself."

That's where the conversation ended.

He didn't even bother taking his turn.

She'd said more than enough for both of them.

The only thing they could do now was wait.

3:45 a.m.

COLE BENT OVER the handheld monitor watching the activity below.

Rather than give his appointment a final destination Clark had ordered two members of his team standing by at Lincoln Park to intercept his expected guest en route to an unknown destination.

Clever.

Stephens had chosen wisely when he picked this one.

Too bad his time on this earth was sorely limited. Clark would be the next to die.

Angel whimpered in her sleep. Cole glanced in her direction. She'd settled on the floor in the corner, her legs pulled tightly to her chest. He looked away. Unable to bear the idea of her getting hurt in the events about to take place. There was only one way he could ensure her safety.

He'd searched the supply cabinets and found duct tape. That should hold her.

He checked his weapons once more. The one in his shoulder holster and the one at his ankle he'd retrieved from his pack. He was ready.

His gaze drifted back to Angel. She wouldn't go along with this. That left him with only one option.

He crossed the small room and crouched next to her. "Angel," he whispered. "Wake up. It's time."

Her lids fluttered opened, revealing those luminescent blue eyes. "What time is it?"

He pressed his finger to his lips. "Almost four."

He assisted her to her feet.

"What're they doing down there?" Her gaze moved to the monitor.

"Turn around," he ordered quietly.

Her gaze swung back to him. "What?"

He made a circular motion. "Turn around."

She looked at him. "What're you doing?"

"Making sure you stay safe."

When she would have argued, he plastered a piece of the two-inch-wide tape across her mouth. She glowered at him and reached for the offending tape.

He shook his head, touched the butt of his weapon in warning. Her eyes widened in surprise. He averted his, not wanting to see the hurt or disappointment that would surely be there, as well.

When he'd turned her around, he bound her wrists behind her, then ushered her back down to the floor. He wound a few loops of the tape around her ankles.

"I assume you know better than to make any noise," he noted. "Giving away my presence wouldn't help your aunt."

He did look at her then. She looked ready to murder him. He almost smiled. Good girl. *Don't let a bastard like me get you down.*

He told himself it was a mistake but he just couldn't resist. He kissed her forehead and murmured, "Take care."

He didn't look back for fear of changing his mind. Instead he unlocked the door and slipped out, keeping a close eye on the monitor.

Before dawn it would all be over.

LUCAS CAMP HAD NO CHOICE but to allow the two men to escort him inside the warehouse. He'd kept the appointment just as the man who'd called had requested. Lucas had insisted his team of Specialists stay as far back as possible. Risking Mildred's life was a chance he wasn't willing to take, not even to safeguard his own. His men wouldn't be far behind. Still, as he walked toward where a man waited in the middle of the main warehouse floor, he couldn't help feeling uneasy. He was unarmed and a pair of police-issue handcuffs rendered him pretty much powerless.

"The master spy, Lucas Camp. Well, well, we finally meet."

Lucas waved off his inspired greeting. "I'm afraid you have me at a distinct disadvantage."

"Ah," the man said in mock surprise. He extended his hand. "Wyman Clark."

Lucas declined the gesture. "One of Leberman's recruits," he suggested.

"I was recruited by Howard Stephens actually."

"Do tell," Lucas said facetiously. "And to what do I owe the distinct dishonor of this clandestine rendezvous?"

Clark gestured for three of the four men present to go outside. He no doubt suspected that Lucas would have backup.

"I'm afraid you've caused me quite an inconvenience," Clark said then. He nodded to the fourth man present and he retreated to what looked like an office only ten or so yards behind his boss.

"I'm certain it wasn't inconvenience enough since you're still breathing," Lucas returned, seeing no point in keeping up the ridiculous chatter.

A red fury rimmed Clark's thick neck. "Cole Danes has proven a far worthier opponent than we anticipated. Since you commissioned his assignment to find and destroy me and the only remaining original member of my team, I thought you might like the pleasure of watching him die."

"Unfortunately," Lucas told him, garnering a great deal of glee from revealing this little tidbit, "I can't take credit for siccing him on you and your team. He's been picking you off one by one for years."

Clark looked bewildered. "Impossible. Only one of my men was killed by professionals, the others had unfortunate accidents."

Lucas smiled knowingly. "Unfortunate accidents orchestrated by Danes. And now, you're the last man standing. Didn't your buddy Stephens tell you before he took that swan dive off that mountain? I'm sure he must have figured out the connection."

The red bloom of fury crept up Clark's neck and over his face. "No NSA paper pusher would be good enough to take out one of my men, much less three."

"I guess we'll just have to agree to disagree. Why don't you ask him for yourself? He's probably here right this minute, watching you."

Clark glanced around, a nervous sweat breaking on his forehead. "No more games," he snarled. "Maybe you're right, maybe he is here. That would be good. He can hear witness to what his elusiveness has caused."

The fourth man emerged from the office. Mildred, bound and gagged, struggled in his hold.

Lucas felt the air rush out of his lungs. He couldn't let Clark kill her. Her frantic gaze landed on Lucas's and she let out a moan that ripped him apart inside.

"Let her go, you son of a bitch. You have me now."

"What I have," Clark countered, "is a helicopter standing by. I know when I'm cornered. But you haven't seen the last of me." He glanced back at the man holding Mildred. "Kill her."

"You don't have to do this," Lucas urged, keeping the desperation he felt out of his voice. "Let her go. Take me."

Clark laughed. "Oh, no. It's far too much fun to watch you squirm knowing there's absolutely nothing you can do to save her."

Clark walked away, leaving his man with a gun to Mildred's temple.

Lucas readied to ram him. If he got off a shot Mildred would die, but, as it was, she was dead anyway.

A shot exploded in the air.

Lucas blinked.

The man holding Mildred dropped to the floor.

The side entrance flew open and another of Clark's men rushed in. Lucas rushed against Mildred, taking her down to the floor and shielding her body with his own.

More shots shattered the silence.

ANGEL'S MOVEMENTS became more frantic when she heard the shot. She didn't know what was happening out there but she had to do something.

She rubbed the tape binding her wrists against the corner of the countertop until she'd succeeded in tearing it. She quickly struggled out of it now. Ripped the tape off her mouth and then from her ankles, ignoring the sting.

The monitor was blank. Had he turned it off?

She didn't have time to figure it out. She resisted the urge to run out the door. A weapon. She needed a weapon.

She dug through his backpack. Her fingers curled around a gun very much like the one she'd purchased. There was a clip in the handle and a similar safety mechanism.

She released the safety and pushed to her feet.

Okay. She could do this.

Angel moistened her lips and forced her respiration to slow, her heart to calm.

Focus. Pay attention to the details the moment you open the door. Don't waste any time.

She eased the door open and moved across the narrow landing to the railing. Below on the warehouse floor, a man lay atop her aunt in the middle of the floor. A scream rushed into Angel's throat but she swallowed it back.

Moving. Her aunt was moving. The man on top of her was checking her.

Safe.

She was safe.

Cole. Where was Cole?

Movement in her peripheral vision snagged her attention. Near the side entrance. Cole and another man rolled around on the floor. How could she help?

She stared at the gun in her hand, then at the men struggling. No way to shoot without maybe hitting Cole.

Another flurry of activity drew her gaze to the left. She looked toward the far corner of the mezzanine just in time to see someone barreling up the stairs toward the roof.

She blinked.

Clark.

He was getting away.

She ran after him.

He couldn't get away.

It would never be over...

She thought of her baby girl.

Mildred was safe. She would take care of her baby.

She had to stop Clark—had to end this.

Dragging in a bolstering breath, she clenched her jaw and ran as fast as she could to the stairs. She didn't slow down to think...didn't lose her focus until she'd reached the very top.

Angel burst through the door and onto the roof. Wind whipped around her.

A helicopter sat near the skylight.

Clark ran toward it.

She took aim. Steadied her arms. Spread her feet apart.

Her left shoulder jerked.

She stared down at it. Saw the blood bubble through a strange hole in Cole's jacket.

The pilot in the helicopter had shot her.

She ignored the burn of pain.

Squeezed the trigger.

Glass exploded.

The man in the helicopter fell to one side.

She hadn't shot him?

Had she?

Clark suddenly turned. His weapon leveled in her direction.

She fired again.

He stumbled back, but didn't drop his weapon.

She fired again.

He fell back onto the asphalt roof. Was he dead? His arm moved.

She shot him again.

His body twitched.

She fired again.

"I think you can stop shooting now, ma'am."

Angel swung to face the voice.

A man dressed in combat gear held out his hands in a calming gesture. "Lower your weapon please."

She glanced back at Clark. "Has he stopped moving?" Tears were pouring down her cheeks. Her whole body trembled so violently she could hardly stand.

"Yes, ma'am, he won't be moving anymore."

She turned back to the man in black. "Who are you?"

"I'm Specialist John Logan. I'm here with Lucas Camp."

Her strength evaporated in a mist of exhaled tension.

She dropped the gun. Fell to her knees.

It was over.

She'd killed him.

The man named John Logan helped her to her feet. "Let's go inside, ma'am. It's clear now."

Her gaze collided with his. "Clear, what does that mean?"

"It means the enemy has been neutralized."

"What about my aunt? Cole?"

"Your aunt is safe. One man inside is injured, one is dead."

God, don't let it be him.

John Logan helped her down the stairs since she felt too weak to walk on her own. The dizziness just wouldn't go away. Her vision faded in and out of focus. She knew the symptoms but she refused to faint just yet. She had to be sure.

When they reached the mezzanine she broke free from the man named Logan and ran to the railing. Her aunt sat in a chair, a man kneeled beside her, visually examining her. An EMT, maybe only he was dressed in black combat gear like Logan.

Where was Cole?

A motionless body lay on the floor near the door. Her heart stalled in her chest.

No. It wasn't Cole.

Thank God.

Then she saw him.

He stood a few yards away talking to Lucas Camp.

Relief rushed through her. She half stumbled down the remaining stairs that took her to the main warehouse floor.

She suddenly stopped, felt torn. She looked from her aunt to Cole and back. His gaze collided with hers across the distance. She pressed her hand to her mouth to hold back a sob. She wanted so badly to run to him.

"Angel!"

Her aunt's voice drew her in that direction.

She hugged the woman she loved with all her heart.

"Thank God you're safe," Mildred Parker murmured over and over as she hugged and kissed her niece.

Angel drew back and swiped at her eyes. "You're okay?"

Mildred made a scoffing sound. "They couldn't kill me," she protested. "I haven't lived this long without learning a few things." Her aunt winked at her and Angel knew then that everything would be all right. Despite the slightly shaken look in her eyes, she wore her usual unstoppable facade.

She kissed her aunt's cheek. "There's something I have to do."

"Go on. I'm fine." Mildred ushered her off so the man waiting nearby could continue his examination.

Angel hesitated for a moment thinking she should be doing that. She was a nurse.

"Go," Mildred urged, a knowing look in her eyes.

Angel nodded. She pushed to her feet, her legs still feeling shaky. A searing pain shot through her arm. She'd forgotten about getting shot. Wasn't it supposed to hurt worse than this?

Shock, she told herself. Shock was setting in.

She turned to go to Cole, but he was gone. She frowned, closed her eyes a second and then looked again.

He was gone.

"Ma'am, I need you to sit down and let me have a look at your shoulder."

She looked up to find the man named Logan standing

next to her. "Where's Cole Danes?" she asked, almost startled by how strange her voice sounded. A sudden wave of wooziness washed over her.

"You need to sit down, ma'am."

"I'm...where's..."

And then the lights went out.

CHAPTER FOURTEEN

Inside the Colby Agency,
9:00 a.m...the morning after

"I can't believe it's really over." Victoria Colby-Camp looked to her husband for final confirmation.

"It's over," Lucas confirmed. He turned to Cole then. "I don't know whether to thank you or have you arrested," he said, annoyance muddying the relief he clearly felt. "You endangered both Mildred's and her niece's life. As well as your own," he added with a raised eyebrow. "Not to mention that of Jayne Stephens and Heath Murphy."

"I did what I was commissioned to do," Cole reminded him. That this assignment coincided with his own personal quest was purely accidental...or fate if one believed in such things.

"Mr. Danes." Victoria leaned forward, the leather of her luxurious executive chair crinkling with her movement. She settled her clasped hands on her polished mahogany desk. "There are no words to adequately convey my gratitude."

Well, that was a change. Most were too furious with him at the end of an assignment to admit he'd done what they'd asked him to do.

She blinked but not before he saw the emotion clouding her vision for that one instant. "You cannot know what Leberman has done to my family." She stared at her hands a moment. "You've read the accounts, of course." Her gaze returned to his. "But you can never really know."

But she was wrong.

"Leberman's legacy is finished," Cole stated with finality. He allowed her to see the weight of what he felt inside, the intimate knowledge that no one else on the planet, excluding his father and Angel, knew. "Lucas's team of Specialists rounded up the last of those involved with Stephens and Leberman at Lincoln Park this morning. Your son is safe. You and Lucas are safe."

She smiled and Cole imagined that it had been some time since she'd smiled in just that way. Without reservation, with profound relief. Her life was her own once more. No more ghosts. No more reading between the lines or looking over her shoulder.

The evil that had haunted the Colby name was gone for good.

"Ms. Parker is well I presume?" he asked, keeping his tone carefully measured, completely professional.

"Mildred is fine," Victoria returned without hesitation. "She asked for some time off to be with her boyfriend."

"Boyfriend?" Cole felt his expression turn amused. So, Victoria wasn't the only indomitable woman at the Colby Agency.

"Yes." Victoria looked pleased. "Dr. Ballard, a long-standing client of this agency. His life and that of his daughter's was endangered a while back. One of my investigators uncovered the scam at his pharmaceuticals corporation. Mildred and Dr. Ballard have been an item ever since."

Another happy ending for the Colby Agency. Cole wondered why it was that real life rarely had so many happy endings. Obviously fate looked kindly upon the Colby Agency. Or perhaps destiny knew that bigger things were in store for the Colby Agency. Certainly the agency's ability to come back from the brink of devastation meant something in the overall scheme of things. Then again, perhaps the past forty-eight hours had softened him somehow, made him start thinking along lines he'd ignored for more than a decade.

If he was lucky, he'd get over it.

Cole Danes didn't rely on fate or destiny. He paved his own way. Just now, however, his destination seemed rather obscure.

He stood, choosing to shirk the sentimental musings. "If you need me for anything else—" he turned to Lucas "—you know where to find me."

Lucas stood, the effort a bit more arduous this morning. Saving his wife's closest confidante had taken a toll on the man. Cole couldn't resist a smile. Some people just didn't know when to quit.

"Thank you again, Mr. Danes."

Cole turned back to Victoria once more before exiting her office. For the first time since meeting her, he realized how uncommonly strong she was. Though silver had invaded her dark hair and decades of pain and suffering marred her dark eyes, neither detracted from her gracious beauty. Victoria Colby-Camp truly was a remarkable woman.

He nodded once then walked away.

He'd long ago surrendered to the idea that there would never be anyone in his life. He could not afford the distraction in his line of work.

The image of an angel flickered before he could block it. Silky white-blond hair, translucent blue eyes. Not even an angel could save a wretched soul such as his.

At the elevator Lucas Camp stabbed the call button and turned back to him. "There were times in the past few days that I had to repress the urge to kill you myself," he said bluntly.

A smiled tugged at one corner of Cole's mouth. "You aren't the first. I doubt you'll be the last."

Lucas didn't look at all surprised by his retort. "In the event that you were asking after the other Ms. Parker—"

"I wasn't," Cole interrupted smoothly.

"I understand," Lucas said knowingly. "Believe me, I do. Just in case you start wondering while en route back to D.C., she's fine. The bullet went straight through soft tissue. No permanent damage. She's taking a few days off to mend and be with her daughter. Otherwise, she's in top form."

Cole stared at the gleaming steel doors refusing to allow Lucas's words to penetrate his defenses. "I'm sure Miss Parker will be fine."

"Me, too," Lucas allowed. "Some young fellow from the hospital assured us that he would take very good care of her. I think he's a doctor or intern or something."

To Cole's relief the doors slid open at that precise instant. "Good day, Lucas." The last thing he wanted was for Lucas to see how his words affected him. Fury mushroomed inside him, unrelenting jealousy. He refused to acknowledge it. Refused to be moved by it.

"You, too, Danes. You, too."

The doors closed, blocking out the view of the grinning man. Cole gritted his teeth. Lucas Camp had no business prying into his life. He'd informed Cole at the warehouse that morning that he knew everything about the coldhearted, relentless Cole Danes. That he knew what he'd done and that he'd better thank his lucky stars that his thirst for revenge hadn't harmed any innocent victims.

And then he'd taken one look at Cole's face as his man Logan brought Angel downstairs and he'd chuckled. Another jolt of fury slashed through Cole. Lucas Camp had known. Damn him, he'd known and there had been nothing Cole could say, for it was undeniably true.

He'd grown attached to Angel Parker. He closed his eyes and let go a weary breath. Damn he was tired. Despite a long, hot shower and a clean bandage on his healing wound, he felt exhausted. He'd gone days without sleep before, that wasn't the real issue. This unfortunate encounter with a bullet was certainly not the first time he'd been shot or otherwise injured. Cole's body had endured many kinds of pain. This nagging hurt felt profoundly foreign to him. Deep and grave. Not a mere wound of the flesh…but closer to the soul.

The wholly amusing part was, Cole considered as he stepped off the elevator into the lobby, all along he'd thought he didn't possess one. Along with a heart, he'd foolishly thought that only the weak lugged around such unnecessary equipment as a soul.

He crossed the parking lot and slid behind the wheel of his SUV. The tightness in his chest would not relent. The knot in his gut refused to relax. He felt empty, hollow.

Perhaps how he felt had more to do with having finished his work than with Angel Parker. He leaned back against the leather headrest. Not likely.

There was one last thing he had to do.

He fished out his cell phone and entered a number from memory. A number he hadn't called in nearly a decade. The fact that he remembered it almost surprised him.

"Hello."

The sound of his father's voice shook Cole in a way he hadn't anticipated. "Hello, Father," he murmured.

"Cole? My God, son, are you all right?"

Of course his father would think the worst. After all, what would one think when abruptly hearing from someone after eight years?

"It's done. Over. They're all dead." He didn't bother to explain, his father would understand.

The heavy sigh that preceded a lengthy silence proved telling. Relief combined with a hefty dose of trepidation.

"Son, you've got to let this go. Surely you can do that now," his father urged. "Your mother and I love you. We only want you to be happy. If sharing your life with us is too painful, we can accept that. What we can't accept is you turning your back on life. Please, please, get on with your life. Put this behind you."

Cole had long awaited this day—had thought numerous times of what he would say to his father, what his father would say to him. He had not expected such simple words to carry such a powerful impact.

"I'll be in touch."

Cole severed the connection, unable to say the rest of what burgeoned in his throat. *I love you, too. I'll be seeing you soon.*

He sat in the quiet of the cold February morning, watched as an unforecast snow started to fall upon the Windy City.

The feeling of emptiness and uncertainty as to what should happen next faded. A kind of understanding took its place.

There was only one thing left for Cole to do.

CHAPTER FIFTEEN

Angel kissed her baby's forehead and covered her with a soft pink blanket.

A sigh of deep gratitude eased past her lips.

Her baby was safe at home in her own little bed. Her aunt was unharmed and as vivacious as ever, taking a much-needed vacation with the man she loved. All was as it should be. Life was good again.

Angel reached up and gingerly touched her sore shoulder. She would live.

The evil that had descended upon her life two years ago was gone, obliterated from existence.

By the man she loved.

Ironically, fate had given her that man and then taken him away in the same fell swoop. Cole Danes had walked away without looking back, without even asking if she was okay. But then, he knew she was.

Mildred always said she'd inherited the Parker stubborn streak. Angel would manage. The shoulder would heal and her heart would, as well. She'd been down this road once already. A smile slipped across her lips as she thought of Keith Anderson. He'd called twice this morning, had rushed to the hospital where she'd received treatment for her shoulder at the crack of dawn.

He was so cute and undeniably sweet.

But he was not Cole Danes.

She thought of the hard-hearted man who'd shown up

at her house barely three days ago. Of how he'd threatened her life more than once when all along he would have risked his own to save hers in a heartbeat. His relentless, brutal reputation might be well deserved, but it, apparently, had not extended to her.

Lucas Camp had warned her when she recovered from fainting—something she'd never done before in her life—not to worry about Danes. He was fine. And, he was gone. The only injuries incurred in the final shoot-out had been to Clark's men and to Angel. He didn't mention Cole having asked about her at all. Only that the mission was complete and he'd gone.

She closed the door to her baby's room and slumped against it. Her eyes drifted shut as she attempted without success to rid her mind of those final images of that evil man. Clark's pilot had shot at her, hitting his target as well as warning his boss that someone had rushed up behind him.

Lucky for Angel, dumb beginner's luck at that, she hadn't let the bullet that passed through her shoulder slow her reactions. She'd done exactly as the guy at the pawnshop had told her. *Don't stop shooting until he stops moving.*

Another lucky break had been John Logan, one of Lucas's men. Though, admittedly, luck had not actually been involved. Lucas's men were expert marksmen and had been ordered to move in at the first sign of gunfire. Logan had taken down the pilot, otherwise Angel wouldn't be standing here right now. Logan's decision to shoot the pilot rather than Clark had saved her life, and at the same time allowed Clark the split second necessary to fire his own weapon had Angel not fired first. She hadn't been able to bear the idea of Clark getting away. That's what had sent her running up those roof-access stairs after him. What had driven her to squeeze that trigger when every instinct had screamed at her not to. It wasn't in her nature to hurt anyone, not even a ruthless killer.

But she'd grown weary of not fighting back, of being a victim.

That was another issue she would have to learn to live with. Lucas had told her over and over that she'd only done what had to be done. That, in fact, it may have very well been a shot from Logan that killed the man. She wasn't sure if Lucas merely told her that to make her feel better or if it had actually happened that way. She'd fired several times. The noise from the helicopter and gunfire combined with the shock had likely prevented her from taking in a lot of detail. She might never know.

Some things, she decided, were better left alone.

Clark was dead. His men had been stopped. That's all that mattered.

A knock at her front door jarred her thoughts. Angel tensed instantly, a habit that would surely be hard to break. She heaved a sigh. "Calm down. It isn't the devil."

Determined not to let old fears hang over her like a dark cloud, she pushed off the door and strode into her living room. Surely Keith hadn't made good on his promise and come to her house. She'd told him she needed time alone with her daughter. Somehow she had to get that through his thick skull.

No longer afraid to open the door without looking first, she pasted on a smile and pulled it open wide, a part of her foolishly hoping it might be Cole. Her smile drooped just a little.

"You're supposed to be glad to see me." Keith smiled

widely, a huge bouquet of red roses in his arms. "I ditched rounds for this."

"Doctors aren't supposed to ditch rounds," she scolded, helpless not to be flattered by his attention. He truly was adorable and had a terrific professional future ahead of him.

"I'll remember that," he teased. "And, for the record, I'm not actually a doctor yet."

"Come in," she allowed, reaching for the lovely flowers.

COLE PARKED AT THE CURB across the street from Angel's house. For an instant he considered what the hell he was doing here. He should be on that plane back to D.C. There was the final report to do. Though he'd been commissioned by the Colby Agency for this assignment, the case against Stephens and Leberman had remained open with at least three government agencies, including NSA.

That case was now closed.

He supposed he owed it to Angel Parker to check on her one last time before he returned to D.C. A common courtesy. Nothing more. She had been the one to take Clark down, as it were. Taking her statement would be appropriate for his report.

The small sports car parked in front of her house gave him pause. Her vehicle was a four-door sedan, certainly not this shiny red two-seater.

Lucas's words echoed in his brain sending a twist of fury through him. Her social life was none of his business. He knew that and still, the talons of irrational jealousy dug deep. Further proof of how far out of control he had allowed this assignment to get.

But he was back on track now.

There was this one last thing to do and he would be on his way.

Still curious as to whether she had company or not, he pulled out his thermal scanner and checked for himself. One image, then another appeared nearby on the screen, along with a third in a deeper part of the house. He bit back a curse. The second image moved close to the first, too close. Before his brain fully assimilated what that could only mean he was out of the SUV and striding across the street.

He would get this over with and go. Let her get on with her life with…what's his name. The doctor-to-be. He shot a seething look at the sports car as he passed. That sort of vehicle was made for playing the field not settling down. Whatever this man wanted from Angel was not permanent.

A new rush of fury seared through Cole.

He knocked on the door, resisting the urge to kick it down and go in with his weapon drawn.

The door opened and to Cole's supreme annoyance Keith Anderson stood there looking as cocky as ever, as if the next big score were already within his reach.

"Yo, pal, you're looking far better than the last time I saw you." He thrust out his hand.

What the hell kind of doctor started a sentence with yo?

Cole glared at him. "Where is Miss Parker?"

"Oh, ah…" Keith grinned. "Angel is making some tea." He dropped his hand and stepped back. "Come in. I'm sure there'll be enough for three."

Tea?

Right.

Cole stepped inside, sized up the situation, noting the enormous bouquet of roses dominating the coffee table, then Mr. Anderson's relaxed visage as he closed the door and said, "Have a seat."

As if he were *home* already.

The roar of blood blasting toward Cole's brain blocked all sense of reason. His fingers clenched. He turned his most intimidating gaze on the other man and decided not to make small talk. "Get out," he told him, in a low, deadly tone.

Keith's eyes widened like saucers. "I'll…ah…just be going then."

He was out the door in three seconds flat.

Angel breezed into the room, a tray laden with a porcelain tea set in her hands. Her startled gaze collided with Cole's but she quickly hid her surprise.

"Cole," she said on a rush of breath before looking around the room. "Where's Keith?"

"He had to leave."

She looked confused but then seemed to brush it off. "Okay." She set the tray on the coffee table next to the obscenely mammoth display of roses and took a deep breath.

"What do you want?" she asked when she'd faced him once more. Her voice had changed…hardened.

That was, he admitted woefully, the sixty-four thousand dollar question. What did he want?

Her cheeks flushed with anger and her right foot started to tap against the well-worn hardwood floor. "You disappeared from the warehouse…" She took a moment, visibly composed herself. "Why did you come here?"

Angel wasn't sure what she expected him to say, but she intended to have an explanation. She'd told herself for the past twenty-four hours to forget about him. It was over. He'd done what he came to do, end of story. So what if she'd fallen head over heels. So what if they'd had the most intense sex of her life. It was over. Over, she repeated.

"I wanted to check up on you." He lifted one broad shoulder in a passable shrug. "Make sure you were all right before I leave for D.C."

"You could have waited two minutes in that warehouse to make sure I was all right." She let him have it with both barrels. She hadn't meant to, definitely didn't want to wake Mia. But she just couldn't help it. How dare he!

He stared directly at her with those calm, intimidating eyes looking every bit the dark, mysterious pirate she'd pegged him for from the beginning. She wanted to scream!

"Nice of Mr. Anderson to drop by," he commented dryly.

Was he jealous? That couldn't be. Impossible! "Yes," she fired back. "Very nice. In fact, we have dinner plans this evening so if you don't mind…" She gestured to the door. "You've come, you've seen, you can go back to where you came from and forget about me."

A line of annoyance, the first she'd seen, appeared between those piercing blue eyes. "Dinner? It's early yet. Surely it won't take so long to prepare for an evening out." A muscle flexed in his lean jaw.

She blinked, her heart thumped. He was jealous! This didn't make sense. As if anything in her life had lately. "What do you want?" she demanded, maintaining her firm stance. She wanted to hear him say it.

He blinked, startled. "I told you. I wanted—"

"I know what you told me," she cut him off. "Now I want the truth." She cocked an eyebrow. "That is if you think I can handle the truth."

He narrowed that laserlike gaze.

"Or maybe you're the one who can't handle the truth."

"What truth?"

Enough. "We made love, Cole," she said bluntly. "I won't ever forget those moments. I won't ever forget you. But I need more than a great climax now and then. I need stability...I need to know what to expect when I wake up in the morning."

Another first. He looked speechless.

He glanced away, set his hands on his hips

What was the point? He wasn't ready for this. If he wasn't man enough to admit it, she was damn sure woman enough.

"Just go." She gestured to the door. "Let's not do this to each other."

He started to turn away but stopped. He closed his eyes and drew in a deep breath before opening them once more. And then he asked a question that startled her all over again.

"Where is Mia?"

Startled that he even remembered her daughter's name, she motioned vaguely to the hallway. "She's sleeping. It's her naptime."

Just when she'd thought nothing else that occurred between them could surprise her, he asked, "May I see her?"

She threw her hands up. "Sure." Why not?

Angel led him to her daughter's room, quietly opened the door. Her baby slept with all the innocence and sweetness a child deserved. Angel's thoughts drifted momentarily to Victoria Colby-Camp and her heart wrenched that this had been taken from her. But her son was home now and the devil who'd haunted her was gone for good.

"She's beautiful," Cole murmured. "Just like her mother."

Their gazes locked a moment. Damn her silly emotions. Damn him. A tear streaked down her cheek. She swiped it away, then whispered, "She did get my hair and eyes."

"And your heart I would venture to say."

Angel couldn't do this, couldn't bear it. She stepped back and closed the door. "I'm sorry, but I don't want to wake her." She lifted her gaze to meet his as she spoke. "She has been through an ordeal, as well. I don't want anything else to hurt her."

"Of course."

A moment of awkward silence passed. Why didn't he just go? Didn't he see what this was doing to her.

"Cole—"

He held up a hand to stop her, his expression turning suddenly, stunningly vulnerable. "I…" He hesitated, seemed to search for the right words.

Angel's heart reached out to him as she watched the monumental battle taking place in his eyes, on his face, deep inside him. But she couldn't do this for him. She couldn't be the one. If he'd come here for more than to simply see how she was doing, as she suspected, he had to follow through. He had to give her something concrete to go on.

Like her, a long-lasting nightmare had ended for him. He'd finished what he set out to do, avenging the murder of his brother and the devastation of his family. But there was collateral damage—a term she'd learned in the last seventy-two hours. That, too, she understood. She doubted her life would ever be the same after the events of the past three days, or the past two years really. But she had to move on…get on with her life. He needed to do the same.

"I need you," he said finally. He exhaled a heavy breath then smiled, the features of his handsome face softening in a way she had never seen before. In that moment her lethal pirate transformed into the most handsome man she'd ever laid eyes on. A man who had needs. A man who wanted more.

She didn't know what to say. Now she was the one speechless. Hope bloomed in her chest but she was so afraid to believe…

"I've never done this before, but I want desperately to try."

His confession and vulnerability solidified her tremulous emotions. She reached for his hand, squeezed it, ignoring the little jab of pain that accompanied the move.

"If I've ever met a man in my entire life capable of shaping his own destiny," she assured him, "it's you."

Those deep blue eyes turned agonizingly serious. "Perhaps. There's just one glitch in my plan."

"What's that?"

He tugged her closer. "I need someone to show me how to do this. *I need you.*"

Well, it wasn't "I love you," but Angel knew it was the best he could offer just now.

He glanced toward the bedroom where her daughter slept then back to her. "And your lovely daughter, as well. I need both of you in my life."

"Now that," she allowed, "is a proposition I can live with." Nothing could have pleased her more than his including her daughter. This was a wonderful new beginning.

He cradled her face in those strong hands. "I'd like to properly seal this contract, Miss Parker."

He kissed her, long and deep. And Angel knew that, whatever the future held, they would face it together. As a team and a family. Maybe a soon-to-be larger family. After all, they hadn't used a condom during those wee, frantic hours of the morning. She could hope. With that she planned her own sweet strategy that included a trip a little farther down the hall…in a minute or two. Right now she just wanted to get lost in his kiss.

* * * * *

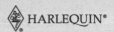

INTRIGUE®

THE NEW EQUALIZERS

Melissa Shepherd's life shatters when her three-year-old niece is abducted. There's only one man, Equalizer Jonathan Foley, who might be able to help. He has refused to commit to her emotionally, but there's no way he can refuse to help the only woman who has ever come close to touching his heart.

Will Jonathan be able to find the child and protect Melissa, while fighting his own feelings?

FIND OUT IN...
MISSING
BY
DEBRA WEBB

Available April 12, 2011, wherever you buy books.

If you enjoyed these stories from Debra Webb, don't miss this exclusive sneak peek at her upcoming book MISSING.

Available April 2011 from Harlequin Intrigue®.

Bay Minette, Alabama
Friday, May 28th, 9:15 a.m.

Calling *him* had been a last resort.

Melissa Shepherd hugged her arms around her middle and stared through the window over the kitchen sink at the drizzling rain. She was desperate.

Or crazy.

She shuddered. Jonathan Foley had disappeared from her life three years ago. The ache, though dull, still swelled deep inside her whenever he came to mind. She shouldn't have called him. Bay Minette's entire police force, aided by numerous volunteers from surrounding towns and counties, hadn't been able to find her niece. Why in the world would she believe *he* could?

Misery washed over Melissa. Polly had been missing for five days. Five endless days and nights.

That was the real reason Melissa had called Jonathan. He didn't like talking about his past career in the military but, from what she'd gathered, during that time he had been connected to extremely high-level people—important people. He could call someone. She was certain of it.

She'd asked him to do that when he'd returned her call in the middle of the night last night. He'd promised to call her back this morning.

So far she hadn't heard a word.

Melissa opened her eyes and searched the backyard of her childhood home, her heart automatically hoping her gaze would land on sweet little Polly playing there. But the yard was empty. The old rope-and-wood swing her father had built for her as a child hung empty from the big old pecan tree's massive branch.

She'd tried. For days Melissa and the rest of the family, along with friends and neighbors, had searched. And nothing. It was as if Polly had vanished into thin air, leaving no trace of the reason or the person behind her disappearance.

After five days…the worst was feared.

A lump rose, tightening Melissa's throat. *Please, God, don't let that sweet baby be hurt.*

A loud chime echoed through the too-quiet house.

Doorbell.

What if they'd found Polly or…Melissa swallowed tightly…her body?

Dear God, no, no, no. Don't let that be.

Holding her breath, Melissa opened the front door.

She'd braced for the appearance of one of Bay Minette's finest or a family friend bearing bad news.

But not this…she wasn't prepared for this.

Jonathan Foley.

The breath she'd been holding whispered past her lips, his name forming there without conscious thought. "Jonathan."

"Melissa."

He was here. After nearly three years without a word… *he was here.*

Don't miss this mysterious and passionate new tale. MISSING by Debra Webb, available April 2011 from Harlequin Intrigue.

REQUEST YOUR FREE BOOKS!

2 FREE NOVELS
PLUS 2
FREE GIFTS!

HARLEQUIN®

INTRIGUE®

Breathtaking Romantic Suspense

YES! Please send me 2 FREE Harlequin Intrigue® novels and my 2 FREE gifts (gifts are worth about $10). After receiving them, if I don't wish to receive any more books, I can return the shipping statement marked "cancel." If I don't cancel, I will receive 6 brand-new novels every month and be billed just $4.24 per book in the U.S. or $4.99 per book in Canada. That's a saving of at least 15% off the cover price! It's quite a bargain! Shipping and handling is just 50¢ per book.* I understand that accepting the 2 free books and gifts places me under no obligation to buy anything. I can always return a shipment and cancel at any time. Even if I never buy another book from Harlequin, the two free books and gifts are mine to keep forever.

182/382 HDN E5MG

Name _____ (PLEASE PRINT) _____

Address _____ Apt. # _____

City _____ State/Prov. _____ Zip/Postal Code _____

Signature (if under 18, a parent or guardian must sign)

Mail to the **Harlequin Reader Service:**
IN U.S.A.: P.O. Box 1867, Buffalo, NY 14240-1867
IN CANADA: P.O. Box 609, Fort Erie, Ontario L2A 5X3
Not valid for current subscribers to Harlequin Intrigue books.

**Are you a subscriber to Harlequin Intrigue books and
want to receive the larger-print edition? Call 1-800-873-8635 today!**

* Terms and prices subject to change without notice. Prices do not include applicable taxes. N.Y. residents add applicable sales tax. Canadian residents will be charged applicable provincial taxes and GST. Offer not valid in Quebec. This offer is limited to one order per household. All orders subject to approval. Credit or debit balances in a customer's account(s) may be offset by any other outstanding balance owed by or to the customer. Please allow 4 to 6 weeks for delivery. Offer available while quantities last.

Your Privacy: Harlequin is committed to protecting your privacy. Our Privacy Policy is available online at www.eHarlequin.com or upon request from the Reader Service. From time to time we make our lists of customers available to reputable third parties who may have a product or service of interest to you. If you would prefer we not share your name and address, please check here. ☐

Help us get it right—We strive for accurate, respectful and relevant communications. To clarify or modify your communication preferences, visit us at www.ReaderService.com/consumerchoice.

HI10R

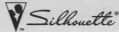

ROMANTIC

SUSPENSE

Sparked by Danger, Fueled by Passion.

NEW YORK TIMES BESTSELLING AUTHOR

RACHEL LEE

No Ordinary Hero

Strange noises...a woman's mysterious disappearance
and a killer on the loose who's too close for comfort.

With no where else to turn, Delia Carmody looks
to her aloof neighbour to help, only to discover
that Mike Windwalker is no ordinary hero.

Conard **C**ounty *THE NEXT GENERATION*

*Available in February.
Wherever books are sold.*

Visit Silhouette Books at www.eHarlequin.com

SRS27709R2

Try these Healthy and Delicious Spring Rolls!

INGREDIENTS

2 packages rice-paper
spring roll wrappers
(20 wrappers)

1 cup grated carrot

¼ cup bean sprouts

1 cucumber, julienned

1 red bell pepper, without
stem and seeds, julienned

4 green onions
finely chopped—
use only the green part

DIRECTIONS

1. Soak one rice-paper wrapper
   in a large bowl of hot water
   until softened.

2. Place a pinch each of carrots,
   sprouts, cucumber, bell
   pepper and green onion on the
   wrapper toward the bottom
   third of the rice paper.

3. Fold ends in and roll tightly
   to enclose filling.

4. Repeat with remaining
   wrappers. Chill before
   serving.

Find this and many more delectable recipes
including the perfect dipping sauce in

YOUR BEST BODY NOW

by

TOSCA RENO

WITH STACY BAKER

**Bestselling Author of
THE EAT-CLEAN DIET®**

Available wherever books are sold!